What Others Are S
About Sharlene MacLaren and

Gift of Grace leaves you breathless. A gifted storyteller, Sharlene MacLaren skillfully weaves together history, romance, and God's divine plan. You can't help but care about her characters, and the romantic tension will have you turning pages until the end. Well done!

—*Sherry Kyle*
Author, *Watercolor Dreams*

Although some of the backstory involves adventure and intrigue, it is pure love that drives the plot, with emphasis on a biblical-style union. In Sharlene MacLaren's *Gift of Grace*, there's some anguish in the romantic journey.

—*Alan Daugherty*
Columnist, Angelkeep Journals, *Bluffton (IN) News-Banner*
Author, *THE flood: A Bluffton History Novel*

Sharlene MacLaren brings the late nineteenth century to life as she creates a dilemma for her characters that will keep the reader turning the pages. This is a book you don't want to miss.

—*Merrillee Whren*
Author, *A Place to Call Home*

Sharlene MacLaren has created a story with great characters, plenty of action, and a whole lot of heart. This emotionally rich read will have you alternately reaching for a tissue, laughing, and getting so angry that you want to jump into the pages of the book and give a certain character a piece of your mind. Treat yourself to a gift and open the pages of *A Gift of Grace*. You'll be glad you did.

—*Keli Gwyn*
Author, *A Bride Opens Shop in El Dorado, California*

Yet again, the amazing and talented Sharlene MacLaren has created a story that will touch every emotion in your heart and soul. A word to the wise: Set aside plenty of time when you pick up *Gift of Grace*, because you won't want to put it down until you've reached the last, sigh-inducing, satisfying page.

—*Loree Lough*
Award-winning author of 100-plus books, including
Currency of the Heart (book one, Secrets on Sterling Street)

GIFT OF Grace

GIFT OF

A NOVEL BY SHARLENE MACLAREN

WHITAKER
HOUSE

Gift of Grace
Tennessee Dreams ~ Book 3

Sharlene MacLaren
www.sharlenemaclaren.com
sharlenemaclaren@yahoo.com

ISBN: 978-1-62911-288-6
eBook ISBN: 978-1-62911-289-3
Printed in the United States of America
© 2015 by Sharlene MacLaren

Whitaker House
1030 Hunt Valley Circle
New Kensington, PA 15068
www.whitakerhouse.com

Library of Congress Cataloging-in-Publication Data

MacLaren, Sharlene, 1948–
  Gift of Grace / Sharlene MacLaren.
    pages ; cm. — (Tennessee dreams ; Book 3)
  Summary: "Grace Fontaine must decide whether to go through with her wedding to a prominent lawyer when an unexpected guest shows up and throws a wrench in the plans"—Provided by publisher.
  ISBN 978-1-62911-288-6 (alk. paper)
  I. Title.
  PS3613.A27356G54 2015
  813'.6—dc23
                        2014035267

1 2 3 4 5 6 7 8 9 10 11   ɰ   22 21 20 19 18 17 16 15

Dedication

To my wonderful, precious, devoted husband, Cecil. Some women would make the same claim about their own husbands, but I am married to the BEST man on earth, hands-down. He loves me unconditionally and fully supports my writing career—as in, he does the laundry, cleans the kitchen, keeps me watered and fed, and gladly eats peanut butter and jelly sandwiches when deadlines loom.

He is a true man of God, full of wisdom, always studying the Word and seeking the Lord's best for his life. On top of that, he happily gives of his time, energy, and finances to those in need. He is a fantastic father to his daughters and sons-in-law and is the most amazing Papa to our five grandJOYs! I can't thank him enough for choosing me out of "all those other girls" he could have had.

He's been my loving hubby since 1975, and I plan to hang on to him clear into eternity.

Honey, I love you more.

1

August 1894 · Paris, Tennessee

It was a drippy day for a wedding-dress fitting, but Grace Fontaine refused to let the rain dampen her spirits.

"You doin' okay back there, Miz Grace?" called Solomon Turner, a former slave now in the employ of her aunt Iris, from his raised seat on the brougham.

Grace felt a trifle embarrassed to be riding in such comfort while he battled the elements in order to get her to her appointment on time. "I'm fine, Solomon, but how are you?"

The loud crack of thunder that sounded must have drowned out her query, for he made no response.

"Solomon? Would you like to turn around? I'm sure Mrs. Jennings will be more than understanding if I decide to reschedule."

"I's jes' fine, miz. A little rain never did hurt a body."

"But you must be soaked," she called, shouting this time.

"We almos' theh, and I's gots my umbrella tha's doin' a fine job."

Ruling it useless to argue further, she settled back against the cool leather seat and watched the rain drizzle down the glass pane that turned her view of the Tennessee countryside into a grayish blur. The carriage bumped along as it made a wide turn. She tried to see past the haze of wetness but couldn't decipher their location. However, when Solomon piloted the pair of horses into yet another turn, she surmised that they'd reached their destination.

To confirm her supposition, Solomon gave a loud, commanding "Whoa!" and the carriage rolled to a stop.

She reached for the door handle but stopped upon Solomon's insistence that she stay put. Although she'd been living with her great-aunt at Brockwell Manor for three months, she had yet to grow accustomed to the pampering that the staff showered upon her, catering to her every want and whim. She'd left her position at Massachusetts General Hospital and traveled to Tennessee to care for her ailing eighty-year-old relative, and in turn, the staff members seemed to have made it their mission to care for *her*. She could only assume it was due to their gratitude for her willingness to come. While Aunt Iris was generally polite and pleasant, her illness had taken a toll on her spirits, turning her into a bit of a biddy, and sometimes the members of her staff were hesitant to even approach her for fear of how they would be received.

Grace hadn't found it particularly easy to pull up her Boston roots; but, aside from leaving behind several dear friends, she had no family keeping her there. Truly, Aunt Iris was her closest relative, unless she counted a couple of aunts and some cousins with whom she'd lost all contact. She'd barely thought twice about her decision to go to Paris after receiving the telegram from Dr. Trumble. How could she *not* go?

With umbrella held aloft, Solomon opened her door, extended a weathered, callused hand, and helped her down. He was an aging gentleman, not much younger than Aunt Iris, but he was far from elderly. Oh, he walked with a limp, winced on occasion when rising from a chair, and didn't stand quite as tall as he once had, to Grace's recollection; but he made sure everything ran as smooth as spun silk at Brockwell Manor, right down to the sheen of every last silver spoon in the bureau drawer.

When Grace planted her shoes in the thick, sodden earth, they sunk fast, but she pulled them out again and, with her hand tucked in Solomon's arm, walked briskly to the tiny abode that housed The Perfect Fit Tailoring Shop, owned by Joy Jennings. The house had been Joy's home before she'd married Lucas Jennings, pastor of Paris Evangelical Church, and moved into the parsonage.

Moments later, the pretty lady threw wide her front door and beckoned them inside.

"Wasn't sure if I should expect you folks in this weather," she called, "but I'm glad you made it safe an' sound." A young face peeked out from behind Joy's long skirts—her daughter Annie, who looked to be about five or six. Such an adorable child, and the spitting image of her mother, with her wispy blonde hair and beaming blue eyes the color of the Atlantic. "I could just as well've driven out to yer place, but I s'pose, in the end, it's best you came my way. Wouldn't want t' take the chance o' ruinin' yer fine weddin' dress in this horrid storm. Come in, come in."

Solomon ushered Grace inside, greeted Joy, then returned to the door. "I'll be waitin' in the carriage, miz. You give me a little wave from the door when you be ready t' leave."

"Would you like to sip some iced tea while you're waitin', Mr. Turner?" Joy asked him.

"That's mighty kind, Missus Joy, but I'll be jes' fine without. I brought m' Bible with me, so I think I'll commence to readin' some Scriptures whilst you ladies do business." He tipped his hat at all three of them, then stepped out and closed the door behind him.

Grace turned her attention to young Annie, giving her hands a tiny clap while bending at the waist. "Well, you're looking mighty pretty today in your flower-print dress."

The child pulled back her shoulders and smiled brightly. "Thank you. My mommy stitched it for me."

Joy grinned. "It plain don't make sense to buy dresses ready-made when I got a perfectly good sewin' machine."

Grace straightened and gave a little chuckle. "I have a perfectly good sewing machine, as well, but I've learned it doesn't make dresses on its own. It takes great talent to sew as you do, and I'm grateful Aunt Iris recommended you. She speaks glowingly of you, and when she showed me her closet full of gowns you'd fashioned for her, it was clear why."

Annie wandered off to a corner where several toys were scattered about—a few dolls and a cradle, a baby carriage just her size, small blankets, and wooden crate overflowing with doll-sized clothes. Clearly, the child didn't lack for things to keep her busy while her mother worked.

A speck of concern glittered in Joy's eyes, and she lowered her voice to say, "How is yer aunt, by the way?"

A rocklike weight seemed to settle in Grace's chest. "Doc Trumble says the disease is progressing. He doesn't see her living until Christmas, but I pray he's wrong. She lives with constant abdominal pain, but you wouldn't know it if it weren't for her awful moods. When she's feeling especially poorly, her spirits drop to the ground. She won't admit to the pain, though; she's much too stubborn for that. When I ask her how she's feeling, she always says, 'Fit as an old fiddle.'"

"Oh, dear." Joy's brow furrowed. "I'm sorry t' hear she's sufferin' so. I knew she was ill, but I had no idea Doc Trumble'd given 'er so little time."

Grace's chest grew heavier. "I'm afraid she has a tumor, perhaps more than one. Of course, he can't be certain, but it's his best diagnosis. Based on recent examinations, he believes it's growing at a rather increased rate. Of course, an operation is out of the question at her age. Don't worry, though; Aunt Iris isn't about to succumb to her illness yet. Just the same, I'm asking that you finish my dress as quickly as you can. We're hoping to hold the wedding date at October fifteenth, but if her condition worsens, we will move it up."

The pretty seamstress gave a thoughtful nod. "I promise you I'll do my best."

"I'm certain you will, Mrs. Jennings, but I didn't mean to put any undue pressure on you."

"Oh, you haven't at all. An' even if you had, I'm used to workin' under pressure. Gracious, would you look at that pile o' mendin' over there? Don't tell anyone, but I've put yer dress at the top of the stack. My other customers will just have to practice patience. I'd say an upcomin' weddin' takes priority. Would you like to see how much I've done so far?"

Grace's spirits shot up a notch. "Oh, could I?"

"O' course, but on one condition."

"And what is that?"

"That you start callin' me Joy. I can't abide stuffiness."

Grace smiled. "Well then, you must call me Grace."

Joy gave a full smile, revealing a nice set of gleaming teeth. "We make a pair, don't we? Grace and Joy. Have y' met my friend Mercy Connors?"

Grace giggled. "I don't believe I have, but you must introduce us. With names like ours, we are all destined to be good friends."

"Indeed. Now, come on over here so we can get you fitted in this gown. I need to check some measurements before I proceed."

Grace followed her across the room. On the left wall was a brick fireplace and, beyond that, two doors, probably to bedrooms, if she had to guess. Straight ahead was a tiny, unused kitchen. On one wall stood a tall, finely crafted wardrobe with two doors, in which she envisioned sewing projects neatly stored on shelves or draped from hangers, and beside it sat a long, bureau-like table, also beautifully designed, housing twenty-five drawers or more. She could only assume it contained sewing supplies, such as scissors, threads of many colors, measuring tapes, pins, yards of ribbon, lace, and other bric-a-brac. Next to that stood Joy's sewing desk and a fine-looking Singer sewing machine, shining like new.

"Did your husband build all the furnishings?" Grace asked her. "I understand he's a talented craftsman."

"Indeed he did," said Joy with a proud smile. "And indeed he is! I've yet t' find one thing he don't excel at. Well, I'll take that back—he's useless when it comes to stitchin', cookin', gardenin', cleanin', and general housekeepin'." She laughed. "I'm not complainin', mind you. I could no more stand behind that pulpit and deliver a sermon than I could pick up a rattler with my bare hands. We all have our gifts, don't y' know."

Grace smiled. "Yes, I suppose we do, although I've yet to find mine."

"Oh, you've got gifts aplenty, Grace Fontaine. Everyone does. I can already tell you've got a big heart, not to mention a spirit o' generosity and compassion. Otherwise, you wouldn't've left the big city o' Boston and come clear down t' Tennessee t' care for yer ailin' aunt. Not everybody would do that, y' know."

Grace liked the southern drawl that characterized Joy's speech, as it did that of most of the residents of Paris. "Well, I appreciate that, but I didn't have to think twice about coming. Yes, I left a job I loved, along with some very dear friends; but Aunt Iris is family, and I have such fond memories of visiting her as a girl with my mother."

Turning her back to Grace, Joy opened one of the wardrobe doors and started fishing through the garments hanging inside. "Are yer parents still livin'?"

"No, I'm afraid not. Papa died in a logging accident when I was very young, and my mother passed some five years ago."

"Oh, I'm so sorry to hear that. My parents are gone, too—my mother passed away just last year. Time's fleetin', isn't it?"

"Yes, very."

"What sort o' job did you leave behind?"

"I worked as a nurse at Massachusetts General Hospital. Someday I hope to go back to my profession—that is, if my fiancé agrees. He sees no need for me to work, but should the opportunity present itself…."

Joy kept digging around in the wardrobe. "You'll prob'ly start totin' little ones soon after you marry. Won't do for you t' work away from the home with young'uns underfoot. Ah, here it is." She produced a fancy, partially finished white gown that far exceeded Grace's expectations.

A gasp of excitement whistled out of her. "Oh, my stars! Is that it? But—it's gorgeous."

"Well, as you can see, I'm not near done." Joy held it up high to keep the hem from touching the floor. "I've yet to attach the lace and tiny pearls, finish the sleeves, shorten the length, and fasten the buttons. I just completed all the buttonholes last night whilst baby Naomi slept. Of course, I haven't started the veil yet." She began to turn the gown around for Grace's perusal, but the mention of her two-month-old infant somehow evoked a tiny whimper from one of the side rooms.

Annie leaped up from her youth-sized chair and abandoned her doll to the crate. "Mommy, Naomi's awake."

"Shh. I know, honey. Let's see if she'll go back t' sleep."

The blonde-haired beauty put on a frown. "If she don't, can I hold 'er?"

"Yes, after I diaper and feed 'er."

"It must be nice to have such a fine helper," Grace inserted with a wink.

Joy smiled back. "If an overly enthused one."

After easing into her wedding gown, successfully evading any pins that might have poked her, Grace stepped up to a stool so Joy could assess the dress's fit. As hoped, baby Naomi quieted, and Annie resumed her play, humming a tune. For the next few minutes, Joy worked, adding more pins to the bodice and bringing in the material at the shoulders and waist, as well as marking off the sleeve and hem lengths. Once done, she assisted Grace in stepping down from the stool and climbing back out of the dress. Grace hastily put on her long-sleeved, button-front, yellow poplin blouse and her ankle-length brown skirt with the braided trim at the bottom.

The fitting hadn't taken long, as Joy had worked with efficiency and skill, mumbling to herself as she'd pinned and sometimes turning to jot things down on a pad of paper. So as not to break her concentration, Grace had kept mum, somewhat buried in her own thoughts about her upcoming wedding—especially the groom, Conrad Hall. He was a fine Christian man—protective, mature, self-assured, handsome, successful, and, all in all, quite captivating. She hadn't fallen as quickly for him as he had for her, but his outright charm and gentlemanly affections had soon won her over. A prosperous lawyer from Chicago, he had started collaborating with Murphy & Wadsworth, Attorneys-at-Law, some eighteen months ago; six months later, he had joined them in their downtown Paris office. Now the fancy placard on the redbrick building in the center of town read "Murphy, Wadsworth & Hall, Attorneys-at-Law." As if that weren't enough, he'd purchased Brooks Hotel and Restaurant in downtown Paris soon after joining the law firm. It was a fine establishment that he'd seen as a good investment, considering many people made it either their ultimate destination or a stopover on their travels between Memphis and Clarksville.

"You must be gettin' pretty excited about yer weddin'," Joy said while she hung the dress in the wardrobe once more. "I s'pose seein' yer gown made it seem more real."

"Yes," Grace agreed. "Sometimes I have to pinch myself. Just four months ago, I never would have dreamed I'd be trying on my wedding dress within a year's time."

"It's been a whirlwind romance, then. Mr. Hall must be very charmin'."

"He is." Her stomach always took to fluttering when she spoke of her betrothed. A few stray strands of hair tickled her cheek, so she positioned them behind her ear, a nervous gesture. "He enjoys spoiling me far more than I deserve."

"Oh, you deserve it. Every bride-to-be needs spoilin'. Sounds like he's a keeper."

"He surely is. They don't come much finer."

"He's a good Christian, I presume. I've seen y' at church, but I regret I've been so busy roundin' up my little ones, I haven't gone out of my way t' welcome you. Lucas tells me you've asked him to officiate at the weddin'."

"Yes, and we're elated he agreed." Grace decided to skip over the comment about Conrad's being a good Christian. Naturally, he knew the Lord; she wouldn't marry him if he didn't. He just had a quieter way of expressing his faith, even though he did voice an occasional "amen," albeit under his breath, when the reverend's sermons called for it.

"Your husband is a fine preacher," Grace went on. "I'm afraid I don't tell him enough how much I appreciate his messages—so thought-provoking and uplifting. Conrad always seems to want to beat the crowd to the churchyard so we can be on our way. For that reason, I haven't had much chance to meet folks. It's for the best that we head home immediately, though, as I don't like leaving Aunt Iris for long periods of time."

"I understand. Yer fiancé—he works with that law firm in town, doesn't he?"

"Indeed, as one of the partners."

Joy pursed her lips a moment. "Maybe I shouldn't mention this, but I don't much care for that Mr. Murphy. He's rather a stinker, if I may say so. A couple o' years ago, he behaved in aquite unseemly manner with me."

"No, really? Did he mishandle a legal case?"

"Um, no, nothin' like that." Joy shook her head. "He, for lack of a better term, mishandled *me*."

Grace frowned. "I don't understand."

"Well, let's just say he brought his business t' me and then tried t' take advantage o' me—in a not-so-appropriate way."

"You mean, he made advances toward you?"

"More than once, I'm afraid. I was divorced—well, I'd never actually gotten married, unbeknownst to me, but that's a different story—and so he viewed me as a…shall we say…loose woman, even though *he* was very much married."

The information gave Grace pause, and she wondered if she ought to bring to Conrad's attention this unfavorable trait of his business partner. She also wondered about Joy's background but decided not to ask about it now. "Did you report the incidents?"

"No, I didn't really need to—nor did I want to. Lucas handled the matter in a rather discreet manner, but that's yet another story. The only reason I told you is so you could be aware. I think he's rather devious, though I've never heard anyone speak ill o' his legal practices. I hope mine was an isolated case. At any rate, you should be cautious round him."

Grace nodded. "I shall, and thank you for telling me."

"I don't mean t' stir up any trouble, so please don't share this information. I'm not one to spread gossip, but since yer husband-to-be works with the man, I thought I'd mention it."

"I appreciate that, Joy. Truly, I do."

"Well, enough o' that. Tell me more about yer fiancé. Is he yer first love?"

The unexpected question took Grace aback. "My first…? No, not exactly."

As if she had seen him only yesterday, the face of her former love, Jess Quinn, flashed across her mind like a moving picture. She envisioned their final moments together, more than two years ago, before he boarded the *Lone Star*, a 300-passenger steamer with forty-plus crew members bound for London; she recalled their tight, clinging hugs and last-minute kisses, and the twinkle in his olive eyes when he said, "I love you, Grace Fontaine. When I return, I shall do something about changing your last name." Even the gentle touch of his finger to the tip of her nose had burned in her a poignant, permanent memory.

"There was someone else," she finally said, "but that was a long time ago. I'm afraid he was lost at sea on a transatlantic voyage."

Joy gasped. "That's terrible! You must've been devastated."

Grace didn't wish to go into detail about love lost while she was being fitted for a wedding dress for a marriage to someone else. "Yes, well, we kept holding out hope for news that he'd survived, but British naval authorities finally concluded that the entire crew had drowned."

Joy shuddered. "How awful for you and all the others left behind."

Grace turned her gaze to young Annie, who seemed oblivious to her presence, still humming away as she played in the corner. "Well, I didn't mean to put such a damper on things." She rubbed her hands together.

"No, I'm the one what started it by bringin' up that dreadful Charles Murphy," Joy said. "Next time, there'll be nothin' but happy things t' discuss, namely, yer weddin'. An' I hope even yer aunt Iris will've improved. Does Mrs. Brockwell have other relatives?"

Grace was glad for the change of subject. "She has a couple of nephews, my second cousins, but she distanced herself from them years ago after they took advantage of her generosity. She'd loaned both of them a good sum of money to buy houses, which they refused to repay, claiming she'd told them it wasn't necessary. And then, if that wasn't enough, one of my cousins found a way to start draining her bank account, having gotten ahold of some private papers. My great-aunt's banker caught him red-handed and had him arrested, but Aunt Iris refused to press charges. I do believe it broke her heart, even though she wouldn't acknowledge it. She cared a lot for them in their growing-up years, but they were spoiled brats, I'm afraid. To this day, they're ruffians, as are their children." She sighed. "Honestly, I'm the only one Aunt Iris has, and I don't care one hoot about her money, so I suppose that explains why she trusts me."

Baby Naomi stirred again, and Annie leaped from her station on the floor where she'd been dressing her dolls, ran to a door off the room, and ducked inside.

"I must say, you have a very patient baby," Grace observed. "Is she normally a sound sleeper?"

Joy chuckled. "She's a good sleeper, yes, until her empty stomach starts sendin' messages to her brain."

"May I have a peek at her before I go?"

"O' course!"

Grace followed the slender woman to the small room and watched from the doorway while she lifted her baby from her cradle, young Annie reaching up to snag hold of the infant's foot and give it a gentle squeeze. *Such a doting older sister,* Grace thought. She tried to imagine the very professional Conrad Hall as a father, but her mind couldn't quite wrap itself around the concept. Odd how the subject of children had yet to come up in their conversations, even though they were engaged to be married. Well, it surely would at some point before they said their vows.

Time was when she'd envisioned Jess Quinn as the father of her children. She gave her head a stern shake to ward off the foolish remembrance. She'd decided some time ago to dismiss all thoughts of him. Chances were that even if he had miraculously survived and somehow returned, she wouldn't have the same feelings for him she'd once had. Having reached the ripe age of twenty-five, she'd put away childish notions and started viewing life with a greater degree of realism, especially considering her sickly aunt, who probably needed her by her bedside even now. She intended to take her leave, but when Joy placed her cooing, wriggling infant in her arms, Grace's heart turned to mush, and she could no more have left in that moment than she could have dragged a mule up a steep mountainside.

2

$\mathscr{G}$race gazed across the table at her future husband, dapper in his dark pin-striped suit and loosely knotted print tie, a kerchief folded to perfection poking out his breast pocket. His wavy hair, parted in the middle, shimmered with splashes of gold, reflecting the light of the chandelier overhead.

He certainly looked the part of wealthy restaurateur. The establishment, Brooks Hotel and Restaurant, boasted fine dining and fashionable accommodations—the best in all West Tennessee. And since he insisted on spoiling her beyond reason, they usually dined here several times a month. She had told him time and again that he need not treat her to dinner so often, when they could easily stay in and enjoy whatever fare Zelda Wiggins, the head cook at Brockwell Manor, had prepared. But he countered by reminding her that he owned the place and wanted to make sure the staff kept it running according to his high standards. Grace had never known such pampering.

Other diners at the restaurant spoke in quiet voices, and the glittering candlelight, the delectable aromas carrying out from the kitchen, and the tinkling of silver on china provided a romantic ambience.

Conrad eyed her with an admiring look. "So, the wedding gown is coming along, is it? I'm sure you'll be the loveliest bride Paris has ever seen."

Smiling, she took up her water glass, swallowed a small sip, and set the crystal glass back on the white linen tablecloth. "Yes indeed, it's most lovely."

Conrad dabbed with his napkin at his well-groomed mustache, then lowered the cloth to his lap and grinned. "Tell me about this fancy gown you'll be wearing the afternoon of October fifteenth."

"Certainly not. Haven't you heard it's improper for the bride to give the groom even the smallest hint about her dress?"

His lips twitched playfully. "I've heard that the groom isn't to see his bride on the day of the wedding, prior to the ceremony, that is, but I've not heard that he isn't permitted to know so much as a single detail about the dress. I suppose it's bad luck, eh?"

Grace gave a little shrug of one shoulder. "I don't believe in good or bad luck, but I do believe in following decorum."

He chuckled. "Ah, so you shall continue to bait me with tiny tidbits but tell me nothing. Is that how it is, my dear?"

She laughed with him. "You know as much as you need to know."

He reached across the table and snagged her hand. "You look lovely tonight. Have I told you that?" he said in a mellow tone that sliced into her thoughts.

She smiled. "Only half a dozen times, but I don't grow tired of hearing it."

His thumb grazed over the top of her hand in a circling motion, his grayish blue eyes piercing clear to her soul. "Good, because I intend to keep telling you for the next fifty or so years. You're irresistible, you know. Are you sure I must wait till mid-October to make you wholly mine?"

Were it not for the dimness of the room, he'd surely have spotted the blush of her cheeks. Good gracious, but he had the power to draw her like metal to magnet. No man—not even Jess Quinn—had ever charmed her with such romantic words. "There is still much yet to do to ready myself for our wedding, Conrad, and I need every spare minute to plan it."

He winked and leaned forward, his shirtfront pressed against the table, and whispered, "I wouldn't mind eloping tomorrow and doing away with all the formalities of a wedding with guests." His foot found hers under the table and flirted with it.

Feeling the heat of another flush rise to her cheeks, she quickly tucked both her feet under her chair, crossing them at the ankles. To date, their intimacy had amounted to nothing more than sweet kisses, and she intended to keep it that way until their wedding night. She fumbled with a few strands of hair that had fallen from her fancily fixed bun. "You know my wish is that Aunt Iris should witness our vows—if she is well enough, that is."

"Oh yes, Aunt Iris." Something happened to the lilt in his voice. It dropped a degree. "How is she these days?"

Grace sighed. "No better, I'm afraid." She sniffed, fighting off her sudden feeling of sadness. "She is a fighter, though. I don't think the doctors gave her an accurate prognosis."

Conrad released her hand, so she put it back in her lap, intertwining all her fingers. He picked up his water glass, took a few swigs, and then settled back in his chair, eyebrows knitted into a small frown. "You think they're mistaken about the presence of tumors? Dr. Trumble has a fine reputation, as do the other physicians he called in from Nashville to examine her."

"No, no, I believe they made an accurate diagnosis. I just don't believe they know how strong and stubborn Aunt Iris can be. She doesn't want to die yet, and something tells me she'll hang on to life with every fiber of her being. Perhaps we should postpone our wedding just so she'll make every effort to live longer."

His frown became a full-out scowl. "Well now, that would be plain cruel—to her, and to me."

"I was only being facetious."

He released a loud sigh. "That's a relief. I don't think I could wait one second past midnight of the fifteenth. You've punished me enough by making me wait two more months, my darling."

"Oh, silly, I'm not punishing you one bit." She lifted her left arm and extended her hand to admire the diamond engagement ring he'd given her. It sparkled in the glow of the candle in the middle of their table.

A waiter dressed in a pristine suit with a spotless white cloth draped over his arm approached with a pitcher of water. "May I refill your glasses, Mr. Hall?"

"Of course," Conrad answered.

The waiter leaned forward and poured until the sparkling liquid came nearly to the rim of both their glasses. Then, straightening, he addressed Conrad again. "Would you care to order your meals now?"

In his usual take-charge manner, Conrad lifted his chin and replied, "Yes. We'll have the roast goose with stuffing."

"Very good, sir." With finesse, the man swiveled on one heel, making his coattails flare, and disappeared as quickly as he'd come.

Grace wasn't fond of goose, and she'd told Conrad so on a former occasion. He must have forgotten, since it was his favorite dish. Well, so be it. She could handle a few bites. Best not to cause a stir over something so trivial.

When Grace entered the massive foyer of Brockwell Manor a couple of hours later, Solomon emerged from the library, a dust cloth in hand. The man worked around the clock—Grace was convinced of it. "Ah, Miz Grace. Welcome back." He took her lightweight cape and laid it across his arm.

She hoped he didn't notice her flustered deportment or detect any evidence of puffy lips, a result of Conrad's overly anxious kisses. Tonight, he'd been far more passionate than usual after helping her down from the carriage. Then, once he'd escorted her up the walk to the front door in a breathless state, he'd kissed her one last time on the porch before hurrying back to his buggy. She much preferred the attentive, gentlemanly side of Conrad Hall to this aggressive one and hoped not to have to fend him off again.

"How is my aunt?" she inquired.

"Missus Blanche brushed out her hair, gave her her tonics, and put her to bed a while back. She ask for you mo' 'n once at the supper table. I kep' tellin' 'er you is out with yo' husband-to-be, which seemed to satisfy her temporary-like."

Grace clicked her tongue and shook her head. "I'm worried about her. Did she eat anything?"

"Miz Ellen, she done coax her till she was pert-near blue in the face, but yo' aunt, she plain stubborn. She kep' on shakin' her head no. I tries her on some soup, and she sipped a few teaspoons and drank some warm milk. Miz Ellen get her to chew on a cracker, but tha's about it."

"Well, I appreciate all of you trying." She felt her brow crimp in worry.

He gave a knowing smile, making his upper gold tooth gleam in the light of the gas-lit chandelier glowing overhead. "Oh, she a stubborn one. We'll jes' have t' wait an' see. It's in da Lord's hands, as you an' me well know."

Grace nodded. "I pray each morning the Lord will allow her to out-live the doctor's predictions. I know she's ready to meet the Lord, but I'm not ready to let her go."

Solomon's dark eyes twinkled, the whites around his pupils having yellowed from age. "No, ma'am, none of us be ready for that. She has her conversations with the Lord. I 'magine she been tellin' 'im 'bout the same thing. She ain't scared t' go, mind y'; she jes' don't want t' go quite yet." He shook his gray head. "She done mellowed out these past couple o' years, yes'm, sort of like a fish what's grown tired o' fightin' at the other end of the line. She don't like to show it much, but it's true as the snow is white."

"I know she can be as tough as crow sometimes, but she's also got a big heart. Mama once told me Aunt Iris donates money to all manner of good causes."

"Oh, that she do, miz. Yes'm, she a mighty generous soul. She gives to Lost Children's Fund of New York, the Paris Women's Club, sev'ral missionary societies, and the First Methodist Church. She used to go there when Mistuh Brockwell was alive. She ain't much for church attendance, but she sho''nough knows the Lord. Missus Brockwell's a private lady 'bout her faith, very private. She had her hurts in life."

Grace assumed he was referring to her aunt's apparent inability to bear children. Her mother had once told her that Aunt Iris had fallen into a deep, dark sadness in her early forties, refusing even to leave her house for the span of a year or more, and that it had to do with her despair over never having children. Grace envisioned Uncle John, Solomon, and the rest of the staff at Brockwell Manor carrying food trays to her room and tending to her every need.

"You've been a wonderful friend to her, Solomon."

"Ah, and she to me. It's goin' to be awful strange around here once she…well, you know, passes on into glory."

"Indeed. I can't bring myself to think about it. I sometimes wonder what will become of this place."

"It'll go t' you, o' course. Ha'n't yo' aunt talked to you about it?"

"No, but if those are her intentions, I couldn't accept it. Why, what would I do with a house this size? Good gracious, I'm accustomed to my small flat in the heart of Boston."

"Well, I don't know, miz, but I's certain you'll come up with somethin' worthwhile t' do with it. You best talk to yo' aunt 'bout her wishes while she's still of sound mind. One thing I don't want y' worryin' 'bout is what to do with me an' the staff. I cain't speak for the others, but I know I'll make do. I has lots o' friends at St. Paul Missionary Baptist Church, and they's already talkin' 'bout me buyin' a small house over in their neighborhood. I'll find some way t' earn my keep, too. I ain't one for charity."

Grace couldn't believe her ears. "Solomon Turner, what are you talking about? You'll not be moving anywhere. Brockwell Manor is much more your home than it is mine!"

He gave a sheepish smile. "Oh, I may've come here as a youngster, Miz Grace, but you is her blood kin."

Over the years, Grace had heard bits and pieces of the story—that Uncle John had bought Solomon off the slave block but treated him as one of the family.

"How old were you when you first came here, Sol?"

"Well, let's see here." He scratched his temple and squinted, his bushy white eyebrows arching. "My mammy died when I was a wee one, which resulted in me bouncin' around from one master to 'nother. Never did know my pappy. When I was right around fourteen, I took real sick. My master, Mistuh Langsley, had no mo' use fo' me, so he put me on the block real cheap. Mistuh John Brockwell was passin' through Atlanta at the time, an' he made eye contact with me. Yes'm, I remember the day. Those eyes o' his jes' went kind o' soft, and he marched right up to the platform an' bought me on the spot. Put me on a train to Paris that very day." He gave a rumbling chuckle. "I kin still remember Missus Brockwell's scowl when she first see me. Weren't nothin' even close to Mistuh Brockwell's reaction, no siree. She put her hands on her hips and looked me up and down. 'He won't be much good to us, John Brockwell. He's skinnier than a fence rail,' she says. But Mistuh Brockwell tells her the Lord tol' him to buy me, so she best not be arguin' with divine orders. That done quieted her." He laughed again, one upper gold tooth catching a fleck of light. "After that, we become real good friends, me an' Missus Brockwell—as long as I remembered my station. I always said she nursed my body back to health, but it was Mistuh Brockwell what nursed my soul an' spirit, teachin' me the ways o' the Lord."

Grace touched his arm. "You've been through a great deal, Solomon."

"Not at all, ma'am. I been nothin' but blessed, an' I got the Brockwells t' thank for that."

"I think my aunt would argue that she is the blessed one, surrounded as she is by so many caring folks. Speaking of Aunt Iris, I'd best go peek in on her."

"You do that, miz. I'll be right along with some tea."

"No, please don't bother. I'll be getting ready for bed soon."

"Tha's jus' fine, then, Miz Grace. I'll have Missus Blanche go turn down yo' covers."

There simply wasn't any point in telling him not to wait on her. Grace had determined shortly after arriving at Brockwell Manor that the staff was a decidedly stubborn bunch whose job it was to make the residents and guests as comfortable as possible. No amount of arguing would change that.

Contrary to what Solomon had told her, Aunt Iris was not asleep but was sitting in her wooden rocker next to the window, unmoving, staring out at the dusky night. A summer breeze blew through the open window, making the sheer floral curtains swell. Her wrinkled hands were folded in her lap, and in the growing dark, her wedding ring gleamed when it caught a tiny ray of light from the kerosene lamp on a nearby side table. Her white hair, neatly brushed, cascaded down the middle of her back, some of it falling over her shoulders to blend with her crisp white nightgown, the yoke and the sleeve edging of which were tatted in an intricate pattern—probably another stitching creation of Joy Jennings.

"Aunt Iris, why aren't you in bed?" Grace glanced at the mattress. The blankets lay in a rumpled heap, evidence that her aunt had been there before moving to the rocker.

The woman made nary a move but merely continued gazing out the window, blank faced.

Grace bent over, pulled off her Lady Jane sling-back pumps with the two-inch heels, and set them next to the door. She didn't want to startle her aunt with the clicking of heels on hardwood, even though a lovely Turkish rug covered a good share of the floor. Her petticoats swished as she approached, but still Aunt Iris sat mute. Grace went down on her knees and stretched out a hand to lay atop her aunt's clasped ones. "Auntie?"

As if coming awake from a long nap, Iris Brockwell's eyes alighted on Grace's face and sparked with recognition. "My, you look so much like your mama, I thought for a moment there you were Hilda."

"No, it's just me, Auntie, your great-niece. Mama died five years ago." Grace's mother had been more like a daughter than a niece to Aunt Iris, and she'd loved the older woman as much as if she were her own mama.

Aunt Iris lifted her hazy eyes to give Grace a better looking over. "I guess you caught me in a bit of a dream. Of course, I know it's you,

Grace, and you don't have to remind me that your mother died five years ago. I have tumors in my abdomen, not my brain."

Her aunt's brashness in spite of her grave condition made Grace laugh. "Oh, Auntie, I know that."

"Well, good. Tell that to the rest of them, would you? Sometimes I think they imagine I can't hear or understand them when they're talking about me. I tell them they can discuss me all they want once the under-taker lays me out for the viewing, just not when I'm lying in my bed. Just because my eyes are closed doesn't mean I'm deaf."

Grace bit her lip to hold back a smile. "I'll tell them."

For a brief moment, Aunt Iris stared at her before returning her gaze to the window. "It's getting dark. Did you see the sky?"

Grace reached across the distance to pull back a corner of the drape, craning her neck to look out. Shades of red, pink, and purple streaked the horizon, making for a perfect August sunset. "Indeed I did. It's pretty, don't you think?"

"I suppose. Seen plenty of sunsets in my day. Did you have a nice dinner?"

"Yes, it was lovely. Thank you for asking." Rather than retrieve a chair, Grace sat on the floor next to her aunt, legs crossed at the ankles, and rested her back against the window wall. "What do you think of Conrad, Auntie? You've never really said."

The woman scowled. "Well, if you want the God's truth, I don't know him well enough to judge. He doesn't come around very often. I can't say I've ever carried on much of a conversation with him."

Her abrupt honesty touched a nerve in Grace's spine, making her go pin straight. "He's a fine man, Auntie. Perhaps he just doesn't know what to say to you."

"Am I that difficult to talk to?"

She almost asked, *"You want the God's truth?"* but held her tongue. Iris Brockwell was known for her blunt candor and outright cheekiness as much as for her generous spirit. Indisputably, many were intimidated by the woman.

"I wouldn't say that, no," Grace fibbed. "But perhaps…well…a tad, um, outspoken."

Iris lifted a thin white brow. "Are you telling me that a seasoned attorney of the law can't handle an old lady who speaks her mind? Perhaps he's in the wrong field."

"No, Conrad's excellent at what he does. You just don't know him, that's all."

"Humph. Then tell him to come over some night and stay awhile."

Hiding the deep sigh that threatened to erupt, Grace gave her aunt's folded hands another gentle pat. "I'll do that. In fact, we'll have dinner with you next week. How would that be?"

"I guess that'd be fine, although I'm none too fond of eating these days—not when most of my food won't stay put."

"I know that's a problem. Doc Trumble says it's common with your condition."

"Yes, well, my 'condition,' as you put it, is wearing on my last nerve."

Grace giggled, then sobered. "It's wearing on mine, as well. It pains me so to see you suffer."

"I'm not long for this world, you know."

"Now, Auntie, I won't have you giving up. Doc Trumble says—"

"I know what the doctor says. He's giving me till Thanksgiving, if that."

"But he also said no one can predict the course of things. Only God knows."

Iris stared again at the golden horizon, fast vanishing. "Sometimes I hear the Lord speak. I know you must think it strange that He'd talk to an old crank like me, especially one who doesn't even go to church. I know my Savior, though. I want to make that good and clear."

Grace gave her a tender smile. "I know you do, and I don't think it's a bit strange that God would speak to you. I have often heard Him speak to me—in still, small ways, of course."

"Of course." Iris winced and clutched her stomach.

Grace touched her shoulder. "Shall I help you into bed?"

"I believe that'd be a good idea." The woman put her hands on the chair arms and pushed up, gritting her teeth as she shakily stood, Grace supporting her with a firm hand under her elbow. Her legs had grown wobblier over the past weeks. Once stable, Aunt Iris slapped her hand away. Grace let go and walked alongside her. Iris backed herself up to the bed and dropped down onto the mattress, then, with help, went into a reclining position. Her breaths came out labored, and again she winced when situating herself on the mattress.

Grace pulled the covers up and tucked them under her aunt's chin. Grasping the blanket by the hem with her withered, crooked fingers, Iris stared up at her, opened her mouth, and then closed it again.

"Auntie? Are you all right? Having some pain?"

"Pfff, I'm fine as a frog's hair." Even dying, she detested having to concede her suffering.

"Well, you looked like you were about to say something."

"Yes, I suppose I was." Her clouded eyes sought out Grace's brown ones. "When the Lord speaks to you in that still, small voice you spoke of, does He tell you in no uncertain terms to marry Conrad Hall?"

The question set Grace aback. *Had* God spoken to her in such a way? She concluded that surely He had. She couldn't put her finger on when, exactly, but she hadn't felt any stabbing prick of her conscience *not* to marry him, so that should be good enough.

"Seems like it's taking you a while to answer."

She hurried to come up with a response. "God led me here to take care of you, and I met Conrad on my very first day, at the train station. From there, things just started moving along. If that's not God at work, I don't know what is."

"Hmm. Well, that doesn't sound like any still, small voice to me, but then, what do I know? Good night, dear niece. And if it means anything, I am glad you came clear from Boston to live with me."

Grace smiled, then leaned down to plant a featherlight kiss on her aunt's forehead. "As am I, Auntie." She sat with her for a few minutes, and when Iris drifted off into a slumbering state, she tiptoed across the room, retrieved her shoes, and slipped out the door.

3

A hot August sun beat upon the crystalline waters of Boston Harbor, transforming its surface into a million glittering mirrors that looked more like flashing fish than rippling waves. Folks stood at the quayside on Liverpool Wharf waving handkerchiefs at the incoming ship. Jess Quinn hefted the bag containing his meager possessions and moved with the masses to the front of the vessel, where they would disembark.

He didn't expect to find Grace awaiting his arrival—or anyone else, for that matter. He'd wired a message to his father six weeks ago, the first one he'd been permitted to send since his capture and subsequent unlawful imprisonment in England. Even so, he would be shocked to find him waiting, since his father had no idea what ship he was to sail home on, much less the exact date or time of arrival.

He hoped his father had honored his wish not to inform anyone else—Grace included—of his impending return. Oh, he had no doubt she would be elated to discover him alive; but his present physical condition might frighten her, and he didn't want to send her into a state of utter shock. Two years of hard labor in a British naval camp had battered his body. He'd lost much weight, and the sight of the pathetic-looking, frail, bedraggled fellow in the washroom mirror upon boarding the ship had nearly scared his own raggedy pants right off. His hair had been beyond unruly, and his thick beard fully masked his identity. In fact, his own father would probably be hard-pressed to pinpoint him in a crowd.

He had much to explain concerning his long absence, yet no matter how many hundreds of times he'd pondered what he ought to tell everyone, it never sounded convincing enough. His stomach fluttered, and for a moment, he feared he might just lose his sparse lunch—a single piece of bread and a cup of water. It wasn't that the options in the commissary had been limited but that his appetite had failed him.

The ship gave a minor jolt as it docked, and a sea of hot, sweaty, smelly bodies bumped against one another as they moved like a herd of cattle toward the gangplank, eager to plant their feet on solid ground. It had been a long, trying journey, so Jess didn't blame folks for wanting to be the first to go ashore. As for him, he hung back. No point in rushing into a muddle of unfamiliar faces.

Once on shore, he found a spot away from the commotion to get his bearings. It would take days to adjust his posture and gait, as his sea legs kept insisting that he was still rising and falling with the waves. If he never boarded another boat, it would be too soon.

Shouts of joyful greetings echoed off the wharf as sweethearts reunited. Wives and mothers dabbed at happy tears, and fathers hoisted into their arms the children they hadn't seen for perhaps months. At the foot of the pier, buggies and carriages waited to bear the arriving seamen and passengers to their destinations, while horse-drawn drays stood by to haul incoming cargo to waterfront warehouses. Jess's eyes traversed the jovial crowd but spotted nary a familiar face. Of course, he hadn't expected to.

Leaving the excitement behind, he tucked his jacket under one arm, hoisted his single piece of luggage with the other, inhaled a heavy breath, and started to make his way up the wharf between clusters of townsfolk. Finding Congress Street, he headed west past the navy yard, crossed over Dorchester Avenue and then Atlantic, wended his way north on High Street, and soon made a left turn onto Pearl. The several blocks' walk winded him, after weeks of sea travel with hardly any exercise to speak of; so, when he reached the familiar corner at High and Pearl, his racing heart hitched, and he paused to take a breath. Setting his luggage on the cobblestone road, he mopped his sweat-soaked brow with his sleeve, then gazed up the street. From what he could see, nothing much had changed in his absence—the same weather-bleached, stately brick apartment buildings lined both sides of the street, standing shoulder to shoulder like aging soldiers, and looking sleepy beneath the noonday sun. A salty breeze drifting off the harbor melded with the scent of flowers in the tiny front-yard gardens. Unfortunately, the stench of horse dung also played into the mix.

Hoisting his bag again, he made his way up the uneven road until his eyes finally settled on the building where he'd grown up—the most ramshackle one on the block. An untended patch of grass and a bed of weeds greeted him at the front entry. Before climbing the concrete stairs to the big double doors, he paused and gazed skyward till he identified his father's front window. The curtain hung crooked, of course. If his mother were still alive, she'd have a fit. She'd always been so meticulous. He exhaled, then climbed the steps and opened the heavy door, wondering if he'd even find his father at home. At the landing, he gathered his strength, mopped his brow one last time, and then proceeded up three flights of dark, dingy stairs, his footfalls echoing loudly. Somewhere in the building, a baby wailed, someone banged on a piano in dire need of tuning, and bacon sputtered in a skillet. When he reached the third floor, he snagged another deep breath of the hot, sticky air, then proceeded to the door bearing the number 314.

He gave the door a light knock, then turned the knob and entered. His father sat slumped in the old green velvet sofa, eyes closed, a smoking pipe hanging out one side of his mouth, and a half-consumed bottle of beer resting on a wooden crate at the end of the sofa. Jess's heart thrummed with some kind of emotion. Before waking his father, he let his eyes roam the unkempt room. The old man had no notion of how to clean house. He'd aged visibly, and his gut had enlarged, no doubt a result of his consumption of ale. His scraggly hair needed a cut, and he could use a good shave; but then, who was Jess to judge a fellow man for his shabby appearance?

He dropped his luggage by the door, tossed his jacket atop the suitcase, and crossed the gritty wood floor to a chair occupied by several tattered copies of the *Boston Globe*. After clearing them away, he lowered himself into the chair he'd considered ancient even as a kid.

His father stirred, made a snuffling noise, and coughed deep in his chest. His eyelids fluttered.

"Hi, Pa."

He startled and sat up, his foggy eyes looking far older than their fifty-one years when they came to rest on Jess's face. "That you, Jess?"

"Yeah, Pa, it's me."

"Ya got a beard."

"I'm a sight, I know."

"A sight for sure."

He could have said the same for him.

"You done working for the day, or are you going in later?"

"Didn't have t' work today. I worked so much overtime, the boss tol' me t' take the day off."

"That's nice."

His father's eyes crinkled in the corners when he fastened Jess with a long stare, perhaps because a bit of moisture had gathered there. Then he dragged himself nearer the edge of the sofa, huffing a bit as he inched forward. "Look at y', would ya?" he said, his faded Irish brogue more gravelly than Jess remembered it. Fergus Quinn had left his homeland as an adolescent but had never fully shed his accent. And now, with the addition of his Boston accent, one had a difficult time exactly determining his country of origin.

"Didn't think I'd ever set eyes on y' again. I reconciled with yer bein' dead and gone, and now here y' are, settin' right here in the old brown chair." He reached out a hand, and Jess detected a quiver that hadn't been there two years ago. Had he been drinking himself to death? The trembly hand went around Jess's forearm and squeezed. "Ya lost some pounds, Son. What happened to y', anyway?"

Fergus Quinn had never been demonstrative—Jess couldn't remember the last time his father had even hugged him—so the gesture meant a great deal. Jess pressed his larger hand over his father's shaky one. He hated seeing how much the man had aged. Were their days for making up for lost time limited?

"It's a long story, Pa, and one I think I'll save for later, if you don't mind."

The man's eyes grew a shade darker. "If yer ma was here, she'd be havin' a conniption. She'd be runnin' ever' which direction, all excited an' about to fall over with delight. She also wouldn't let ya keep shut about what happened to ya, but I can see ye're tired. We were told some pirate ship robbed yer vessel, took ya hostage, and that the Royal Navy gunned down the ship. No survivors."

"That's the gist of it, yes. I survived, though—as you can well see."

The man nodded and swiped a hand through his unruly gray hair. "I'll wait till ye're feelin' stronger to get the details. It's good fer now just knowin' ye're alive."

"Thanks, Pa. I appreciate that." The mention of his mother had brought on a strong sense of nostalgia. He missed her, would give anything to wrap his arms around her small frame, but another part of him celebrated the fact that she hadn't had to endure the news of his ship going down. She'd been gone three years now, a result of a traffic accident on Rutherford Avenue. The incident had so rattled his father that it seemed he'd been trying to kill himself ever since with booze.

The man blinked hard, tried to pull himself straighter, and resumed drawing on his pipe, filling up the room with the acrid stench of tobacco. With every breath, his lungs hissed. Time was when Jess had found the aroma comforting; but ever since he'd given up smoking, he actually found the smell quite nauseating.

He swallowed down a hard lump of emotion. "I know I asked you not to tell anyone about my coming home, but did you speak to Grace about the wire I sent?"

"No. Ya told me not to, so I honored yer wishes. 'Sides, Grace ain't around anymore. She left Boston a few months back, but I don't recall just where she went."

"What?" Jess sat forward in his chair, half choking on the word before continuing. "What do you mean, you don't know where she went? Why'd she leave?"

"Don't know offhand—somethin' 'bout takin' care o' somebody. She brought me a meat pie and a plate o' cookies. I told her she was a good cook."

Jess didn't want to hear about Grace's cooking. He wanted, he needed, to learn where she'd gone.

"She preached at me 'bout my health, too. Told me I needed to start eatin' better. Weren't ya gonna marry 'er?"

"Yes, and that's still my intention."

"Ye'll have to find 'er 'fore ya can do that."

Jess withheld a sigh of frustration. "You sure you don't remember where she said she was going? Think hard."

"I am thinkin' hard, but I tol' ya, I don't recall. Maybe she'll send me a letter someday."

"Someday? Pa, I'm not waiting till *someday*. Have you seen Josiah lately? He might know where she went."

"Ain't seen 'im since he got married."

"Married? Josiah's married? Did he marry Ruthie?"

"I guess that's her name. Stiles was her maiden name, I b'lieve. They just had a little'un, too."

Jess looked up from his clasped hands. "Well, I'll be. They're a regular family. Boy or girl?"

"What's that?"

"The baby—did they have a boy or a girl?"

"Pssh. How would I know?"

"Well, Josiah is my best friend."

"Yeah, but I ain't seen 'im in a while. He don't come round here much like when y' was here. One of the neighbors told me 'bout the baby."

"Okay." A wave of wistfulness raced through him. Josiah and Ruthie, Jess and Grace—they'd been a regular foursome before he'd set off on the *Lone Star* to make some fast money. Had he known that he'd wind up kidnapped and hauled aboard a pirate ship, forced to work in the galley for a bunch of filthy crooks, he'd have stuck with his job at the barrel factory and forgotten the extra money. "I've got to go see them." He stood up, suddenly energized.

"Now? But ya just got here."

"I know, and I'll be back." He needed to find out where Grace had gone, and he figured Josiah and Ruthie would know.

"Y' ain't eaten. I can tell by lookin' at ya."

"I'll be fine, Pa. I'll grab a bite somewhere. Don't wait up for me, okay?"

"But—y' ain't even tol' me the first thing about them pirates kidnappin' ya."

"Pa, I promise I'll give you the whole story later. Get some rest. You look pretty rough. You should lay off the booze."

"Pfff, ya should talk. Ain't y' at least goin' t' shave?"

"Ain't you?" Jess asked, his lips twitching in the corners as he bent at the waist and drilled his eyes into the fellow's.

If his father caught his playful tone, he didn't let on. "All right, then. Be gone with ya."

"I said I'll see you later. I just don't know what time I'll be back." He looked around the tiny apartment. "You got a room cleared for me to stay in, or should I ask Josiah and Ruthie to put me up for a few days?"

"Yeah, yeah, I got room for ya. Go see yer friends. They're livin' in Josiah's parents' old place."

"Thanks, Pa. If you're sure." Jess walked to the door, then turned and gave his father a quick glance. "It's good to see you again."

The fellow nodded, and for all of ten seconds, they each drank in the appearance of the other's face. Finally, the older man flipped his wrist. "Go on with ya, then. Ya been gone for two years; I s'pect a few more hours ain't goin' to bother me none."

⌒

In preparation for Conrad's arrival, Grace donned a gored peplum jacket with a matching gathered skirt, the dainty floral pattern and lightweight fabric suitable for an evening in. Sitting at her vanity table, she gathered her hair in a loose bun and fastened it with two hand-carved bone hairpins, allowing a few dark strands to dangle loose, framing her face. Next, she rubbed a bit of color into her cheeks and lips—a daring move for her. To top off her look, she pinned an ivory Victorian camellia brooch just below her stand-up collar on the left side. It proved the perfect complement to her outfit, but the brooch stirred up memories of her beloved mother, who had given it to her. Oh, how she would have loved to participate in planning Grace's wedding. In fact, she likely would have been at the center of all the organizing, which would have suited Grace just fine. Event planning, no matter that they intended to keep their wedding small and simple, just wasn't her specialty. Thankfully, Zelda Wiggins and her assistant, Nellie Flanders, had the food aspect under control, and Solomon had given a list of chores to Horace McMartin, the groundskeeper, and to Blanche McMartin and Ellen Waters, the housekeepers, to ensure that the manor would be perfect inside and out before her big day.

Briefly, she wondered what her parents would have thought of Conrad Hall. Surely, they would have approved, for he was a successful lawyer with much drive and enthusiasm, not to mention charm and good looks. Of course, his Christian witness made him particularly appealing. Grace's father had died when she was but a young child, so her memories of him were few. But her memories of her mother, who had died just five years ago of complications from scarlet fever, remained as vivid as ever. Grace was an only child, and her mother had never remarried after the death of Grace's father, her heart having died a little the day her beloved husband had passed into glory. She'd always claimed she didn't have it in her to give what remained of her heart to another man, although she would have had her pick of any number of suitors. Grace glanced at her dresser, which displayed a tintype of her mother and father taken on their wedding day in August 1865. My, but they'd made a handsome couple.

For reasons she couldn't identify, a blurry image of Jess Quinn's alluring face flashed across her mind. Perhaps it was because she had slipped into a rather melancholy frame. It rankled her that, in the two-plus years since Jess had disappeared and been presumed dead, she still hadn't managed to fully eradicate him from her thoughts. How long before she would finally put the matter behind her? Perhaps her marriage to Conrad would be the key. It wasn't that she still loved Jess; she loved Conrad and no other. But her recollection of him remained unusually vivid, right down to the single freckle above his left eyebrow. He'd had a broad chest and tall frame, and his piercing green eyes had been warm and inviting one minute, fierce and determined the next.

She hadn't wanted Jess to take the job on the Allan Line steamship—working in the galley sweeping floors, peeling vegetables, washing dishes, and running errands—but the promised salary had been no small amount, and it would have increased their little nest egg, bringing them that much closer to buying their first house after they married. It was to be a four-month commitment, during which he would earn five times the money he'd been making as a cooper, and they'd figured they could manage a temporary separation if it would mean being able to marry and move into a home that much sooner.

Jess had never returned, however. She'd stood waiting at the pier on that cool, windy October day when the *Lone Star* had sailed into port, her heart dancing wildly with excitement to see her beloved fiancé following such a long absence. Accompanied by Jess's father and her friends Josiah Woodbridge and Ruth Stiles, she'd watched the passengers disembark, keeping an eager eye out for her first glimpse of him. An hour later, when the crowd had mostly dispersed, one last passenger—a uniformed crewman—came strolling down the gangplank. They had raced over to him and asked if he could shed any light on the matter of Jess's absence, and that was when they'd learned the terrible news: Pirates had attacked the ship and smashed the communication room beyond repair, making it impossible for the captain to wire ahead to Boston. The pirates had kidnapped someone from the galley, the crewman had said, but he couldn't give them a name. He'd explained that the incident had created untold chaos among the passengers, many of whom had been robbed of money, precious jewels, and extravagant possessions.

Unable to console Grace's shock and disbelief, Josiah and Ruthie could do little in the way of comforting her but to insist she go home with Ruthie to stay for a few days. As for Jess's father, Fergus Quinn, he'd stood there in silence, looking as confused as the rest of them. They would wait for investigators to start piecing things together and hope that, within days, they'd receive encouraging news of Jess's release. However, six long torturous weeks passed before Grace finally learned that the Royal Navy had blown up the *Neptunia*, the pirate ship reported to have carried the crew that robbed the *Lone Star*, and that there were no survivors. The news had squeezed the life out of Grace and shattered her dreams into a million pieces.

Shaking off the memory, she frowned at her reflection in the vanity mirror, then rose from the brocade-covered bench. Why did she allow herself to dwell on such thoughts—especially now, when she was about to enjoy an evening with her betrothed? Granted, she knew that Conrad wasn't overly anxious to dine at Brockwell Manor. He'd wanted to take her to the theater, where a group of traveling minstrels was performing.

"But I've already promised Aunt Iris that we'd spend Friday night with her, Conrad," she'd told him earlier that week when she'd stopped by his office to say hello. "She wants a chance to get to know you, and, frankly, I think she deserves it."

"You do, do you?" He'd granted her a coy smile and a wink. "Then I'll have to put on my most mesmerizing charm, so she won't try to talk you out of marrying me." He'd ambled to his office door and quietly closed it before crossing the room and taking her in his arms.

Giggling, she'd allowed him a quick embrace, then had playfully untangled herself from him and begun fiddling with his tie. "Conrad Hall, she wouldn't dream of doing that. Once she gets to know you better, she'll love you as much as I do. Well, maybe not quite as much, but enough."

He'd bent to kiss her, but she'd teasingly turned her cheek, then ducked her head and slipped out of his reach.

"Are you flirting with me, Miss Fontaine?" he'd asked.

She'd laughed again, enjoying their repartee. "I don't know, Mr. Hall. Am I?"

A light rap came to her bedroom door, and Grace turned abruptly, her petticoat swishing. "Come in," she called.

Ellen Waters peeked her head inside. "There is a handsome man come callin' fo' you, miz." She winked. "He's waitin' in the parlor."

Grace smiled. "Thank you, Ellen. Would you please tell him I'll be right down?"

"Yes'm."

"Oh, and how is my aunt this evening?"

"She's doin' quite good for a change, miz. I got her all dressed and prettied up for the occasion. She's settin' downstairs on the divan, talkin' to yo' man."

"Then I'd best get down there before she scares him off."

Ellen gave her gray head a couple of quick shakes. "We all knows no one can make a body feel so quivery with just a glance o' the eye like Missus Brockwell can. Yes, you best hurry down."

"I will, and thank you."

The door closed behind Ellen, and after making a hasty scan of her bedroom and a hurried move to extinguish the lamps, Grace exited and descended the stairs.

Before rounding the corner at the bottom of the staircase, she paused to eavesdrop a moment on Aunt Iris and Conrad.

"So, you joined Gerald Wadsworth and that Murphy fellow, did you?" Aunt Iris was asking. Her voice sounded stronger than usual. Perhaps her long afternoon nap had revitalized her, or perhaps the new treatment Doc Trumble had prescribed was making a difference. This past week, it did seem that her level of discomfort had decreased and her appetite improved.

"Yes, ma'am," Conrad affirmed. "And that would be Charles Murphy."

"Humph. Don't care much for that fellow. Gerald, however, is a very good man. I have trusted him with my estate for many years."

Aunt Iris was the second person Grace had heard remark negatively about Charles Murphy in one week's time, the first being Joy Jennings. It made Grace curious.

"Yes, I understand he handles your estate. I have deep regard for Gerald Wadsworth."

"And you practiced law before coming to Paris?"

"Yes, I worked for a reputable firm in Chicago."

"Chicago. How strange that you would desert the big city, with all its opportunities, for a small town like Paris, Tennessee."

"Not strange at all, ma'am," Conrad countered. "I much prefer small-town living. Besides, I met your beautiful great-niece in lovely Paris, which makes me all the more thankful I came here."

"Yes, she is beautiful, and she deserves the very best a man can give her."

A slight pause followed, making Grace wonder if Aunt Iris hadn't sent Conrad one of her signature piercing scowls to emphasize her words.

Conrad cleared his throat. "I...I completely agree." His voice had caught a frog.

"Good. I'm glad to hear it. Where did you live before Chicago?"

"I lived in the Chicago area most of my life."

"And do your parents still reside there?"

"No. Unfortunately, my parents are both deceased. One died of consumption, and the other perished in a train wreck."

"Which one?"

"Pardon?"

"Which one died in the train wreck?"

"My father."

That was odd. Grace could have sworn he'd told her his mother had died in the train wreck on a return trip from visiting her sister in Pennsylvania, and that his father had died of consumption. She would have to ask him about that later.

"That's unfortunate." Aunt Iris clicked her tongue. "Where did you go from there? That is to say, who cared for you?"

"That would have been my aunt—my mother's sister. She was quite wealthy, you see. She'd never married, so she had no children and was happy to take me in."

"Never married? Then how did she acquire her wealth?"

"Well, that's a fine question, one for which I never learned an answer. My belief is that she inherited it from an uncle. Or perhaps it was a friend of the family."

"Humph. If she'd inherited it from an uncle, seems to me your mother would've shared in the inheritance."

"Well, yes, my parents did come upon some money. Unfortunately, Mother and Father both squandered their share."

"So then, it wasn't a family friend at all?"

Conrad cleared his throat. "As I said earlier, I never fully learned how she acquired it."

My, Aunt Iris could be relentless. Grace decided it was time to rescue Conrad from her aunt's barrage of questions. Straightening her posture, she entered the room. Not surprisingly, Conrad wore a flustered face that suddenly flashed with relief at the sight of her.

4

Conrad had never been so thankful to see Grace enter a room. He needed saving from her great-aunt, who gave the impression of possessing some mysterious power to see straight through him. The sooner he ceased conversing with her, the better off he'd be. He left his station at the fireplace and went to greet Grace.

"Ah, there you are, my love." As he lifted her soft, feminine hand to his lips for a kiss, he could have sworn that the old biddy Iris Brockwell watched with a dour expression. She clearly didn't like him one bit, though he didn't know what he'd ever done to earn her disapproval. Surely, she had no idea of his past. No one did—not even Grace.

Grace swooned in her usual way. He had indeed won her over, even managing to make her forget about that dead sailor to whom she'd been betrothed. He had only his lucky stars to thank for the man's misfortune. Marrying Grace would mean inheriting her aunt's million-dollar estate. With access to the files of every client at Wadsworth & Murphy, he'd quickly learned whose purses were the largest. Iris Brockwell had won by a long shot, all thanks to her deceased husband, a former railroad tycoon and a shrewd investor. Conrad relished the thought that this lavish estate would one day be his.

Luck could not have worked better in his favor. The moment Grace Fontaine had stepped off the train in Paris, he'd been at the station to see a client off to Nashville. She'd looked like a classic damsel in distress, so as soon as he'd bidden the fellow farewell, he'd approached to ask if she needed assistance. She'd looked so relieved to see him. They'd introduced themselves, and she'd explained that she was expecting a ride to Brockwell Manor, but her train had arrived three hours ahead of schedule, and all the cabs had been hired by other passengers, leaving her stranded at the station. Naturally, he'd offered to take her there, and she'd happily consented, though not without making it clear that she didn't want to put him out. "Nonsense," he'd said, assuring her that he had no pressing appointments till late that afternoon. He'd made sure to take full advantage of that spare time by driving her around Paris to show her a few of the sights before directing his pair of horses to the grand estate situated outside the city limits on a large parcel of land with well-manicured lawns and gardens.

They'd covered several topics in that brief period, enough for him to know he wanted to pursue a relationship with her, and so, before dropping her off at her aunt's mansion, he'd asked if she might consider accompanying him to the theater the following week to view a community play sponsored by the Paris Women's Club. She'd turned him down, which hadn't surprised him, considering she barely knew him; but the following week, he'd returned to Brockwell Manor and inquired of the butler if he could see her. She'd come to the door moments later, looking just as beautiful as he remembered. He'd invited her on a walk around the premises, and to that, she'd acquiesced. The friendship had blossomed from there, and at a rather fast pace, to his great delight. Of course, it helped that charm seemed to come naturally to him. It had been his ticket out of many a sticky situation in life, had even helped earn him a higher mark in one of his classes in law school.

Grace pressed her palm against his chest and looked at him with shining eyes. "You're looking dapper, Conrad. Isn't he handsome, Aunt Iris?"

The woman fashioned her mouth into a straight, stalwart line and pulled her hunched shoulders back. "Handsome, indeed." Her tone was rigid, as if it pained her to admit it. Conrad could tell that she'd been a beauty in her day. Unfortunately, time had stolen that feature from her, and now all he saw was a sick old woman whom he hoped wouldn't waste much more time moving into the hereafter.

"Dinner is served," the butler announced from the doorway. Conrad breathed another sigh of relief.

Iris Brockwell winced when she tried to stand, and Grace rushed to her aid. Conrad followed suit, albeit begrudgingly, stepping up to take her by the arm. He was almost certain the old crank tried to resist his touch, but weakness forbade her to fight him.

The dinner conversation went as well as could be expected. Conrad sat across the table from both ladies, which meant that he had to look Iris in the eye when addressing her, as well as endure her censorious glances. He much preferred having Grace all to himself, but she'd insisted they make a habit of dining in with her beloved aunt. "After all," Grace had argued, "she won't be with us much longer, and I want you to get to know her—and she, you—before it's too late."

He couldn't see the necessity of that, but if complying would mean keeping the peace with Grace, he'd go along with it. The day would come when it would be just the two of them—and the servants, of course—and that thought alone would make the visits with her elderly aunt more bearable. Besides, getting his hands on some cold, hard cash would mean ridding himself of Carl Petrie, the shylock he'd been fool enough to seek out when he'd started falling behind on his monthly payments to Fred Brooks, former proprietor of the establishment he'd arranged to buy. He could hardly wait to get Petrie off his back. The worthless scoundrel had been making all manner of threats if he didn't pay the full amount of his loan, plus the astronomical interest—and soon. In retrospect, he never should have bought the hotel, but he'd wanted to make a name for himself upon relocating to Paris, and what better way than to purchase a thriving establishment and show off his entrepreneurial finesse? To be sure, it had helped attract clientele right from the start. Of course, Grace knew nothing of the loan, as he'd told her that he'd paid for the business in full—with cash.

"How is your prime rib, sir?" one of the servants asked, standing to his left.

Oh, but he loved the cosseting that accompanied wealth. "Excellent."

"It's all very good, Nellie," Grace put in. "You and Zelda have outdone yourselves."

Nellie curtsied. "I'll tell Zelda you said so, missus."

"No need. I'll tell her myself after dinner."

"Yes'm. We'll be takin' yo' dishes soon, then servin' dessert and coffee. How is Missus Brockwell holdin' up?"

"I'm doing just fine, Nellie, and you can address me if you have a question," the woman nearly barked. "I'm not deaf, you know."

"Oh, yes'm. I wasn't sure if—"

"If I was awake tonight?"

"Aunt Iris...." A frown creased Grace's pretty brow.

"No, I—I didn't mean that," Nellie stammered. "I...." The woman's eyes went as round as a full moon, and Conrad nearly laughed. Poor thing didn't even know how to finish her sentence. At least he wasn't the only target of Mrs. Brockwell's abuse.

Grace dabbed at her chin with her napkin, then laid down the linen and gently touched her aunt's forearm. "Nellie meant no ill will. She's merely looking after your welfare."

The biddy harrumphed, and Conrad thought then that Grace had an extra measure of patience and compassion, undoubtedly due to her close walk with God. He didn't have the same kind of relationship with the Almighty, but he knew plenty *about* God, including enough of the proper lingo to use when speaking about his faith. After they married, he would drop the façade. Grace wouldn't be happy, but, fine Christian woman that she was, she wouldn't even consider divorce.

She was the kindest, sweetest soul he'd ever known, and he loved her—as much as he was capable of loving, he supposed. He'd never met another woman like her. Chances were, they'd have a good marriage—maybe not the happiest, but it would be above average; he'd see to that. The money would help, for he would take her on grand trips around the world. They would dine at the most exclusive locales and perhaps even purchase a weekend retreat somewhere in the mountains.

Who would have dreamed that he, an orphan boy with nary a coin to his name, would one day inherit such wealth? He'd worked hard for that law degree, taking the occasional shortcut. It wasn't easy climbing to the top, so getting there sometimes required a little conniving. However, he needed more than just his successful career and thriving restaurant and hotel to make his way to the top of the financial ladder. Now that he'd snagged the hand of Grace Fontaine, it was only a matter of time until folks started recognizing him as the richest man in West Tennessee.

Ah, but life held promise.

⌒

Josiah and Ruth Woodbridge lived in Josiah's childhood home on Savin Hill Avenue, several blocks southeast of Jess's father's apartment and not far from Dorchester Bay. Josiah had inherited the two-story colonial after his parents had taken up residence in southern New York to be closer to his two older sisters and their families. Jess and Josiah had met as young boys working at the wharf cleaning fish and selling them on the streets in cooled fish carts for a local merchant. They'd had fun, getting themselves in a little trouble but learning and growing from their experiences, and had become fast friends. They'd given their lives to Jesus the same summer night at a revival tent meeting Ruth Stiles had invited them to attend. Beneath that giant canvas tent, Jess had heard a rousing gospel message such as he'd never heard before, one that tore at his heart with sweeping waves of conviction and compelled him to run down the sawdust aisle to the altar.

After his conversion, he'd remained rough around the edges, hadn't spent much time reading his Bible, and had nearly fallen away from his faith. Still, he couldn't manage to forget that all-important decision, because God had kept hounding him about it, His Spirit always tugging, always reminding, always chasing after him. It wasn't until he'd found himself behind bars in a British naval prison, alone, afraid, and helpless to save himself, that he'd once again come to God in complete surrender, this time giving Him his everything and begging Him to take control of his circumstances. From that point on, he'd laid down his life to his Maker, determined to spend the rest of his days in service to Christ, no matter the cost—even if it meant remaining in prison and never seeing his beloved Grace again.

God had honored his obedient heart. One of the prison guards had befriended him and, believing Jess's story, had set out to investigate, ultimately obtaining Jess's early release. Now, all that remained was to find Grace and renew his promise to love and cherish her till death parted them. He could only hope that Josiah and Ruthie would be able to give him the information he sought.

The first time he knocked on the front door of his friends' house, no one answered. So, he went to a local eatery to kill time sipping coffee. His stomach growled repeatedly, but he couldn't do much about it, considering he had little money to his name and needed to hang on to every penny until he secured a job. It would be pointless to ask his father for a loan, seeing as he spent every spare cent on booze and tobacco. If only Jess had dug through the cupboards for even a tiny morsel to eat before setting out.

When Jess rounded the bend to the Woodbridges' a second time, two lanterns glowed in the front window—an encouraging sign. He strode up the flower-lined path, his pulse hitching at the thought of seeing his dear friends again. He only hoped they wouldn't keel over in a dead faint at the sight of him. Because his father had honored Jess's wishes and kept quiet about his reappearance, everyone still presumed he was dead. How to go about greeting Josiah and Ruthie for the first time completely evaded him. There just was no way to go about it but to shock their stockings off. He mounted the front steps and crossed the covered porch, the heels of his worn boots clicking on the wood slats. A wicker chair and matching settee graced the porch, along with several pots of blooming geraniums. The outdoor gaslight glittered, as if they expected a visitor. Perhaps they did, in which case he'd have to keep his own visit short. Before knocking, he reached inside his breast pocket and pulled out the fob of his scratched watch. It was a quarter past seven. He dropped the watch back in his pocket, gulped, and took a breath of heavy, moist air. "Here goes, Lord."

He rapped on the door and immediately noticed moving shadows on the other side of the window, confirming his belief that someone was home. He cleared his throat and straightened his filthy collar. He'd been wearing the same clothes for three days now, since his only change of clothing was even dirtier. At least he'd had a bath yesterday, such as it was, in the bathroom of the ship. Passengers in steerage enjoyed about as many amenities as a mosquito. They were fed and watered twice a day and given a single berth but were otherwise on their own. Oh, there were fancier ships, to be sure—ones where even the accommodations in steerage were comfortable—but he'd sailed on the *Sea Rogue*, an old, beat-up ship that offered the lowest fares in London. He'd had no choice but to take it. Thankfully, the prison warden had funded his one-way pass and had also given him a meager amount of money for incidentals, all of which was as good as gone by now.

He knocked once more, this time a bit louder. His stomach lurched when he spotted Josiah rounding the corner and walking at a fast pace to the door. With nary a glance through the windowpane, he threw wide the door. "Come in, come—" Instantly, the poor fellow's face blanched white as a summer cloud, his jaw dropping, his brown eyes staring a hole straight through Jess. His broad chest ballooned, then flattened when his lungs expelled air. "What—in—the—name—of—Moses?"

Jess managed a shaky smile. "Hey, Josiah." He half choked on the two words, his throat clogged with emotion.

"Jess, is that you behind that beard?" Josiah crinkled his brow, which caused his eyes to narrow to slits, and leaned forward. "Ruthie, come here." He twisted his body around when he called but kept his eyes fastened on Jess, as if afraid taking them off him would make him vanish.

Jess spread his arms. "It's me, Josiah."

"You're alive?"

The simple question rather humored him. "Would I be standing here if I weren't?"

Around the corner came Ruth, a blanketed bundle in her arms. She gave much the same reaction as Jess, except that she teetered a bit and forgot to breathe, and Jess worried she might fall. He reached over the threshold and steadied her at the elbow. "Careful, Ruthie."

She sucked in a loud gasp. "Jess!" she bellowed, coming to life and waking the baby, who immediately took to howling. "Jess!" she exclaimed once more as she handed the infant to Josiah, who still wore a befuddled, unbelieving expression. Then she snagged hold of Jess's arm and pulled him off the porch. "What—? How—? I don't understand, but I'm thrilled—*we're* thrilled, aren't we, Josiah?" She glanced at her husband as she dragged Jess inside, but he hadn't yet closed his mouth. "Josiah, it's Jess!" she squealed. There she was, the old Ruthie. "He didn't drown when the pirate ship went down. He's alive!"

The wave of emotion washing over Jess at the sight of his old friends threatened to bring him to tears, but he held them at bay by focusing on the scruffy hat he'd taken off and now turned in his hands. "Yes, I am," he affirmed. "Very much so."

Ruthie stared at him for another moment, then quickly swept him into a hug. Jess closed his eyes. It was the first real human touch he'd experienced in over two years, and he found himself almost melting with warmth.

When they separated, he smiled at her. "You look good, Ruthie."

"Oh, pooh. That baby did some permanent damage to my waistline. But look at you!"

"Well, I'll be swallowed by a whale!" Josiah managed to utter, sweeping a hand through his dark hair. "Come in and rest yourself—and tell us where you've been all this time." Still holding the baby in one arm, he used the other to give Jess a hard pat on the back.

"Let me have a look at that little one first," Jess said.

Josiah peeled back the blanket to reveal a pink-skinned, wrinkly-faced infant, now calm once more.

"Boy or girl?" Jess asked.

"It's a girl," Josiah said. "Jess, meet three-week-old Edith Ann."

"Well, hello there, Edith. I'm happy to say you favor your ma instead of your pa."

Josiah tossed back his head with a laugh. "You haven't changed much, have you? Well, except for losing a few pounds."

"Yeah, and I see you've put on a few," he teased, allowing Josiah to lead him to a chair. "Ruthie keeps you well fed, I see."

"She does, she does. Here, sit." He pointed to an overstuffed upholstered armchair. "Ruthie, see if you can rustle up something that'll put a little fat on this fellow's bones."

His mouth watered at the mere mention of food. "Don't go to any trouble," he told her, not meaning a word of it.

"Nonsense. I'll warm up a bowl of beef stew. And would you care for some fresh bread topped with big pats of butter?"

"That sounds like something straight from heaven."

Ruthie cast him a worried glance and shook her head. "Oh, Jess, we're so glad you're alive, but I'm concerned about what you've been through. Are you going to tell us?"

He nodded. "Sure."

She breathed in through her nostrils, and a noisy sigh rushed back out. "But not till I come back, you hear? I don't want to miss a single word."

He smiled as she rushed from the room, her blue striped skirt flaring when she turned the corner.

When she came back, Jess tried to pace himself with decorum rather than devour his stew. They conversed about lighter topics first, Jess choosing to reserve his questions about Grace until after he'd finished his meal and shared his story.

"I thought perhaps you were expecting company, since your porch light was on, and you opened the door without checking to see who it was."

Josiah nodded. "Some friends mentioned they might stop by tonight to show us their new horse-drawn carriage, but that was only if they had time. They said not to expect them much past seven, so I'd say they're not coming, which is just as well. We don't want anybody interrupting our time with you. By the way, are you staying at your father's, or do you need a place to stay?"

Jess swallowed another delectable spoonful of stew. "I'd happily stay with you two, as my father's apartment is in a state of decay, but I'd better stay with him anyway. He'd feel bad if I didn't."

"Well, if you change your mind, you're welcome here," Ruthie said from her spot on the sofa next to Josiah. "We have two spare bedrooms upstairs."

She had no idea how tempting the offer was, but he needed to take a few days to reconnect with his father.

"Now then, it's time you told us where you've been these past two years."

It was a long, rather drawn-out story, much as he tried to abbreviate it. He talked about his job in the galley aboard the *Lone Star*—mainly serving the passengers breakfast, mid-afternoon tea, and dinner. Then he told about the journey itself—how the trip to London had been uneventful, aside from a few squalls, which the ship captain had handled with great skill. But the return trip had been altogether different. First, they'd encountered a number of fall storms they hadn't anticipated, which put people on edge and made a number of them quite ill. In the midst of that, one of the ship's main boilers had shut down, slowing their speed. While the maintenance crew worked on the problem, a pirate ship had taken advantage of the situation.

"I was down in the galley with the chef and a few other staff members, and we had no idea what was happening," Jess explained to his rapt listeners, both of them perched on the edge of the sofa, bodies frozen, eyes wide. The baby still slept in Josiah's arms. "There was a kind of jolt and a booming noise, which we presumed to be thunder. I found out later that it was a gunshot. Everybody else scrambled up to the deck to see what was going on, but I didn't think there was much of anything to fear, so I continued with my kitchen duties. After several minutes, no one had returned, so I went to investigate. The corridor off the galley was eerily quiet. The next thing I knew, someone jumped me and secured my hands behind my back, making a threat on my life.

"It all happened so fast, I barely had time to fight. In the next moment, a dark scarf or kerchief covered my eyes and was knotted at the back of my head. And then I was dragged away. I stumbled several times, but the strong hands forcing me above deck had no intention of letting me go. My captor ordered his men to grab the last of their booty, shoot anybody who dared belay them, and skedaddle back to their ship.

"There was no doubt in my mind that we'd been invaded by a band of pirates. The one hauling me around yelled such phrases as, 'Ye'll be keelhauled if ye so much as try to foller us, ye pustulant, pox-ridden flounder.' Nobody else spoke, though I heard a few whimpers from some of the women and the cries of a baby or two. Before debarking, the guy jerked me around to face the onlookers and said with a cackle, 'The Lord's blessings be upon thee, ye scurvy dogs!'"

Jess combed a hand through his scruffy hair and studied his friends through weary eyes. "Would you believe that bandit's evil laughter haunts me to this day?"

5

Oh, Jess, I still can't believe you were kidnapped!" Ruthie exclaimed. "What was their reason for taking you?"

"I was the only one they found in the galley area, and they needed a cook, since theirs had taken ill and, from the tale told me, died and was tossed overboard. Only God knows if that's true."

Ruthie shivered, then hugged herself. The night had cooled off with the setting sun, giving way to a faint breeze that blew through the side windows and resulted in a comfortable cross ventilation perfect for sleeping. Jess sure hoped he could sleep, with his nerves on edge from the sordid memories he'd stirred up.

"How long were you on the pirate ship, Jess?" Josiah asked, his brow crumpled with intense curiosity. "We heard that the Royal Navy set fire to it, and it sank in less than fifteen minutes, presumably drowning everyone aboard. How in the world did you manage to survive? And why didn't the Brits escort you back to Boston—in first class, no less?"

Jess took a deep breath. "My best guess is that I was on the pirate ship for anywhere from six to eight weeks. They treated me like a prisoner, with someone assigned to hold a gun to my head at almost all times, especially while I was preparing their meals. At night, they locked me in a tiny, closet-sized room with a cot.

"A British officer told me that the Royal Navy had been hunting down the *Neptunia* for a couple of years. The crew was notorious for their sea crimes, including the murder of several sailors during one of their raids. When the Navy finally came upon the vessel, about seventy-five miles off the English coast, they showed no mercy, firing off a canon that nearly split the ship in two. The pirates had dragged me to the upper deck a little while before this to help with the fishing nets. A number of scalawags on the upper deck were killed instantly, and a roaring blaze ignited. A few of us jumped overboard, and I managed to swim to the wooden dinghy tied to the back of the naval ship. The Navy didn't shoot the others who were in the water, but they certainly didn't help them to safety, either. The assumption is that they all drowned. Meanwhile, I climbed inside the lifeboat and lay low, basically awaiting my own demise. I know now it was only by God's grace that I made it to that little dinghy. When the Navy finally discovered me, they hauled me out of the boat and dragged me aboard. I'm shocked to this day that they didn't blow my head off, because they surely believed me to be a pirate. I tried to explain my plight to them—that I'd been kidnapped from the *Lone Star* and forced to do labor on the *Neptunia*—but not a one of them swallowed my story, calling it a 'real dandy' and jeering me, even as they put me in chains and jammed me into a four-by-four cell aboard their ship."

"Jess!" Ruthie cried. "Why on earth wouldn't they believe you? Couldn't they see you were different from the others?"

He chuckled. "Not really. I wore the scruffiest clothes, sort of like what you're seeing now; I had grown an unsightly beard; I hadn't bathed in days; and I stunk so bad, even I couldn't stand myself. Besides, I was so exhausted at that point that I'd lost a portion of my fight. I figured once we reached British soil, I'd be able to speak reason in a court of law and finally reclaim my freedom.

"Problem was, I didn't have my day in court. Instead, I went to a British naval prison where no one listened to anything I said. As a matter of fact, if I so much as opened my mouth to speak, I got a good slap across the face. And, depending on which guard was on duty, I often got a punch to the gut for good measure. As far as I know, nobody inquired about any kidnappings having occurred on the *Lone*

Star. I can't even tell you how many black eyes I got while locked in that cell."

Seeing the pallor of Ruthie's complexion, Jess regretted having revealed so much. Unfortunately, she and Josiah were the first friendly faces he'd seen in years, and he found it hard to distinguish just how much detail was too much.

"Maybe I should stop there," he said, frowning. "I fear I've upset you, Ruthie. Are you okay?"

She swallowed and cleared her throat. "I'm all right, Jess—just heartsick, is all. And angry...yes, that's it. Angry. Furious, actually!" The baby started to squirm in Josiah's arms, and Ruth gave her daughter an anxious glance. "I think perhaps I'll take Edith Ann upstairs and get her ready for bed. I'll let Josiah fill me in on the rest of the details later. It's not that I don't want to hear them, because I think it's important for you to tell your story; I just don't think I can bear to hear another word right now. It makes me want to take the next ship to London and tell them what's what."

Jess couldn't contain the rumble of laughter that escaped his lungs. "You've always been a spitfire, Ruth Giles—er, Woodbridge. When did you two marry, anyway?"

"We celebrated our first anniversary in June," Josiah said as he handed Edith Ann to his wife. "Too bad you couldn't have been here to witness our vows, my friend. I thought about you a lot that day. In fact, I've thought about you nearly every day since you left us. I have to say, I'm still so flummoxed—but so happy, mind you—to be gazing at your face right now."

Jess longed to mention Grace, to ask where she'd gone off to, but a strange sense of dread kept him from doing so. Perhaps it was the fact that neither Josiah nor Ruthie had brought her up even once. Hadn't Ruthie and Grace once been best friends? He wondered if Grace had attended their wedding.

Ruthie exited the room and started her ascent of the creaky stairs. When she reached the second level, every floorboard squawked with her steps.

Josiah adjusted his position on the sofa, sliding further forward and resting his elbows on his knees, his hands dangling between them. "So, how did you manage to escape prison?"

Jess nearly laughed. "I didn't escape. They released me. About a month into my imprisonment, a new guard entered the rotation—a friendly sort. He said I was the only prisoner who never gave him any trouble when he brought the inmates' meals, and he started striking up conversations with me—brief exchanges, at first, but they eventually turned longer and more inquisitive. He asked me how I'd gotten hooked up with such a rowdy bunch of pirates, since I didn't seem their type. When I told him that I'd been kidnapped, he didn't believe me at first, and I begged him to do some research. He said he could get in trouble, even lose his rank, if he dug too deep, so I laid off.

"Eventually, curiosity or compassion—maybe both—got the better of him, and he went to the library and got his hands on some Boston newspapers dating back to the October day when the *Lone Star* had returned home to port. Sure enough, he read that one Jess Quinn was missing, presumed kidnapped by pirates, the article said, but also presumed dead, a later article reported, after the Royal Navy fired on the *Neptunia*, the vessel under the command of the pirates who'd robbed the *Lone Star*.

"Once I got this guard behind me, the wheels of justice started spinning. He contacted a higher-ranking officer to report his findings. There was never any sort of formal apology, no compensation for my trouble, and no press covering my unlawful imprisonment. I'm told the Royal Navy has no tolerance for piracy, and if they ever received any inquiry regarding my existence, they neglected to acknowledge it."

"So, they held you up as an example," Josiah said. "I totally agree with their stance on piracy, but you weren't a pirate, Jess. They had no right to keep you prisoner. Heck, they didn't even allow you to make contact with the outside world, did they?"

Jess shook his head. "Not so much as a single telegraph. In fact, they robbed me of every last one of my rights. But it's over and done with, and I'm not going to pursue justice. I'm just glad to be free again."

Josiah asked a few more questions, which Jess freely answered. Then, seemingly satisfied, he rubbed his day-old beard and arched one eyebrow. "I expect you'll be looking for work. As Ruthie said earlier, the welcome mat is out for you as long as you need it."

The moment of truth had come. After a bit of hemming and hawing, he decided to just come out with it. "Where is she, Josiah? Where is Grace?" He braced himself for the response.

His friend hesitated, still massaging his jaw. "Tennessee, in some little town called Paris."

"Tennessee? What in the world is in Tennessee?"

"Do you remember Grace talking about going to see her great-aunt who lived in the South? Apparently, she's dying, and Grace volunteered her services to care for her. I believe she's the old lady's only living relative, or at least the only one she trusts."

Tennessee? That was manageable. More than manageable, actually. Jess's stomach did several somersaults, and he grinned. "That answers your question about my looking for work, Josiah. I'll find something temporary around here, to raise just enough cash to buy myself some essentials and a train ticket bound for Paris, Tennessee. Don't you wish you were a little bird and could fly down there to catch her expression when she sees me?"

Josiah shifted uncomfortably in his seat. "Oh yeah, a little bird, all right. That's just what I want to be." He studied Jess's face with utmost solemnity. "Jess."

"Yes?"

"You need to know something."

"What is it?"

He seemed unable to bring himself to speak.

Somehow, Ruthie had managed to creep back down the stairs unnoticed. "Grace has met somebody else, Jess," she murmured from behind him.

Jess whirled around, his heart suddenly crashing hard against the walls of his chest.

Ruthie clasped her hands so tightly, they went white, and she wore a sheepish face. She bit her lip for a moment before continuing. "She's to be married in October. Josiah and I plan to attend the wedding. In fact, she's asked me to serve as her matron of honor, and I've agreed."

6

Doc Trumble paid a call on Aunt Iris the last Friday in August. According to the calendar, summer was drawing to a close, but nothing about the wet, soggy morning seemed to back it up. The humid air hung heavy like a thick blanket, making it hard for a body to breathe. Grace had been wearing the lightest fabrics possible, her dresses as loose and airy as fashion deemed acceptable for a lady, and yet still she perspired like a cattle farmer, despite frequent baths and subsequent applications of a new product known as Mum deodorant cream.

It didn't bear saying that Aunt Iris was unhappy. If folks had labeled her cranky before, the uncomfortable weather made her more ornery than a stuck mule. When Solomon Turner greeted the doctor at the door and ushered him inside, Grace left her aunt's bedside and whisked down the staircase at the first sounds of his low, rumbly voice.

"Doc, I'm so glad to see you. Aunt Iris's pain seems to have worsened, and you know how that affects her disposition. Is there anything you can do for her?"

Frowning, he set his dripping-wet doctor bag on the floor and removed his sopping hat, giving it a little shake over the entry rug. Solomon took it from him and hung it on the brass coat tree by the door. The doctor's white hair stood up in mussed tangles, and Grace had the urge to smooth it back in place. Instead, she focused on his wrinkled expression.

"I'm afraid I gave her the maximum dose of laudanum last week. It should make her groggy enough to sleep a good share of the day."

"She has been sleeping more," Grace acknowledged, "but she dislikes that because she wants to remain alert, so she balks every time I offer her a dose."

"Stubborn woman," he muttered with a teasing grin and a shake of his head. "Let me examine her and see if I can determine whether the most pronounced tumor has changed in size."

Grace detested his having to do that, as it always caused her aunt extreme discomfort, sometimes to the point where she cried out in agony.

He must have read her worried expression, for he added, "I'll go easy, my dear. If it's too painful, I'll stop immediately. But it's important that I check, as this will determine the length of time we can expect her to remain with us."

She bristled at his matter-of-fact tone, but she supposed he had to treat his patients with as much objectivity as possible. Becoming emotionally involved might blur his professional judgment. "I understand. Do you think it's…getting worse?"

"Whenever vital organs are compromised—in her case, the pancreas—the outlook is not good. How has her appetite been?"

"Some days, she eats fairly well; others, very little. I'm afraid she's been having a great deal of trouble holding down what she does manage to consume."

"Hmm. That's to be expected, I'm sorry to say."

Solomon stood off to the side, saying nothing, the fingertips of both hands grazing the hem of his long jacket. His eyes glittered with moisture, and it occurred to Grace that he was likely despairing as much as she at the notion of losing a lifelong friend.

"Sol, would you like to come up to the room with us?" Grace asked him.

"Oh, Miz Grace, I don't want t' impose none."

"Nonsense. Your presence would be a comfort to Aunt Iris."

Doc Trumble retrieved his bag, and the three of them ascended the stairs, a shroud of silence encasing them, and halted just outside the open door to her aunt's bedchamber. Across the room, Aunt Iris sat where Grace had left her, in her rocker facing the window that overlooked the massive estate. Her lap was covered by a lightweight afghan, which she'd insisted on using, despite the hot, stuffy temperature. Even on the days when she seemed to suffer the most, she refused to lie in bed, claiming that giving in to the temptation would preclude her from ever getting up again. She preferred to rest sitting up whenever possible.

"I'm not dead, for pity's sake," she announced without turning her head. "Not yet, anyway. Come in, come in, the lot of you. And that means you, too, Sol. Good grief, you might have thought to invite the cooks and housekeepers, too, while you were at it—and why not the groundskeeper?"

How she knew, without looking, who had come to see her, Grace couldn't say, unless her sharp ears had overheard their discussion downstairs. She made a mental note to ask the staff to keep all future talk about her well out of earshot.

"Doc wants to examine you, Auntie. I invited Solomon to come along because he's worried about you."

"Come here, Sol," Iris said, her tone softer.

The butler left Grace's side and soundlessly made his way across the room. "Yes'm? What can I do fo' you?"

She turned to look at him, but no words passed between them. He set his dark hand on her shoulder, and for all of a minute, they did nothing but stare out the window together, she from her ancient rocker, he from where he stood, somewhat stooped, at her side. Grace's throat pinched, and she wasn't one bit surprised when a lone tear slid down her cheek.

"You've been a good friend, Sol," Iris finally said, "ever since John brought you home from Atlanta." She paused. "Well, maybe not right off. I'll admit I was put out with him at first."

Solomon chuckled. "You sho' were. You didn't want nothin' to do with me."

"He was always bringing home strays, and you were just one more. Scrawny thing, you were."

"Yes'm, I was that. Sickly to the point o' death."

More silence swathed them, and for a moment, Grace suspected her aunt had drifted off to sleep.

After a time, she lifted her head. "John told me you needed a friend; but, in truth, I think he thought I stood in greater need of one."

"I guess we both did, ma'am."

"Yes, yes, that's true. We were an unlikely pair, you and me, but somehow we made our friendship work, didn't we, Sol?"

"Yes'm, we sho' did. You nursed me back to health, an' I'll always be grateful for that."

She gave a little scoff. "I don't recall doing very much."

"You forced gallons o' chicken broth down my throat. I remember that."

"And now you're trying to get even with me."

Solomon chuckled. "I s'pose you could look at it like that."

Doc Trumble cleared his throat and approached the two of them. "How are you feeling, Iris? Grace tells me your pain has worsened."

Grace came up beside the doctor. Iris gave a slight turn of the head, then flicked her feeble wrist. "Pfff, it's no worse. My niece likes to exaggerate."

"Auntie." A tiny smile touched Grace's lips. At least the woman hadn't lost her feistiness.

"How about you let me check you over?" Doc Trumble opened his bag and retrieved his stethoscope and several other items.

"Oh, for pity's sake, I can tell you for a fact that my heart is still beating."

He grinned. "I've no doubt about that."

"We'll be right outside, Aunt Iris," Grace told her.

"How do a cup o' hot tea sound, Missus Brockwell?" Solomon put in.

"I suppose that would be nice," she conceded.

As they tiptoed toward the door, Aunt Iris groused under her breath to Doc Trumble something that Grace couldn't quite make out.

Solomon closed the door behind them, then winked at Grace. "She ain't goin' nowhere for a while, miz. She still got too much vim an' vinegar in 'er."

⌒

"What do ya mean, ye're leavin' for Tennessee in the mornin'? Didn't ya say Josiah an' Ruth said Grace is marryin' somebody else?"

"That's what they said, Pa, but I'm not about to let that happen. Not when she was promised to me."

"That was two years ago, Son. It's not like ya disappeared a week ago. A lot can happen in two years."

Jess knew that all too well. According to Josiah, much of the gang he used to hang around with had left the old neighborhood and, in some cases, moved away from Boston altogether. Some had gotten married, taken jobs in other states, settled down with families of their own, or changed so much that he said they didn't even seem like the same people. Josiah and Ruthie had made almost all new friends. One former friend had even died a year ago, much to Jess's despair, when he'd contracted a bad case of diphtheria. He'd been such a cheerful, spirited character, and the thought of his succumbing to a premature death had taken Jess a few days to process. It seemed so many of the people he'd wanted to catch up with weren't even to be found. Most of them would probably live out the remainder of their days still believing him to be dead.

"That doesn't change the fact I need to see her," he answered while adding a couple of newly purchased secondhand shirts to his satchel. "I'd never forgive myself if I just allowed her to marry the guy without letting her know that I'm still alive. We were in love, Pa—like you and Ma once were."

"And still are," his father insisted.

Jess wondered if the man would ever get beyond his grief and start truly living again. He was a good-looking fellow, when he spruced himself up, and still had a lot to offer—if he would just cease with the heavy drinking and incessant smoking and let the Lord breathe new life into him.

Of course, it didn't do any good to preach at him. Jess had tried that yesterday and been shut down immediately for his "holier-than-thou" attitude. He'd decided it was best to keep a lock on his trap and spend time in prayer as opposed to wasting his breath trying to change his father. That was God's job, not his.

He picked up the two pairs of trousers he'd also purchased, folded them as neatly as he could, and stuffed them into the bag.

"Ya got enough money?" his father asked, blowing out a puff of smoke that made the stuffy little apartment a whole lot stuffier. Even with the windows wide open, hardly an ounce of air moved.

"I told you I got a sizeable check from the Allan Line. At Josiah's suggestion, I paid a visit to the police station to file a report. He went with me for purposes of identity verification. They looked up my records, asked me a bunch of questions, and then filed some kind of report for the courthouse. After that, they advised me to drop in at the administrative offices of the *Lone Star*."

"Yeah, ya tol' me that. Ya said they gave y' about five times what they would've paid ya for that galley job."

"Indeed. They also made me sign some papers promising I would neither go to the press nor hire a lawyer to file a lawsuit against them. I wouldn't have done either, but I signed the thing to make them happy."

"They should'a probed a little deeper, in my opinion," his father said with a scowl. "I even went to the ship's captain myself when ya di'n't come back, but he said the Royal Navy made it clear no one survived the destruction of the *Neptunia*, an' he wasn't about to question 'em further. Lookin' back, had they just done some diggin' o' their own, they might've discovered y' still alive."

"You went to *The Lone Star* office?"

"Ya bet yer hot snakes in the desert I did. Lot o' good it did me."

"Well, I appreciate that, Pa." And he did. In fact, it gave him a warm feeling deep in his soul to know his father cared enough to do that. Jess had spent much of his time in jail wondering what people back home were thinking and doing in his absence. It helped to know that his father had been making an effort to find him, even if it had proven to be a waste of time.

"But who's going to go up against the Royal Navy?" he mused. "I don't blame the *Lone Star* for accepting their word as truth. To be fair, the Navy believed me to be a pirate, so why would they say to anyone, 'Oh, by the way, one scummy pirate did survive—he's holed up in an eight-by-eight cell'? Anyway, it's over, and I'm alive."

"Yeah."

His father blew out another puff of smoke just as Jess zipped up his suitcase. He supposed that when he left here in the morning, he'd smell like a smokestack; but then, so would everybody else on the train, so he'd blend right in.

His father scratched a spot above one of his bushy gray eyebrows and let his shoulders drop. "We-e-e-ll, so, ye're goin' to Tennessee to see if y' can win back yer girl, eh?"

Jess gave a slow nod, then hefted his bag and set it next to the door.

"Don't be surprised none if she don't want to give ya the time o' day. If she's gettin' married in a few weeks, chances're pretty good she won't want much to do with ya. Sounds like her heart belongs to somebody else."

Jess sighed. "Thanks for the encouragement."

"Just tryin' to be realistic, Son. That's all. Are ya comin' back to Boston if it don't work out?"

He felt a deep crease form between his eyebrows. "I'm not exactly sure what I'll do, to be honest. You want to roam the countryside with me?" He chuckled.

"Never can tell. I ain't got much keepin' me here. A few friends, is all, an' a job that don't bring me much satisfaction."

"You ought to be doing something that makes you happy, Pa. Why did you stop coopering? You were a fine cooper."

"Oh, the competition's too stiff. I'd prefer to have my own business if I'm gonna do that."

"Well, maybe a door will open up for you. First, though, you've got to lay off the booze. You'll drink yourself straight into your grave if you don't."

"I tol' ya yesterday not to preach at me. I live my life the best I can."

He knew he was just blowing smoke by speaking his mind, but he could no more keep himself from doing it than he could keep from jumping on that train to Tennessee in the morning. "I don't want to be looking down at you in a wooden box the next time I see you, Pa. I'm leaving you a Bible—it's on the crate next to my bed. I bought it for you yesterday, and I want you to promise me you'll start reading it."

His father's head jerked back. "A Bible? Why'd ya want to do that?"

"Because if you start pouring yourself into it, you'll discover that there's something more to life than sitting around staring at dust balls on the floor. You were put on this earth for a purpose, Pa, and the reason why is written in those pages. I'll be sending you letters from Paris to keep you posted and to check in and see if you've been reading your Bible."

He grunted. "We'll see."

We'll see. Jess ducked into the kitchen so his father wouldn't see his hopeful grin. "We'll see" was better than nothing. Yes, he'd take "We'll see."

⌒

The rain continued through Friday and into the night, but by noon on Saturday, the sun did a fine job of wiping the sky clean of every last cloud. It was a good thing, too, as Grace had plans to attend an outdoor picnic luncheon with the ladies of Paris Evangelical Church. At the most recent wedding dress fitting, Joy Jennings had invited her to sit with her and Mercy Connors, saying that it would be the perfect time for the three of them to get better acquainted. Grace had finally met Mercy at last Sunday's service, and she'd liked her and her husband, Sam, immediately.

Unfortunately, Conrad had already gone out the door, having gotten himself involved in a dialogue with another parishioner about a legal issue. Grace would have preferred that he ask the man to come to his office later that week to discuss the matter, and she'd told him so on their carriage ride back to Brockwell Manor.

"The Sabbath is no time for talking business, Conrad," she'd openly complained.

He'd apologized right off and promised not to be so rude ever again, and she'd softened like warm butter when he'd brought her hand to his lips for a soft kiss, then granted her a heart-melting smile. How easily he bowled her over with his charm! Gracious, had she lost her last particle of horse sense?

She only hoped her aunt wouldn't mind her stepping out for the afternoon. At the conclusion of his visit yesterday, Doc Trumble had told Grace that the prognosis had not changed; if anything, the outlook had improved since his previous visit, as the tumor had not changed in size. The result was that the mood around the house had lifted. Even Aunt Iris's spirits had improved, and this morning, she'd taken Solomon up on his offer to help her downstairs, where he'd gotten her settled in a chair in the living room facing the big window that overlooked the immense front yard and its splendid array of colorful flowers.

For the picnic, Grace donned a practical lime green walking skirt with a wide waistband, a back-button closure, and a center back pleat that started below the hip. She'd dressed up the skirt with a white light-weight cotton blouse with a scooped neck and capped sleeves. A floral hat complemented the outfit, as did her Austrian crystal cross neck-lace and matching clip-on earrings, the set a hand-me-down from her mother's collection. When finished, she examined her reflection in the tall mirror and decided she looked ready for an outdoor picnic—not overdressed, but certainly not shabby, either.

"Are you sure you don't mind my leaving?" Grace asked her aunt when she went downstairs. "I shouldn't be more than a couple of hours."

Aunt Iris slowly twisted her neck around and extended one of her long-fingered, scrawny hands. Grace quickly took it in hers, the purple protruding veins putting her in mind of a geographical map. The hand was unusually cool to the touch.

"You look lovely, my sweet niece, and of course you should go. It's about time you got to know some of the fine ladies of Paris. Good gracious, the only person you ever socialize with is that—that lawyer."

"'That lawyer' is my fiancé, Auntie."

"Yes, yes. Well, to be well-rounded, one must branch out in her friendships."

Grace smiled. "I'm well aware. And that is precisely why I accepted Joy Jennings's invitation. I have a long way to go if I'm to become as socially active as you."

Over the years, Aunt Iris had held several prestigious positions in the community, from president of the Paris Women's Club to chairwoman of many charitable groups; had attended dozens of political events and campaign dinners; and had participated in countless social functions, such as community teas and fund-raising suppers. Why, in her day, some would say she'd been the belle of the ball. It thrilled Grace to pieces every time a couple of her aunt's old acquaintances dropped in to visit. Whenever her aunt was feeling up to receiving callers, she always perked up. She'd ask Grace to straighten her hair and rub a little blush into her cheeks, and then she'd assume her place in the chair by the window and summon Solomon to escort the ladies upstairs. It pleased Grace that someone from the Paris Women's Club stopped by at least once a week, for it always lifted her ailing aunt's spirits.

Grace peeked out front and saw Solomon waiting at the ready beside the carriage parked in the circular drive.

"I guess I'll be going, then."

"You have a lovely time, dear," her aunt bade her from the chair.

"I wish you were going with me, Auntie. I'm sure the ladies would enjoy seeing you."

"Well, we both know that's not possible, but please give everyone my best."

She bent and kissed her aunt's cheek. "I will, and I'll be back as soon as I can."

"Don't hurry, Grace, and I'm quite serious. I'll be fine."

Her voice did sound stronger today. It gave Grace hope.

The weather couldn't have been better for the occasion, with a flawless blue sky overhead and a pleasant breeze making the air perfectly comfortable. The lawn of Paris Evangelical Church was filled with tables covered in linen cloths, with jars of flowers for centerpieces. Many women had already arrived, their horse and buggies or single horses beginning to fill up the lot. Grace assumed some of the ladies had been transported by their husbands or menservants, just as she had been. There was a general sense of anticipation in the air as the women greeted each other and began to gather in small groups.

Grace had always considered herself to be an outgoing individual, but a wave of shyness came over her when she didn't immediately spot Joy Jennings. She'd been in Paris for more than three months now, long enough to meet and fall deeply in love with her future husband, but she had taken little time to acquaint herself with any of the other ladies in town. Of course, she primarily spent time with Conrad, so it was no wonder she hadn't formed any friendships. She considered Joy Jennings a friend, but their relationship had begun on a professional level. Perhaps her aunt was right—it was high time she made some female friends.

"I'll be back in two hours, miz, unless y' want me to come sooner," Solomon said as he helped her down from the carriage.

She took his hand and set her feet on the ground. "That sounds fine, Solomon. Thank you."

"If'n you ain't done with yo' visitin' when you see me drive up, you jes' take yo' time, hear? Like Missus Brockwell says, you enjoy yo'self and get to know these nice church ladies."

"I'm sure I'll be ready to go in two hours, Sol. Besides, I don't like leaving Aunt Iris alone for long periods."

He patted her arm. "She be jes' fine, miz. I'll set with her a spell an' keep her company."

"That would be wonderful, Solomon. I'm sure she would enjoy that."

He turned and headed for the carriage. Before mounting the step, he stopped and looked at her, then shooed her forward with his hand. "Go on, now."

She took a deep breath and approached the clusters of ladies already engaged in lively conversation. Laughter and cheerful chatter rang across the churchyard, and for the first time in a long while, she missed her beloved Boston and the friendships she'd left behind—particularly her best friend, Ruth Stiles Woodbridge.

She had a beloved husband-to-be, but all of a sudden, all she wanted to do was go home.

7

The ladies of Paris Evangelical had been more than welcoming to Grace, so much so that before the picnic ended, she'd made five new friends. Of course, it had helped that she'd sat with the vivacious Mercy Connors and Joy Jennings. More than a few people had remarked on the coincidence of three women with such hallowed names striking up a friendship, and that had helped open the door to lively, entertaining conversation. It had also helped to lift her previous gloom about missing the dear people she'd left behind in Boston. Clearly, God had brought her to Paris for more reasons than one. Small towns definitely had something lacking in big cities, and that was a sense of community and belonging.

Once the socializing wound down, a representative from the local medical community named Howard Turnbull gave a brief talk about his vision for a hospital facility to serve Henry County. "The need is great, for while the doctors put forth their best efforts to provide excellent care, without a sickbay, their resources are limited at best. Many of you have already dug deep into your pockets to fund this effort, and for that, we are deeply appreciative. We must spread the vision to meet the needs of the poor and sick of our community who may be suffering without the luxury of family nearby. Some often die untimely, even needless, deaths for lack of proper care and medicine."

Grace's heart broke at the mere thought of dying alone with no family nearby, and she wondered what Aunt Iris's condition would be today had she not answered the call to come to her aid. *What can I do to help, Lord?* she silently probed. *I'm just one person.*

You are a nurse, My child. You can do much.

The inner voice spoke with such clarity that it seemed almost audible, and Grace caught herself glancing around the gathering of women to see if anyone else had been affected in the same way. If so, it didn't show. Yes, all the other women fixed their eyes on the speaker, many of them leaning forward, as if to better soak in his every word; but even Mercy, a nurse herself, didn't appear as moved as she was—which indicated one thing. God had chosen *her*, Grace, for something specific, though she knew not what. All she could be certain of was that she'd detected His voice, and it set her heart to thrumming faster than usual.

When Mr. Turnbull concluded his talk, a couple of things became clear to Grace. The first thing was that the town stood in need of a large medical facility, as well as a "holding place," of sorts, where the sick, poor, and elderly could either recuperate with proper care, nutrition, and attention, the doctor coming to lend his expertise and administer medications as needed, or die with dignity, surrounded by loving caretakers. Her second realization was that Brockwell Manor could serve well as that "holding place," and the very notion made her pulse quicken. Had the Lord planted that thought in her mind, or had she thought it up on her own? It struck Grace with fresh awareness how deeply she cared about the elderly. During her employment at Massachusetts General Hospital, her favorite patients had always been the aged ones, even though they could also be the crankiest and most demanding.

"I'm so happy you decided to join us today," Mercy said later while bidding her and Joy good-bye. Solomon had pulled up in the carriage some ten minutes earlier, but it had taken Grace a bit of time to make her way over there, for all the friendly farewells and calls of "Come again!"

"I'm happy, too," Grace replied, meaning it. She'd thoroughly enjoyed herself, and she couldn't believe it'd taken her three long months to jump in and meet some new people. It would seem Conrad Hall had a bigger hold on her than she'd realized. Not that he would disapprove of her mingling with the church ladies, but he always insisted they spend no fewer than three nights together every week. With her days consumed by caring for Aunt Iris, she seldom rationed time for anything else, unless it was attending church, riding into town with Solomon, or stopping by The Perfect Fit Tailoring Shop for a dress fitting.

"Mr. Turnbull certainly did present us with a challenge, didn't he?" said Mercy. "I'm so glad Mrs. Grassmeyer invited him. It was a message we all needed to hear. While I have some nursing experience, my hands are full caring for my own family. I'd still like to talk to Sam about contributing more to the hospital fund, though. I understand your aunt has been a steady contributor, Grace. Paris truly admires and appreciates her for her generosity."

Grace smiled. "Thank you, Mercy. I'll tell her you said so. I, too, would like to do my part, but I'm not quite sure what that might entail."

Joy smiled and touched her arm. "Wait on the Lord, and He'll reveal it to you in due time."

The words jarred her to the soul, almost as if her friend had laid some sort of prophecy on her. "Thank you." She glanced behind her at the ever-patient Solomon, waiting with the rig. "And now I should be going. I've left Aunt Iris alone long enough."

The ladies said their final good-byes to Grace, asking her to give her aunt their best regards, and then Grace strode to meet the carriage, her heart full, her mind awash with ponderings.

When they pulled up outside the manor, Grace found herself too impatient to wait on Solomon to open her door. She hopped out of her own accord. "You go on ahead to the stables, Sol," she told him. "I don't mind seeing myself inside."

His dark eyes widened, his gray eyebrows arching. "You sho' 'bout that, miz?"

"Of course. I'm anxious to go upstairs and visit with Auntie."

"All right, then. You jes' go on and make yo'self at home. I'm sure Miz Ellen be real happy to get you some ice-cold tea."

"That would be nice. I'll ask for some if I see her."

When she stepped into the spacious foyer, Ellen was nowhere in sight; so, rather than go in search of refreshment for which she had no need, she headed directly for the expansive staircase leading to the second floor. Her skirts rustled as she climbed the winding stairs, turned right at the landing, and proceeded down the long corridor, passing her own closed door first, then two guest rooms on either side of the hall, before finally reaching her aunt's bedchamber. The door was slightly ajar, and she gave a light knock before letting herself in. She found Aunt Iris in her usual station, sitting before the towering window overlooking the grounds, rocking ever so gently, a thin shawl tossed across her lap.

"I'm back, Auntie."

Startled out of her reverie, Iris gave a slight jolt. "Ah, so you are."

"I didn't mean to disturb you. How are you feeling? And what were you thinking on?"

She waved a thin wrist. "I'm fine as peach fuzz, and I suppose you could say I've been sitting here evaluating. Come, pull up a chair and tell me all about the church picnic."

She slid the ornate cushioned stool that sat beneath the mirrored vanity over to her aunt's chair. She wondered how long it'd been since Aunt Iris had sat there primping. "It was quite enjoyable," she said, situating herself next to the elderly woman. "I met so many lovely ladies."

"Good. Then you're glad you went?"

"Indeed, although I hated leaving you behind."

"Pssh. I'm not much good for going out these days. I tire too easily. But that doesn't mean I don't like hearing all about your experiences. Tell me everything."

"I will, but first, you must tell me what you meant when you said you've been 'evaluating.' What, exactly, have you been evaluating— besides the grass below and those beautiful rosebushes climbing up the arbor?" She bent forward and pushed the drapery aside to give herself a better view of the property below. It seemed to stretch as far as the eye could see.

Aunt Iris hardly blinked; she just kept staring out over the vastness, her eyes somewhat glazed over, as if she were lost in thought. "Oh, I don't know. I suppose it happens with most anybody who knows he or she is on the way out of this world. You grow introspective."

"You shouldn't talk like that, Auntie."

"Why ever not? It's the truth, you know."

"But if you persist in dwelling on it, you might—" A catch in her throat made her stop mid-sentence.

Her aunt tipped her head to one side and tossed her a glance. "What? Die before my time?" She chuckled. "I think not. The good Lord's already ordained my time, has known it since before I even breathed my first. No changing that." She picked a tiny ball of lint from her shawl and rolled it around between her arthritic thumb and forefinger, her eyes dropping to her lap. "I wonder sometimes if I've done enough for one lifetime. I fear I spent too much time and money on myself and not enough on others. Of the two of us, your uncle John was the more generous."

Grace sat straighter. "Now, Auntie, I happen to know that's not true. You've given generously to so many worthy causes. Why, just today, someone made mention of your charitable spirit with regard to the hospital fund. If you're planning to beat yourself up for inadequate giving, then I will just have to put a stop to it this minute."

Aunt Iris actually laughed, albeit quietly. "My dear, you do have a way of putting your foot down, don't you?" She pressed a hand to her stomach and gave an awful groan.

Immediately worried, Grace touched her aunt's arm. "I'm sorry for your pain, Auntie. Is there something I can do for you?"

"No, no, I'm fine," she said, flicking her wrist. There was simply no coddling the woman. "Now then, tell me about the picnic."

Grace settled back and proceeded to tell her about the afternoon—the ladies she'd met, most of whom Iris knew at least by name, and Mr. Turnbull's presentation.

At this, Aunt Iris compressed her mouth and crumpled her brow. After some meditating, she said, "It's a shame to hear about elderly folks dying alone. I can't imagine how frightening that must be for them. Is there no place for them to go?"

"Not if they don't have family close by."

"Humph. That could've been me, you know—if you hadn't dropped everything in Boston to move here. I'm not sure I can ever repay you."

"What are you talking about, Aunt Iris? I want nothing in return. We're family, for heaven's sake. I'm just thankful I could come—and that you had the presence of mind to summon me. I had no idea you were so ill."

"Well, I probably wouldn't have said anything, but that Doc Trumble had to put his nose in my business. He finagled your address out of me and then sent you that telegram, the old whippersnapper."

"And I'm glad he did."

There was another pensive pause between them, until Aunt Iris finally broke it. "I suppose you'll be spending the evening with...that *man* again."

"With Conrad, you mean. And no, not tonight, Auntie. He had to leave town yesterday on business, and he won't return till Tuesday morning, I'm afraid. I dearly miss him."

"What sort of business?"

"He's meeting some clients. That's all I know, really."

"Where?"

"He took the train to Chicago, but I try not to delve into his professional life. Conrad says a lawyer must hold his business contacts in strict confidence, lest an individual come across some piece of pertinent information and unwittingly or purposely divulge it to another."

"He doesn't trust you, in other words."

"Of course he trusts me, it's just best he not tell me about his communications with clients. If I should slip up in the wrong company, I might compromise one of his cases, and I'd rather not be responsible for that."

"I suppose that makes sense," her aunt conceded. "Still, John always kept me abreast of his professional decisions. I should think your husband-to-be would provide you with at least some details, such as the name of the hotel where he intends to spend the next few days."

Grace would admit—but not to Aunt Iris—that she'd been somewhat disturbed when Conrad had refused to disclose even the least little detail. "You needn't trouble yourself over such matters, my darling," he'd told her at the train station. "Just know I'll be back on Tuesday morning, and my very first stop shall be Brockwell Manor. Be forewarned, I will be stealing you away for a brief moment to sweep you into my arms, so take care that you don't go riding off to town with Solomon before I drop by, or I shall have to hunt you down."

She'd blushed at his brazenness. "You would do that?"

He'd touched her nose and winked. "You bet I would. I'll be good and hungry for your kisses. Don't forget that I love you very much, and I'll be thinking about you every second I'm away from you."

She'd giggled at his teasing, forgetting all else—until now.

"I'm not concerned, Aunt Iris," she fibbed. "Nor should you be. Conrad is a busy man, and it's not at all unusual that he keep his occupational dealings private."

A loud huff issued from the woman's scowling lips. "You say that now."

Not wishing to belabor the topic, Grace asked, "Would you like to play a board game or perhaps have me read to you?"

Aunt Iris shook her gray head. "Maybe later. For now, I believe I'll lie down."

"Certainly. That would be good for you. I'll return before supper and help you dress. Perhaps you'd like to wear your purple gown tonight—the one with the eyelet buttonholes on the white collar."

Iris gave an overstated sigh. "No need to primp. It's just the two of us."

"True, but you enjoy dressing up, no matter the occasion."

"Humph. We'll see."

She extended a bony hand to Grace, who helped her to a standing position on shaky legs. Oh, how Grace longed to make each second with her count. "Would you like me to just sit with you while you rest?"

Her aunt gave a slight shrug. "Suit yourself."

Grace had a feeling the woman was still a bit miffed at Conrad for keeping his whereabouts a secret.

⌒

"You bring me what you owe me?" Carl Petrie stared down his bulbous nose at Conrad, then let his eyes fall to the briefcase Conrad held under his arm. A big cigar hung out the side of his mouth, the smoke from which hovered around his fat face.

The chill in the night air, intensified by Carl's frigid sneer, sent a shivering pang up Conrad's spine. He hated Carl's bullying—hated the memories it stirred of his days in the orphanage when the bigger boys terrorized him with their ugly words and threats of violence.

"I brought *some* of what I owe you. I told you, I need a little more time."

"And I told you, I've waited long enough!" the man bellowed, his voice echoing down the dark alley. "How much you got in there?"

"Enough to make up for the payments I missed."

"That ain't goin' to catch you up. I'm sick o' foolin' with you, Hall. You ain't made good on your word. We made a deal that you'd pay this loan off in a timely manner."

Conrad's ire shot up. "And I'm working at doing just that." As it was, he'd had to "borrow" money from a couple of his clients' trust funds to produce the necessary cash. He'd tied up the bulk of his earnings in other investments and in his month-to-month essentials—mortgage, meals, and entertainment. He fully intended to return the money to the clients' accounts as soon as that old biddy Iris Brockwell passed on into glory and his wife-to-be inherited her wealth.

"You ain't workin' hard enough. I went three months without gettin' one red cent from you. My patience is runnin' thin. I told you when you bought that hotel I'd give you ten months to settle your debt. Well, we've passed that mark, Hall, and I ain't waitin' any longer."

"You're getting money today, so stop your grousing." Conrad opened the case and withdrew a small wad of bills.

Petrie wasted no time snatching it from his clutches. He gave it a quick glance, then met Conrad's gaze with a beady-eyed stare. "I'll expect to see you in a little over two weeks—Monday, September twentieth, to be exact. I'll meet you at this exact location at eight p.m. on the dot, and you'd best have the remainder of your debt on your person. Understood?" Petrie spat on the ground, just missing Conrad's shoe.

"I can't come up with the rest of the money in that short a time."

"Yes, you can, and you will. You shouldn't have bought that hotel if you couldn't pay for it."

"You'll get your money, Petrie," Conrad growled. "Just get off my back, would you?"

The man snorted. "I ain't gettin' off your back. You got two weeks and some odd days to pay your debt—in full." He fanned the small wad of bills under Conrad's nose. "If you don't make good on this deal, I'll sic my dogs on you—if you get my drift."

Oh, he got his drift, all right. He'd seen his so-called dogs, and they weren't of the canine nature. No, these guys were big-muscled brutes who toted fists for guns. He didn't doubt for one minute they could make mincemeat out of him with just a couple of punches. He swallowed a big dose of bitter bile but determined not to let Petrie smell his fear.

"You'll get your money," he grumbled.

"I better," Petrie said.

Half an hour after they parted ways, Conrad was still steaming mad, if not deeply troubled, as he pushed through the swinging doors of Ruby's Saloon. How was he supposed to keep coming up with money he didn't have? He should have known better than to buy that wretched hotel and restaurant. He'd have to "borrow" from more of his clients and hope nobody noticed.

Ruby herself greeted him when he approached the counter. "Well, lookie what the wind blew in," she said, giving him a gap-toothed grin. "If it ain't Buster himself, all dressed up like some fancy schoolboy. Haven't seen you for a while. You still lawyerin' down in Tennessee, or they done kicked you out?"

He'd always hated the stupid nickname Ruby had attached to him as a boy. She used to pay him a few cents a week to sweep off her back stoop and pick up garbage from the alley. She'd say something like, "Hey, Buster, you wanna earn a nickel?" Back then, he'd do just about anything for money. The poorhouse he'd lived in until the ripe age of thirteen had sorely lacked in comfort, with inadequate ventilation promoting the rampant spread of disease. Chicago Poorhouse and Orphanage, as someone had so aptly named it, had been brimming with kids, and he'd lost count of how many had died due to lack of basic care, inadequate food and clothing, and the general shortage of overall provisions, such as beds and bedding. Medical care was sporadic, at best, and many who might have lived if they'd had suitable care simply died there and were buried in the poorhouse graveyard, often with no ceremony or even a grave marker. Babies born in poorhouses to unwed mothers and prostitutes hardly stood a chance of surviving, as their mothers usually abandoned them.

It was a wonder Conrad had made it out of there alive. He'd never met his parents and didn't know their identity. From what he'd been told, his mother hadn't given birth to him in the poorhouse; she'd merely wrapped him in a few filthy rags, stuck him in a wooden crate, and dropped him off on the front stoop. For all he knew, she'd gotten pregnant from a rape. It didn't matter; she hadn't wanted him, and that was the bottom line. That, or she hadn't had the means for caring for him. He still didn't know why he'd survived when so many others had died a few pitiful weeks or months after birth. He sure couldn't say it was due to compassion or proper care, so he'd always chalked it up to pure, dumb luck.

"Yeah, I'm still 'lawyering,' as you put it—as if you give a rusty red penny what I'm doing."

She tossed back her head and cackled, her two long white braids shaking, her big bosom bouncing. Years of hard living had put deep creases in her wide face, and they only deepened when she grinned. "You don't have to get all cantankerous on me, Buster. It was a simple enough question. You come in for some refreshment?"

"Not the sort you're referring to. Is she here?"

"Who?"

He propped his elbow on the counter and shifted to the side, leaning in and lowering his voice. "You know very well who I'm talking about. Lorinda. Is she upstairs?"

"Might be. You got an appointment?"

"I don't need an appointment, and you know it. Just tell her I'm here."

Ruby pulled at one of her long, droopy earlobes. "You're pretty sure of yourself, aren't you? What if I said she's gettin' married?"

He chuckled and leaned closer. "What if I told you I am?"

She jerked her head back. "You aren't! Are you?"

"Maybe. Is she?"

"No, I was just joshin' you."

"I figured. Everyone knows Lorinda's not the marrying sort."

"And I suppose you think you are?"

"I have my reasons."

She took up a soiled rag and started wiping the weathered countertop. "Huh, ain't that somethin'? Who's the lucky girl?"

At the other end of the bar, a couple of cronies perched on stools were carrying on a conversation of a political nature. A few other customers drank at tables scattered around the dingy, dimly lit room, a couple of them talking louder than necessary. Booze did that to a person—made him forget his inhibitions. That was why Conrad mostly stayed away from the stuff. He couldn't risk losing his bearings.

"You don't need to know her name," he told Ruby. "But we're hitching up in about six weeks."

"Yeah? I s'pose that means we won't be seein' much of you from here on out, then."

"Depends."

"On what?"

He gave her a crooked grin. "On how much I miss Lorinda."

Ruby tipped her face to the side, making her jowl sag. She turned down her thin lips. "You're a regular scoundrel, Buster—have been since the first time I laid eyes on you. I know you stole plenty of food from me back in the day, but I didn't say much. I knowed you wasn't gettin' much at the poorhouse. I think you also dipped into my cash drawer a time or two. There were nights I couldn't get my figures to balance, and always right after you'd been hangin' around."

He didn't crack a grin. "You think you're clever, don't you, Ruby?"

Rather than respond, she took to working on a tiny stain she'd found in the countertop. "You ever go back there?"

"Where?"

"That institution what raised you."

A lump of repugnance balled up in his gut. "No, and I don't intend to, either. Why would I? I don't have one thing to say to those people—except maybe 'Thanks for putting within me a strong determination to escape this rat hole and make something of myself.'"

Ruby chortled and looked him up and down. "Yeah, you did that, all right. Look at you—high-and-mighty lawyer in fancy duds. What d' you wanna come showin' your face around a place like this for?"

He sneered at the wench, then pointed at the ceiling. "What do you think?"

"Connie! Is that you?"

He swiveled at the familiar, buttery smooth voice, and his mouth went instantly dry.

"Hello, Lorinda." She still looked plenty good to him—tall, with curves in all the right places.

Lorinda—whose last name he'd never learned, and didn't want to know—issued him a coy smile as she fairly floated down the staircase in her low-cut, full-skirted emerald taffeta gown with the fitted waistline that came to a flattering point at the front. In her delicate hand, she held a brightly colored fan, which she kept situated just beneath her demure chin. As usual, she wore thick color on her cheeks and eyes, but it went with her profession, and it suited her fine.

Conrad couldn't hold his grin at bay. He stepped away from the bar and went to meet her halfway across the room, grasping hold of one of her hands, the nails of which were long and bright red.

"You came to see me, I presume?"

"I did." He bent and kissed her cheek. Rarely had she ever allowed him a kiss on the lips, and it was just as well. He had no emotional connection to her whatever, and he liked it that way—as did she.

She touched his lapel and batted her long, fake eyelashes at him. "Well, you can't stay long. I have a customer coming in an hour."

That should have put him off, made him jealous, but it didn't. It was hard to feel jealousy when his insides were mostly dead. Shoot, it was hard work telling Grace he loved her. He'd be glad for the day when he could drop the charade.

He took Lorinda by the arm and pointed her toward the stairs.

"You goin' to tell her the good news, Buster?" asked Ruby.

Lorinda slowed her steps and glanced up at him. "What news?"

"He's gettin' married in a few weeks," Ruby blurted out.

Conrad waited to see what effect the news would have on Lorinda, but her expression didn't change. She shrugged. "Well, lucky for you. Too bad I can't say the same for her." She tossed back her head of thick blonde hair, her curls cascading down her bare shoulders, and gave an empty laugh.

Neither of them cared one hoot about the other. Some pair they made.

8

$\mathcal{J}$ess Quinn's boot heels clicked loudly on the sidewalk as he strode along Wood Street in downtown Paris, Tennessee. He paused in front of Grandy's Best Meats and cast a glance up the street to gain his bearings. Folks passed, carting crates and boxes of food products, household wares, and various other items to their horse-drawn wagons. The locals seemed a friendly lot, and those few who gave him a curious stare quickly followed it with a courteous tip of the hat. Others merely smiled as they walked past. Jess did the same, not ready to strike up conversation with anyone before getting acclimated to his surroundings.

Foremost on his mind was, of course, seeing Grace. Finding the best way to do it was another matter. He couldn't very well walk up to someone and say, "I'm looking for Grace Fontaine, my fiancée"—not when most folks about town probably knew that she was promised to another man. He could always march straight into the law office where her fiancé worked and say, "Hand her over, bud—she's mine," but he doubted that method would gain him any favor. For all he knew, Grace had thoroughly put him out of her head and heart, giving her affections to this fellow named Conrad Hall, instead.

Jess had Josiah and Ruthie to thank for passing along what few details they knew about the man. They'd even given him permission to read the one and only letter Grace had written them since moving to Paris, telling about her new love and her subsequent plans to marry on

October 15. He'd nearly retched at the sight of those statements. How could she have fallen in love with another man after a mere month in Paris, when she'd loved Jess so thoroughly, no matter that she thought him dead?

He would go to where she was staying and win her back! First, though, he really needed to find himself a restaurant to fill his empty stomach.

He set off walking again, eyeing the storefronts on either sides of the dirt street. He passed the Paris Fish Market, the county courthouse, and the post office before stopping at an intersection, where he looked both ways, then crossed to the next block. His heart thudded to an abrupt halt at the sight of the law offices of Murphy, Wadsworth & Hall just across the street, the placard above the door swaying in the mild breeze. His gut churned at the thought of coming face-to-face with the man who had stolen his woman. Should he go in there and confront him directly?

Be still, My son. Let Me guide your steps.

The quiet voice interrupted his thoughts, and he realized with chagrin that he'd failed to pray even once about the matter. "Lord, forgive me. I do want You to show me how I should proceed." He meant the whispered prayer with all his heart, but there was still a small part of him that wanted to take matters into his own hands and race ahead. "Whom should I ask about locating Brockwell Manor, Lord? Please lend me Your wisdom."

If he thought the Lord would give him a hasty response, he was mistaken. He pulled his gaze away from the office building and walked on, not slowing his pace till he reached Brooks Hotel and Restaurant. Surely, this swanky place wasn't the only hotel in town. He surveyed the street once more, looking up one side and down the other, searching for another hotel sign. The last thing he wanted to do was waste all his funds on lodging. He wanted his money to last as long as possible. He'd just as soon sleep under the stars. Jess's stomach growled again, and he thought about walking inside to partake of a midday meal; but again, he didn't want to part with his cash. Besides, the establishment appeared to be the type that required one to wear a suit and tie, both of which he was a bit short on right now.

He moved on, passing a general store, a hardware store, a drugstore, and Paris Bank and Trust. Finally, he came upon a little run-down structure called Juanita's Café that seemed more suitable. He swallowed, wiped his sweaty palms on his pants, and pulled open the screen door. It whined in protest, causing a few heads to turn in his direction. He removed his hat, raked his hand through his thick, longish strands, and nodded at a couple of fellows. They nodded back.

He situated himself at an empty table near the front of the room. He worried that the rickety chair might not hold his weight, but after a minute or so passed without its breaking, he started to relax.

A stout Hispanic woman approached. "Hello, sir. I get you something?" she asked, her accent lilting.

"How about a tall glass of water to start out with?"

"Yes sir, I bring. You like something to eat?"

He grinned. "What's your specialty?"

She smiled back, and he was thankful for her friendly demeanor. He figured she'd been around long enough to know just about everybody in town.

"I make you cold meat sandwich and bring you bowl of tomato soup, no?"

His taste buds started doing a jig. "You got it."

"*Sí, señor*. I be back." She whipped around, her colorful skirt flaring behind her.

He sat back and glanced around. Being that it was neither the lunch nor the supper hour, there were very few customers in the small, somewhat dilapidated eatery. However, the delectable aromas coming from the kitchen made up for the lack of adornment.

"You won't be disappointed in the food, mister. Juanita's a fine cook."

He inclined his head at the man who'd spoken, sitting not ten feet away. He'd been reading a newspaper but had lowered it to the tabletop.

"That's good to know," Jess said. "I'm mighty hungry."

The dapper-looking fellow smiled. "You new to town? I don't think I've seen you before."

"Is Paris really that small?"

The man gave a congenial laugh. "I suppose it is a little strange, my instantly identifying you as an outsider. By your accent, I'd say you hail from somewhere out East. Am I right?"

He'd never considered that he spoke with any sort of accent. "I thought it was you Southerners with the accent. And, yes, I come from Boston. Born and raised there."

"Ah. I'm a Michigander, myself. Married to a Southern gal, though." He took a swig of his beverage—coffee, no doubt—then eyed Jess with particular care. "So, how does a fellow from Boston find himself in Paris, Tennessee?"

Jess wondered how much information he ought to divulge. The guy seemed friendly enough, but he didn't want to spout off specific details to a complete stranger. "Just passing through, is all."

"Ah. Well, you enjoy your stay—however long it lasts." The fellow set down his mug, gathered up his newspaper, and pushed his chair back, the legs scraping loudly against the floor. Then he stood and advanced on Jess, extending his hand. "I'm Lucas Jennings, by the way. I pastor a fine little country church called Paris Evangelical. If you still happen to be in town tomorrow, feel free to join us for the Sunday service."

Like a bear out of hibernation, Jess came to life. "You're a pastor?" He hastened to stand, his own chair squealing when he rose. He shook the reverend's hand. "Name's Jess Quinn. It's an honor to meet you, sir. Please, would you care to join me?" He waved a hand at the empty chair across from him.

The preacher hesitated, then pulled out his pocket watch and glanced at it. "I'm afraid I have an appointment in about ten minutes. But it's only a short walk away, so I can give you a few minutes of my time." He pulled out the chair, which wobbled, and lowered himself into it. He was a hefty guy, so Jess figured that if the chair held him, he'd be safe in his own rickety one.

He sat once more. "Meeting you is like...well, it's an answer to prayer, sir."

The reverend's eyebrows shot up. "Oh? How so?"

"I need to talk to somebody."

"I'm all ears." The reverend folded his hands on the table and leaned forward, sincere interest glowing in his friendly, caring eyes.

Jess decided to take the gamble. How could he go wrong in confessing to a minister of the Word? "I misled you when I said I was just passing through town. I'm actually here for a specific reason."

The man raised his eyebrows again. "Is there something I can help you with?"

"I don't know. Maybe. I'm looking for someone in particular, and I'm not sure how to get to the address where she's living."

"Well, I've grown familiar with many of the local townsfolk, but I certainly don't know everybody. Who are you looking for?"

Jess swallowed hard and discovered that the lump in his throat actually hurt. "A young woman who's caring for an ailing aunt."

A tiny flicker lit the reverend's face, but he said nothing.

"Her name is Grace...Grace Fontaine. And her aunt's name is Iris, although I don't know the woman's last name."

The preacher shifted in his seat, then pressed his index finger to his chin, as if contemplating how to respond. After a moment, he asked, "And why would you be looking for this particular young lady?"

"Do you know her?"

"I might."

His heart pounded so hard, he heard the thump-thump in his head. "She's staying with her aunt at a place called Brockwell Manor, and I need to find her because...well, she and I were engaged to be married back in Boston. Then I took a job on a ship heading to England. The short of it is, everybody presumed me dead after news reached Boston that I'd been kidnapped by a band of pirates whose ship later went down. But the reality is that I was held prisoner in London for eighteen months."

The preacher's eyes widened for a moment. Then he lowered his chin and arched his eyebrows. "You were in prison, you say?"

Jess sighed. "It's a long story, and you probably don't have time to hear it right now."

"I regret that I don't, but I'll admit I'm intrigued."

"Can you tell me where she is?"

Reverend Jennings steepled his fingers, his brow furrowed in thought. "I'm afraid that Miss Fontaine is engaged to be married to someone else. In fact, I'm to officiate at the ceremony."

Jess nodded. "I've been informed of her engagement, Reverend. That's precisely why I'm here. I need her to know that I'm not lying at the bottom of the ocean. Just moments before coming in here, I asked the Lord to direct me, and then I met you. I believe you might be the key to my finding her."

"Well, put like that, how could I not assist you?" The reverend smiled. "You're right, of course. She deserves to know you're alive." The man pulled out his watch once more, looked at it, and got to his feet. "I'm afraid I have to be going. Brockwell Manor sits on a large piece of property some four or five miles outside of town. I've driven there on a couple of occasions, but it would be hard to give you directions. Some of those roads aren't marked well. I'd be pleased to take you there later today, though, if you'd like."

"I was intending to rent a horse, assuming there's a livery in town."

"Indeed there is. A couple of blocks south, on the corner of McNeil and South Poplar streets. Perhaps it would be best if you got yourself a horse and then followed me out there. That way, you'd be able to ride back to town on your own. Shall we meet at, say, four o'clock?"

"Yes." Jess nodded eagerly. "That'll give me time to freshen up a bit. Could you tell me if there's another hotel besides the Brooks?"

"There're a couple of small establishments about three blocks north of here. Nothing fancy about either one, though."

"That'll suit me fine. Thank you, Reverend. I appreciate your help."

The man nodded. "It's my pleasure, although maybe 'pleasure' isn't the word I should be using here. I'll confess I'm a little uneasy about getting involved."

"You're not the least bit involved," Jess assured him. "All you're doing is showing me where to find Grace. You don't even have to go with me as far as the front door. Just point me to it, and I'll take it from there."

The man nodded soberly. "I hope it goes well for you. She's very taken with Conrad Hall."

Jess gave a grim smile. "I won't deny your words sting, yet I simply must do this. You understand."

"I do. If it were me, I'd do the same. I'll be praying for you."

Was it possible? Could it be this easy? A wild thrum of expectation pounded through his veins at the thought of laying eyes on Grace again.

How would she react? Only time would answer that question.

⌒

Grace sat curled in a comfortable chair in the front parlor, a large book propped in her lap, and worked on a letter to her dear friend Ruth Woodbridge. She'd been delighted to receive word that Ruth would happily serve as matron of honor in her wedding, and also that Josiah would be looking on with their baby daughter from the back row.

Upstairs, Aunt Iris napped quite restfully, to Grace's relief. It had been a joy to see the gleam of interest in her eyes as she'd shared about the picnic festivities that afternoon, and she planned to do all she could to keep that spark alive for as long as possible.

Grace reread the lines she'd written, pondering what to say next. She'd already thanked her friend for agreeing to join the wedding party and gotten her caught up on Aunt Iris's condition. Should she mention Conrad's business trip? No, that'd be silly, since he'd be back in Paris by the time the letter reached her. She tapped her chin with the end of her pen, still thinking. Finally, she decided to talk about the dreadfully hot summer they'd been having in Tennessee.

The sound of horse hooves pounding up the driveway awakened in her an acute sense of curiosity. Perhaps someone from the women's club had come to visit her aunt. She set her pen in the inkwell on the table beside her, tucked the letter inside the book, and laid it on the desktop, then stood and went to the window. Pulling back a corner of the drapes, she peered outside. The sun shone with blinding brilliance, as it often did on summer afternoons, so it was difficult to identify the caller. At the foot of the lane, a carriage turned around, as if the driver had changed his mind, and started heading back toward town. Meanwhile, a man on horseback came up the pebbled path, his hat blocking his face from view.

Solomon was already on his way to the door. Ever the watchful keeper of the estate, he had the ears of a bat and usually detected approaching visitors before anyone else did. He passed through the big dining room and entered the front foyer, then peered out one of the vertical glass panes next to the double-door entry.

"Who is it, Sol?" Grace asked.

"Don't reckon I know 'im. He's a tall one, kind of on the gaunt side."

She smiled at his observation. "Probably one of those traveling salesmen."

"Nope, wouldn't say that. He ain't pullin' a cart o' wares." He opened the door to the mystery traveler. "Help y', sir?"

Grace moved closer to the door, preparing to peer around the corner at the stranger.

"I'm looking for Miss Grace Fontaine."

The familiar-sounding voice rocked her to the core of her being. A wave of dizziness overtook her, and she stopped dead as a statue, grabbing hold of the wall to maintain her balance.

It was nearly identical to the voice of her former love, but that would be impossible. Surely, she was dreaming. A nauseous sensation surged through her, and she clutched her gut as another wave of light-headedness threatened to steal her equilibrium.

"Who may I say is inquirin'?" Solomon asked.

"Just tell her it's someone…well, someone she thought dead."

Her heartbeats and breaths hastened, then went wild. In an instant, the room spun out of control, her body turning from hot to cold to hot again, her mind a blur of crazy, incomprehensible thoughts. Against her will, her lips formed his name, but her voice refused to utter it. What was happening? Somehow, her feet moved without her brain's consent, and she found herself standing in the doorway, staring at what she thought at first to be a mirage.

"Miz?" Solomon asked. "You all right? You look a bit white in the face." He reached out and seized her by the arm. "Do y' know this here man?"

Again, she opened her mouth to speak, but still nothing came out. Every bit of air whooshed out of her.

The man standing on the stone terrace removed his hat. "Hello, Grace. I'm sorry to throw you into such a shock. It's me. Jess."

He'd lost weight, but not so much that she didn't recognize him. He still had that longish, unkempt light brown hair with flecks of gold, those distinctly piercing green eyes with the arched brows, and that stubble of growth on his square-set face that always appeared by midday, no matter that he'd shaved in the morning. He stood tall and straight, his sleeves rolled up to the elbows, revealing tanned forearms.

"J-Jess?" she finally stammered.

He gave a shaky, slanted smile while she struggled to conceive the inconceivable. Jess Quinn, alive? "Yes, in the flesh."

"But—you were lost at sea."

"So the story went." His voice held a gravelly tone.

"Miz?" Solomon asked again.

She'd never told him about Jess Quinn, had never seen the need. He must be thoroughly confused.

"This…this is…someone from my past, Solomon." It was the only explanation she could manage.

"I see. Did you wish to, uh"—he paused, clearly unsure how to proceed—"invite 'im inside?"

She didn't have an answer for him, for her mind had frozen in place.

"Miz?" Solomon repeated.

"May I come in?" Jess asked, his voice still husky. "I think you'll agree we have much to talk about."

"I—I don't know what to say." Hers barely made it above a whisper.

Solomon waited; she could feel his eyes boring into her. Meanwhile, her heart pounded out of control—she thought it might explode from her chest—and her mind spun at almost the same speed. One thing became clear, and one thing only: She did need answers.

Finally, she blew out a loud breath. "All right," she said, "you may come in, but only long enough to tell me where you've been." Somehow, she'd succeeded in sounding much calmer than her churning insides should have allowed.

Nodding, Jess stepped over the threshold, his hat clutched in both hands. Grace turned away and walked through the parlor to the living room, putting on the strongest air she could muster. "We'll take some sweet tea, Sol." She sat on the divan, straight as a stick, and folded her hands in her lap.

"Very good, Miz Grace. It'll take me but a minute." Even Solomon had assumed a rigid posture, his shoulders more erect, his demeanor stiff, if not protective. He gestured to the upholstered armchair next to the fireplace. "Have a seat in this here chair," he said to Jess.

Grace felt herself shake her head in disbelief when Jess thanked him and did as instructed. Was this really happening? Could she truly be looking at her former fiancé? She found she had no notion of what to feel. She didn't love him anymore—how could she, when she loved Conrad? Yet there was *something* churning inside her. She just couldn't identify it.

He exhaled a breath that made his chest cave in, and she was struck again by how much weight he'd lost. So many questions circled in her head that she hadn't a clue which one to pose first. Perhaps he would supply the answers before she even asked. She glanced down at her left hand, where her diamond engagement ring glittered, and rested it atop her right hand, hoping he'd notice it and understand the implications without her having to explain. If he saw it, he didn't let on, for his eyes had not moved from her face since he'd situated himself in the chair.

Oh Lord, help me make sense of all this, she prayed silently. *Right now, none of it seems real.* The plea somehow helped to settle her heart, but it did nothing to tame her whirling thoughts.

9

Grace looked so trim and pretty in her white blouse and lime green skirt—better, even, than he remembered, with perfectly coiffed chestnut hair, coffee-colored eyes, delicately carved cheekbones, dainty mouth, and exquisite nose. He doubted a finer-looking female inhabited the town of Paris, let alone all of Tennessee. Did this so-and-so, Conrad Hall, have the slightest idea what sort of treasure he had found? Jess doubted it. The man hadn't known her long enough. Jess, on the other hand, had the clear advantage of having known her since youth.

He sat forward in the chair, knees spread, elbows resting there. "You look wonderful, Grace. It's so good to see you."

"Where have you been, Jess?" she asked, skimming right over his compliment.

"It's a long story. Do you have time?"

She shifted in her chair, taking great care to wave her left hand about as she adjusted her skirt. He could tell she was flaunting that good-sized diamond ring. As if he could miss it. But he would be whipped in the britches before he acknowledged it. No, he'd leave it to her to call attention to it. To say that she'd given up on him and had promised herself to another.

"I have a bit of time, yes," she finally said.

"How is your aunt? I understand you came here out of concern for her health."

Her head shot up. "Who told you?"

"Josiah and Ruthie. They were the first people I went to, after seeing my father."

"Your father—how is he?"

He took in a shaky breath and tried to relax. "Aging, I'm afraid—and not well."

She frowned and gave a silent nod then fidgeted with her ring while casting her eyes at something over his shoulder. No question, they were both uncomfortable. Somehow, he had to find a way to ease the tension.

"Josiah and Ruthie said you left Boston just a few months ago."

"Yes. Late April, to be exact."

"So…I missed you by a mere three months or so."

Before she had a chance to respond, the butler returned with a silver tray of tall crystal glasses and a china pitcher. He set the tray on the sofa table in front of Grace and proceeded to fill both glasses almost to the rim. Grace thanked him, and the fellow nodded. "You needin' anything else, miz?"

"No, Sol. That should do just fine. Thank you again."

The man angled Jess a glance that lingered only long enough to send a flash of warning. Jess liked the man, for he could tell that he had Grace's best interests in mind. He wondered what he thought of Conrad Hall. When the butler retreated from the room, Jess noticed two dark-faced women peeking their heads around the corner, their brown eyes round with curiosity. They quickly disappeared when he smiled at them.

"Would you like some tea?" Grace asked.

"Maybe later."

"You won't be here later," she shot back, as serious as the end of a gun barrel.

He swallowed, cleared his throat, and pressed his palms together as he selected his next words. "I spent the last eighteen months in a British naval prison, Grace. That's where I've been. I couldn't write, I couldn't send a telegram, I couldn't even let my own father know I was still alive."

She gasped, her face blanching. "Prison?"

"For a crime I didn't commit," he added hastily. "The Royal Navy mistook me for one of the pirates that raided the *Lone Star*, who had captured me and taken me prisoner. I survived going down with the burning pirate ship by climbing into a little rescue boat and lying low, but it wasn't long before they discovered me and hauled me aboard. Once on land, there was no trial, no going before a judge, no fair treatment of any sort—no questioning at all, really. They just threw me in a cell, fed and watered me daily, and allowed me to bathe about once a month."

She covered her mouth with her left hand, making that perfect diamond gleam with radiance in the afternoon sunlight streaming through the window. "That's awful, Jess," she murmured.

At least he'd gotten her attention. That had to count for something.

As he filled her in on the remaining details, she said little but listened with utmost intentness, her brown eyes as round and deep as the glass in her hand. He told her about his grueling stay in prison—about the times he'd taken sick but gotten no care, and the times he'd gone hungry because of the bugs he'd found in his soup; about the rat he'd befriended in his cell; about the cold that had kept him from sleep for days at a time. He told her more, much more, than he'd told Josiah and even his own father, because…well, because she was Grace, his beloved, and he found he couldn't withhold a single detail from her.

From time to time, she dabbed at her wet cheeks with one of the linen napkins the butler had left on the tray. When, at last, he reached the end of his story, the clock on the wall struck five gongs, and he realized he'd talked a full forty-five minutes with nary a break, except to hear the few questions she'd inserted.

"You've been through a great deal, Jess," she said, smoothing her skirt. "I'm so very sorry. I hardly know what to say. We all…we thought you were dead. That's what they told us."

"I know. My father—"

"Miz Grace?"

The female voice startled both of them. Jess swiveled around and saw one of the women who'd been peering wide-eyed at him from around the corner. He wondered if those women, and perhaps even the butler, had been listening in on his whole wretched tale from the doorway.

"Y' want that I should go upstairs and get Missus Brockwell ready fo' supper, or was you goin' to do that?"

Grace glanced at Jess. "I usually get my aunt up about now."

He stared at her for a full three seconds before it dawned on him that he'd probably overstayed his welcome. Resisting the urge to insist on spending more time with her, he rose to his feet. "Grace, I need to see you again. I still have so much to say, and I need—I need to know what you're thinking."

She stood, as well, smoothing out her skirt again as she straightened. "I'll walk you to the door." She spoke so quietly, he had to strain his ears to hear. He let her lead the way, praying all the while that she wouldn't turn him away.

She opened the door and stepped out onto the front terrace. Jess followed, closing the door behind him. Tension as thick as a shroud of fog surrounded them. He wanted to reach out and take her hand, but he'd be hard-boiled before he'd take that left hand, and she'd conveniently tucked the right one behind her back.

"Grace."

"Jess."

Their voices mingled simultaneously.

"I've been doing all the talking," Jess said. "It's your turn."

She nodded, then lowered her chin to her chest, as if to gather her thoughts and choose which words to say first. Then, raising her head and staring straight at him, she said, "I'm engaged, Jess. I'm to be married on October fifteenth. Surely, Josiah and Ruthie told you that."

"They did, and that's exactly why I'm here. You can't marry him, Grace."

She bristled, and he immediately regretted the way that had come out.

"What I mean is, you can't marry him—yet—especially knowing that I'm still very much alive, and you first promised yourself to me. You were to be mine, Grace Fontaine. Mine alone." He couldn't help it; he reached up and snagged hold of her arm. She tried to pull away, but he refused to let go. "We loved each other, Grace, and you can't deny it."

To her credit, she didn't so much as blink an eye, although he thought he saw her partially parted lips tremble, if only slightly. "You're right—I can't deny it. And I won't," she said quietly. "But I can say that I am in love with another now, and it's no longer appropriate for you to be here."

Desperation prompted his voice to rise in pitch. "How long have you known this fellow? Two, three, months, at most? How can you say you love him when you can't possibly know him through and through?"

Grace wrinkled her delicate brow. "One need not know someone 'through and through' before falling in love. Conrad is a wonderful man, Jess—successful, generous, interesting, doting, and committed. He loves me, and that's enough."

Something didn't sit right with Jess. He released her arm and took a step back. "What about his faith? It seems to me you'd have listed that ahead of all his other attributes."

She gave a taut jerk of her head. "It was a mere oversight, Jess. Of course, Conrad is a Christian. We attend Paris Evangelical Church together. The reverend—"

"Lucas Jennings," he finished for her. "I know. I met him today at Juanita's Café. He's the one who told me where your aunt lived, even brought me out here. But don't worry; he was very hesitant to get involved in our reunion. He told me he's to officiate at your nuptials."

In a bold move, he snagged her left hand and brought it close, giving the diamond a good perusal. He hadn't intended to so much as glance at it, and now here he was, examining it up close. "Nice. I didn't have the money to put one of these on your finger."

"Stop it." She tried to pull her hand from his grip, but he held it fast.

"I intended to give you one when I returned from England, but I clearly recall your saying you didn't want anything big or showy." He studied her eyes, glimmering with moisture. "You know why? Because you said our love was bigger than any diamond could ever be. That was most important to you. Remember, Grace?"

This time, she succeeded in freeing her hand, immediately tucking it behind her back with her right one. "I think you'd better go now, Jess."

"I will, but if you think I'm leaving Paris just yet, you have another think coming. Grace, I know you believe you love another man, but—"

"I *do* love another man," she inserted, poking out her chin and pulling back her shoulders.

He'd always admired her spark. Had she had occasion to show that side of herself to Conrad Hall, or was she still too enamored of him to stand up to him on any issue?

Without thought, he took hold of her upper arms. She stiffened and held herself erect as his fingers tightened. "It's been since June of ninety-two, Grace—that's when we last laid eyes on each other. When I promised to come back to you."

She sucked in a long breath through her nostrils. "But you didn't come back, Jess. Everyone thought you died. It took me two years to get over you."

He lifted an eyebrow. "Ah, so you're saying you didn't get over me till this past June—when you met your new love? Is that it?"

She remained stiff and somber. "New love does have a way of helping one heal."

He clenched her the tighter. "But not helping to forget, Grace. Never that."

He ogled her lips, and she locked them tight, as if she knew he longed to kiss them. He couldn't pull his eyes away, so it was no wonder her solemn expression turned to one of foreboding. As quick as an eagle sweeps down to snatch its prey, he closed the space between them and pressed his lips to hers, kissing her with an impatience that had been growing for months, even years. His mouth covered hers, tasting and testing, their bodies crushed together like two trees in a dense forest. All sense of time and place vanished as his hands moved to the small of her back and drew her closer. The biggest wonder was that she allowed it, even parted those stiff lips and tasted back—until she reared back with a gasp, her hands pushing against his chest to force a separation.

"You shouldn't have done that, Jess." With a scowl so severe that hard lines formed between her eyebrows, she took a giant step back, out of reach.

"You enjoyed it, and don't deny it," he whispered in a raspy voice.

"I'm an engaged woman."

"You were mine first."

Her eyes were luminous with unshed tears and reflected an emotion he couldn't quite name. "You must go now."

"When can I see you again?"

"You can't."

"I'm not leaving Paris, Grace."

"I don't know why you'd stay. Today is September fifth, and I'm getting married on October fifteenth."

"We'll see about that." He gave her a hard, assessing gaze. "Are you going to tell him about me?"

"He knows about you."

"But are you going to tell him I'm in town?"

She lifted one shoulder. "I suppose I'll have to. I don't want you making trouble, Jess. Please."

A round of chilly laughter rolled out of him. "Oh, there'll be some trouble, Grace. Count on it."

He saw her throat constrict, watched her fingers twist into a tight knot, and in that instant he knew—if he didn't know anything else—that his love for her had not dimmed. And when one experienced a love this deep, this complete, this intense, one didn't walk away from it without a fight.

"Will you be seeing him tonight?" he asked.

"No. He's out of town till Tuesday."

"Tuesday." Hope swirled around in his chest.

"Don't get any ideas about seeing me again, Jess, because I won't allow it. First off, it wouldn't be respectable."

"No, I suppose not—unless we kept it a secret." He winked.

Unblinking and sober-faced, she returned, "Please go. Now."

He reached up to touch her cheek but managed only a tiny brush, as she quickly put her back to him and grasped the door handle. "I'm going inside now," she said without turning, "and I expect you to mount up and ride out of here."

"I guess you leave me no choice."

Grace couldn't help it; she stood at the window and watched him ride off, his back still broad, despite his significant weight loss, his shoulders still wide, arms solid. She'd felt their strength in his embrace—a brazen act she should have resisted immediately rather than indulged momentarily. How had her life grown so complicated and difficult in the span of a moment? She tried telling herself that there was nothing complicated about it—that she was engaged to marry Conrad Hall, and nothing would change that. Yet the complexity remained.

"Miz Grace?"

Startled, she jerked and turned around.

Ellen stood at the bottom of the stairway, wringing her apron in her hands. "Yo' aunt be askin' fo' you."

Aunt Iris! How could she have forgotten her?

She rushed upstairs and found her aunt sitting on the edge of her bed, her thin white hair in disarray, her dress wrinkled and rumpled, and her face wearing its usual tired, wincing frown.

"Who came calling?" Aunt Iris asked in a craggy tone. "It's some sort of big secret I can't seem to wrangle out of anybody."

"Oh, Auntie." Grace went to her and sat down beside her, the mattress drooping under her weight and causing their shoulders to touch. She took her aunt's hand and studied the veins, the frail fingers. "He's alive, Auntie. Jess Quinn is alive. He just left a few minutes ago."

"Jess Quinn?" There came a pause, and for a moment, she wondered if her aunt had had a memory lapse—until she released a shaky breath and turned to look at her. "That fellow from Boston who first had your heart?"

She gave a slow nod, saying nothing. Skeletal as her aunt's shoulder was, she found herself resting her head there, longing for solace. "It was like looking at a ghost, Aunt Iris—only he was living and breathing."

"Where has he been all this time?"

"In a prison cell in London."

"In prison, you say? London? What on earth put him there?"

Not finding the consolation she'd hoped for, she lifted her head from Aunt Iris's bony shoulder and angled her body toward her aunt, tucking one foot beneath her skirt. Over the next several minutes, she relayed the condensed version of Jess's story.

"Well, I'll be dad-sizzled," Aunt Iris said after letting the information digest. "If that don't put a crease in the parson's pants."

In spite of herself, Grace giggled to hear her habitually proper aunt utter something so foreign to her formal nature.

"What did you tell him?" Aunt Iris asked, evidently not humored in the least.

"I told him I'm engaged to Conrad, of course."

"He traveled all the way from Boston to tell you he's alive, and all you could think to say in return is that you're marrying someone else?"

A surge of frustration coursed through Grace. "Well, what else was I supposed to tell him?"

"You loved him long before you loved Conrad, my dear."

"True, but I'm promised to Conrad now."

Her aunt raised her eyebrows. "Well, you don't have to marry him until you get your feelings all sorted out."

"But I never said I needed to sort out my feelings."

"Fiddle-faddle! Of course you do. Look me in the eyes and tell me you're not just a little bit confused right now."

Something had sparked to life in the older woman, to Grace's fascination. Yet it also troubled her to realize her aunt spoke the God's truth. Seeing Jess had turned her world upside down; and, as if that weren't enough, he'd kissed her almost into oblivion—until she'd had the common sense to step away and break the spell.

"I...I do need a few days to sort out my feelings, I suppose. And I'll need to tell Conrad that Jess is alive. But I can't imagine it will make me stop loving Conrad. Oh, Aunt Iris, why did this have to happen?"

"Why did what have to happen? Are you wishing he'd died, after all?"

She gasped. "No, not at all! But—but why did he have to come back now? Why couldn't he have waited till after I married? Then I'd have no choice in the matter. Nothing to think about."

"Nothing to think about? That's hardly reality, my dear. Had you already married, you would have been guaranteed to spend the rest of your days asking yourself 'What if?' God knows it's better this way, and I do mean that. God *knows*. Do you think any of this comes as a surprise to Him?" She didn't give Grace a second to answer. "Certainly not. God knows exactly what He's doing, and if you know what's good for you, Grace Fontaine, you'll ask Him to make His plans for you good and clear."

Her forthrightness set Grace aback, but the energy of her response encouraged her, at least. "Aunt Iris, listen to yourself. Your voice is so strong, and—why, you're sitting up straighter than usual. It's almost as if you aren't even ill."

"Humph. Well, perchance the Lord lent me a temporary strength. Maybe He's trying to say something to you through me."

Grace scratched her head and squinted at this dear, aging woman, who had, in the span of a few moments, miraculously acquired a certain fire in her deep-set blue-gray eyes.

"I believe you may be right," Grace said with a sigh. "Tonight, before I go to bed, I'll spend an extended period of time reading the Scriptures, and I'll ask the Lord to enlighten me as to His purposes."

"Good. Start with Jeremiah twenty-nine, verse eleven, which says, 'For I know the thoughts that I think toward you, saith the LORD, thoughts of peace, and not of evil, to give you an expected end.'"

"I didn't know you had committed certain Scriptures to memory, Auntie."

Aunt Iris clutched Grace's hand and gave it a squeeze. "When a person knows she's dying, she takes special care to get things straight with God. I only regret I didn't do it a lot sooner."

10

$\mathcal{G}$race had slept little on Saturday night, so she found herself yawning as she did her hair at the vanity table in preparation for the Sunday church service. She chose to do the top half of her dark brown tresses in a knot and allow the bottom half to flow down her back. A few loose strands fell around her pink cheeks, giving her a more carefree appearance. Odd how, inside, she felt anything but carefree. Instead, her stomach had tied itself up tauter than the bun on her head. In fact, when Ellen called her down to breakfast, she declined, saying that she'd have a small bowl of fruit and a cup of tea instead. Her poor gut couldn't handle much more than that.

In a fitful night of rest, she'd dreamed off and on about Conrad and Jess. In one instance, they'd had a shouting match while standing in a boat. Jess had rocked the vessel back and forth until Conrad lost his balance and fell headlong into the water, flailing his arms in an attempt to stay afloat. Watching helplessly from the shore, Grace had waded in up to her neck but failed to reach him.

Another nightmare had featured Jess and Conrad working together to bind her from her neck to her ankles in rope so tight that it paralyzed her. Still another vision had her sitting at the dining room table next to Aunt Iris with both men situated across from them. Aunt Iris gave them both a calculating glower and then said, "I vote for the horse."

Of course, none of the silly dreams made an ounce of sense—unless she counted the last one, which seemed to imply that neither suitor fit the bill.

Her coiffure finished, she stood and assessed herself in the oak-framed full-length mirror on the other side of the massive bedroom. From head to toe, she looked completely put together in her yellow cotton calico day blouse and matching skirt. If only she could say the same about her befuddled mind. The night before, she had read from Jeremiah 29, as instructed by her aunt, as well as from an assortment of other books of the Bible—all of which had only obscured her thinking the more. Naturally, it thrilled her that Jess hadn't gone down with the pirate ship—that he was still very much alive. She also got butterflies just thinking about seeing Conrad in two days. She loved him—truly, she did. However, seeing Jess yesterday had cast a cloud of confusion over her, making it difficult to think rationally, let alone pray.

The clock on her dresser registered ten minutes after nine. She had time enough to go downstairs for a few bites of breakfast. Next, she'd look in on Aunt Iris while Solomon prepared the carriage to drive her to Paris Evangelical. The church he attended was conveniently located just down the road, so he never had to go out of his way in order to drop her off.

A light rap sounded at her door.

"Come in," she called, turning around.

Blanche McMartin opened the door and stepped inside. "Miz Grace, you must come immediately." Her cocoa-colored eyes had gone so round that Grace could see the whites of them from across the room.

"What is it, Blanche?"

"I cain't tell y'. Y' just got to see it fo' yo'self, miz."

Grace didn't know whether to panic or to remain curiously calm. Blanche lifted her skirts and abruptly exited, leaving Grace no choice but to follow.

In the wide hallway, Grace saw nothing out of the ordinary, but Blanche didn't linger there. Instead, she hurried down the staircase, her full skirts trailing behind her like an assemblage of ducklings. "Come, miz," she called over her shoulder.

Grace picked up her own skirts and darted down the stairs as fast as her high-heeled shoes would permit. At the bottom, she stepped through the archway into the formal living room. There, she halted in her tracks, her own eyes bulging, her mouth gaping. "Aunt Iris, what are you doing?"

The woman, dressed to the hilt, floral hat and all, glanced up from the wingback chair next to the fireplace, then lifted a gloved hand to the brim of her hat. "Why, what does it look like? I'm going to church."

"You're...going to church? But you haven't gone to church in months...perhaps years."

"Well, I mean to go today, now, don't I?"

"Who got you dressed and did your hair?"

"I'll have you know I got my own self ready."

Grace's mind whirled with all manner of thoughts. Had her aunt recovered? Had the Lord touched her in some divine way? Grace had no doubt that He could, but *would* He? Had Aunt Iris been praying for healing? She scolded herself for not having prayed along those lines. Instead, she'd asked God to grant that her aunt would die as peacefully and painlessly as possible. Where was her faith?

"Do you think it's wise?" she couldn't help asking. "What would Doc—"

"I don't give a turtle's tail what Doc Trumble says." Aunt Iris flicked her white-gloved wrist. "I feel well enough to go to church, so I'm going, and don't anybody try to talk me out of it."

"Well, lookie here. If it ain't Missus Brockwell, all gussied up," said Solomon as he rounded the corner in his black suit. He always looked dapper, but on Sundays, he got especially spiffed up.

Grace worried her lower lip. "She says she's going to church, Solomon."

Aunt Iris extended her hand. "Help me up, Sol. All this fussing has gotten tiresome."

Solomon took her hand, and she stood, admittedly unsteady on her feet, but upright nonetheless. Grace could do little but shake her head in amazement.

Aunt Iris looped her arm through his, and he placed his dark-skinned hand over her pale one as they headed for the front door.

"What church y' wantin' t' go to, Missus Brockwell?" Solomon asked her.

"I'll go to Grace's church, of course."

As Solomon walked her slowly out the door and to the waiting carriage in the circular drive, it registered with her that her aunt did not intend to change her mind. Grace scuttled back upstairs to retrieve her small clutch purse. When she returned to the ground floor, she found all the staff gathered in the parlor, peering with wonder out the front windows.

"Well, if that ain't enough to make a house fall down," Nellie exclaimed.

The others gave slow, methodical nods.

As Grace passed the group, Ellen touched her arm. "You take good care o' yo' aunt, now, hear?"

She paused and smiled at the group. "Don't worry, I will. And God has His hand on her, don't forget."

"He sho' 'nough do," Blanche affirmed as she gazed outside. "He up t' somethin', yes, sir."

Grace thought about Blanche's comment while Solomon finished helping Aunt Iris into the backseat of the carriage. Admittedly, the woman huffed and puffed, but then, so did Solomon. They weren't as young as they used to be. Even had she been healthy, the walk to the carriage might have winded Aunt Iris. After all, it was the longest stretch of exercise she'd had since Grace's arrival in Paris.

She continued pondering Blanche's statement. Just what was God up to, anyway?

Jess had found a small, somewhat dilapidated boardinghouse run by an elderly woman named Phoebe Arbogast about three blocks north of Juanita's Café on the corner of Church Street and North Poplar, just as the reverend had said he would. Miss Phoebe's Boardinghouse lacked luster and charm, but it would serve its purpose just fine, as far as he was concerned. He didn't need anything more than a mattress, lumpy though it was; a pillow; some blankets; and two warm meals a day. Miss Phoebe had made it clear he'd have to use the outhouse at the back of the property, and if he had need of a shower—did he look like someone who didn't?—he would have to use the bath facilities in town.

"Be forewarned: Rose's Bathhouse will cost y' twenty-five cents a bath," she'd told him from her post behind the front desk. Apparently, he gave the impression of being destitute—but it was no surprise, considering he'd just traveled from Boston by train dressed in secondhand clothes, sporting a two-day-old beard, and probably smelling like a smokestack. Every train car had been filled with a dense fog from passengers' cigarettes and cigars. Never had he been so glad to get off a train as when that big locomotive had come whistling into Paris.

Jess sorted through the small pile of clothes he'd laid out last night on the wood floor, for lack of any other place to put them. The tiny room had no chest of drawers for storing clothes. It was furnished with only an old bed, which was so short, his long legs dangled over the end; an upturned wooden crate holding a kerosene lamp, above which hung an ancient-looking painting; and a stand with a bowl and pitcher, along with a block of lye soap, a raggedy cloth, and a small mirror propped against the wall.

Miss Phoebe had informed him that, in the morning, he'd have to go down to the kitchen and fill the pitcher if he wanted to wash his face and shave. Then she'd eyed him in a peculiar manner.

"What?" he'd ventured to ask.

"You don't much look like someone who cares about his looks," she'd muttered.

He might have said the same to her, but instead he'd grinned and replied, "Underneath all this grime is another person, Miss Phoebe. I'll introduce you to him after I get that bath."

He looked forward to attending the service at Paris Evangelical Church. One reason was that he would see his new friend, the Reverend Lucas Jennings, no matter that Grace would probably be there and assume he'd come expressly to see her. "No," he would explain to her if she asked, "the reverend invited me." Of course, he desperately hoped he would see her, but he had no wish to ruin her reputation by calling attention to himself. At the same time, he had no intention of standing back and watching some guy—no matter that he might well be a respected, honorable Christian man as kind as a kitten—steal the woman whose heart he'd once claimed.

He dressed in the nicest pair of secondhand trousers he could find, donned a striped cotton shirt, and fitted a blue silk tie around his neck, then fashioned it into a knot in front of the mirror. It had been a long while since he'd worn a tie, so it took about four tries to get it perfect. Next, he tried to do something with his shaggy hair, but there was little hope for it without the help of a barber. He tossed the comb back in his bag and swiped at the beads of sweat gathering on his forehead. He'd be a wet mess before he reached the church, being that his second-floor room was hotter than a cookstove, the nine o'clock sun already beaming its rays through the single window.

His stomach gave a low growl, reminding him that he hadn't eaten since noon yesterday, when he'd run into the preacher at Juanita's Café. He gave himself one more useless gander in the mirror before stepping out of his room. The hallway was a welcome relief, for two open windows allowed a bit of a crosswind blowing from end to end. He made his way to the staircase and got his first scent of breakfast. Bacon, his nose told him, and he couldn't help but smile. If nothing else, Miss Phoebe might put some meat back on his bones—especially if he used a little charm on her.

He was surprised to discover only one other boarder at the long table in the dining room. He nodded at the middle-aged fellow and received a swift glimpse over his spectacles and a noncommittal nod in return. Miss Phoebe poked her gray-haired head around the corner when she heard his approach. Her eyes widened. "Is that you, Mr. Quinn?"

"Yes, ma'am."

"No, it ain't. The Mr. Quinn I met yesterday didn't look nothin' like you."

His grin evolved into a chuckle as he pulled back a substantial chair with a stained cushion and sat down, the other fellow now giving him a more thorough inspection. "Amazing what a bath and a shave will do."

"Humph. You don't look half bad t'day," she muttered. "Yer breakfast'll be right up—I hope you like it. Bacon, eggs, fried taters, grits, 'n cornbread. You want some coffee?"

He'd never tasted grits, but his appetite made him game for trying them today. "That'd be great. You need any help?"

She stuck her head out the kitchen door again, her brow a mass of wrinkles. "Ain't many boarders who ask me that, but no, I ain't needin' any help. You meet Mr. Harper, there?" She nodded at the man across the table.

Jess leaned forward and extended his hand. The other fellow did the same, though not with a great deal of exuberance. "Jess Quinn, sir."

"Tom Harper." They shook hands. "You passin' through?"

"Think I'll stay awhile." Jess glanced toward the kitchen. "As long as Miss Phoebe will put up with me."

She grunted, this time not bothering to peek around the corner. "I'll let you know when you get to be a nuisance." There was almost a hint of humor in her tone. Almost, but not quite.

"How about you, Mr. Harper?"

"I'm stayin' two nights. Doin' some business with a local merchant."

"Just you two boardin' right now," Miss Phoebe said from the kitchen. "Ain't that many folks needin' housin'. Or, if they do, I guess they prefer that uppity place called Brooks Hotel and Restaurant. That or the other boardinghouse up the road. I ain't complainin', though. I make do."

Jess felt a pang of sympathy for Miss Phoebe. Here she was, preparing a nice breakfast, and he wondered how she found the money to provide it.

Miss Phoebe emerged from the kitchen carrying a steaming metal coffee carafe and filled his cup to the rim. "Where you off to this mornin' all spiffed up?" she asked, straightening.

"I thought I'd go to church. Can you tell me where Paris Evangelical is located?"

"Hmm." She thought a moment before answering. "That's out on Morton Street. Y' take East Wood till you come to South Highland. Make a left there, then turn right on Morton. It's right near the corner on yer right."

"Sounds easy enough." He glanced across the table at his fellow boarder. "Would you like to join me, Mr. Harper?"

The man jerked back his head and gawked as if he'd just noticed a large growth on the end of his nose. "Haw, I ha'n't set foot inside a church since I got married, and don't plan on startin' up now."

"I see."

The fellow took up the newspaper from the middle of the table, unfolded it, and proceeded to read, marking an end to their conversation.

11

*E*ven though Aunt Iris tried to talk him out of it, Solomon decided to join the ladies for the service at Paris Evangelical. He insisted that his own congregation wouldn't miss him, although Grace doubted that. She knew his reasons. He wanted to make certain no harm came to his friend and employer. Of course, his dark skin stood out amid the otherwise all-white congregation, and, to Grace's dismay, his presence there earned him a few adverse stares. Mostly, though, folks kept their gazes where they belonged. Several people approached Aunt Iris before the service to shake her hand and say how happy they were to see her out and about. Among them was the kind reverend, who gave Solomon's hand a hearty shake.

It wasn't until she stood for the first hymn—Aunt Iris remained seated at Grace's insistence—that she caught sight of Jess, situated two pews back on the opposite side of the aisle. Their eyes connected, and in that moment, a flash of elation at seeing him burst within her heart—followed quickly by a rush of anger for his putting her in this compromising position. Hadn't she given him strict orders not to attempt to see her again? In two days' time, she would be in Conrad's arms, and she didn't need Jess Quinn hanging around to meddle with her heart and mind!

He had the nerve to smile at her. Rather than reciprocate, she hastily faced forward again as the song leader announced the next hymn:

"O Love That Wilt Not Let Me Go." She could hardly believe it. As she flipped through the pages of her songbook, she came upon "In the Hour of Trial"—a far more suitable title for her situation.

Aunt Iris did amazingly well throughout the service, but at the conclusion, she let out a tremulous sigh, and Grace worried she might be in pain. She looked a little pale, but if she was feeling poorly, she didn't express it. In fact, she stood to her feet with barely any help from Solomon.

"Let me get you out to the carriage, Missus Brockwell," he insisted. "You's lookin' a little white round the eyes."

In typical Iris Brockwell fashion, she scowled and straightened her slim shoulders. "Now, don't be making a fuss in public, Sol. I want to say hello to a few folks."

"I'll be right at yo' side, ma'am," he said with a nod. "You jes' tell me when you wants t' go."

Grace chewed her bottom lip. "Aunt Iris, I really think we should leave." Of course, her reasons for desiring to hurry along had more to do with the presence of a certain someone she wished to avoid.

"Stop doting, both of you."

"Mrs. Brockwell, oh, my stars in garters!" A woman Grace didn't know approached with a broad, toothy grin. "I'm so delighted to see you. You're looking wonderful!"

Aunt Iris smiled. "Well, hello there, Evie. Have you met my niece? Grace, this is Evelyn Mercer. Her husband, Orville, used to help John with the account books."

"My, that was a while back," Mrs. Mercer said. Unlike most of the other ladies, she sported no hat but wore her white hair in a tight bun. Her yellow dress gave her complexion a rather washed-out appearance, but her warm smile made up for it.

"At least thirty years," Aunt Iris said. "My John's been gone twenty-nine years this November."

"My goodness, has it been that long? Time sure don't waste itself in passin', does it? I have seven grandchildren, you know, all gettin' up there in age. I'm no young peach anymore, Mrs. Brockwell."

Aunt Iris chuckled. "Is any of us?"

It didn't take long for others to gather around Aunt Iris, and Grace worried that all the attention would tire her out. Surprisingly, Aunt Iris seemed to blossom, her face brighter than usual. Yes, she'd lost a great deal of weight and probably appeared emaciated to most people, but how wonderful for her to feel well enough to visit with old friends. Even though Paris Evangelical was not the church she and Uncle John had attended, there were few people in Paris who were unfamiliar with them and their philanthropic spirit.

"Hello, Grace."

The low-timbered voice from behind made her breath catch. She turned and tried to appear nonchalant, even as she met Jess's mesmeric olive eyes. Thankfully, everyone around them remained focused on her aunt and seemed oblivious to the stranger vying for Grace's attention— the ever-observant Solomon included.

Even so, Grace stepped away from the circle of folks and moved to the pew behind her, where Jess stood. Whispering, she said, "I thought I told you not to—"

"You're not suggesting I skip church, are you? The reverend himself invited me yesterday." He issued her a mischievous grin.

He had her there. Of course, everyone had a right to attend the church of his or her choosing.

"Who, by the way, delivered a fine message. Were you listening closely, Grace?" He kept his voice low, for which she was grateful.

She would admit that the sermon subject *had* touched a chord deep within, challenging her on many levels. To conclude, Reverend Jennings had asked three questions of his congregation: How devoted are you to personal Bible study and prayer? When did you last sense God moving in your life? Are you running toward God or away from Him?

"I heard every word he said, and, yes, it was a fine message," Grace agreed. "But why would you ask me such a question?" At present, she knew that her faith fell short of where it ought to be, but she wasn't about to share the details of her spiritual life with the man she was trying to evict from her life—or to anyone else, for that matter.

Jess shrugged. "No reason, really. I just wanted to know where you are with God right now."

"You know very well I'm a devoted Christian. I seem to recall your being a bit of a black sheep while we dated. I used to worry that you'd fallen from God's grace. You sowed some wild oats." She felt like a hypocrite, even as she spoke the words; but what else could she say?

"That I did," he agreed. "But it's interesting that you allowed me to court you, anyway—even agreed to marry me. Was that because you believed I'd come around in my faith?"

"I suppose. And have you?" She couldn't help but ask, for she was just as curious about his standing with the Almighty as he seemed to be about hers.

He shifted his weight and stared off for a moment. "You didn't give me much time to elaborate last night, Grace, but just let me briefly say that I wouldn't trade the time I spent in prison for all the money in the world. It brought me to my knees before God Almighty. For the first time ever, I experienced a tremendous need for Him—for His divine strength. I knew that if prison ended up being my lot, I'd need more to go on than my human might, and God provided far beyond my expectations. It taught me a great deal about depending on Him and dealing with injustice. As a result, I didn't walk away bitter; I walked away triumphant."

His comments left her speechless and feeling small—not what she'd expected. He had changed, to a point where she wasn't sure she knew him anymore, and she didn't know how to feel about that. After some thought, she replied, "I'm glad to hear that what could have been a very negative experience developed into something quite positive for you."

"Oh, it wasn't a walk in a garden, by any means, but I lived through it by the grace of God. Someday I may tell you more—if you give me the chance."

Her lungs tightened. "I can't."

Behind her, Grace heard Aunt Iris clear her throat. "And who might this be?"

Grace turned around. "Auntie, we must get you home now." She'd wanted Jess gone before anyone noticed him. Thankfully, the cluster of folks who had been hovering around her aunt had dissipated, for the most part.

"Afternoon, ma'am." Jess gave Aunt Iris's shoulder a gentle pat. "I'm sorry to hear you've been ill. I'm Jess Quinn. Your niece and I—"

"You're Mr. Quinn!" she exclaimed. "Well, I declare! Grace told me about you."

"Did she?" He glanced hopefully at Grace, who abruptly shook her head.

"Well, not as much as I would have liked," Aunt Iris continued. "And I believe this to be the reason why the Lord compelled me to come to church today." She glanced at Solomon, standing nearby. "Sol, help me sit again, would you? I'm fatigued." She looked at the few remaining folks, who were probably as curious as kittens as to the newcomer's identity. "Thank you all for your warm welcome. I hope to see you again sometime soon."

Evidently taking her statement as their cue to leave, they smiled, nodded, and slowly departed.

Then Aunt Iris turned back to Jess. "Sit, young man. Sit." She patted the hard bench beside her, and he dutifully walked to the end of the pew where he'd been standing, rounded the corner, walked the length of the next pew, and lowered himself next to her.

Even ailing, Iris Brockwell had a commanding way about her, and Grace couldn't help the low sigh of dread that escaped her lungs. What in the name of glory did that woman have up her silk sleeve?

"Now then, I want to hear all about you. Start from the beginning." Jess raised his eyebrows. "The beginning?"

"Aunt Iris…." Grace hated to whine, but she couldn't help it.

Scratching his head, Solomon sat down on the other side of Aunt Iris.

Grace dropped resignedly onto the pew behind the three and folded her arms.

"Well, maybe not from birth on, but from at least the last couple of years," her aunt amended. "Tell me how you came to find yourself in prison."

"I already told you, Aunt Iris," Grace murmured.

The woman angled her head around. "Yes, you did. But, quite frankly, I would prefer to hear him tell me himself."

A few congregants glanced at the group as they made their way down the center aisle toward the door, but no one else stopped to speak to Aunt Iris. Even Reverend Jennings, who had returned to the front of the church to collect leftover bulletins and personal effects from the floor and pews, carefully avoided eye contact as he quickly finished his task and headed for the back. It was as if he deliberately left them space for private discussion.

Then Grace remembered that he knew of Jess's relationship to her. Good grief—what must the reverend think of her, considering that he'd agreed to officiate her marriage to Conrad in a matter of weeks? Grace wondered if folks had already begun questioning her reputation. Had Reverend Jennings revealed Jess's identity to anyone? No, that would border on gossip, something she wouldn't expect from the principled preacher. He might have said something to his wife, but Grace hadn't seen Joy that morning. She assumed that she'd stayed home to care for an ailing child.

As Jess relayed his tale of imprisonment to Aunt Iris and Solomon, they gave him their rapt attention, and the fact that her aunt remained so alert for the telling, after hearing a long and engrossing sermon and then conversing with so many people, astounded Grace. Had they been at home, her aunt likely would have grown weary long ago and asked for assistance in getting to her room. The stairs were always a chore for her, so she generally remained in her room, journeying to the first floor only at suppertime. Today had been an altogether different story, though—one that still stumped the daylights out of Grace. Where had her aunt found the strength to come to church? Had God truly ordained that she be here today for the sole purpose of meeting Jess? If so, then why? Jess had shown up too late. Grace had already promised herself to Conrad Hall.

She soon realized that Jess had finished his story and was chatting amicably with Aunt Iris.

"Well, I think you should come for Sunday dinner," the older woman was saying.

Coming to life, Grace scooted forward on the hard, slippery bench. "Aunt Iris, that's impossible."

She looked to Solomon for assistance, but he merely shrugged and showed her those big, helpless brown eyes, the whites of which were rounder than two marbles.

Jess craned his neck to look at Grace and slanted her an impish smile. "I'm not sure your niece approves, Mrs. Brockwell."

"Pfff. She's just being stubborn."

"Aunt Iris, how can you say that? I'm engaged to Conrad."

"Yes, yes. How could I forget?" Aunt Iris leaned over to Jess and whispered something in his ear. Grace couldn't quite make out the words she uttered, but she was certain she'd confided in him her disapproval of Conrad. Jess stifled a tiny snort and nodded, and then Aunt Iris made a half turn toward Grace. "You don't have to join us, dear. In fact, you may take your meal in your room, if it suits you."

In her room? Grace's ire shot up. Sometimes her aunt could be quite insufferable. Did she not care one cent about Grace's reputation? But then, who was to know that Jess had come for dinner? As long as he didn't follow them directly to Brockwell Manor, they should be fine.

What was she thinking? She would have to tell Conrad. One didn't keep secrets of that nature from one's fiancé. No doubt, he'd be most unhappy about the news, and how could she blame him? She wouldn't want him entertaining another woman while betrothed to her. What a terrible quandary!

"Well then, it's decided," said Aunt Iris. "Sol, you and Mr. Quinn help me up, please."

"Yes'm," said Solomon.

Each man grasped one of her arms, and Aunt Iris stood. It took several moments for her to steady herself, but once she did, she lifted her gaze to Jess. "My, you're a tall one. I do believe you'd tower over Mr. Hall. Isn't he a piece taller than Conrad, Grace?"

Anger sizzled just below the surface. She turned eyes of annoyance on Jess, then narrowed them to slits.

He lifted one shoulder and gave his head a couple of shakes. The sparkle of humor in his eyes added to her dismay.

She pursed her lips, huffed a little breath, and marched up the aisle ahead of them to the double doors at the back of the church, which had been propped open by two large bricks. The reverend met her at the cement stoop just outside, probably waiting for the four of them to exit so he could lock the doors behind them.

"Everything all right, Miss Fontaine?"

She cast a glance over her shoulder toward the sanctuary. "Aunt Iris has invited Mr. Quinn for dinner."

He folded his hands in front of him. "I see. Is that a problem?"

"Well…yes. I'm engaged to Conrad Hall, and it's obvious she's trying to change my mind. She puts me in a rather awkward position."

"It's remarkable how well she's looking." He rubbed his square chin pensively. "What do you think has brought about this sudden change?"

She pressed the back of her hand to her forehead, which had suddenly started beading with perspiration. Who needed an oven to bake a chicken when one had the Tennessee September sun? The reverend had changed topics on her, and she didn't know what to make of it. "I—I can't understand it, myself."

"A divine touch from the Lord, perhaps?"

"Perhaps, but I don't know what that has to do with my utter frustration at these untimely circumstances."

"Hmm."

They both glanced up as the threesome approached the tiny vestibule, both men holding Aunt Iris firmly by the elbows. Jess leaned over and muttered something to her—words of assurance and praise for her accomplishments? Grace would have to ask Solomon later.

"I met Mr. Quinn yesterday, you know," Reverend Jennings said.

"Yes, he told me."

"I hope you're not upset that I showed him the way to Brockwell Manor."

"No, Reverend, of course not. You did what you believed right."

He continued to rub his chin. "Why don't you come out for supper some night? Joy asked me to invite you. Our little Annie is down with a cold this morning, so she couldn't come to the service, but she asked me to let you know that we'd love for you to join us sometime."

The invitation both surprised and delighted her. "It would be good to get a woman's point of view"—she leaned forward and lowered her voice—"besides what I'm getting from my aunt, however well-meaning she may be."

The reverend chuckled. "Well, if I can be of any help, I'll gladly lend an ear, too," he put in.

"Did Joy mention a specific night?"

"She did, in fact. How does Wednesday after next sound? Around, say, six o'clock?"

It took her only a moment to think about it. "That sounds lovely. Please tell Joy I accept."

He smiled. "Indeed I shall."

"Reverend." Her aunt's voice had lost a bit of its luster. Exhaustion had at last begun to catch up with her. "That sermon...it was exactly what these old ears needed to hear."

"Why, thank you, ma'am," he said, taking one of her hands in both of his. Jess maintained his hold on her elbow to steady her. The way he conducted himself, it almost seemed that he'd known her for some time and had a deep love and respect for her. Such a contrast to the manner in which Conrad treated her!

Grace's breath hitched at the realization, and she had to swallow a hard lump of emotion. Rather than stand around and ponder it further, she turned and headed for the carriage. The sun scorched her shoulders. Any other day, she would have rejoiced in the late-summer radiance, but her present circumstances only weighed her down.

12

$\mathcal{J}$ess could not believe his good fortune—rather, God's favor. He didn't believe in luck, or even coincidence. No, this was a case of God's good hand at work in granting Iris Brockwell the strength and wherewithal to attend church that morning, and then the notion to invite him to her home for Sunday dinner. She easily could have insisted on going to the Methodist church where she'd long been a member and which she still supported financially, according to Solomon Turner, with whom Jess conversed before the meal while Grace tended to her aunt upstairs. Yet the woman had insisted on visiting Grace's church. Mr. Turner also told Jess that he considered it quite the miracle, especially since the critically ill woman hadn't ventured beyond the front garden for several months.

"I must say, it sho' did knock me over when I seen 'er settin' over there on that wingback chair, all ready an' waitin' on me to cart 'er off t' church this mornin'," said Solomon, gesturing at the chair in the other room. "I reckon it had the same effect on Miz Grace, and the rest of the house-hold, too, the way they all stands around her with they mouths hangin' open. I don't rightly know whether she'll be up fo' suppin' with you or not. I know she invited you 'cause her intentions were the best, but I cain't say fo' sho' if she'll have the strength to come down to the table."

"It won't matter a bit, Mr. Turner," Jess said with a shake of his head. "If she can't make it, I'll take my leave."

"Oh, no you won't, suh. An' please, call me Solomon. The kitchen staff done prepared a scrumptious meal, as they do most every Sabbath. Miz Wiggins'll block the door iff'n you tries t' leave before partakin'."

Jess laughed. "Well, I thank you for your hospitality, but I wouldn't want to impose. As you can tell, Grace isn't too thrilled about my presence. Did you see the way she marched across the churchyard and climbed into the carriage? She's more than a mite put out with me for barging back into her life."

Solomon clutched his coat by both lapels and rolled back on his heels, giving Jess a shiny-toothed grin with a flash of gold from a metal filling. "She does have a bit of feistiness in 'er, don't she?" He chortled. "I'll admit I ain't never saw that before. Didn't know that side o' her e'en existed."

"Oh, it exists, all right. But since you haven't seen it, I can't help but wonder if Mr. Hall ever has."

Solomon chuckled again. "I'd tend to doubt it. She ain't got nothin' but smiles and dreamy eyes for that lawyer man." He quickly sobered and lowered his chin, folding his hands at his waist. "Pardon me for mentionin' that, suh. I don't 'magine you wants to hear such talk."

With a slight frown, Jess raked his hand through his hair. "It's okay, Solomon. Just a reminder that my work's cut out for me." He ventured a glance up the broad staircase with the luxurious banister to see whether Grace and Mrs. Brockwell had started making their way back down. Seeing no sign of them, he surveyed the massive parlor with its soaring ceilings, its long buffet bookended by two brocaded wingback chairs, and its shiny oak floor covered partly by a lush Persian rug. To Jess's left was a rounded archway that led into a stately living room, where he spotted a Steinway grand piano in one corner and an impressive fireplace between a set of floor-to-ceiling bookcases. The showpiece of the room had to be the crystal chandelier, hanging directly over a glass-topped coffee table perfectly centered upon another Persian rug.

The staircase wall displayed various pieces of artwork that Jess would have enjoyed examining at closer range but wouldn't consider doing without permission. Indeed, the enormous home deserved the designation of mansion, and it contrasted almost comically with the shabby third-floor apartment on Pearl Street where he'd grown up. Possessions didn't matter much to him, though. In prison, where he'd been forced to live with next to nothing at all, he'd quickly learned that possessions alone did not generate true peace and contentment. Those he'd attained through trusting Christ with all his heart and learning to praise Him in the midst of even the toughest circumstances. Oftentimes, he'd reflected on the experience of the apostle Paul, who'd lived a good deal of his Christian life enduring jail and persecution, and yet had been able to say, *"I have learned, in whatsoever state I am, therewith to be content."* Philippians 4:11 was just one of the many Bible verses Jess had committed to memory during his imprisonment, and it was one that had greatly encouraged him.

Seeing that Solomon seemed disinclined to leave him alone in the parlor, Jess decided to strike up further conversation with the man. Not only was he a pleasant conversationalist, but he might also be able to shed some light on Grace's relationship with Conrad Hall.

Jess cleared his throat. "Earlier, Mrs. Brockwell made it clear to me that she doesn't much care for Conrad Hall. Do you happen to know why that is?"

"No, suh, I cain't say I do," the man replied. "But I do know she's one who don't put her trust in folks till she knows 'em good an' well. I don't want to be speakin' out o' turn, but I'll say this much: Mistuh Hall, he makes hisself quite scarce round here. Miz Grace been workin' on tryin' to get him to be a little friendlier toward her aunt. It's not that he ain't friendly, mind you. Maybe jes' a bit...unsociable. Yes, that's a better word. Or might be he jes' plain shy."

"A lawyer who's shy and unsociable?" Jess almost laughed. "Solomon, I must give you credit for your generosity, but I've known a few lawyers in my day; and though most of them have been upstanding, law-abiding, hardworking individuals, I've also known a few shysters. That begs the question: Which category does Mr. Hall fall under? And, if it's the latter, why hasn't Grace seen through him? She's intelligent enough."

Solomon lowered his chin and raised his thick, white eyebrows. "If you pardon my sayin' so, suh, Miz Grace be a woman, an' Mistuh Hall, he be a man who's, shall we say, real enchantin'."

An uneasy feeling crept over Jess like a colony of ants tickling up his spine, making the hair on the back of his neck stand on edge. "I sense you don't much trust him either, Solomon."

"Oh now, suh, I plain didn't say that. No, suh."

A grin made its way to Jess's mouth. "You're quite the diplomat, my friend. Ever considered running for political office?"

Now the man laughed outright. "No, suh. I's the wrong color fo' that."

Unfortunately, he spoke the truth.

⤸

"Aunt Iris, I wish you'd listen to me. You're plain tuckered out, and I'd much prefer you lie down as attempt to go back downstairs for Sunday dinner. Mr. Quinn will understand if you change your mind."

Aunt Iris winced, and Grace knew it was the result of chronic pain. Even so, it gave rise to a straightened spine and a face filled with stubborn resolve. "I'm rested enough," Iris announced from her chair by the window. "Now, help me up so I can tend to my guest."

"Your *guest*?" Grace couldn't help the low growl that came out of her. "What are you doing, Aunt Iris? Be honest with me."

With more gusto than Grace thought she had in her, Aunt Iris removed her feathered hat and tossed it on the window seat. "You were in love with him, Grace. How can you pretend it isn't true?"

Grace's eyes went suddenly wet in the corners, so she quickly turned, crossed the room, and began fiddling with the comb and brush set on the dresser. She picked up the hand mirror and gazed at her reflection, then quickly wiped away the dampness with her index finger. "I am not pretending any such thing, Auntie. I'll admit it wholeheartedly—I *was* in love with him. Past tense." She whirled around. "But that is no longer the case. I love Conrad, Aunt Iris, and it's high time you accept that."

She hated the harsh tone she'd just used. It wasn't her nature, and she couldn't imagine what had come over her. She hurried back to the window and knelt down in front of Aunt Iris, taking hold of her frail, bony hand and bringing it to her own cheek. "I'm sorry for speaking to you in such a manner, Auntie. I just truly wish that you'd come to terms with my betrothal to Conrad."

Aunt Iris met Grace's eyes, and her expression softened. She turned her hand over and caressed Grace's cheek. "I believe that you love Conrad, dear. It's just that I want you to keep an open mind and heart— and make sure you're marrying for love and not mere infatuation. This romance with your Mr. Hall has moved too fast, in my humble opinion; but then, I've grown weary of telling you what I think." She expelled a heavy sigh. "Well, are you going to help the dinner conversation along, or should I expect to carry the load?"

"I'll join in, but are you sure you're up for dinner? Do you have an appetite?"

Aunt Iris pulled back her skinny shoulders. "I'll manage just fine," she insisted.

The quaver in her voice didn't escape Grace's notice, and she marveled once again that her aunt had gathered the strength to attend church. Would the exertion required by such an outing set her back for the next several days? Grace couldn't help but worry a little. *Oh Lord, what is Your purpose in all this?*

I long for your trust, My child—all of it.

The still, small voice echoed in the chambers of her heart, even as she helped her aunt out of her chair and guided her slowly down the hall and then the staircase, Aunt Iris clutching to the banister with Grace holding her other arm. When they'd made it halfway down, Jess raced up the stairs two at a time to relieve Grace of her duties. The generous move prompted a similar thought to one she'd had earlier that day— that Conrad never would have acted on such an impulse. She longed for Tuesday to arrive so she could test her heart's reaction to seeing him again.

Over dinner, the topics of conversation ran the gamut, but when Aunt Iris dozed midway through the meal, having downed only a spoonful or two of mashed potatoes, her head dropping until her chin touched her chest, Ellen and Solomon came to her rescue. "Come, Missus Brockwell," Ellen coaxed her. "Time fo' you t' rest."

Aunt Iris didn't object when the two of them pulled back her chair and helped her stand, but she did gesture at Jess to sit back down after he leaped to his feet. She gave him a tiny smile. "I'm happy to have met you, young man. You come back and see me, hear?"

With no hesitation, and without so much as a single glance at Grace, he said, "The feelings are mutual, ma'am, and you can count on me to do just that."

"Hmm...tomorrow would suit fine," she muttered while shuffling toward the staircase, Ellen and Solomon supporting her.

"She's quite the lady." Jess smiled at Grace from across the table after the threesome had disappeared from view.

"She is that." She looked at her unused spoon, gleaming spotlessly in the sunlight streaming through the dining room window.

"I see where you get some of your stubbornness."

Grace jerked her head up and cocked it at him, giving him a pointed stare. "I am not stubborn."

"No? Then why can't you admit to being happy that I'm alive—and that I'm sitting across from you, no less?"

"I never said I wasn't happy you were alive. It's just that my heart belongs to another now, and I can't easily turn from that." She resumed studying her spoon.

"Although you'd like to."

She glared at him. "I never said that, either."

"You're confused."

"No, I'm not."

"Of course, you are. When I boarded that ship in June of ninety-two, the last words you shouted to me were 'I love you.' Do you know how many times that memory kept me alive in that tiny jail cell?" His voice broke.

She threaded her fingers tightly together and lowered her hands to her lap. Her plate of food sat mostly untouched. She hadn't done much better than Aunt Iris. Jess's words had cut through to her core, for they were true. She recalled all too well standing on the docks on that foggy June morning, watching her beloved wave frantically from the ship's deck and hearing him shout back the same three words.

"Well," she said softly, "there's nothing to be done for it. That was then, and this is now."

"Time cannot dictate how I feel, Grace Fontaine." His determined gaze nearly burned her, so she averted her eyes and brushed a few tickling strands of hair behind her ear.

"You can't even look at me."

"Stop it."

"Admit it—you still love me."

Immediately, she raised her gaze again. "I— I—" She could only stammer as she allowed her eyes to study the strong curve of his jawbone, shaded by new whisker growth, and his longish, tawny brown hair, brushing his shirt collar and giving him a burly, wholly unsettling appeal. "Please, Jess," she finally managed. "You mustn't come here again. It isn't proper."

He pushed back his chair and stood. "I'm sorry, Grace," he uttered thickly, "but even the most savage of animals couldn't keep me away. Besides, I want to honor your aunt's request that I visit her."

She had watched him stand but made no move to do the same. Instead, she gave a loud sniff and straightened her spine. "Then I shall have to leave the minute you arrive."

He came around to her side of the table, and her stomach formed an instant knot. "If that's what you think you have to do…. Just know that running isn't going to solve anything." He stepped behind her and gently clasped the back of her neck.

She gasped in shock.

"I still love you, Grace, and I don't mean to quit fighting for you."

Hearing the emotion in his voice made her pulse take off like a herd of wild horses. She felt helplessly stuck, even trapped. She focused on a tiny spot on the wall, afraid even to blink. The next thing she knew, he was leaning down, his lips brushing her cheek. She ceased to breathe, her eyes still fastened on the wall, his breaths hot and moist. "Did you hear me, Grace? I still love you."

She nodded three times fast, hands tightly clasped in her lap. His own fingers closed more firmly around the back of her neck, and beads of sweat broke out across her forehead. *Lord, help me,* she muttered in her head as memories of his closeness rushed to the surface of her mind like a thousand hungry minnows. *This can't be happening.* Again, his lips brushed her blistering cheek, but this time they kissed—and kissed again, roving from her earlobe to her chin. Then, with his finger, he turned her face so that their eyes met.

"I'm going to kiss you again," he said in what sounded like a confession.

"No, you're not," she answered back, her temples aching with panic.

"Try to stop me," he said, then closed in on her, one hand gently grasping her shoulder, the other cupping her chin and raising it to meet his lips.

Though she trembled uncontrollably, she found herself acquiescing. *Lord God, what is happening? Save me from this predicament!* When his lips met hers, her heart rate leaped to an alarming pace, until she worried she wouldn't be able to catch her breath. Perhaps she would collapse and die right there in the dining room, pounding on the pearly gates of heaven ahead of Aunt Iris. And all over a kiss!

At the sound of footfalls on the staircase, Jess released her and straightened, dropping his hands at his sides. "Tell me you didn't like that, Grace," he whispered with a half smile.

"Stop it," she hissed, picking up a napkin and pressing it to her mouth. She pushed back her chair and prepared to stand, gripping the edge of the table for support, just as Solomon reentered the dining room. For fear he would suspect something, she kept her eyes averted as she said, "Mr. Quinn was just leaving, Sol. Would you see him to the door?"

There was a pause. "Why, yes'm, I be mighty glad to do that."

"I'll see you again soon, Grace," Jess whispered in her ear.

She wanted to say, "No, you won't," but the words wouldn't come. Why, she couldn't even find it in her to utter a decent good-bye, with her heart still pounding an awful racket in her ears and her throat as dry as desert dust. If Jess hadn't heard Solomon coming down the stairs, Sol would surely have caught them kissing, and where would that have left her? In disgrace, for one thing!

Not until she heard Solomon bid Jess good-bye and the door click shut did she rise from the table, pass through the kitchen with nary a word to either Zelda or Nellie, and slip out the back door to run, unseen, to the wooded area behind the stables. She needed to find a peaceful haven behind a massive oak tree and let a whole batch of tears roll down her face.

13

On Monday morning, Jess set out in search of employment, going door-to-door in downtown Paris. He wasn't necessarily looking for a permanent position, but he needed a means of income if he was to stay in Paris for any length of time. While he still had plenty of money left from the settlement granted him by the Allan Line, it wouldn't last forever, and he didn't want to grow complacent. Besides, he loathed loafing around. To him, being industrious was essential to a fulfilling existence.

On his journey up Wood Street, he passed the law offices of Murphy, Wadsworth & Hall and briefly considered applying for any position they might have available—perhaps a filing clerk, for example—never mind that he had no experience. A cooper by trade, he could hardly fathom the thought of an office job. He simply thought it would be a great surprise for Conrad Hall to come home from his business trip and discover the "dead" former beau of his fiancée employed at his firm. It would be worth it just to see Hall's contorted face when he learned the news. Laughing to himself, Jess moved on.

After several dead ends, he finally found an opening at Paris Feed Sale and Livery Stable. A former stable hand had up and moved to Georgia without prior notice, forcing Bill Hansen, the liveryman, to double his workload. He told Jess that his job inquiry had come at the perfect time, and he hired him on the spot, asking him to start the very next morning.

No experience was required for the position, and while it didn't pay much, it would suffice for the time being. He would have preferred working in a cooperage, but there was none in Paris, as folks ordered their casks, barrels, buckets, tubs, butter churns, and so forth from a shop in nearby Buchanan. Perhaps, if things ever worked out with Grace, Jess would coax his father to move down to Paris and open his own cooperage. Jess would work alongside him, but his father was the one with the real talent, not to mention passion, for the trade. Bringing him here might also give the old guy an incentive to lay off the sauce.

Jess's mind filled with all manner of images and thoughts on his walk back to Miss Phoebe's Boardinghouse—yesterday's sermon; dinner at Brockwell Manor; the delicious, daring kisses he'd planted on Grace's lips; his father, isolated at home in Boston; and gratitude that he'd landed a job. Who but God knew how long he'd be here? All Jess could say with certainty was that October 15 would be his absolute last day in Paris if Grace went through with her marriage to Conrad Hall.

He wondered if he ought to go back to Brockwell Manor today. Iris had invited him, after all; though she was likely still recovering from the exertion of her Sunday outing. Phooey! It was almost equally likely that she'd forgotten the invitation altogether. Chronic illness often impaired the ability to recall persons and events, especially among the elderly, and he had no idea the condition of her mental state. Yes, she'd somehow managed to rally enough strength to attend church yesterday—a true miracle, according to Solomon Turner—but would she pay for her adventure with a rapid decline in health? He didn't understand the progression of diseases, but he did know they often took strange twists and turns. In some cases, God chose to fully heal the sickest of individuals. Jess could cite several such examples from the Bible, and he prayed in earnest that such might be the case for Iris Brockwell. Experience had proven the scriptural truth that with God, all things were possible. *All things*, he told himself, including a change of heart when it came to matters of love and marriage.

He carried that thought with him as he made the trek up the dilapidated staircase at Miss Phoebe's to his tiny room. His afternoon plans included penning letters to his father and to the Woodbridges. He'd tell them about Paris, but as for his reunion with Grace, he hadn't a clue what to say.

⌒

Late Monday, after stopping by Ruby's Saloon to see Lorinda one last time, Conrad headed to Chicago's Grand Central Station and boarded a passenger car bound for Tennessee. He arrived in Paris early Tuesday morning, physically and mentally exhausted, and hungry, to boot. He'd tried to sleep some in the night, but the screeching whistle announcing every stop, the chug-a-chug of the big locomotive, just four cars up, and the brash hum of flanged steel wheels spinning on clanking rails had kept him mostly staring out his scuffed-up window at pitch blackness. Of course, the thoughts of Lorinda storming his mind hadn't helped. He should have felt at least some measure of guilt for stepping out on Grace, but somehow he didn't. Maybe it was because Lorinda meant nothing to him, nor he to her. Alas, Grace didn't mean all that much to him, either—but her inheritance sure did.

After hefting his bag and disembarking with several other travelers, several of whom he recognized but didn't know, he decided to break-fast at Juanita's Café, an approximate six-block trek from the station. Then he'd go home to freshen up before taking a drive out to Brockwell Manor to see Grace prior to going in to the office. He'd told his partners that the purpose of his trip to Chicago was to meet with some former clients and their new attorneys regarding some old files that needed clarification. His claim had come off sounding so legitimate, neither man had batted an eye; and he doubted they would ask him about it on his return to the office later today. In a couple of weeks, when it came time to return to Chicago with the rest of the money, he'd simply tell his partners that there were several more loose ends to tie up.

In the meantime, he had to figure out a way to dig up enough money to pay off that weasel Carl Petrie. The guy got under his collar some-thing fierce, and he'd about had it with him. Time to siphon additional funds from his clients' trust accounts so he could pay off his loan in full.

Of course, he'd need to figure out a way to replenish the funds—maybe by increasing profit margins from his hotel and restaurant. Marrying into wealth would also help. He hoped that, during his absence, Grace's aunt had taken a few steps closer to the pearly gates. It couldn't be much longer now. Not when she looked frail enough to blow over in a gentle breeze.

He arrived, slightly winded, at Juanita's Café just as the Mexican woman unlocked the door and hung the "Open" sign in the front window. Another man approached at the same time. He acknowledged Conrad with a friendly smile, so Conrad nodded and feigned good cheer, although he'd sooner lift his lip in disdain than show a friendly demeanor. He had far too much on his mind to put on a happy pretense for some stranger he didn't care one fig about.

"Nice morning, isn't it?" the guy said, his New England accent similar to Grace's. "Going to be a warm one."

"Like we need another steamer," Conrad muttered.

They both started for the door, and the other fellow waved a hand for him to go first. Once inside, Conrad hung back to see where the guy intended to sit so that he could situate himself as far away as possible, thereby dispensing with any further talk. When the man pulled out a chair at the table closest to the front window, Conrad walked to the very back, sat down with a sigh, and reached for his case. He needed to review some important legal documents before a meeting he'd scheduled with one of his clients later that week. Time for reeling in his wayward thoughts and getting back to business. No more thinking about Petrie, no more fearing the future—and no more dwelling on Lorinda.

⌣

"I see you come back again, sir. You like coffee?" asked Juanita, holding her coffeepot at the ready.

Jess grinned at her. "Please." He watched her pour the steaming black brew. "You have a good memory."

"Ah, no, I just remember a good face." This she followed with a low titter. "See, I can say these things, since I at least twice your age."

He laughed. "Twice? You can't be a day over thirty-five."

Laughing, she finished pouring and straightened her posture, sticking her spare hand on her plump waist and smiling an ultra-red-lipped grin. "Flattery is good thing. You come back any time."

"I would've eaten at the place I'm staying, but Miss Phoebe, the owner, is feeling under the weather today, so I told her I'd just as soon come here. She seemed to appreciate that."

"Ah, you nice man, I can see that. You stay at Miss Phoebe's Boardinghouse, no?"

He nodded. "For now, anyway. You know Miss Phoebe?"

"*Sí, señor*. She's nice lady once you get to know her. At first, she's… how do you say? Gruff."

He laughed. "She is that, but I'm getting her to come over to my side."

She stepped back and tipped her head to the side, giving him an assessing glance. "I think you be very successful."

At the back of the café, the other gentleman cleared his throat loudly and held his coffee cup aloft.

"Oooh, I be right there, Mr. Hall," Juanita called. Then she whirled around to face Jess once more. "You like bacon, eggs, and fried potatoes?"

He paused, a muscle in his cheek twitching upward involuntarily. "Did you call him Mr. Hall?"

"*Sí*. Now, you want bacon, eggs—"

"Conrad Hall, by chance?" he asked quietly.

"I don't know first name, just Mr. Hall. I go give him coffee now, okay?"

He leaned to look around her plump body at the man, who appeared to be shuffling through some papers. *It can't be*, he told himself. *It would be too great a coincidence.* Then again, he didn't believe in coincidences.

"*Señor?*"

"Yes, yes. Bacon and eggs sounds perfect."

She turned, her full red skirt flaring as she scurried across the room.

In between bites of breakfast and sips of coffee, Jess stole glimpses of the man named Mr. Hall. The occasional incoming diner obscured his view, but he managed to catch an overall picture. He supposed the man was handsome, as men went, though Jess wouldn't claim to be a good judge of looks when it came to his own gender. Hall appeared to be in his mid-thirties, and he had a professional air about him; however, his suit, while fashionable, had wrinkles galore, perhaps the result of hours of wear. Had he just debarked from a long train ride? Jess had heard the whistle as the locomotive had lumbered into town some thirty minutes ago, and he happened to know that Grace expected her fiancé to return to Paris sometime today.

If this fellow were truly Conrad Hall, Jess would have liked to walk up to him and have a few words, namely, "Keep your gritty hands off my future wife." He wouldn't, but he would've liked to. He recalled his first impression of the man as he'd approached the café—curt, aloof, and even somewhat rude. He certainly hadn't seemed interested in conversing; but then, Jess had to admit, most folks weren't all that talkative first thing in the morning. The fellow had also been demanding of service, exhibiting blatant impatience with Juanita for her failure to promptly fill his coffee cup. Loathsome sort!

Juanita returned to Jess's table, coffee carafe in hand. She'd been running almost nonstop since first filling his coffee cup, to make sure her several customers were well taken care of. She started to refill his mug, but he stopped her. "No more, but thanks, Juanita. I'm starting a new job today, and I don't want to be late. Thank you for the tasty breakfast." He reached in his pocket and pulled out enough coins to cover his meal, plus a generous tip, then tossed them on the table next to the handwritten bill Juanita had left there several minutes ago.

"New job, eh? Where you work, *señor?*"

"Paris Feed Sale and Livery Stable, over on Poplar."

"*Bueno.* You have good first day on job." She turned to go, then whirled back around. "Oh, *señor*, I find out Mr. Hall's first name. Eez Conrad, as you thought. He's lawyer in town."

Jess had started to stand, but he dropped back into his seat with a plunk at the confirmation of his speculations. "Really?" he squeaked out.

"*Sí.* I ask gentleman over there, and he tell me." She pointed at a white-haired fellow sitting a few tables away from the man in question. "I not ask Mr. Hall himself. He might think me nosy. You understand."

"Yes. Thank you."

"You okay? You look…what is the word? Pale. Your food no good?"

"No, no, it was very good. Thanks."

She left him, his head spinning, his mind a crazy mix of emotions—shock, indignation, confusion, resentment, and, strongest of all, envy. What did Conrad Hall have that he didn't? Well, other than a successful career that brought in a handsome salary. Furthermore, what did Grace see in him that attracted her so? Still numb from the realization that he'd come face-to-face with his foe, he took out his watch to check the time and saw that he was to report to his new job in twenty minutes. No time for any further dawdling. He simply had to put this guy's face out of his mind and get on with his day—and ask the Lord to forgive him for his instant hostility.

14

Grace had no idea what time to expect Conrad, so she'd been moving around the rambling mansion all morning, as anxious as a schoolgirl on her first day of class. When she finally heard a horse's neigh and the rattle of approaching wheels, she ran to the door ahead of Solomon and threw it open. Instead of Conrad, though, she saw Jess Quinn, perched high on the seat of a wagon whose side bore a sign that read "Paris Feed Sale and Livery Stable" in red letters. She stepped onto the terrace and walked to the edge just as he drew back on the reins, bringing the wagon to a halt.

Grace raised her hand to shield her eyes from the sun's blinding rays, her treacherous heart racing at the sight of him. Blessed saints, but he looked good to her. Far too good to a woman who was engaged to another man. He wore an off-white cotton shirt with a standard collar, the leather tie string closure left unlaced to reveal a tuft of chest hair, the blousy puff sleeves rolled up just past his elbows. He'd tucked the shirt into brown trousers, and pulled low on his head was a battered-looking wide-brimmed hat, covering his eyebrows and shading his expression.

She hated the way her emotions ran the gamut, from annoyance to exhilaration. One part of her was angry at him for riding into Paris, thinking to reclaim her in an instant, with no consideration for the long months—even years—it'd taken her to defeat the suffocating pain and sorrow of her loss. Another part of her rejoiced that he'd survived, and why not? He'd been the love of her life before setting sail on the *Lone Star*.

Which led her to recall another irritating tidbit: She hadn't wanted him to go on that overelaborate passenger ship. She'd even begged him not to, insisting that they didn't need the extra money; that his staying back and continuing with his coopering would mean far more to her than a few extra dollars in their savings account. Yet he'd stubbornly insisted on going, arguing that they'd be able to marry sooner and have a bigger nest egg with which to start their lives together—even though she hadn't cared one hoot about a bigger nest egg. She'd simply wanted him in Boston.

When she'd learned of his most certain death, she'd cried for months before finally beginning the healing process; and by the time she'd received word from Doc Trumble that her aunt lay critically ill, she'd been ready to leave Boston, having regained a sense of purpose and even viewing the move as an opportunity for change and renewal. Not only that, but she'd prayed about it and had sensed God telling her it was the right thing to do. Later, she'd presumed He'd led her to Paris for the express purpose of meeting her charming Conrad.

"What are you doing here, Jess? And why are you driving the livery wagon?" She couldn't help the indignation in her tone.

Keeping a loose hold on the reins, Jess pushed back the brim of his hat and tossed her a lackadaisical smile. "I started working there just this morning."

"You just started— You took a job in Paris? At the livery?"

"Yes, ma'am." He glanced over at the entry door where Solomon stood. "Good morning, Solomon. I brought the oats and other feed you ordered from Mr. Hansen. Would you like me to drive it down to the barn and unload it for you?"

"Mornin', Mistuh Quinn." Solomon came out to stand behind Grace. "That'd be mighty nice o' you. You'll find Mistuh McMartin down there, muckin' out stalls. You workin' for Mistuh Hansen, is y'?"

Jess looked right past her as though she wasn't there. "Yep. Walked in there yesterday, and he offered me the job. Started bright and early this morning. I think it'll be a good fit."

"Wull, ain't that sumthin'?" Solomon made a clicking sound with his tongue, and Grace could imagine him slowly nodding his head up and down as a sign of approval.

She sucked in a deep breath and released it out her nostrils in one loud gust. "I don't know why you'd go and get a job in Paris, Jess Quinn."

He gave her his signature crooked grin—one she'd always found enchanting, but she refused to let it affect her now. "It's a lovely town. Why wouldn't I want to settle here?" he said with a shrug. "It's big enough for both of us, isn't it?"

She closed her eyes in frustration and swept a hand across her clammy forehead. With Solomon standing directly behind her, she couldn't spout off half of what she wanted to. Instead, she just glared at Jess and gave her head a slow shake.

"How is your aunt doing today?"

"She's been resting a great deal."

"I suspected Sunday would have tired her out. I thought I'd ask, though, since she did invite me back for another visit."

"Iff'n you'd like, suh, I can go let her know—"

"No, Sol!" Grace whirled on her heel. A gust of wind picked up her yellow skirt, and she had to use both hands to settle it back down. More quietly, she said, "It's best you don't disturb her."

Solomon scratched his jaw. "You prob'ly right about that, Miz Grace."

"Will you at least tell her I asked about her?" Jess asked. "I don't want her thinking I forgot my promise to come back and visit."

Grace did have to admire his concern for her aunt's well-being, and she couldn't help observing yet again the differences between him and Conrad.

"I'll be sure t' tell 'er," Solomon said.

"Good." Jess gave Grace a lingering glance, which Solomon must have taken as his cue to leave. Without another word, he turned around, walked back inside, and closed the door behind him.

Grace almost wished he had stayed. Whatever Jess was about to say, she wasn't sure she wanted to hear it.

"Well, I saw your Mr. Hall this morning, Grace," Jess announced.

Immediately her head swirled and her heart thudded. "What do you mean, you saw him? Where?"

"At Juanita's Café. We were her first customers and, for a while, her only customers. We even spoke briefly, although I have to say he wasn't that friendly. I initiated the greeting—not knowing at the time whom I was addressing—and if I hadn't, he never would've acknowledged me. He looked a bit rough around the edges, even in his professional attire. He must've been on the train all night. Where'd he go, anyway?"

She could barely find the words to answer him. "To Chicago on business—not that it's any of your concern. What made you think it was Conrad?"

"I know it was Conrad. Confirmed it with Juanita herself. Don't worry—I didn't go introduce myself to him once I found out."

That detail did give her a measure of relief.

"Don't think I wasn't tempted to, though. I figured if I did, I might end up in a little unchristian altercation with him, and since I don't cotton to the thought of landing in another jail cell, well, I restrained myself—with the Lord's help, mind you."

"That was generous of you."

He stared at her for all of five heartbeats. "You want to jump up here and ride with me down to the barn?"

She stared at the wagon seat. Of course, she knew that she shouldn't. What would Conrad think if he found out? Then she reminded herself that she was in love with Conrad, and that an innocent ride down to the barn with a former beau couldn't hurt anything. They were old friends, after all. She started to step down from the porch, then stopped and raised a finger. "If you promise no monkey business."

He lifted one eyebrow under that wide-brimmed hat. "You know you can trust me."

"Pfff. About as far as I can carry a rattler." Even so, she found herself descending the steps and approaching the livery wagon. Jess jumped down from the seat, hitting the ground and sending dust flying in every direction, and then offered her his outstretched hand to help her up. "I could just walk out there, you know. It's only a short distance." It wasn't two days ago that she'd run out there for that good, old-fashioned cry.

"Yes, but that wouldn't be half as fun."

With his help, she situated herself on the hard wooden seat. When he hoisted himself up next to her, she couldn't help but marvel at the strength of his legs—surely far exceeding Conrad's—and was fully aware of how the hair on his bare forearms had grown thicker and longer. She wondered if he'd been forced to do hard labor in jail, for while he'd lost a great deal of weight, he hadn't lost his muscle tone or his shoulder breadth.

"Hah!" he shouted at the horse.

The animal jerked forward with such force that it thrust Grace's body hard against the back of the seat. She clutched hold of a side rail to steady herself. Once she'd regained her balance, she decided to ask him about his experience in prison. "Did they work you hard?"

"Who?" he asked, maneuvering the reins to coach the roan up the winding gravel path that led to the stable area behind the mansion. His elbow brushed against her side, but rather than move, she tried to ignore the ping of nerves it set off in her body.

"The prison guards."

"Oh. Yeah, from morning till night most days."

"They must not have fed you in proportion to your workload."

"Of course not. They didn't much care whether I lived or died. The Lord cared, though, and I give Him all the credit for my survival. He kept me strong through it all." He looked down at his frame. "I think I've gained a little weight since coming to Paris. Miss Phoebe feeds me well."

"Miss Phoebe?"

"She runs the boardinghouse where I'm staying. It's a few blocks north of Wood Street."

"Oh. I don't think I've ever seen the place."

"I doubt you'd have occasion to."

She took a moment to digest the fact of his staying in a boardinghouse. There were so many things she didn't know about, but if she asked too many questions, he'd mistake her curiosity for care, and she didn't want to mislead him. Never that.

"Like I said, God kept me alive through the worst of ordeals. He had plans for me—many of which are yet to be fulfilled."

As water can overflow the banks of a fast-moving river, a wave of unexpected guilt washed upon her. Would she have exhibited the same degree of faith and courage under similar circumstances? She doubted it. *My stars, do I even have that sort of faith under normal circumstances?* She cleared her throat, trying to regroup. "I—I'm sorry you had to endure all that, Jess. I don't think I've said that yet, but I needed to. I know it couldn't have been easy for you."

"As I said, God's been faithful to me. In those cramped quarters, I learned a great deal about His love for me. I'm just thankful the guards allowed me to keep the Bible I received from a visiting clergyman. I was stripped of everything else, but I was given the most important thing, and for that, I'm forever grateful."

She couldn't imagine being grateful to one's prison guards for anything. She also couldn't remember Jess ever being so vocal about his faith. During their courtship, they'd talked little about their Christian journeys. Oh, she'd had no doubt he'd accepted Christ as his Lord and Savior, just as she didn't doubt Conrad's salvation. It simply had never been something they'd discussed. Now, she realized, she was coming to enjoy talking about matters of faith, had even longed to broach the topic with Conrad. In truth, she didn't know how closely he walked with God, and that realization challenged her own faith. Shouldn't it matter greatly to her? Or was one's faith intended to remain private between an individual and God? Her own parents had been believers, faithfully attending church every Sunday, but they'd spoken little about their faith to her as a child—and even as an adult.

Jess reined in the horse at the big double doors of the barn, which were open to the elements. Horace McMartin stepped into view, a rusted pitchfork in one hand. "Howdy!" he said, removing his worn hat and knocking it against his overalls to shake out the dust. "You brung out some feed fo' the critters, I see. Mistuh Turner done place the order yesterday whilst he was in town. Don't take Bill Hansen long t' fill 'em. You new t' the job, suh? Ain't never seen y' before." It wasn't till he stepped fully out of the barn and into the sun that he caught sight of Grace perched high on the seat, sitting somewhat in Jess's shadow. "Why, Miz Fontaine, I din't rightly see you up there."

"Hello, Mr. McMartin. This is Jess Quinn. He's…an old friend of mine."

Jess looped the reins over the brake handle and jumped down, then extended a hand to Horace, who looked at it before shaking it a little hesitantly. "Mr. McMartin, I presume? Pleasure to meet you, sir. Solomon Turner told me I'd find you down here."

It wasn't often that folks greeted the hired help in such a way, especially those with dark skin. A swell of emotion akin to pride came over Grace. Conrad would have done no such thing. She couldn't really fault him, though, considering he came from different breeding. Back in Boston, she and Jess had been mere common folk, which had suited her just fine. It didn't suit Conrad, however, who seemed bent on doing everything in his power to elevate her status.

"I can put them bags o' grain right over here." Horace hooked a thumb over his shoulder.

"I'll help you," Jess said, then started to follow Horace around to the back of the wagon.

Horace stopped in his tracks. "Oh no, suh. I'll not be needin' any help."

Jess chuckled. "If you say so."

The stable hand stepped onto the back of the wagon and hefted a bag. When he prepared to climb back down, he discovered Jess right behind him, arms uplifted and ready to relieve him of his load. "We call this teamwork, Mr. McMartin," he said with a sly grin.

Horace grinned back. "If you says so, suh."

As soon as they had completed the job, Jess mounted the wagon, its bed rocking like a puny rowboat under his weight, then plunked himself down next to Grace. Without a second's warning, his closeness set off a stream of vivid memories from days gone by.

In early adolescence, they'd often taken long walks with their good friends Josiah Woodbridge and Ruth Stiles. Josiah had been Jess's best friend since the age of thirteen, whereas Ruthie and Grace had met in grade school. Josiah and Ruthie started courting when both were fifteen. Ruthie's parents, strict and religious, hadn't approved, but there simply was no separating the two. To try to appease her parents, Ruthie had insisted that Josiah attend church with her, which he'd happily done for her sake.

At first, Jess had made fun of Josiah for giving in—until Ruthie had closed in on Jess and guilted him into attending a revival tent meeting with her and Josiah. It was there, under the powerful preaching of a well-known traveling evangelist, that both young men had asked Jesus Christ to forgive their sins and to fill their hearts with His love and joy. Grace hadn't been there to witness the event, but she'd certainly heard plenty about it from Ruthie, to the point that she'd even felt envious for having missed it.

One hot summer evening, the foursome had found themselves walking by the docks in Boston Harbor to watch the big ships, barges, and tugboats come and go, some transporting passengers, others carrying imported or exported commodities. They'd all looked on with interest as they'd talked back and forth, laughing and enjoying one another's company. Whereas Josiah and Ruthie considered themselves a couple, Jess and Grace were still just friends at this point. All that changed when, upon arriving at a patch of rocky shoreline, he reached out and took her hand and wouldn't let go. Grace could still conjure the sensations she'd felt—how her heart had soared and her stomach had turned over with glee. They'd continued holding hands for the rest of the night, even when their fingers and palms grew sticky with sweat.

After that, everything changed between them. A new bond took hold and molded their friendship into something far more substantial. The foursome of friends became two inseparable couples. Rarely did a person see one pair without the other, no matter the function. It took Jess a while to plant that first kiss on Grace's mouth, though.

It happened several weeks into their courtship. That day, around dusk, the foursome was separated. Ruthie's family was preparing for a weeklong vacation at her grandparents' cottage by the coast, and her father wanted her home by eight o'clock so that she could finish packing and get a decent night's rest before they set off by train in the early-morning hours. That moist, muggy night marked the first time Jess and Grace were alone, just the two of them, and Grace remembered marveling that he couldn't hear the thunderous thumping of her heart.

They'd stood on a hillside overlooking the harbor. At first, it had seemed that neither knew what to say to the other—after all, this business of being alone was completely novel to both of them. Kissless weeks of holding hands had passed since they'd started courting, but this night seemed different, and they both appeared to sense it. A stunning sunset had painted the sky with a palette of colors that reflected off the still waters of the harbor, lending to the already romantic atmosphere.

Grace had shivered, and when Jess asked her if she was cold, she said no. *Just nervous,* she thought to herself.

She'd wondered how to get him to make the first move so that they could get the inevitably awkward first kiss out of the way. Yet, she hadn't wanted to rush him, desiring that this be his moment as much as hers. Still, when all he did was stare down at her, as if trying to think where to start or what to say, perhaps wondering whether he ought to ask permission, she simply touched his arm, and that was all it took.

They held their breaths and leaned haltingly toward each other. First, their noses bumped, and they giggled; then, they angled their heads just enough until, finally, it happened. Their mouths met in a tentative exploration of taste and texture. That first kiss led to another, and then another, until common sense intervened and warned them of what could happen if they continued. They were indeed naive, but they weren't totally ignorant of the dangers of kissing into the winds of oblivion.

Now, perched high on the wagon seat with Jess, his bare forearms grazing the thin cotton of her sleeve, his knee gently bumping against hers as he maneuvered the horse with a tug of the rein and a gentle "Gidd'up," a tiny prickling at each point of contact alerted Grace to the danger of his closeness. No longer were they that naive youthful two-some. No, far from it!

Oh, saints, why had she agreed to ride out to the barn with him? The smart thing would've been to stay back at the house and watch him from her upstairs window—as if watching were even smart. Stars above, she shouldn't even be looking at him or talking to him, let alone bouncing along beside him on a wagon seat.

When they reached the house, he reined in the horse. "Well, time to make some more deliveries. I'll help you down." He moved to dismount.

"Please, stay put. I'll manage on my own." She hurriedly took hold of the side rail, swiveled her body, and held her skirts out of the way as she got her footing. Then she climbed down, eyeing him only after securely planting her booted feet on the ground. "I…I'm glad you were able to find a job, but I wish you would just go back to Boston."

As sober-faced as a funeral director, and without moving a single facial muscle, he answered, "No, you don't, Grace. All you can think about are the kisses I gave you recently, and how long you'll have to wait till the next one."

She sucked in a noisy gasp. "How dare you say such a thing!"

He grinned. "I don't hear you denying it."

Like a flustered schoolgirl, she compressed her hands into tight fists and stomped her foot down hard. "I will thank you to leave now."

He tossed back his head and let out a teasing chortle. "You've got that move down quite well, Grace."

A horse neighed, drawing both their gazes to the lane.

"Looks like company's coming," Jess observed.

Grace felt her heart crash to her toes at the sight of the dray making the turn off Nobles Road and onto the stony drive leading to Brockwell Manor. *Conrad!*

"Go!" she shouted at Jess, her panic rising.

"Must be your beloved Conrad, eh? Are you as excited to see him as you were to see me this morning?"

"You—you conceited oaf!"

"No, Grace, not conceited. Just confident."

With no time to argue, she glared at him with wide-open eyes. "Go!" she hissed.

"I'm going, I'm going." Straight-backed, he set his eyes on the road ahead, put his horse in motion, and headed down the drive without so much as a glance back at her. As he passed Conrad, she could have sworn that she saw him slow in order to make some sort of comment. Conrad merely nodded curtly and kept moving forward, his adoring eyes set on her.

"Conrad!" she called, then ran to meet him, her skirts flowing behind her. She kept one eye on Jess, who'd reached the end of the drive at last and had begun to turn onto Nobles Road. Whether he observed Conrad leap to the ground, lift her into his arms, and spin her around, she couldn't say. For now, she had eyes only for her betrothed.

Conrad laid a hard, unyielding kiss on her mouth, and she immediately compared it to her most recent kiss, after church on Sunday. Confound that Jess Quinn! Still, she didn't let the memory deter her from wrapping her arms around Conrad's neck as he continued to swing her around, her skirts flaring. Secretly, she hoped Jess had gotten a glimpse of her elation, but when she shot a quick glance down the drive, she saw that he'd already set his horse at a gallop up Nobles Road. She returned her gaze to Conrad. "Oh, I missed you so much!"

"And I you!" he said, kissing her square on the mouth again. She didn't stop to analyze the kiss, just took it for what it was, fervent and possessive.

At last, he set her back and gave her a quizzical look before casting a glance toward the road. "Who was that fellow who just passed me on the drive?"

"Oh, him? He— Why do you ask?"

"Because I saw him for the first time this morning at Juanita's Café. I didn't meet him officially, by any means, but he made a most unusual remark to me just now."

"Really?" Just as she'd thought. "What did he say?"

"He said, 'You have your hands full with that one, don't you?' and used his head to indicate you, my dear. Then he tipped his hat at me and said, 'You have a nice day, now, Mr. Hall.' How would he know my name? He apparently works for the feed store and livery stable, and I've never done business with them."

A long, heavy sigh rolled out of her. "Oh, Conrad. I'm afraid I have some news for you."

A line of worry etched itself in his forehead, and he reached up to finger the end of his mustache. "What sort of news?"

She looped her arm through his and smiled up at him. "Don't look so worried, dearest. Come, let's walk out to the gazebo and sit a spell. We need to have a little talk."

He followed her, but she sensed a slight faltering in his steps.

15

"What do you mean, he's still alive?" Conrad roared in the middle of Grace's abbreviated account of Jess's return from the dead.

"Shh," she hushed him. "No need to get so worked up over it."

He leaped from the bench they'd been sharing and turned in a circle, then rubbed his hands over his greased hair, ruining the neat part down the middle. "But I am worked up! He's taken a job in Paris. What does he hope to accomplish by doing that? Surely, he's not of the assumption he can win you back."

"No, no, of course not," she fibbed. "He's…well, I don't exactly know what his intentions are. He said that he's found he likes the area and might as well stay awhile."

"What?" he shrieked. "That's impossible! He can't stay here, and you know it."

"Well, it's not as if I'm planning to have tea with him."

"This is not a joking matter, Grace, so stop treating it as such. I cannot, will not, have your former beau living in the same town as us. The whole idea is preposterous. Moreover, what were you discussing with him when I arrived? When I rounded the bend on Nobles Road, I saw you standing there, looking up at him in the wagon seat."

She'd never seen him so angry, and she couldn't tell if his rage was directed more at her or at the situation in general. "I—I don't know. Oh, Conrad, if it's any consolation, I have asked him to leave town."

He sniffed loudly, then crossed his arms in an imposing manner and gawked down at her. "And what did he say to that?"

She tried to remember. "He said, 'Paris is a lovely town, and it ought to be big enough to fit all of us'—or something to that effect. I don't remember his exact words. Goodness, Conrad, don't let it concern you so. Come, sit back down and tell me about your business trip." She patted the empty space on the bench. "How did your meetings go?"

"What?"

"Your business trip to Chicago—I'd like to hear about it. By the way, you never did tell me the name of the hotel where you'd planned to stay. Aunt Iris found that quite odd."

"Odd?"

"She assumed that you would have told me those details, and when I explained that I hadn't thought to ask, she said that I should have demanded to know."

He unfolded his arms, but she could see that he had a long way to go before he relaxed. Once more, she patted the spot on the seat next to her, inviting him to sit. But he didn't take the bait, instead striding over to the other side of the gazebo; folding his long, slender, professional-looking fingers around the railing; and, with his back to her, looking out over the miles and miles of wide-open space.

After several minutes, he finally spoke, though he didn't turn to face her. "I don't even recall the name of the hotel, to tell you the truth, and the details of my business in Chicago would bore you. I met with former clients, talked about old accounts, answered their attorneys' questions, and then got a few hours of sleep before starting all over again." Then he shifted around, leaning back against the post. "I'm afraid I must return there soon to iron out a few final details. After that, I should have to make only occasional trips to Chicago. I have a few long-term clients there, you see, from my former days at the law firm of Roberts and Cline. You understand."

She didn't, really, but she supposed it wasn't for her to know all the aspects of his career. After all, she wasn't the one who'd gone to school for years to earn the degree. All she knew was nursing, a profession she missed. At least some of her skills had stayed fresh in her mind due to the care Aunt Iris required.

He studied her for all of five breaths before his eyes went suddenly bright and eager. "Grace, I've just had the grandest idea."

She stared up at him. "What?" His sudden excitement caught her off guard.

He stepped away from the balustrade and crossed the gazebo, then plunked down next to her and grasped her hand in both of his. He brought it quickly to his lips and kissed it. "Marry me."

She giggled. "I believe you've already made that request of me, and you know my answer hasn't changed."

"But I'm asking that we marry sooner than later. What do you say? Can we make it soon? Perhaps even elope? I love you too much to wait much longer. How does this Saturday sound?"

She wriggled her hand free. He could have told her he'd just spotted a flying machine skimming over the treetops, and she wouldn't have been more surprised. "You can't be serious, Conrad."

He snatched her hand again and squeezed it so tight, her fingers went numb. "Oh, but I am serious, darling. It would show that Mr. Quinn a thing or two. You are my wife-to-be, and I'll not allow him to set up camp in Paris with the intention of stealing you out from under me. I simply won't have it. Our stepping up the wedding date—eloping, no less—will get the point across to him like nothing else. Surely, he would put himself on the next train to Boston."

Her head started spinning while her heart quaked. "But the invitations have already gone out, Conrad. It's too late to change the date."

"We'll just send out announcements after the fact," he countered. "We can still have a celebration when we return from our elaborate honeymoon. We'll receive the guests then."

"But I don't want to elope. I want to have a regular wedding. Besides, Aunt Iris—"

"Your aunt wouldn't mind it one bit. Every day is touch and go with her, anyway."

That point rang true. Her aunt may have felt well enough on Sunday to attend church, but ever since then, she'd spent the majority of her time resting in bed, even taking most of her meals there. The sudden decline was so disheartening.

"We don't have to elope, if you'd rather not," Conrad hurried to say. "We could have the ceremony in the grand hall of Brockwell Manor. You would process down the majestic staircase and proceed to an altar we'd set up by the fireplace. Wouldn't that be lovely? The reverend would still marry us, to make it a fully Christian wedding, and you could invite a few choice guests—just not that loathsome Jed Quince."

"It's Jess Quinn."

"I don't give a split hair what his name is. I want to marry you, and I want to marry you *now!*"

He put such strong emphasis on the last word that she rocked backward.

"I'm sorry, darling—I didn't mean to sound so harsh," he rushed on. "Granted, we couldn't have all the pomp and circumstance that goes with a larger, more traditional wedding, but the end result would be the same. We'd be married. Isn't that all that matters?"

She licked her lips, which had gone as dry as sand, then tried to swallow but without success. "You've sprung this on me so suddenly, I—I don't know what to say."

He hurriedly kissed her hand, his eyes darting all over her face. "Say yes. Say it, Grace."

"What? I—I don't—"

"This Saturday, Grace. Say you will."

"But—it's already Tuesday. That gives us less than one week to prepare."

His smile came off sly and devilish and dripping with charm. He leaned close, lifted the hair covering her ear, and kissed her right on the earlobe. "You know I'll make it worth your while, Grace Fontaine," he whispered, his lips gliding over her skin. "I have amazing plans for you and me, plans you can't begin to fathom. Oh, the places I want to show you, the things I want to share with you, the romantic spots around the world I intend to carry you off to—after we marry. Please, darling. I simply can't wait beyond a week to make you fully mine."

Hardly giving her time to respond, he pulled her into an embrace and kissed her so completely, it nearly stole her last breath. When they finally came up for air, she gasped. "Oh, Conrad, you are so—charming. But I'm afraid I must decline."

"What?" His eyes burned into her.

"Please calm down, darling. I'm still going to marry you; I just want to stick with our original date."

"Let me talk to your aunt. Alone. I bet I can convince her of the wisdom in moving up our wedding date."

"My aunt? I've already told you, I don't want to change the date, and it has nothing to do with Aunt Iris. Besides, the mere mention of the word 'elope' would greatly upset her."

Conrad smiled condescendingly. "I won't upset her, I promise. I just need the chance to speak privately with her, in part to give her an opportunity to get to know me better. You said yourself that she wishes for me to spend more time at the manor. My initiative in arranging a personal chat with her will speak volumes. It should at least help set her mind at ease about me. I want to assure her that I'll take good care of you, and also give her the chance to ask me anything she wants to about my past."

"Oh, Conrad, that's sweet," Grace conceded. "I'll admit, your spending quality time with her would be a nice idea. Unfortunately, we'll have to wait and see how her condition progresses. By the way, something you just said pertaining to the past reminds me of a question I myself have wanted to ask you."

"Oh?" A tiny flicker of concern crossed his face. "What is it, darling? I want to put your mind at ease." He had ceased squeezing her hand so tightly and had taken to caressing it, instead.

She gathered a deep breath. "Well, you once told me your mother had died in a train wreck on a return trip from visiting her sister in Pennsylvania, and that your father had died of consumption."

He looked down at her hand, which he continued to stroke with great care. "Yes, it was a tragedy of tremendous proportion, my losing both parents within such a short span of time—and at such a young age, no less."

"But I distinctly heard you tell Aunt Iris the opposite—that it was your mother who died of consumption and your father who'd perished in a train wreck."

Furrows of confusion etched his brow. "That's odd. Either you heard me wrong, or I had a simple slip of the tongue. Indeed, my mother was killed on a train on her way home from visiting her sister. Of course, you know my dear aunt assumed care of me from that point on."

"And did she then move to Chicago? Because you told Aunt Iris you'd spent your life in Chicago, and yet your mother had just returned from visiting your aunt in Pennsylvania."

"Oh, that," he replied without hesitation. "Yes, my aunt sold her estate and bought a lavish Chicago apartment on Lake Shore Drive. I'm surprised you don't recall my telling you that."

"I don't believe you ever did."

"Well then, it was a simple oversight. At any rate, after she passed away, some five years ago—apparently about the same time your mother did—she left all her wealth to me, which, of course, paid for my college tuition, among other things. The Lord has been so very good to me. Then, when I met you, why, it seemed He'd chosen to doubly—no, triply—bless me. I can't even begin to tell you how wonderful my life has been since you walked into it."

He trailed a series of soft, tiny kisses all over her face, beginning at her jaw and working his way up to her temple, sending a surge of shivers down her spine. "The Lord is so good, is He not?"

"Indeed He is," she whispered. "Indeed."

Even as she uttered the single word, a tumultuous knot rolled around in her chest, and she couldn't tell whether it came from eagerness or unease—or, perchance, a bit of both.

⁓

Working as a liveryman wasn't Jess's dream job, but it would certainly do for now. Since he spent the majority of his day delivering product to area farmers, he didn't think he could have landed a better position. He enjoyed driving the livery wagon, as it allowed him to soak up the warm sunshine and breathe in the fresh air, all the while learning his way around Paris and meeting new people at every turn.

At day's end, sweaty, tired, and famished, he would brush down his horse, feed and water him, hang up the tack, and finish off whatever additional chores Mr. Hansen may have assigned to him. The boss usually went home to his wife, Dora, at suppertime, leaving Jess in charge for an hour or so while the other two hands went out for a bite to eat. When they returned, it freed him up to go back to the boardinghouse.

The other hands were two brothers, perhaps in their early twenties, named Harv and Morris. They made their home at the livery, where they slept in a corner of the office on two iron cots with sagging springs. Their bedding consisted of horse blankets and discarded quilts, none of which had ever been laundered, as far as Jess could tell based on the overwhelming odor. A cast-iron stove had been placed in the middle of the livery for cold winter nights, and on one side of the stove sat a shallow wooden box full of ashes to accommodate the tobacco chewers who came and went. That, and other smells peculiar to a typical horse stable, made working outside all the more pleasurable for Jess.

This particular evening, after sweeping the front entrance of the livery to make it more presentable to customers, Jess propped the broom in the corner, then proceeded to the back of the building to check on each horse's supply of food and water. A sound at the front alerted him to an incoming customer.

"Be right there," he called.

No answer came, so he hastened to the front without ado. In the light of the open door, he saw the silhouette of a man, hat on, hands at his waist, legs parted somewhat.

"Hello?" he ventured. "Are you in need of a horse, or did you need to board one?"

Still no response. Odd, unless the fellow suffered from deafness.

Jess moved closer, then halted in his tracks when recognition dawned on him. "Well, if it isn't Conrad Hall. I'd been wondering when we would run into each other next. I have to say, I'm a bit surprised you chose to make the first move. Honored, actually." He came within five feet of the man and stopped. "Jess Quinn. But then, I suppose formal introductions aren't necessary." He extended a hand, knowing good and well the man wouldn't take it. After three seconds, he dropped his arm at his side once more. "To what do I owe the honor of this visit?"

"You can drop the pleasantries, Quinn," Conrad grumbled. "I'm not making a social call."

"No? Well, I'm disappointed. Here I'd been thinking we could be great friends."

The man issued a cold, hard smile that never made it to his eyes. "Hardly. I'm here to tell you to pack your things and leave Paris first thing in the morning."

"Really. On what authority?"

"On the authority that if you don't make tracks, I'll make trouble. Is that authority enough?"

Jess didn't much appreciate threats. Thankfully, he had the presence of mind to ask the Lord for an extra dose of self-restraint. Otherwise, he very well might have walked up to the chap and done some serious damage. It wouldn't require much effort, for Hall couldn't possess more than half his strength. In fact, what *did* he possess besides looks, and the obvious ability to turn on the charm?

Jess put on a calm demeanor. "I'm sorry to disappoint you, Hall, but I'm pretty happy in Paris for the time being."

For a moment, their gazes pierced one another, like two wild boars facing off.

A muscle twitched in Conrad's jaw. "I will not have you interfering with my plans to marry Grace Fontaine. Is that clear?"

"Clear as rain," Jess said with a nod. "'Course, she'll have to make the final decision, you know." He winked as he added, "May the best man win."

Conrad gritted his teeth. "You stay away from her, or I'll—"

"You'll what, Hall?" Jess lifted one eyebrow. "You're not seriously threatening me, are you? You can't do that, you know. I thought I was speaking to a man who knew the law frontward and backward."

"What will it take for you to leave? Every man has his price. Is it money you want?"

Jess threw back his head and laughed, then combed his hand through his mussed hair. "Man, that sounds like blackmail. Are you that desperate? Desperate men are usually that way because they lack confidence, which tells me you're worried your 'beloved fiancée' might turn tail on you."

Now Hall laughed, a chilling chortle. "Not in the least. I have every confidence she'll be mine, and sooner than you think. I'm working on convincing her to move up our wedding date. I just thought you'd want to leave town ahead of time so you wouldn't have to suffer humiliation at such close range. My offer of money came merely as a gesture of kindness, but since you prefer to call it blackmail, well, I'm afraid I'll have to renege."

It took abundant fortitude for Jess not to react to the news that Conrad was trying to move up the wedding date. Surely, Grace wouldn't agree to that. Or would she? What sort of hold did Conrad Hall have on her that she wouldn't give Jess the chance to reignite the flame that had once burned so powerfully between them? Had he only imagined that she'd enjoyed his recent kisses? He desperately wanted to tell Conrad about them—about how Grace had not only allowed them but participated actively—but to do so would amount to a form of betrayal. Those kisses had been between him and Grace, and, though she refused to admit it, he knew they'd affected her deeply, and he intended to keep them sacred. He also resisted the urge to inquire as to why Hall thought it necessary to expedite the wedding.

"Well then, since you're withdrawing your offer, I suppose you have no more reason to hang around the livery," Jess observed. "Unless you'd like to rent a horse and ride out of town yourself." He chuckled at his own joke.

Conrad didn't reveal the faintest hint of a smile. "I'd sooner walk than rent one of these mangy critters."

The horses Bill Hansen kept were a superior breed, his operation more upstanding than most; but Jess wasn't about to argue those points. He didn't want to talk with Hall any longer than was necessary. Stepping over to the door, he gestured with his arm for Conrad to exit.

Saying not a word, just huffing a loud breath, Conrad Hall straightened his spine, lifted his upper lip in a sneer, and brushed past Jess, his unmistakable fury almost palpable.

"Thanks for stopping by," Jess called after him. "I'd say it was a pleasure meeting you, but the Lord doesn't look too kindly on lying."

16

The remainder of that week went by in a flurry. Although Conrad made every effort to convince Grace to move up their wedding date to that Saturday, September 12, he failed. He still hoped she'd succeed in arranging a private tête-à-tête with Iris Brockwell, but that remained to be seen. It wasn't that he planned to do much talking to her. Their conversation would last only as long as was required for him to lace her tea with a special ingredient.

He'd found the bottle of arsenic in the cellar of his house, presumably left there by the previous owners. One never knew when one might need the stuff to rid one's living quarters of such pesky critters as rats, raccoons, and the like. In fact, most households kept a stash for that very reason, so he need not ever fear any questioning from the authorities. Although he'd never opened the violet-colored bottle, he knew, from conferring with lawyers who'd handled a murder case in Chicago, that the poison was tasteless, colorless, and odorless—the perfect combination of properties.

It wasn't his intention to murder the old woman, for that would incite a thorough investigation. No, he simply wanted to spike her tea with just enough poison to make her condition more precarious, thereby giving Grace an incentive to move up the wedding date. He knew how much she wanted her aunt to witness their vows. And that was another reason to keep the old biddy alive—her death would only propel Grace into a period of mourning, with the likely result of her postponing the wedding indefinitely.

His plan would work. It *had* to work. With the inconvenient resurrection of Jess Quinn, he had no time to waste in making Grace Fontaine fully his. It still irked him plenty that he'd failed to convince that worthless clown to leave Paris. Imagine Grace settling for some smelly duffer who worked in a livery stable! He couldn't begin to guess what she'd ever seen in him, and he reveled in his sense of confidence that she had no desire for the two of them to reconnect. She'd even asked him to leave Paris, or so she'd said. The guy didn't have much in the way of brains if he couldn't see that Grace had eyes for him alone.

Conrad glanced up when his associate Charles Murphy paused in his office doorway, briefcase under his arm, apparently heading out for the weekend. The other associate, Gerald Wadsworth, had left just minutes ago. "I suppose you're taking that pretty little lady of yours out tonight," the stout man said.

Setting down his pen, Conrad glanced at the Junghans pendulum box clock on the wall. It was a quarter to six, past time for going home, but there were things needing tending, and he wanted the office to himself.

"I'm afraid not tonight," he answered. "Grace wanted to spend time with her aunt this evening, just the two of them. I'll be seeing her tomorrow, though."

"Humph. How is that old woman doing these days, anyway?" Murphy asked. "Last I heard, she was hangin' on by a thread."

"She has her good and her bad days."

"Ah. Well, I imagine those good days will all turn to bad before too long. From what I hear, she has tumors, and we all know those are usually deadly. You're sure to inherit quite a sum after you marry and the old lady passes. Have you thought about that?"

Had he thought about that? Conrad nearly laughed out loud. "It's occurred to me, yes." He tried to force a calm tone into his voice. "That's not why I'm marrying Grace, of course."

The plump fellow grinned and gave a few nods of his balding head. "Uh-huh. It's fine by me if that's your reason. Lord knows I'd have done the same if I were in your shoes. Actually, it's one of the reasons I married Gladys. Her parents didn't have near the fortune of Iris Brockwell, mind you, but they had enough that she and I have never suffered financially. How do you think we acquired a fine house on North College Street?" He leaned his head in the door and lowered his voice to add, "Her parents paid for it with cash. 'Course, that's between you and me."

"Of course." He'd known Murphy to be a bit of a jerk, but he hadn't expected him to practically admit it. He'd witnessed the man flirting with other women on various occasions. The guy must consider himself quite debonair. However, Conrad couldn't understand women's attraction to him—unless his money was the main draw. He wondered how much Gladys knew of his roving eyes and wandering ways, or even if she cared.

The man fingered one end of his thin mustache and sniffed. Then, as if he'd read Conrad's mind, he said, "Gladys and I get on fine, as long as I let her make most of the decisions. You know women. Sometimes a man has to give a little to get what he wants, if you understand my drift. Gladys is a bossy little thing, but I allow it because it makes her feel like she's holding the reins." He chuckled. "Gotta do whatever you can to keep your woman happy, as you'll soon learn."

Conrad had met Murphy's wife, and he knew that the reality was, Gladys henpecked her husband to the ground. So much for his "allowing" her to make most of the decisions. Conrad would never tolerate that sort of behavior from Grace. He had put up with other people pushing him around his entire life, and he'd had enough of it. No, when he married Grace, he'd make it clear from day one that he intended to run their little ship—or, in the case of Brockwell Manor, their ocean liner—and everyone on staff would learn it soon enough, as well.

"Yes, I think I do get your drift, Charles, you old conniver, you." He gave an obligatory chortle. "How long have you and Mrs. Murphy been married?"

"Oh, let's see." Charles squinted at the ceiling and rubbed his double chin. "Going on twenty years, I think. Don't worry; she'll remind me when our anniversary draws near. She always does, and expects me to take her somewhere special for dinner. I do it just to stay in her good graces."

Stupid fool let the woman walk all over him. "I forget if you have any children," Conrad said.

Charles shook his head. "Never did. No time for them. Kids require too much energy and commitment."

Conrad couldn't agree more. Although he and Grace had not conversed about the topic of kids, he assumed she'd want them someday, so when the time came for discussing it, he'd put the kibosh on the whole idea. In his estimation, children created too much havoc. All he could think about in regard to youngsters was the noise they made. Memories of a time when he'd been seven or eight haunted him yet. Someone at the orphanage had acted out, and to teach them all a lesson, the headmistress had shut them in a small, closet-sized room. There must have been fifteen or more of them, all close in age, crammed together for hours, half of them crying, the other half squawking that they were scared, hungry, thirsty, or needed to use the outhouse. He had no idea how long she'd kept them locked up, but it had to have been hours, for when she finally opened the door, a few girls had wet themselves, and everyone else, including him, had made a beeline for the outhouse.

He'd never been so glad to escape that panic-ridden space and all the hysteria that went with it. To this day, he hated overcrowded rooms and screaming, bratty kids. Of course, his true anger always pointed back to Mrs. Gould, headmistress of the Chicago Poorhouse and Orphanage. He'd hated that woman more than vomit, and he recalled telling her just that on the day he'd finally been old enough to walk out the door—at all of thirteen years of age. Her cackle at his admission still echoed in his head.

Conrad exchanged a few more words with Charles Murphy before his fellow attorney bade him a pleasant weekend and left the office. When he shut the main door with a click, Conrad rose, passed the vacant reception desk, where their assistant, Garfield Heaver, sat daily from 7:30 to 5:30—typing dictated letters, receiving clients, and performing other clerical duties—and walked to the door to turn the brass lock. Once done, he made sure the "Office Closed" sign had been hung, then lowered the shades.

There. Now he could accomplish his mission with no distractions or interruptions. It pleased him that he hadn't made plans with Grace for this evening, as it afforded him the chance to stay at the office well into the night. He would need that time to finish his task.

⁓

Grace sat in the parlor with Aunt Iris, whose bony legs were draped in a light blanket, and tried to carry on a conversation. It was difficult to concentrate, however, knowing that, within minutes, she would hear a horse's hooves pounding the earth and clattering up the quiet driveway. Initially, it was to be just the two of them for dinner, but Aunt Iris had just broken the news that she'd asked someone else to join them.

"Aunt Iris, you didn't," Grace said, instinctively knowing without inquiring that she'd invited Jess. "You must cease with taking matters of my personal life into your own hands. You know very well I plan to marry Conrad Hall. In fact, truth be told, he wanted to marry me this very weekend."

Aunt Iris jerked her head up, and the sudden movement made her face go almost as pale as her white hair, pulled into its usual knot at her nape.

Worried, Grace hastened out of her chair and lowered herself onto the settee next to her aunt. "I didn't mean to upset you, Auntie. Are you all right?"

Aunt Iris pressed her lace handkerchief to her damp brow and took a few breaths, starting to regain some of her color. "Why would he wish to hasten your wedding date?"

"He loves me and says he simply cannot wait. By the way, he would like the chance to speak to you in private."

The woman scowled, making her already wrinkled face look even pricklier. "About what does he wish to speak to me? I already don't approve of your moving up the date, not when you have so many things to sort out in your heart and your head."

Grace exhaled. "He just wants the chance to get to know you better, to assure you that I'll be in good hands as his wife. You said yourself he doesn't come around here often enough."

"He's been coming around more lately, but I just don't get a good sense about him."

"Aunt Iris." She released a laborious moan. "Must you be so stubborn?" She took her aunt's hand in both of hers and looked deep into her cloudy eyes. "Truly, Conrad is a good Christian man, a fine gentleman. I don't know why you can't see it." She rubbed her aunt's shoulder and found its protruding bones quite alarming. She'd lost so much weight that only a thin layer of almost transparent skin covered her tiny frame. "Would you do it for me—meet with him, that is?" She hated that she had to grovel.

Clutching her abdomen, Aunt Iris gasped and grimaced. Grace felt a new surge of apprehension about the pain her aunt was experiencing.

"Oh, all right, all right." Aunt Iris gave a loud sniff and waved her frail hand. "I suppose I can agree to a visit with him if it will make you feel better, but on one condition."

Stipulations always seemed to play a part with her shrewd aunt. "And what might that be?"

"While I am busy trying to better understand just why you want to marry Conrad Hall, you must work at trying to understand why you won't give Jess Quinn a second chance. That means that if I agree to talk to Conrad, you must also agree to meet with Mr. Quinn."

"Well, that shouldn't be difficult, since you've taken the liberty of inviting Mr. Quinn to supper tonight."

Her glib remark came just before the sound of hoofbeats thundering up the drive, which provoked a slight hitch in Grace's chest.

17

Mrs. Brockwell didn't eat more than three or four bites from her plate, as far as Jess could tell, but her slight appetite didn't deter her from keeping the dinner conversation moving. She wanted to know nearly everything about him, and he willingly answered every question she asked, holding back nothing, including the story of how he and Grace had met in early adolescence through their mutual friends Josiah and Ruthie, and how the four of them had spent endless hours together. He told her about his boyhood jobs, his upbringing as an only child, the death of his mother in an awful buggy accident, and the sad trajectory his despairing father's life had taken ever since.

When she inquired about his spiritual life, he gladly told her about his conversion to Christ, relaying that he'd lapsed into a lazy Christian until he'd landed in a London prison, where he'd discovered his utter dependency on the strength of God to make it through each day. Only then had he reestablished his thriving relationship with the Lord.

"I can relate to that," Mrs. Brockwell told him. "The good Lord and I were what you'd call distant partners for some time, but over the last couple of years, I've come to terms with some important areas of my life and finally realized I couldn't go on hiding from God. We've since reunited, so to speak." She frowned. "Well now, I've put that in a strange way. God isn't one to move away from us; rather, we're the ones who walk away from Him. He, in His gentle manner, continually beckons us back, and it's up to us to choose whether we will respond to His loving summons."

"Beautifully put, ma'am."

As he inquired further about her life, he noticed that Grace merely picked at her food, mostly keeping her eyes directed at her plate. He could tell she was trying to appear neutral and indifferent, but he also sensed her inner fascination with the two-way conversation. He would break through that barricade yet, and when he did, it would come crashing down around her, leaving her fully vulnerable and unable to hold back her feelings a second longer. He had only to practice patience and allow God to do the work.

"Your husband must have been a captivating sort of fellow to have caught your eye, Mrs. Brockwell," he remarked next.

"Please, call me Iris"—she glanced quickly at Grace, then looked back at him—"or Aunt Iris, if it suits you."

To this, Grace did raise her head. Her eyes connected briefly with Jess's before she lowered them to her plate once more. Stubborn girl.

Jess smiled broadly at the older woman. "That would suit me fine, Aunt Iris. Thank you for the offer. Getting back to Mr. Brockwell, how did you meet him?"

"Oh, my stars, you don't want to know about that old tale."

"But I do."

Grace lifted her face again, her expression brighter this time. "Tell him, Auntie. It's so romantic."

Aunt Iris lifted her water glass with a shaky hand and slowly sipped, then set it down and cleared her throat. Her voice had grown a bit weak and raspy, making Jess wonder how much longer she would last at the table. The kitchen staff had already removed most of the dinner dishes, and now their dessert of apple pie sat in front of them. He'd been dying to slice into his, but seeing that neither Iris nor Grace had made a move in that direction, he held back.

The old woman offered a wobbly smile. "Well, I'll give you the short version, then."

He sat up straighter, and Grace did, as well. Jess, for one, didn't want to miss a single word, so he leaned closer, glad to be seated directly across from both ladies so that he could watch their expressions.

"I met my John at a church function when I was nineteen. He was a dozen years older, and it seemed almost scandalous for a girl my age to be so taken with a man of thirty-one years. My parents, however, thought nothing of the age difference and encouraged the relationship because he was such a good man, already successful and wholly devoted to God. I suppose they felt fortunate that someone as fine as he would take their daughter off their hands. For you see, I'd already surpassed what was then considered to be the marriageable age. Some of my friends had married at fourteen and fifteen, and not so much for love as out of necessity."

Grace chuckled. "I guess that makes me an old spinster, then."

"Humph." Aunt Iris clucked. "Better to be a spinster than married to a man you don't love."

Her assertion made Grace's smile fade to nothing.

Jess decided to try to lighten the mood. "Twenty-five is getting up there, Grace," he said, playfully pointing his index finger at her. "I'm surprised I don't see any gray hairs in those brunette locks. Are you sure you're not hiding them?"

Her light laughter warmed him. It pleased him to see her finally start to relax in his company.

"You should talk, old man. At twenty-six, it's a wonder you're not going bald." She turned her glinting gaze away from Jess. "Please go on with your story, Auntie."

"Well, all right, but I told you I'd be sharing the shortened version. I'm starting to grow weary, and I want to give you two a chance to spend some time together."

At that, Grace's eyes rounded, and Jess felt his brows rise of their own accord. Happily, though, Grace made no verbal objection, and it gave him hope for what the night might hold for them. He'd already decided not to make any moves; the kisses he'd gotten recently would have to suffice for the time being. Right now, his focus needed to be on getting back inside her head and heart.

Iris resumed her love story, sharing how her parents needn't have worried about convincing her that she and John were a perfect fit. In fact, he'd swept her clean off her feet so that, not five months later, they'd found themselves walking down the aisle and exchanging vows. From that point forward, they had grown to love each other more each day, his occasional absences due to business trips only enhancing the sweetness of their time together when he returned home. Iris said that he had a special love for her that even she couldn't explain, other than to say that it contained an element of the divine. "Were it not for God granting John abundant patience, understanding, and forgiveness toward me, he couldn't have loved me as he did. Certainly, no other man on earth would have had that ability."

"Aunt Iris, you are not a hard person to love," Grace assured her. "And I'm certain that, at nineteen, you had very little need of Uncle John's forgiveness."

Her aunt chuckled and shook her head. "We all stand in need of forgiveness, child—some of us more than others. At any rate, your uncle John fitted the bill to a tee. I look back now, loath to wonder where I might have ended up on life's journey, had John not shown me his abiding, unconditional love—and then convinced me that God loved me even more than he did. Yes, it took me countless years to fully accept unconditional love—from both him and the Lord—but that's only because I'm a slow learner." She smiled at her own admission.

Then she put a hand over her mouth to cover a yawn. "I'm about petered out, I'm afraid."

Solomon and Blanche appeared as if on cue. They must have been hovering just around the corner.

"I'd say it's high time we took you upstairs, Missus Brockwell," Solomon said. He carefully pulled her chair away from the table, and then he and Blanche each took her by one of her scrawny arms and helped her to stand.

"Let me go with you," Grace said, quickly rising.

Jess jumped to his feet, as well.

"No, dear." Iris waved off her great-niece. "You stay here and tend our guest, and don't be sending him away before you've had your chance to talk, hear?"

"I'll see to that, ma'am," Jess put in, stepping around the table to give Iris's shoulder a gentle squeeze. "Thank you for the dinner invitation. I thoroughly enjoyed the meal and the wonderful conversation. And I'll keep praying for you."

He stood at least two heads taller than the tiny woman, so she really had to crane her neck to meet his eyes. "I appreciate that. You're a good man, Jess Quinn." She nodded slowly, shakily. "If only a certain someone in this room—ahem—would come to her senses."

Grace exhaled a loud breath that nearly made Jess laugh. Somehow, he managed to contain himself. It made her plain nervous to be alone with him, and he suspected, even hoped, it was because she dreaded having to admit that her great-aunt was right—she still cared; she needed only to come to her senses.

⟨⟩

It was a glorious evening, if Grace did say so, the blue sky turning to shades of pink, purple, and red as the great bright ball of orange began to settle in the West. A warm breeze chased through the tall grasses at one side of the property, where Horace McMartin allowed them to grow at will, and wildflowers of every color danced and swayed, as if to some angelic symphony. An evening hush had settled on both her and Jess as they stood side by side on the stone front terrace.

With his hands tucked into his trouser pockets, Jess turned his body to face the building and gazed upward. "Tell me about this old place. Did your uncle have it built for your aunt?"

She turned with him, and as she did, her arm brushed against him, starting her heart to thrumming. She scooted aside and nearly lost her balance until Jess reached out and took her arm to steady her. How clumsy of her. Why did he make her so nervous? She turned her attention back to the mansion and collected her bearings. His hand went back in his pocket, and he assumed a casual stance once more, as though nothing in the world were amiss.

She breathed deeply through her nostrils to calm herself before responding. "The former owner was in the process of building it when he went bankrupt. I heard that Uncle John bought it from the bank for far less than market value, then hired an architect and a contractor to finish it to Aunt Iris's liking. It's quite the monstrosity, in my opinion. I can't imagine residing in so massive a place, or having to manage it."

She felt his gaze on her. "And yet it will probably be yours someday, don't you think?"

"Perhaps. Unless I can talk Aunt Iris into doing something sensible with it—something that won't deprive the staff of their positions and housing, mind you. Their living quarters take up the entire third floor. I've never gone up there, but I know Aunt Iris provides well for them. They've spent a good share of their lives here, never as slaves but always as paid servants. The slaves who worked here when Solomon came have all passed on.

"Horace and Blanche McMartin have probably been here the longest—after Sol, that is. They even raised three children here, so, for a time, there were youngsters running up and down the manor hallways and stairs. I have a vague memory of playing with them some when Mother and I used to visit. By the time I reached adolescence, they had all grown old enough to move away and find jobs. Last I heard, they'd scattered, one living in New York, one in Michigan, and the other in Ohio, I think. Sol told me Aunt Iris paid for their educations."

"She's an amazing lady."

Grace's nerves began to settle. "She is, but she's too humble to think of herself as anything of the sort."

"Indeed."

Her gaze landed on the gazebo situated to the right, a rust-colored brick pathway lined with flowers leading to it.

As if reading her mind, Jess pointed at the structure. "Shall we?"

She hesitated, remembering how, just days ago, she had sat there with Conrad. Yet the loveliness of dusk made the invitation hard to resist. She lifted her skirts a few inches and descended the steps, then followed the winding pathway just wide enough for two adults to stroll side by side. Every so often, Jess bumped against her, and it always managed to make her heart race. Meanwhile, he conducted himself with total nonchalance. How irksome she found his erratic behavior!

Once they seated themselves on one of the benches, a safe distance away from each other, Jess clasped his hands in front of him and set them on his lap, then peeked back at the mansion. "What sort of 'sensible' plans did you have in mind for the manor?"

The question caught her off guard, for she had yet to discuss her idea with Aunt Iris or even with Conrad. She swallowed before proceeding. "I haven't fully thought it through, but I recently attended a ladies' picnic luncheon at the church, and the guest speaker talked about the need for a home for displaced elderly folks in the community. There are many who require medical attention, whether for illness or injury, yet have no family close by to look after them. Some even die prematurely for lack of care. He said that if there was a facility for them, it could be staffed by doctors from neighboring counties, making for an efficient system, and many of the patients could probably be nursed back to a state that would allow them to return to their homes. And I was thinking…well, wouldn't Brockwell Manor function perfectly as that facility? I also thought that, with my nursing degree, I could assist in providing care. It would give me great satisfaction to know I was making a difference in the lives of others."

Jess gave her a tender smile. "You've always had a heart of compassion, Grace. It's one of your God-given gifts. You should use it to the best of your ability."

"Thank you for that vote of confidence."

"I know you pretty well, remember?"

She looked down at her lap, where her own hands rested, her fingers intertwined.

"Anyway, I think it sounds entirely worthwhile—and something your aunt would likely approve of. What does your…fiancé…think of the idea?"

"Oh—well, I haven't brought it up with him just yet. As I told you, I'm still in the initial stages of thinking about the possibility. But I'm sure he'll agree it's a good idea."

Jess raised his head in a half nod. "Ah, yes. No doubt." His tone conveyed a hint of uncertainty and perhaps even sarcasm. "I met him, you know."

"Yes, you told me you saw him at the café; and then, of course, you passed each other in the driveway."

"No; I mean, I met him—as in, he paid me a visit at the livery. He didn't tell you?"

Grace's head snapped up. "No, he didn't mention it, and he just stopped out last evening to see me briefly. You say he introduced himself to you?"

Jess's jaw twitched, as if he might laugh. "I wouldn't describe it that way, exactly."

She sat straighter, a spiky sensation crawling up her back. "Well then, how would you describe it, exactly?"

He arched one eyebrow. "You might say that he threatened me."

"Threatened you? How so?"

"He strongly suggested I leave Paris, and the next day would have suited him. As you can see, I'm still here. He even offered me money, but"—he fastened his eyes on her, crinkled his brow, and angled his mouth into a sideways grin—"I don't scare easily, and I certainly can't be bought."

Why would Conrad have done such a thing? Making threats hardly sounded like something her fiancé would do. Surely, Jess had misunderstood his intentions. Even so, she felt the need to apologize. "I'm sorry—"

Jess raised his hand. "No, don't apologize, Grace. I understand why he did it. He's merely trying to protect what he considers rightfully his." He bent, picked up a twig from the floor of the gazebo, and snapped it in half. "But then, so am I." He tossed the two halves back to the ground and brushed his hands together, then spread his knees, propped his elbows on them, and lazily lifted his gaze to meet hers once more. "He did tell me something else of interest."

"What?" She almost didn't want to know.

"He said he's been trying to convince you to move up your wedding date."

She pursed her lips for a moment, growing more aggravated with Conrad by the minute. "Well, he shouldn't have said that. He only wants to ensure that Aunt Iris will still be with us when we exchange our vows." She gave him a hasty glance. "This is an awkward topic to be discussing with you, Jess."

"Are you sure his real reason for wanting to move up the date isn't because I've suddenly appeared on the scene?" he asked, passing over her last remark.

She tilted her head, thinking for a moment, then nodded. "I'm sure that plays a part, yes."

"He's not very confident of your love, then, is he?"

"Jess, may we please stop talking about him?"

"What is it about him, anyway, Grace? What has you so attracted to Conrad Hall?"

She didn't hesitate to answer. "First and foremost, he's a Christian. He's also smart, successful, thoughtful, kindhearted, and he treats me like a queen." She glanced down at the diamond on her finger.

"Really. I can understand his treating you like a queen—you deserve that. But 'kindhearted'? That I don't see."

"Of course you don't. You don't know him."

"Why do I get the distinct feeling your aunt doesn't like him? What does she know that you don't?"

"Aunt Iris knows nothing, at least when it comes to Conrad. She hasn't even given me a concrete reason for her dislike. All she can say is that she has a certain 'sense' about him."

"Well, maybe you ought to take her words to heart."

"I do take her words to heart." Suddenly she felt short of breath. She inhaled, longing to drop the subject. She should have known it would come to this. "I do, Jess, but...well, she doesn't know everything."

They sat in silence for a few moments, the only sounds being their breaths and the cooing of birds as they settled in for the night. Two black squirrels scampered across the yard mere feet away, twigs crackling beneath them. The peaceful serenity came to an end when Grace slapped at a mosquito that had alighted on her bare arm.

"Do you actually have any fun with the man?"

His query caught her unawares. "Of course, we have fun!"

"What does he do that makes you laugh?"

She hated that she had to rattle her memory to come up with a specific example. "Oh, different things. I can't think of any one example off the top of my head. Why would you ask that?"

"Because I was recalling the times you and I laughed for hours about nothing and everything."

She remembered those times, as well, and she wanted to remind him that they'd been much younger then.

"We'd stroll along Boston Harbor, and I'd tell you something about my day that would get you giggling. Remember the time we decided to amble through the cemetery, of all places, and we started reading the names on the tombstones? God rest their souls, but we did get a good laugh out of some of them. Do you remember any offhand?"

She needed only a second to recall one. "Thomas Loser." She felt the corners of her mouth turn up in a tiny smile.

He laughed. "Yeah, and then there were Rusty and Pearl Gates."

"I'd forgotten about them! And Fanny Brain—oh my goodness!"

"And the one that beat all: Cornelius Slobbercorn."

She laughed so hard, she had to hold her stomach. "My stars, how do you remember that?"

"I had a lot of time to mull over distant memories while sitting in a jail cell."

With that, their laughter died. Jess kicked at a pebble, sending it across the gazebo floor. "We always had a grand time with Josiah and Ruthie," he remarked, his tone brighter.

"Yes, we did. I'm recalling a certain Sunday afternoon when we borrowed that creaky wooden rowboat from Mr. Ivy, Ruthie's kindly old neighbor, and took it out on the river, only to find it had a hole the size of a melon under one of the floorboards. We got about ten feet from shore before the thing started to sink."

"And we all had to bail out, you girls with your dresses on, and Josiah and I in our Sunday suits. Ruthie started screaming in panic because she couldn't swim. We laughed because the water was only five feet deep, and we could all touch bottom."

"And it was a squishy bottom!" Grace remembered. "I lost my best shoes in that muck, and Mama was so upset with me. She didn't care about the fact I'd ruined my dress, or that I might've drowned, had we gone any further out—only that I'd lost my shoes!"

They chuckled at the silly reminiscence, and Grace felt refreshed and, well, free. After spending so much time fretting over Aunt Iris's health, poring over wedding plans—changing and refining certain aspects of the ceremony to make it perfect, discussing details of the reception and guest list with Solomon, traveling back and forth from The Perfect Fit Tailoring Shop for dress fittings—and trying to spend as much time with Conrad as possible, she found it relaxing, almost magical, to let her worries fall away in a hearty round of laughter.

Almost too relaxing, considering it was Jess and not Conrad who was working the magic.

18

So far, so good, Jess thought. As long as he kept a physical distance from Grace, maintained a composed and tranquil atmosphere, didn't push too hard when it came to the character of Conrad Hall, and even got Grace reminiscing over fond memories, they remained on good terms. The question was, could he keep it that way? He found himself treading a fine line. He truly wanted to discuss some deeper issues with her, but doing that would mean crossing that line and potentially offending her loyalties to Conrad.

He silently prayed for wisdom and asked the Lord to pave the way by providing him with discernment and bountiful amounts of patience. He didn't know Conrad Hall well enough to pass judgment. Perhaps he truly was a good man, and Jess had only to accept that Grace intended to marry him. If that was the case, he would likely wind up going back to Boston a bachelor who'd failed to win back the heart of his one and only love.

To avoid that outcome, he proceeded with caution. "Tell me how you happened to fall in love with Conrad."

Grace gaped at him with surprise in her eyes.

"Seriously, I want to know the story," he assured her. "Maybe if you tell it to me, it'll give me a better understanding of the man."

She quirked her dark, perfectly plucked brows and tilted her flawless oval face to one side. A few wisps of hair fell around her face, and he had to resist the powerful urge to reach over and tuck them behind her ear.

"If you're sure," she said, her tone tentative.

He leaned forward, hands clasped, and gave her a slow nod. "I'm sure—and I promise to keep my trap shut while you talk."

She hesitated, probably trying to determine where to begin, or perhaps whether to believe that he would actually remain quiet the entire time. He pretended to turn a key beside his mouth, indicating that his lips were locked.

Apparently satisfied, she gave him a tremulous smile. "All right, then." With closed mouth, she inhaled a loud, vast breath of air, then swallowed.

Jess refolded his hands and stared down at his scuffed boots as he waited for her to begin.

"You'd been gone a full year before I finally realized I was drowning, too—in despair. When I learned you'd been lost at sea, I cried until there was nothing left in me. Pardon the pun, but I cried an entire ocean for twelve solid months.

"Maybe life stood still for you, Jess, but there came a time for me when I resolved that I wanted—needed—to survive the pain of my loss. Doing that meant taking my eyes off of myself and focusing them on others. I made a point to begin socializing again, jumped headlong into my work at the hospital, sought sound counsel from our pastor at Boston Central Church, and, with God's help and the encouragement of friends, started finding new purpose and meaning in life. A full year later—two years since hearing that you'd died at sea—I received a telegram from Doc Trumble detailing the critical condition of my great-aunt. I sensed God calling me to move to Tennessee to help tend to her, and the thought of getting a fresh start someplace new also appealed to me. So, I obeyed what I believed to be God's will and went.

"On April thirtieth of this year, due to a number of circumstances, my train arrived in Paris well ahead of schedule. Solomon was to pick me up three hours later, and, having no way to contact him to ask that he come earlier, I prepared myself for a long wait at the station, since all of the cabs had been rented. Within minutes, a handsome gentleman in professional attire approached me. He introduced himself as Conrad Hall, Esquire, and explained that he'd just seen one of his clients off. When he learned of my predicament, he kindly offered to drive me out to the manor. We struck up an easy conversation right from the start, and I found him quite friendly, warmhearted, and charming. Rather than driving me directly to the manor, he first showed me around Paris, which immediately endeared me to the town. I know it's difficult to believe, but during the course of that drive, I learned a great deal about him, including that he shared my faith in Christ and attended Paris Evangelical Church.

"When he dropped me off at the manor, he asked to court me, but I declined, thinking it inappropriate to accept a date with him so soon after meeting. Gentleman that he was, he didn't press me to accept; but, a few days later, he returned to the manor and invited me to take a stroll with him around the grounds. I accepted. After talking and walking for what seemed like hours, he telling me about his upbringing—how both his parents had perished when he was young, leaving him in the custody of his well-to-do aunt—and about his determination to study law and make something worthwhile of his life, I discovered that he quite enthralled me. I felt comfortable enough to share about my own upbringing, even going as far as to tell him about you and your certain demise at sea. He was most sympathetic, and assured me that he would pray for my continued emotional healing. I thought that was so generous and thoughtful of him.

"After that, our courtship began. We would go out to dinner—he owns Brooks Hotel and Restaurant, in case you weren't aware; attend social functions, such as concerts, plays, and the like; and, of course, go together to Sunday services at Paris Evangelical. Not long into our courtship, he professed his love for me. It didn't surprise me when he told me, for I had sensed our relationship moving in that direction. Still, it took me a week or more to echo the words back to him. As soon as I did, he proposed marriage, and I readily accepted."

At last, she paused and looked at him with guilt in her eyes. "Oh my, I've talked your ear off, and I fear I've bored you, to boot."

"No, no, not at all," he assured her.

Bored? If anything, she'd attached a two-ton weight to his heart so that it dragged on the ground. He tried to come off as unaffected, but even taking a simple breath now proved difficult.

She proceeded. "We set the date for October fifteenth, a little over five months since our initial meeting. I immediately started making the arrangements. Conrad said that he didn't care to be involved in the planning process, because he fully trusted my ability to make good decisions and plan a tasteful ceremony and reception. I sent a letter to Ruth Woodbridge first thing, asking her to be my matron of honor. Within two weeks, she replied, expressing congratulations and telling me how eager she and Josiah were to witness our vows. They are both very happy for me."

As Jess had promised, he'd kept mum while she talked, but by now, his throat was too clogged with emotion for him to speak, anyway.

"Would you say something?" she finally sputtered after a few moments' silence, her own voice gruff with emotion. "Please?"

He really didn't know what to say. All he wanted to do was take his leave. It was his own fault for asking her to bare her soul. "Thanks for… your openness," he managed. "I appreciate it. But I think I should head out now." He stood and stretched his back muscles, which had gone as tight as fiddle strings.

Grace rose to her feet, her brown eyes wide with an unreadable expression as she stared up at him.

Suddenly his gaze was riveted on her every facial feature. He had to leave before he kissed her. She'd just told him she loved another man. What was he doing entertaining the thought of kissing her—again?

He started to turn but stopped to add, "Please thank your aunt again for the dinner invitation. I thoroughly enjoyed myself."

"I will." She pressed her lips together. It appeared that she had something more to say, but he didn't feel like sticking around to hear it.

"Good night, Grace."

"Good night."

He pivoted on his heel and walked with hurried, purposeful strides to the hitching post to retrieve his rented horse. He couldn't even remember the critter's name. His eyes had blurred, so that he barely made out the path. What was the matter with him? He couldn't recall the last time he'd shed a wretched tear. Eighteen months in a British naval prison, and he hadn't cried once. Why, now, did he feel so vulnerable, so dead, inside?

You asked for it, he told himself. *You persuaded her to tell you the story of her and Conrad, so you'd have a "better understanding."* It accomplished that, all right. He finally saw the situation plainly. How had he been so blind not to realize that his two-year absence had erased all chances of ever reclaiming Grace's heart? Evidently, her love for Conrad Hall far surpassed anything she'd ever felt for him.

Reaching his horse, he mounted up and grabbed the reins. On the ride down the drive, he didn't waste a second looking back to see if Grace watched from the gazebo. Surely, she'd gone inside already. No sense in letting her gaze linger on a man she no longer loved.

Conrad couldn't believe his luck. Grace had sent word with the butler early Saturday afternoon that her aunt would receive him in her parlor at six o'clock on Monday evening. She also sent her own regrets that she preferred to rest that evening rather than see him, but she'd had a very busy week. She added an assurance that she looked forward to seeing him in the morning when he picked her up for the Sunday service.

He should have been disappointed, and perhaps a trifle miffed, that she'd canceled their Saturday date. What if he'd made special arrangements? Of course, he hadn't—scratching his name from the reservation book at Brooks Hotel and Restaurant posed no problem whatsoever. If anything, he relished the thought of two nights in a row to himself. He grew weary of having to constantly manufacture new methods of entertainment, and looked forward to the day when he could walk through the doors of his rambling brick mansion, kick off his shoes at the front entry, recline in one of the leather chairs in his mammoth library, and order Solomon to bring him the *Paris Post-Intelligencer* and a tall glass of a refreshing beverage after a long day at the office.

That evening, after supping on a simple beef sandwich at his dining-room table, he carried the dish to the kitchen and set it in the sink, then meandered down to the fruit cellar. There, in plain sight, sat that lovely violet bottle labeled "Arsenic." He picked it up, heart pounding, and popped the cork for his first real sniff of the stuff. Sure enough, it emitted no odor. He wouldn't test it for taste; no, he'd trust his sources that it lacked any flavor.

Grinning, he dusted off the bottle with his bare hand, secured the cork, and set it back in place on the shelf. Tonight, he would dream up a scheme for transferring just the right amount into Iris Brockwell's cup of steaming hot tea come Monday evening.

19

This morning, unlike last Sunday, Aunt Iris did not express a desire to go to church. She did, however, insist on getting up and dressing earlier than usual. Grace helped her into a floral dress that had been hand-stitched by Joy Jennings, then worked her thin white hair into a neat bun, which she secured with a pink herringbone comb.

"Thank you, dear."

"You're very welcome. Would you like to go downstairs and sit by the parlor window? It's a beautiful day. You can watch the swallows and jays come and go and keep your eyes out for wildlife. I've seen a few turkeys crossing Nobles Road of late, and the deer seem to be multiplying in huge numbers. A couple of days ago, I even spotted a fox in the wee morning hours—a rare sight, indeed."

"I can get a better view from my own window. I'll just go over to my chair."

"All right."

Iris planted her hands on the vanity top and managed to push herself up from the cushioned bench.

"Here, let me help you," Grace offered.

Rather than refuse assistance, Aunt Iris looped her hand in Grace's arm, and they set off across the vast room. "You're a good girl."

She smiled. "Thank you, Auntie. I happen to think you're a very special lady."

"This house is going to be yours someday, you know."

The statement seemed to have come out of nowhere. "Oh, Aunt Iris, I don't need this big house."

"But it's going to be yours nonetheless. I settled it long ago with Gerald Wadsworth. Of course, Solomon and the rest of the staff will be well taken care of, too, but you will get the manor. Gerald will sort out the details of my will after I'm gone."

"Aunt Iris...." Her throat had gone suddenly raw and scratchy, making swallowing most difficult. "May we discuss this later? I don't think now is—"

"Of course, dear. Here we are." They arrived at the old rocker, Aunt Iris panting more than usual. Grace eyed her with concern as she carefully lowered her into the chair.

"Would you prefer that I stay home from church and sit with you? I wouldn't mind at all."

Aunt Iris flicked her gnarled wrist. "Heavens, no," she said, her voice shaky. "You go on, and I'll sit here and talk to the Lord while I count the deer that pass through the yard. When you return, I want a detailed summary of the preacher's sermon."

Grace stared down at her. Why had she mentioned her will just now? It was the first time her aunt had done so, and it made Grace wonder if the woman had some uncanny sense of something just beyond the horizon. The notion of putting the manor to good use after Aunt Iris's passing persisted in her thoughts, and she wondered if she ought to bring it up for discussion this afternoon. If her aunt approved of the plan, would the manor remain in Grace's charge, or would it become a publicly owned facility? Should it go to Tennessee, so that the state would govern its policies, or would handing it over to Henry County be the better arrangement? Perhaps it should remain a privately owned institution so that a carefully selected board of trustees would make the important decisions.

So many questions, so few answers. But why worry with the details now, when she would have Conrad to turn to for legal counsel and financial wisdom? Surely, he would know how best to go about converting the home into a medical facility—again, if Aunt Iris approved of the idea. And with the way she'd been talking this morning, something told Grace she needed to broach the subject sooner than later.

As was usually the case on any given Sunday morning, Paris Evangelical Church filled up quickly. Between Reverend Jennings' fine preaching, song leader Tom Walters' worthy selection of hymns, and pianist Wendy Hodgin's excellent playing, folks had begun attending the church in droves. Seldom had Grace ever heard the piano played quite so beautifully as when Mrs. Hodgin sat at the keys. In her experience, churches out East had little use for pianos, seeming to find them too informal, if not worldly and sinful, for church worship. Many folks preferred the pipe organ—or even a cappella singing—over what they considered to be an instrument fit only for tavern music. Personally, Grace favored the piano over no instrument at all, for it aided in covering up the voices of those sopranos whose piercing, high-pitched voices nearly shattered the eardrum.

One had to arrive a good quarter of an hour early to be assured of finding a seat. Unfortunately, because Grace had fussed a bit excessively over Aunt Iris that morning, she and Conrad arrived at precisely five minutes to ten and almost didn't find a place to sit. Fortunately, the people seated in a pew five rows from the front squeezed together to make room for them. Conrad grumbled under his breath that they would have been better off standing in the back than crowding together on such a hot and humid morning. Already, various odors of a bodily nature assaulted the senses, in spite of all the windows' being propped open.

Attempting to ignore Conrad's tetchiness, Grace glanced about the sanctuary. That's when her eyes alighted on Jess, sitting two rows ahead of them at the opposite end, along the center aisle. Next to him sat a pretty, fair-haired lady she'd never seen before. He leaned over and whispered something in her ear, and she smiled, then laughed. The sight made Grace's stomach drop and stirred within her a mix of ire, jealousy, and confusion. When she'd last seen him, just two nights ago, he'd made no mention whatever of having made a female acquaintance in Paris. How could he possibly have met someone between then and now—someone in whose presence he already appeared entirely comfortable, even going so far as to invite her to sit with him in church? He'd professed his undying love for Grace upon coming to Paris, and now, here he was, involving himself with another woman already.

Grace felt the area between her eyes crumple into a frown so deep that it pained her brow.

Conrad leaned close. "Looks like your old beau didn't waste any time finding himself a new woman."

"What?" She tried to feign ignorance.

He chortled. "Don't pretend you didn't notice, Grace. I saw you staring at him."

The heat of a blush crept across her face. "I wasn't staring. I just happened to see him, that's all. How could I avoid it, with him sitting right in front of us?"

"Humph. You're not peeved, I hope."

"Shh, don't talk so loud. And, no, I'm not peeved," she hissed just as loudly.

Floretta Grassmeyer gave a stiff turn of her head and scowled, sending a clear message that she and Conrad were causing a disturbance. Embarrassed, Grace pressed her lips together, turning them slightly under, and straightened her spine.

Tom Walters approached the podium and invited the congregation to rise for the opening Scripture, taken from the book of Hebrews. "'Let us hold fast the profession of our faith without wavering; (for he is faithful that promised),'" he read with great fervor. "I hope you brought your songbooks, because we are going to raise the roof with our opening hymn, 'Standing on the Promises.' Please turn to page one hundred fifty-seven."

There was a rustling of pages as the people searched their hymnals. Those who did not have a copy of their own either hummed along or shared books with nearby congregants. Blessedly, Joy Jennings had given Grace an extra hymnbook the first Sunday she'd visited Paris Evangelical.

On cue, Mrs. Hodgin played the introduction with great gusto, after which Mr. Walters raised his hand and directed the congregation to start the first verse. "Standing on the promises of Christ my King, through eternal ages let His praises ring...." The flock of worshippers sang with considerable volume and fervor.

Grace sang along, but her heart couldn't work up the same degree of exhilaration exhibited by those around her. She figured she knew the reason why. Jess Quinn had a girlfriend!

⁓

Jess enjoyed the service, the music, the message, and the atmosphere of worship. However, the woman next to whom he found himself sitting wasn't exactly what one would term his cup of tea. She was pleasant, of course, and even pretty, with her head of long blonde hair and her cornflower-blue eyes, but too forward for his liking.

Her disposition confirmed something Jess had heard from Sam Connors, who owned and operated the local blacksmith shop with his uncle and often fashioned horseshoes for Bill Hansen. In the course of their conversation several days ago, when Sam had stopped by to drop off a few items, he had joked that if Jess continued coming to Paris Evangelical Church, it wouldn't be long before the single ladies began emerging from the far corners of the county. He explained that until the Reverend Jennings married, all the eligible women had vied for his attention Sunday after Sunday, each one eager to fill the role of preacher's wife. Ultimately, the woman living next door to the church had won his heart.

Apparently, word traveled fast when a bachelor moved to town, because no fewer than four women had encircled him as soon as he'd entered through the church's main doors that morning. It wasn't that he didn't enjoy the attention. What man wouldn't? Especially since none of them was too hard on the eye, with the obvious exception of one who didn't have all her teeth, yet smiled most broadly. If he could look beyond that troublesome detail—alas, he feared he couldn't—all her other features exceeded those of the average woman.

Of course, none of the women appealed to him, for his heart belonged to one Grace Fontaine. As it turned out, he'd had no plan of escape when Idalene Berry had unabashedly, and to the dismay of the other ladies, taken him by the arm and led him straight down the center aisle to the third row from the front of the church, as if they were courting. He'd humored her by chatting quietly for a few minutes before the service had begun, but when the song leader had announced the opening hymn, he'd welcomed the interruption and made a joyful noise unto the Lord as never before.

However, at the close of the ceremony, Idalene immediately picked up where she'd left off, apparently determined to monopolize his attention while holding the other women at bay. She spoke about the wonderful music, the preacher's fine message, the friendliness of the people, and even the lovely sunshine pouring through the open windows. He thought the whole thing almost amusing, as he'd never considered himself a female magnet, especially with his unkempt hair, secondhand clothing, and otherwise rugged appearance—not to mention the fact that he'd been around so few ladies over the past two years, he hardly remembered the proper way to act in their presence. When Idalene looped her hand through his arm again, it caught him off guard; but, not wanting to hurt her feelings, he didn't remove it. He just proceeded down the center aisle, certain that she would release him once they stepped outside.

The center aisle quickly filled with attendees endeavoring to make their way to the back of the church, many conversing with one another as they moved like cattle on the way to market. Idalene kept up a constant chatter, but Jess managed to make out only mere bits and pieces because of his resolve to pinpoint just where Grace had been sitting—or if she and Conrad had made it to church at all. He soon discovered them working their way to the back via the outside aisle, which appeared to be just as clogged as the center one. At the sight of Conrad's hand firmly planted at the middle region of Grace's back, a possessiveness came over Jess, though he knew that, as her fiancé, Conrad had the right to touch her. By contrast, Jess had no claim on her whatsoever—hadn't, ever since he'd disappeared and been presumed dead. If only things could return to the way they had been before he'd set off for England. He could kick himself a hundred times for taking that job against her wishes.

He noticed Conrad bending forward to say something in Grace's ear, to which she merely nodded and continued facing forward, with an apparent goal of escaping the crowd. Was concern for Aunt Iris the reason for her haste? Jess wondered whether the woman's health had improved, held steady, or declined since last he'd seen her.

As Jess and Idalene proceeded up the aisle, at the same pace as Conrad and Grace, it soon became apparent that they were going to meet in the middle. His heart stuttered at the thought of coming face-to-face with the two of them—together—for the first time. As politely as possible, he tried to unlatch himself from Idalene, but she was having none of it. The woman had turned into a regular leech.

Conrad's eyes met his, and the guy gave a token nod that fell far short of sincere. "Well, if it isn't Mr. Quinn. Good seeing you again." He turned to Grace. "Darling, did I tell you I had the pleasure of meeting your former fiancé?"

Grace met Jess's gaze, then quickly skimmed over Idalene's face. He could have been mistaken, but he swore he saw something akin to fury in those dark diamond eyes that glimmered and sparked. "No, you didn't mention it, but Jess told—"

She'd nearly slipped and told him that she knew, thanks to Jess—which would have clued Conrad in on the fact that the two of them had spoken alone. Jess gave an inward chuckle. Then he whisked over her blunder by slapping Conrad on the upper arm, perhaps a little harder than necessary. "Yes, awfully good seeing you again, Hall."

"Fiancé?" Idalene asked, clenching Jess's arm a little tighter.

"Former," Conrad clarified.

"I see."

A traffic jam of sorts kept them stalled where they were. Idalene took advantage of the halt in progress by outstretching her free hand to Grace. "I'm Idalene Berry. And you are…?"

Ever courteous, Grace extended her hand, as well, and they shook. "Grace Fontaine. And this"—she gave a hasty glance at Conrad, but Jess noticed a lack of warmth in her eyes—"is my fiancé, Conrad Hall. Nice to meet you, um—Idalene." She cleared her throat. "How long have— That is, when did you two...?"

"Oh! We—us?" Idalene giggled. "Well, gracious, we just met, didn't we, Jess? He was most eager to share a pew with me this morning, and I must say we have enjoyed getting to know each other."

Eager? Jess wouldn't go anywhere near that far. But, at the risk of embarrassing Idalene, he didn't dispute her assertion. He noticed how she clutched even more firmly to his arm, as if to signify ownership. He would need to set her straight, and soon. For the moment, though, he quite enjoyed the interesting expression Grace made, pursing her lips in a forced smile.

The line of people began to move forward again, so the four of them did, as well, Conrad urging Grace to take the lead, his hand still pressed to the center of her back. Grace granted Jess the tiniest of glances as she passed in front of him, and he had the strongest desire to reach across the space that separated them and snag hold of her, take her in his arms, and kiss her. She was the only one he loved. The only one he longed for. Yet he could only watch, helpless, as another man laid claim to her.

20

$\mathcal{O}$n Monday morning, Aunt Iris had strength enough to come down to the sunroom that faced the backyard gardens for a cup of tea and a biscuit with a bit of honey drizzled on top. She drank all the tea and digested half the biscuit before her appetite dwindled, but it was more than she'd had the morning before. In private, Doc Trumble had told Grace a few days ago that if her aunt didn't increase her food intake, she would decline at a much faster rate going forward. His intimation had ripped at her heart, but she couldn't fault him for his honesty. He'd forced her to face the cold reality of Aunt Iris's condition—that she was indeed dying, and that, while good days were always a possibility, such as the Sunday when she'd felt well enough to attend church, the bad days were sure to start outnumbering them. The statement had also caused Grace to rethink Conrad's suggestion that they move up the wedding date.

Solomon stepped into the sunroom and asked if either of them needed anything, and Grace assured him that they didn't. He then announced his plans to drive into town for supplies, saying he'd return before noon. Blanche and Ellen were busy changing bedsheets, shaking out rugs, and sweeping and dusting the upstairs bedrooms, he'd said, and the cooks were giving the kitchen a thorough cleaning. "Won't be long now 'fore that weddin' takes place. We gots a lot to do in the way of preparation."

Just how would Solomon react if she announced the possibility of moving up the date? She didn't want to think about it. The mere thought set her heart to sprinting, and she couldn't tell if her nervous jitters came more from excitement or from trepidation. Lately, when she pictured herself as a bride processing down the grand staircase of Brockwell Manor, she got a blurry image of Jess standing there waiting for her instead of Conrad, and it frightened her no end. How could she be thinking such things with her marriage to Conrad just weeks away? Yes, she'd once loved Jess with all her being, but she'd adjusted to his being dead, for goodness' sake! His coming to Paris had complicated everything and completely unnerved her. Further, seeing him at church with another woman yesterday had only confused her the more. The outright jealousy she'd felt at the sight of that woman clinging to his arm not only surprised her, it outraged her. Blessed saints! She'd turned into an indecisive ninny.

Aunt Iris cleared her throat. "I wish to speak to you about a few things." Her voice carried a determined strength, despite its shakiness.

"Yes, Auntie."

Nellie treaded in nearly unnoticed and removed their breakfast dishes, leaving their water glasses behind, then slipped back out just as quietly. Aunt Iris fiddled with the lace doily under her glass, her fingers trembling. "I've been thinking about this big house. I mentioned it earlier, but you asked that we discuss it later. Now seems like a good time to me."

Grace sat forward and issued a silent prayer for wisdom in her reaction to whatever it was that her aunt wanted to say. "All right, then. What did you have in mind?"

Aunt Iris glanced up. "When I first mentioned that the manor would one day be yours, your first response was dismissive. You told me that you didn't need this big house."

Again, Grace prayed for the right words. "Indeed. I know you have loved Brockwell Manor, and it's suited you perfectly, but you were a socialite in your day and entertained many dignitaries. That's just not who I am, Auntie."

"As humble and soft-spoken as he was, your uncle knew many people of influence, and it was my responsibility to host many social events. While I acknowledge that today is a different era, the house goes to you, regardless. Have you and your fiancé"—she spoke the word almost as if it pained her—"discussed any alternatives for its use?"

"Conrad and I have not discussed the matter, but I did talk to Jess—"

She stopped abruptly when it occurred to her, in a most unsettling way, that it was Jess in whom she'd confided with regard to the manor, not Conrad. How would he react if he discovered her error? Moreover, what would he say about the entire notion of turning the mansion into a home for ailing elderly folks? For that matter, what would Aunt Iris say? She decided that now was as good a time as any to broach the subject with her.

"Do you recall my telling you about Mr. Turnbull, the man who spoke at the ladies' picnic at church? He expressed a serious need for a medical facility to lend aid to the sick and aging of our community who have no close relatives to assist them. Many are dying for sheer lack of care."

Aunt Iris's aging eyes sparked with interest, and she gave a slow nod. "Keep going."

Something like a small fire ignited at the base of Grace's chest and started to burn with passion. "Well, I was thinking that at some point— not right away, mind you, but after plenty of prayer and sage counsel— we could look into the possibility of converting the manor into just such a place." She had ceased to breathe while stumbling awkwardly over the sentence.

"Well, forevermore, you don't have to be so timid about bringing this idea to the forefront," her aunt said in a scolding tone. "You act as if I'm going to jump all over you for even considering such a thing."

Grace jerked back her head and felt her eyes grow large. It had been a while since she'd heard this sort of spunk come out of Aunt Iris. She smiled. "Are you?"

"Good gracious, no. You might not believe this," Aunt Iris said, continuing to finger the doily on the table, "but ever since you told me about the gentleman who spoke at the ladies' picnic, I've had similar thoughts about this big old place. When your uncle John built it for me, we had it in our heads that we would someday fill its hallways with a passel of children. Who knows? It could be that the good Lord had plans way back then to fill it with a passel of elderly folks, instead. Of course, I'm not foolish enough to think I'll ever see such a thing come to fruition. But if it's my blessing you're seeking for such a project, then, child, you have it."

Instant tears formed in Grace's eyes and started to drip down her cheeks. "Really, Auntie?" She pushed her chair back and scurried around the table to embrace her aunt.

Iris held up a bony wrist. "Now, don't go getting all mushy on me. You know that's not my style."

Disregarding the remark, Grace gently wrapped both arms around her aunt, alarmed to find there was so little to hug, and planted a light kiss on her paper-thin cheek. Then she pulled out the chair next to Aunt Iris and sat down. "I haven't the foggiest idea how to go about initiating such a thing, but with his knowledge of law and legal proceedings, Conrad should know just what to do."

"We should draw up the paperwork while I'm still of sound mind," her aunt suggested.

"So soon?"

Aunt Iris picked up a napkin and carefully wiped away the wetness on Grace's cheeks. The gesture only made the tears start up again. "Child, we don't have long to dwell on this."

"But nothing need be settled ahead of time. I now know you approve of the idea, and Conrad will help me—"

"Do you really believe Conrad will be in favor of such a thing—turning this estate into a home for the elderly?" Her aunt raised an eyebrow at her.

"Why wouldn't he be? It's a very worthy endeavor that would bode well for him in his career. Besides, it's not as if the entire house would be converted. We will have to section off at least part of it for our own dwelling, or perhaps build a smaller house somewhere on the property. Of course, the staff will remain in their upstairs quarters."

Aunt Iris cocked her head slightly to one side. "Has the suspicion ever crossed your mind that Conrad might want to marry you primarily for your inheritance?"

Grace suppressed a gasp of shock at the implication. "No, of course not. His own aunt left him with plenty of money."

"Did she? Have you ever sought to learn more about his background? I understand his wealthy, unwed aunt took him in. Did he have no other relatives who could have helped to raise him?"

"I don't know."

"You don't know." Aunt Iris pursed her lips for a pensive moment. "He did tell you that his father died in a train crash and his mother perished of consumption, correct?"

"Well, actually, it was the other way around. His mother died in the train accident on her way back from visiting her sister, his aunt. That particular aunt was the one who took him in. It was his father who developed the awful disease."

Aunt Iris grimaced. "Why would he tell me the opposite? I clearly remember our conversation."

As did Grace. She'd been standing around the corner when she'd overheard him answering Aunt Iris's question about his parents, but his later explanation for his blunder made perfect sense. Her mind cluttered with silly doubts. "He merely misspoke, that's all."

"I see." Clearly, her aunt wasn't convinced. "Regardless, you should endeavor to learn everything possible about him before you say your vows. I believe that his success in sweeping you off your feet was due, at least in part, to his having found you at a particularly vulnerable point in your life."

"Oh, Auntie, listen to yourself. Didn't Uncle John do the same to you?"

"It was different with us. He had my parents' blessing, and, in fact, they convinced me he was right for me even before I'd convinced myself."

Gloom started seeping into the recesses of Grace's mind, replacing her earlier joy. "Are you implying that we don't have your blessing?"

Aunt Iris drew an unsteady breath. "Well, I certainly don't recall Mr. Hall's ever having asked for it."

"Auntie, I assure you it was purely an oversight. I'll speak with Conrad about it before he comes to see you tonight. I'm so sorry for having slighted you. Please forgive me."

A silent pause stretched between them before her aunt spoke again. "What of your Jess Quinn?"

"He's not 'my' Jess Quinn, Aunt Iris. Besides, I saw him sitting with another woman at church yesterday, someone by the name of Idalene Berry."

Aunt Iris gasped, which provoked a coughing spell. Grace stood and started patting her frantically on the back, worried that she'd choke. Zelda and Nellie flew into the room, their eyes wild with concern. They all hovered over her and assisted in whatever way they could, offering her sips of water and stroking her back for what seemed like several minutes but was probably more like seconds. At last, she regained control, raised her palm at the three of them, and put the other hand over her chest. "Good grief," she mumbled. "I liked to have died on the spot—and not from those ghastly tumors, either. Zelda, Nellie, please. I'm fine. Go back about your business." The ladies remained stationary until Grace gave them a nod. Even then, they retreated with hesitant steps and worried expressions. Grace sat back down, tentative herself.

"Mr. Quinn brought a woman to church, you say?"

"I don't know as he *brought* her. I believe they met at the service, and he invited her to sit with him."

Iris picked up a napkin and dabbed at her eyes, which were still wet due to her coughing spasm. "I see. And how did you feel about that?"

"I...." Grace had no idea how to answer, since she hadn't known how or what to feel. They sat in prolonged silence.

"Jealous, that's how you felt."

"Auntie."

"And don't try to deny it. You once loved him, remember?"

"I know, but I'm engaged to another."

"Yes, yes, you needn't keep reminding me."

Grace sighed. Outside, a rumble of distant thunder alerted her to an impending storm. She glanced out the window of the sunroom and saw that the sky had gone completely dark.

How perfectly the weather mirrored the emotions in her heart.

21

For at least the tenth time, Conrad fingered the small violet-colored bottle in his jacket pocket and tried to tamp down his raging nerves. He'd thoroughly researched the properties of arsenic and had discovered that one tablespoon would cause almost sudden death in an adult, while a teaspoon here and a teaspoon there, administered over time, would cause violent illness leading to eventual death. He'd already decided that he didn't want to kill Iris Brockwell—the cancer would do that trick in due course. He merely wanted to hurry the process along. Surely, seeing a sudden decline in her aunt's health would motivate Grace to move up their wedding date. He would remind her how important it was for Aunt Iris to witness their vows, and how, if she didn't, Grace would regret it for the rest of her life.

That being the case, slipping a mere trace of the deadly liquid into her cup of tea just had to work in his favor. The difficulty would lie in putting it there without anyone catching him. Hence his insistence on meeting alone with her. If he could pull that off, he could pull off anything.

As he guided his horse up the long drive leading to the enormous estate, the carriage rolled along at a slow, steady pace. His heart, on the other hand, raced like an animal gone wild. From his position on the carriage seat, he admired once again the splendid mansion and envisioned the entire place being his someday soon—perhaps sooner than he'd even imagined.

When he parked the carriage in the circle drive, Grace stepped outside to greet him, a timorous smile on her alluring face, as if something nagged at her. He dismissed the notion, quickly descended from the vehicle, and went to her, their paths intersecting in the middle of the driveway. Upon reaching her, he took her in his arms. She smelled of lavender soap, and it thrilled him to think she'd prettied herself up just for his arrival. It would always be this way, she fancying up before he returned home from a hard day at the office. She would greet him with assurances that all was in order; would have his daily newspaper spread out in the library, the evening meal prepared, and a cold, refreshing drink awaiting him on the stand next to his favorite chair.

He held her at arm's length. "I could get very used to you greeting me in this manner, my darling." Then he leaned forward and kissed her forehead. "How is your aunt today? I trust she's still expecting me."

"She is, but...but I need to speak to you first, if you don't mind."

"Why should I mind, sweetheart? You know you can talk to me about anything." He kissed her cheek and then, squeezing her shoulder, led her to a pair of wooden lounge chairs situated under a nearby shade tree. Overhead, a pair of crows argued back and forth. The thunderstorm that had swept through Paris earlier that day had left the air hot and heavy, and the sky was still overcast, the sun having made only a few appearances throughout the day.

Once they had sat down and angled themselves toward each other, their knees touching, he took her hands in both of his. "Now, what was it you wanted to say?"

She swallowed hard, and in her eyes, he detected a glint of anxiety. "A couple of things, actually."

He didn't know why, but his stomach lurched as an unbidden thought came to mind. This didn't have anything to do with Jess Quinn, did it? "Go on, then," he urged her, dread plaguing his gut.

"Aunt Iris and I had quite a long talk this morning about several matters, but we mostly talked about the estate...and also our engagement."

He relaxed somewhat, but then he tensed again. "Oh? What about our engagement?"

"Well, she expressed disappointment that we never sought her blessing with regard to our betrothal. And as for the mansion, we discussed its future, primarily what purpose it might serve."

He didn't much care about the blessing part, but the matter of the estate's future certainly made him sit straighter. He chose his next words carefully. "I guess I didn't think it necessary to ask her permission for your hand, since we're two grown adults, and it's usually a father's blessing one seeks, anyway. But I'll certainly try to make that right with her today."

Grace smiled, although he noticed that the expression didn't quite reach her eyes. "Thank you. Aunt Iris can be quite old-fashioned."

"What are her concerns about the estate? Is she worried you won't take proper care of it—or that you'll fire the staff? In my opinion, they—"

"No, no, that's not it at all. This pertains to what we might do with the estate and the surrounding property. I've learned that Aunt Iris wishes to donate Brockwell Manor, and a good share of the grounds, to Henry County—with the stipulation that the staff remain for as long as they so desire. She's designated a generous stipend for all of them, particularly for Solomon Turner. Naturally, she will see that I am also left with a reasonable settlement, probably much more than I need or even deserve."

He felt his spine stiffen like a steel rod but tried to keep his expression calm. "I don't think I understand this—this donation to Henry County." His throat went as dry as sand.

"Well, naturally, you don't. And why should you?" She gave a nervous giggle. "That's why I'm bringing it up with you now. You see, this morning, Aunt Iris and I were talking about the possibility of using the manor as a sick bay for the elderly. Being a nurse, I would be able to lend my skills and do exactly what I believe God has called me—"

"A sick bay for the elderly?" Had he heard her correctly? Sheer anger flamed in his chest.

"Yes!" She barely seemed to take a breath. "Did I ever tell you about the ladies' picnic I attended and the man who spoke about the dire need in this community for some sort of facility that would provide care for those who have no family nearby?"

Conrad frowned. "You may have mentioned something about it, but I hardly think...." His head was a muddle of panic and confusion, not to mention disdain for the outrageous notion. No way would he approve such a preposterous suggestion. At the same time, he had to play his cards with utmost care. "What I mean to say is, a three-story estate is hardly conducive to elderly care. Many modifications would have to be made in order to render it usable for such a purpose."

"I do realize the manor isn't properly set up at the moment, but I also knew that you, as a lawyer, would have ideas, not to mention the necessary legal resources, to iron out the specific details pertaining to any potential obstacles. Naturally, the plans would fall to an architect and contractor. Aunt Iris has the financial resources to make it happen. The stairs can be a problem, but Aunt Iris, even in her state, has been able to manage them with assistance. An elevator would certainly prove helpful, and I'm most certain an architect could easily draw that into the plans. Many of the rooms are much too large and lavish, but the architect could design a configuration of new walls to divide them into smaller quarters, thereby increasing the number of patients we could accommodate."

"And just where do you propose *we* live?" He figured he may as well play along. Let her entertain her little fantasy. Because that was all it would ever be—a fantasy.

"Aunt Iris thought my idea of a much smaller home somewhere on the property sounded reasonable—something large enough for an eventual family, of course, but nothing as massive as this place. There again, an architect would prove helpful."

"Yes." He skipped over her mention of a family. He'd wondered when the topic of children would arise between them. Of course, it would have to be now. He chose to ignore it for the time being.

"This is something that will take a lot of forethought and extra planning," he pointed out. If he had his way, no architect or contractor would ever get as much as one second of their time, nor would there be any sort of contribution to Henry County.

The corners of her mouth curved upward in a hopeful smile. "Oh, I know, I know. There will be months of planning necessary to be sure everything is done correctly and according to regulations. You must admit, it is a worthy cause. How wonderful to have this opportunity to support this fine city and county. I think we will call it 'Brockwell Manor Medical Facility,' or maybe 'The Iris Brockwell Home for the Sick and Aging.' But then, I'm jumping way ahead, aren't I?"

Her enthusiasm was extremely off-putting. "Worthy?" Conrad sputtered. "Um, yes, but…well, it would've been nice if you hadn't sprung the idea on me so abruptly."

Her smile disappeared, her lower lip jutting out in a tiny pout. "I'm sorry, Conrad. It's just that Aunt Iris and I talked about it for the first time at breakfast this morning. Until today, it was nothing more than a silly notion in my head. It's her home, and I didn't want to allow myself to hope for such an eventuality unless I knew she would approve of the idea. That's why I thought it best to speak with her first. I'm sorry if I did it backward. It's just that, all along, I've wondered what in the world I'd ever do with this monstrosity of a mansion once she willed it into my hands."

"Monstrosity?" He could barely believe his ears.

"I don't mean that in a negative way. This wonderful estate has served its purpose well, accommodating large groups of dignitaries for dinner parties and various political functions. My aunt has hosted a countless number of teas and other charitable events. She once told me that she and Uncle John even entertained the governor of Tennessee a time or two, back in the fifties. Isn't that amazing? This house has a wonderful history, but it would be unfair of me—of *us*, I should say—to keep it to ourselves. Why, it wouldn't even be Christian."

He attempted to tamp down his bottomless exasperation, afraid that if he didn't, he would say something he'd soon regret—something that would cause her to question his love for her or, worse, her wisdom in marrying him.

"Well, it's certainly something we can discuss in the future," he finally said. He could only hope she didn't sense his insincerity.

"Aunt Iris would like to draw up the papers as soon as possible. She intends to speak to you about it tonight."

He sat forward a bit and squinted down at her. "What papers?"

"The papers stating her wishes regarding the future of the estate. I told her you would be happy to get them started for her—unless you prefer that I speak to Mr. Wadsworth, since he has been her financial adviser and representative for all these years and does have her will and testament in his possession. Right now, it simply states that everything will go to me. But since I've discussed these alternate plans with her and gotten her approval, I would like to have it put in writing, as would Aunt Iris. I suppose Mr. Wadsworth—"

"No, no, that's fine. I'll speak to Gerald myself."

She gazed at him with hopeful eyes. "You approve, then?"

"Yes, darling," he barely managed to say. "But you do understand this isn't something that's going to happen in a day, don't you?"

"Certainly, Conrad. You don't think I'm that naive, do you?"

He took her chin in his palm and smiled, then leaned forward and kissed the tip of her nose. "Not for one second."

As he uttered the falsehood, he felt the weight of the violet-colored bottle in his pocket and knew he needed to place a few more drops of the noxious liquid into Iris Brockwell's tea than originally planned. Unfortunately for her, he hadn't a second to waste.

Grace took him to the living room, where Iris Brockwell sat waiting for him, her sunken eyes making her look almost skeletal. He removed his hat and dipped his head in a quick bow. "Good evening, ma'am. It's very nice to see you. You're looking quite fine."

"Yes, Auntie, indeed you are," Grace agreed. "Did you get a good rest?"

The woman scoffed. "Either I'm looking better than I feel, or you're both exaggerating. Come in, Mr. Hall. Have a seat right there." With nary a smile, she pointed at a gilded French armchair identical to the one she sat in, on the other side of a small coffee table. "You may leave us, Grace." As usual, the woman minced few words.

Grace gave an uneasy smile as her eyes passed from her aunt to Conrad. Because his stomach had formed a painful knot, he had no grin of reassurance to give her in return.

"Would you mind seeing to it that the kitchen staff provides us with some hot tea?"

No sooner had he spoken the request than Solomon entered. "Yes, suh. The tea is on the way, along with some wafers. I trust you's well, suh."

"Yes, I'm fine, Solomon. We'll await the tea, then."

Solomon bowed and left the room, and Grace followed him.

Alone at last with the vinegary woman, Conrad situated himself on the chair, wondering just how he would manage to add a few drops of the venomous liquid to her cup without her seeing. It was the only part of the plan he hadn't been able to prearrange in his head.

"I understand you suggested to Grace that it might be to your advantage to move up your wedding date." Mrs. Brockwell's voice had a shaky quality to it, but it certainly didn't lack resolve. He couldn't help but admire her for it. Considering the fragile state of her health and her rack-of-bones appearance, he wondered how she'd managed to hang on this long.

"Just to set the record straight, I'm not in favor of it."

He crossed one knee over the other and picked a tiny stray leaf off the woolen fabric of his pant leg. Beads of sweat had popped out across his forehead, so he removed his neatly folded handkerchief from his front jacket pocket and swiped at his brow. He couldn't imagine drinking anything hot right now. Actually, he could use something strong to calm his nerves, never mind that he wasn't a regular drinker—unless Lorinda was pouring. Those were about the only times he had the urge to imbibe.

"I love her very much, and I'm most anxious to make her my bride," he offered by way of explanation.

"I see. Your wanting to rush the process doesn't have anything to do with Jess Quinn's appearance on the scene, does it?"

Good thing the tea hadn't come yet. If he'd had a cup in his hand, he might have spilled it. "Of course not. I'm very confident of Grace's love for me."

A woman from the kitchen staff walked in carrying a tray on which were balanced a silver teapot and two dainty teacups, along with a plate of delicate-looking cookies. He had neither the desire nor the appetite for either, with his stomach roiling at the thought of what lay ahead. The woman set the silver tray on the table between him and Mrs. Brockwell, then picked up the teapot and prepared to pour.

"Here, allow me," he offered.

She stopped mid-pour and set the silver pot back down, casting him a stupefied glance. She clearly wasn't accustomed to ceding her jobs to others.

When she didn't move, just stood there staring at him, he said, "You're dismissed." He found no small thrill in the way that she bowed slightly, turned, and exited the room without hesitation.

"Let me serve you, ma'am." He scooted forward in his chair, lifted the pot, and poured the steaming liquid into one of the cups, his nervous hands making pouring difficult. Thankfully, Mrs. Brockwell didn't seem to notice. Now to figure out a way to administer the special ingredient.

"I take a dash of sugar with my tea," she muttered.

"Yes, ma'am." He lifted the lid of the sugar bowl and found it full. "Oh, it appears the help forgot to fill it. I'll just take your cup to the kitchen."

"Never mind, then." She shook her head. "I can go without this one time."

"It's really no problem at all." Standing, he picked up her steaming cup, then left the room and hurried around the corner to the parlor, where he set the cup on the large buffet. He removed the bottle from his pocket, his hands dripping with sweat, and hastened to remove the cork, upturn the bottle, release a few drops of the noxious liquid into the cup, and then replace the cork and drop the bottle back in his pocket.

"Mistuh Hall?" Solomon's voice startled him so that his body lurched. "May I help you with somethin'?"

"Me?" Conrad whirled around to face the butler. "No, no. I—I was just coming into the kitchen for some sugar."

The man's eyes glinted with something like suspicion. "Sugar? I done checked the bowl 'fore Miz Flanders delivered the tray."

"Really? I'm certain it was empty."

"No, suh, I don't believe so." He moved past Conrad and walked into the living room. Conrad followed, his hand that carried the scalding teacup still shaking. Solomon bent to lift the lid on the sugar bowl. "They's plenty o' sugar in here."

"Really? Something must be wrong with my eyes, then. I could have sworn I was looking into an empty sugar bowl." He stepped closer and stared into the small silver container with the ornate design. "Well, I'll be. You're right as rain. Good grief, I'd better get my eyes checked." He let go a gush of laughter, hoping to ease the tension.

Solomon picked up a silver spoon and dipped it into the bowl, then turned toward Conrad, dropped half a spoonful into Iris's cup, and stirred. The big man's eyes never left Conrad's while he agitated the liquid, and for all of ten seconds, the two faced off. As quickly as Conrad had acted, Solomon couldn't possibly have witnessed his scheme. No, the man clearly just didn't like him, no doubt due to the influence of his employer. Well, so be it. Before long, Conrad would be the one controlling the estate and setting the rules, and he didn't give a rat's tail what the butler thought of him. If he gave him any trouble, he'd just show him the door.

Solomon was first to break the stare when he took the cup from Conrad's grip and passed it down to Mrs. Brockwell. "Careful, ma'am. It be steamin' hot."

She reached up with two unsteady hands and seized the cup. Conrad held his breath when she took a couple of small sips. That sealed it. If the butler had truly suspected something, he wouldn't have let her drink from that cup. Conrad blew out a quiet breath of relief and settled himself back in the chair. "You may leave us now," he said to Solomon as he poured a bit of tea into his own china cup.

"No," Mrs. Brockwell stated. "Sol, why don't you sit yourself down on the sofa? You may as well listen in, since it's you who will be making sure all the wedding details fall into place."

Ire rose in Conrad's chest, but he shoved it back down.

"Yes'm." Without hesitation, Solomon walked to the long divan and lowered himself onto it.

"Mr. Hall wants to move up the wedding date. What do you think about that?"

Solomon's eyes rounded like two boulders. "I think the date of October fifteenth oughtta hold. It's only four or so weeks away. Movin' up the date don't make much sense t' me."

Conrad would have spat at the pitiful man, had Mrs. Brockwell not been in the room. What right had a household servant to speak his mind about such matters?

Mrs. Brockwell took several more small sips of the hot liquid, and he grew intensely excited, if not edgy, having no idea what sort of reaction to expect once the poison traveled through her system. Nor did he know how long it would take to do its work. All sorts of questions rose in his mind. Had he added enough? Too much? Would she keel right over or merely complain of stomach troubles? Would she lose consciousness or remain fully alert? He wished now that he could better remember what he had researched, but his anxiety seemed to be impairing his mental faculties.

"Well, I would at least appreciate your blessing on our marriage," he told Mrs. Brockwell. "That, of course, is of utmost importance to Grace and myself alike."

The frail woman leaned over and shakily set the teacup on the table next to her, then grimaced. "It's hard to bless a union I'm not entirely certain is right."

He sat a bit forward, putting his elbows on his knees and folding his hands. "Surely, you must know how very deeply I love her, Mrs. Brockwell. I will take excellent care of her through the years."

"Hm, yes, and she will take fine care of you."

He didn't like her tone or the obvious implication of her words. "I shall do my best to keep it more the former than the latter."

"I assume she's told you about my wishes for the estate." Her gaze trailed to Solomon. "You've been away on errands a good share of the day, Sol, so I haven't had time to speak with you. But Grace and I have talked about the future of the estate, and I think you'll approve of the decision we have reached."

Solomon pulled his bent spine a bit straighter. "Yes'm. Whatever you decide will be fine with me."

"You're always so good, Sol." She cast the man a warm smile that faded as she turned to Conrad. "Mr. Turner is an overly generous soul. He's been a part of my family for many years, and so I've named him in my will."

"Now, Missus Brockwell, no need to be talkin' 'bout stuff such as that."

"I think that's very…noble," Conrad said, holding his teacup, from which he had yet to take the first sip.

"What sort o' plans did you have in mind for the estate, ma'am?" Solomon asked her.

The woman opened her mouth, but before she could answer, she winced and clutched her stomach.

"Ma'am?" Solomon stood as fast as his aging body would allow.

The lady's wrinkled face went instantly pale. "I'm not…feeling so well."

"Mrs. Brockwell?" Conrad got to his feet and stepped in front of her at precisely the same moment she uttered a groan and spewed a stream of bilious vomit that hit him square in the chest. He staggered backward, overcome with revulsion, and it took all the strength he could muster to keep his own stomach from rebelling. At the same time, the entire household came running from every direction, Grace arriving first.

"Aunt Iris, are you all right?" She bent over her aunt and looked into her dazed, confused eyes, getting no response. "Solomon, quick, ride into town for Doc Trumble."

"Yes'm, right away."

To the kitchen staff, she issued orders to bring wet cloths for cleaning up her aunt—there was no mention of Conrad's sullied jacket. From the house staff, she asked for assistance in getting the elderly woman to the divan so she could recline. Mrs. Brockwell moaned and closed her eyes. Was she dying, then? He could only hope.

Rather than assist the ladies, he stood helplessly by, his own stomach continuing to roil.

"I think I'm feeling a bit better," the woman mumbled after a few minutes of mollycoddling.

Blast it all! That was not the response Conrad had been expecting.

"Just the same, you'll lie still till Doc Trumble arrives," Grace told her.

The members of the kitchen staff hurried back to the room with a basin of soapy water and a cloth, and they set to cleaning her up.

Finally, Grace angled her head to look at Conrad. "Oh, dear. It looks like you'll need to have that suit jacket laundered."

22

Grace, Zelda, Nellie, Blanche, and Ellen all hovered over Aunt Iris until the older woman finally closed her eyes and slept, her breathing labored but steady. Her emaciated cheeks, temporarily drained of all color, were finally returning to their original, sallow shade. The only one not sticking close was Conrad; he'd nestled himself in a chair across the room next to the parlor entry, looking a little pallid himself. If Grace were to describe his expression, she would have called it "fatigued" and perhaps "a trifle irritated." She imagined it was because the evening hadn't gone as he'd hoped it would, considering that he'd barely had a chance to talk to Aunt Iris before she'd taken ill.

"It's probably a good thing that she cleared her stomach," Doc Trumble said. "What has she had to eat today?"

"Not much," Zelda answered. "She had some tea and part of a biscuit with honey this mornin'. Then, fo' lunch, she sipped on a bit o' chicken broth and downed half a cup o' coffee. I couldn't get her to eat more 'n a couple o' bites of bread for supper, but she didn't do no spittin' up till after she done sipped on that hot tea she had whilst sittin' here with Mistuh Hall an' Solomon. I think that new medicine you done gave her has helped with the nausea. Well, until tonight, that is. I guess them tumors are gettin' the better of 'er."

Solomon reentered the room, having gone to empty the basin of water and to rinse out the cloths. He'd also tended to Conrad's soiled jacket, a task Grace probably should have taken care of herself. But right now, her main concern rested with Aunt Iris.

Doc Trumble stared down at his patient. "She's resting now, and that's a good thing. Her vital signs are still strong, and she feels warm to the touch, which means her circulation is still good. I'm not sure this particular episode relates to the tumors. I don't know why she vomited, particularly since you say she ate very little today—unless the tea was bad. Did you happen to use old water?"

"No, Doc, o' course not. It comes fresh from the well every day, and we keep it cold in the icebox," Zelda said.

Solomon turned his body and cast Conrad a long, curious stare, one that Grace didn't understand. Conrad rose from his chair and advanced on Grace, putting an arm around her shoulder and drawing her to him, perhaps in an effort to lend comfort. "Will she make it through the night, Doctor?" he asked. Grace appreciated his concern.

All eyes fell to the older gentleman. "I'd say she'll pull through, yes."

Grace felt a whoosh of air come out of Conrad. "Well, that's—a relief, now, isn't it?" he said.

"She's a tough cookie," said the doctor with a half smile. "I don't think anyone but Iris knows exactly how sick she is, and she certainly isn't one to complain—even to me."

Grace inwardly agreed. Aunt Iris rarely shared her physical condition, often making light of it with pat answers like "I'm as fine as feather hair," even as she winced with pain. Still, it did comfort her to hear the doctor say that her vital signs remained strong.

"I'm afraid I must be going," Conrad announced to the lot of them. "I shall be in deep prayer for Mrs. Brockwell tonight." And to Grace, he said, "Walk me to the door, darling?"

"Of course."

The others bade him a good evening, and the pair headed for the entryway. As they turned to go, Grace noticed Solomon casting Conrad another peculiar stare. She crumpled her brow at him, but he was too busy looking at Conrad to notice.

Out on the front terrace, Conrad grasped her upper arms and bent to kiss her forehead. "Unfortunately, I didn't acquire your aunt's blessing on our marriage. She took ill so suddenly. I hope you'll consider tonight's incident as a warning that we do need to hurry things along if you wish for her to witness our vows."

Grace's stomach twisted with inexplicable dread. "Did she have a chance to talk to you about her wishes for the estate?"

"Well, she started to, but that's about the gist of it."

"When will you start drawing up the papers so that Aunt Iris can sign them?"

"Soon, my dear." He touched her nose. "No need to worry yourself over it."

"All right, then. I assume you'll speak to Mr. Wadsworth about the matter."

"Absolutely. He will probably want to advise me on it, as well. As I said, don't worry. We'll settle this shortly. You do know I'll need to return to Chicago very soon."

"Already? But it seems that you were just there."

He smiled. "This trip won't take more than a couple of days."

"When are you leaving?"

"Early Monday morning, a week from today."

Grace sighed, then swallowed in an effort to keep from crying. It was difficult to control her nerves, a reminder that she hadn't been giving her worries over to the Lord. "Thank you for praying for Aunt Iris. We all appreciate it."

"Of course." Beyond his silhouette, the moonlight gleamed off a distant hillside, giving it an ethereal glow. "I can't wait to make you mine, Grace. Very soon."

She touched his brow, dotted with perspiration. "We will be married soon, dear. October fifteenth is fast approaching."

He cupped her cheek with his palm. "Not soon enough for me, darling." Without warning, he planted a hard, demanding kiss on her mouth and then, just as quickly, stepped back. "You're mine, and I don't want you forgetting it." He stood stern and unmoving, staring deep into her eyes, as if willing her to challenge his claim.

She shifted her weight and examined his countenance, trying to recall what it was about him that had made her fall so madly in love. She began to panic when it didn't immediately come to her. "You worry too much," she managed.

Her answer must have satisfied him, for he silently nodded, then turned and walked to his carriage. She stood there and watched until he turned onto Nobles Road.

Over the next couple of days, Aunt Iris improved enough so that, by Wednesday, Grace felt confident enough to leave her for a few hours. The Reverend Lucas and Joy Jennings had invited her for dinner, and she didn't want to cancel on them, although they surely would have understood her reasons for declining. In truth, she sincerely anticipated the opportunity to bare her soul to another woman. Lately, so many questions had been pestering her mind and plaguing her heart.

Solomon dropped her at the parsonage at six o'clock on the dot. Upon her arrival, the preacher came out to tell Solomon that he would gladly drive her back to the manor later. At first, Solomon wouldn't hear of it, but with a bit of persuading, the butler finally gave in.

Dinner was most pleasant, with lively conversation and plenty of laughter. Grace couldn't even put into words how much she relished the chance to escape the all-too-quiet mansion that forever carried a sense of foreboding. Young Annie entertained them with her animated stories, and baby Naomi, awake and happy, smiled widely from her daddy's lap. Their big, friendly dog, a mutt named Rusty, lay sprawled on the floor nearby, watching closely for any morsel of food that the young Annie might drop.

Midway through the meal, Naomi started yawning and rubbing her eyes, so while the rest of them ate, Lucas excused himself to go put her in her crib upstairs. By the time he returned, everyone else had finished eating.

Joy pushed her chair back. "I hope you like apple pie, Grace."

"Oh, my goodness, I do, but I'm so full already."

"Nonsense. There's always room for dessert." She started to rise, but Lucas stopped her, saying that he and Annie would carry the dishes to the kitchen and also serve the pie and coffee.

"Why, thank you, honey," Joy said, her face beaming at her husband's kindness. For the life of her, Grace couldn't picture Conrad ever serving her in the way that Lucas did Joy. She could, however, envision Jess doing so, and that troubled her.

When Lucas and Annie had left the room, Joy reached over and pressed a hand to Grace's arm. "You must tell me how you're feelin' 'bout your approachin' weddin'. Are you nervous? Excited? Apprehensive? Overwhelmed?"

"My goodness, so many adjectives," Grace said with a tiny giggle. "All of the above, I suppose."

Joy smiled. "Mostly excited, I'd assume."

"My emotions are so scattered, I can't really pinpoint any particular one. We should probably add 'confused' to the list."

Joy's face held no hint of surprise. "Might that have t' do with the arrival of a certain Jess Quinn in town?"

"You're perceptive, indeed."

"Not really." Joy shrugged. "I'm a woman, so I can imagine your dilemma. D'you still love Mr. Quinn?"

The question should have set her aback, but it didn't. She'd come to appreciate Joy's no-nonsense approach. No one could accuse her of beating around the bush. "I honestly don't know. I do know that when I saw him seated with another woman at church on Sunday, a Miss Idalene Berry, it made me feel...well, jealous, which makes no sense at all."

Joy nodded. "I noticed the two o' them sittin' together, but I didn't recognize her. D'you think you should marry Mr. Hall if you're experiencin' this sort o' thing?"

"Well, I...I keep thinking that once I marry Conrad, any doubts will dissipate."

Joy raised her blonde eyebrows. "That's yer rationale? What if it don't turn out as you plan? What if you spend the remainder of yer life regrettin' yer decision?"

She opened her mouth to respond at the same moment Lucas and Annie entered the room carrying dessert. Annie placed a slice of pie in front of Grace, and Lucas served his wife. "I'll get your coffee," he told them, "and while you two enjoy some more private conversation, Annie and I will take our desserts outside, then go out to the barn to tend to the animals. You two take your time, and, Grace, when you're ready to leave, Annie and I will take you back to the manor. It's a nice night for a drive."

"You're too kind," Grace said.

"Not really. I just recognize the importance of leaving women alone when they're in the midst of a deep discussion. I'd gladly lend an ear, and even my opinion, but I have a feeling you two have everything under control." He winked at them. "We'll go get your coffee. Come on, Annie." He took the little girl by the hand and led her back to the kitchen. Moments later, they returned, Annie carrying an empty cup and saucer, and Lucas carrying the same, along with a coffeepot. They set everything on the table, then went back to the kitchen for their own desserts before exiting out the back door.

"My, you are a blessed woman," Grace said. "Not many wives have husbands as kind and thoughtful as yours."

"Believe me when I say I don't take that man for granted." Joy chuckled and shook her head. "I still don't understand what he ever saw in me."

"Oh, please, Joy. You have so much to offer, not to mention you're a beauty."

"Well, thank y' kindly, but what I have is a sordid past, somethin' certain members of our congregation didn't consider worthy of a preacher's wife a few years back. But, my goodness, that discussion's for another time and place. Tonight, we talk about you."

Grace had heard only a few tidbits about Joy's past, but even the little that she knew made her respect this woman the more. "I'm rather boring, I'm afraid."

Joy laughed. "You're about to be married. I call that anythin' but boring."

In the next moment, the women dove into their pie and took sips of coffee. Between bites, Joy said, "Well, back to what I asked you earlier. What if you marry Conrad in hopes of forgettin' all about Mr. Quinn, only t' discover you still love Mr. Quinn? Do you truly want to live a life o' regrets? I'm not sayin' Mr. Hall ain't—isn't a good fit for you, but at the same time, you've gotta go with yer heart—and, o' course, you've gotta go in the direction you believe the Lord is leadin' you. Do you feel strong in yer convictions that Conrad Hall is the man the Lord wants you to marry?"

That last question unsettled Grace. She fingered the rim of her coffee cup. "It's funny you should ask that. All along, I've thought that Conrad was one of the reasons God brought me to Paris, but ever since Jess's arrival in town, I don't know what to think. I loved Jess deeply at one time—and perhaps I still do, I just don't want to admit it. I've professed my love to Conrad, so I feel tremendous guilt for thinking I might still have feelings for Jess."

Joy said nothing, just sipped her coffee and leaned in, her eyes intent on Grace.

"Conrad would love to elope and get the whole thing behind us, and I'm sure it's because of Jess's arrival. He doesn't want to give me a single day to dwell on the fact that the man I loved and then thought dead for two years is still very much alive. It has shaken Conrad's sense of security in our relationship. Admittedly, I'd probably feel the same way, were I in his shoes."

Joy's brow crinkled as she studied her coffee cup. "Let's just remove Jess Quinn from the picture altogether for a moment. Would y' say Mr. Hall would still be overly eager to marry you?"

The question seemed odd to Grace, but she answered it anyway. "Yes…why do you ask?"

Joy frowned. "Well, it's been brief, as far as courtships go—and I know somethin' about that. I also personally know very little about Conrad Hall." She bit her lip before continuing. "I shouldn't ask, but I've got to: Does it ever concern you that Conrad might want you for yer inheritance? I mean, have you ever put that partic'lar question to him an' then watched his reaction?"

Grace thought long and hard before responding. "Not in so many words, but I don't think he's after my inheritance. He's successful in his field and makes plenty of money. Besides that, he acquired a substantial inheritance from his own aunt, so he doesn't suffer financially."

Joy gave a knowing smile. "I'm not sayin' this is the case with Conrad, but with some, no amount of money is ever enough. They acquire a little, and all they can think about is gettin' their hands on more. That was the case with Annie's father. I can tell you that pledgin' yerself to the wrong man will bring y' nothin' but grief—not that I'm suggestin' Conrad isn't right for you, only that I speak from experience."

A large knot tightened in Grace's chest. "You aren't the first to suggest that Conrad may have ulterior motives for wanting to marry me. My own aunt doesn't trust him."

"But you do?"

Rampant emotions threatened to unleash a flood of tears, but she held them back. "Like I said earlier, I don't know what to think anymore—or *feel*, for that matter."

Joy covered Grace's hand with her own. "I understand, maybe better than most. I was so madly in love with Annie's father that I could barely think straight. I agreed to marry 'im, not knowin' nearly enough about 'im, thinkin' surely everything would turn out perfect once we said our vows. I wish I'd prayed more about it. I'm certain that, if I had, God would've intervened."

That last statement struck a powerful chord in Grace's heart. Had she ever consulted the Lord in regard to her relationship with Conrad? She found herself doubting the degree to which she'd surrendered her heart to God.

"Somethin' is bubblin' up inside me, and I want to share it," Joy said. "You are a precious gift, Grace—a beautiful, cherished treasure. We all know that gifts are t' be given away, but take care that y' don't give yerself to just anyone. God designed you to love Him first. And in order for us to enjoy a successful, happy union with another individual, we've gotta first love God. Puttin' Him above all others is what makes a marriage work best—God first, others second." She tilted her pretty face at Grace and smiled. "Keepin' our priorities in proper order just makes for a much more joyous existence."

Over the course of the next hour, Joy shared one nugget of truth after another with Grace. When the time came to leave, Grace's head and heart overflowed, not so much with thoughts of Conrad or Jess but with an intense need to dig out her Bible from the bottom drawer of her dresser and reacquaint herself with God's promises to her.

23

On Wednesday, Jess heard from Bill Hansen that Iris Brockwell had taken a turn for the worse on Monday. He decided to leave work early and drive out to the manor to inquire after her. Grace would likely resent his coming, but so be it. He'd found a friend in the elderly woman, and he meant to visit her. For all he knew, it could be his last opportunity to do so.

He left the livery around six that evening. It had been a long, busy day, the weather hot and humid, so he went back to the boardinghouse first to wash up before heading out to Brockwell Manor. What he needed was a visit to the bathhouse for a good, long shower, but there was no time for that now. A sponge bath would have to suffice. If he'd learned one thing about working the livery stables, it was that he wasn't born for the job. It was an honest living, though, and he appreciated the income he drew from it, however meager it was.

Miss Phoebe was dusting bookshelves when he came through the door. She turned, gave him a brief smile, and announced that she'd prepared a pot of beef stew and biscuits. He could have predicted as much, since he'd smelled the delectable aroma on his way up the narrow walk. He bustled upstairs to his room to wash up, then went back down to the dining room and downed a bowl of stew in five minutes flat.

There was an abundance of stew for seconds or even thirds, as no other boarders had shown up for dinner. Miss Phoebe had accommodated a few additional boarders after Mr. Harper's departure, but most of them had stayed for only a night or two. Given the limited facilities, Jess could understand why. He'd told Miss Phoebe that she'd do a better business if she made some improvements around her place, but she'd claimed she didn't have enough money and didn't believe in borrowing it. He'd shrugged and said, "Suit yourself." Still, he worried about her future. She'd apparently never married and had no children and no relatives nearby. How would she survive if her business failed? Or, worse, her health?

"You want another bowl?" she asked, breezing past him with the dust cloth still in hand. "There's plenty to be had."

He polished off the rest of his second biscuit and rubbed his full belly. "Thanks, but that's all right. I'm heading out to Brockwell Manor to pay a call on Mrs. Brockwell. I'm told she's not doing well."

"She won't last much longer, is what I hear."

"I'm afraid you might be right."

She opened the door to the closet beside the kitchen entry, hung the cloth on a hook, and grabbed a corn broom. Leaning on the long handle, she heaved a breath. "Hope that big ol' mansion don't go t' waste."

He had a mind to tell her of Grace's hopes for its use, but the idea wasn't his to share.

After a bit more conversation, he thanked Miss Phoebe for the meal, then excused himself and headed for Brockwell Manor.

As expected, Solomon Turner answered the door. Upon seeing Jess, he gave a friendly grin, his gold tooth gleaming. "Why, if it ain't Mistuh Quinn. Come in, come in. I's sorry t' say Miz Fontaine ain't about."

He was disappointed to learn of Grace's absence. No doubt, Conrad Hall had stolen her away for the evening, which only irked him further. "Actually, I came to check on Mrs. Brockwell. I heard she took a bad turn on Monday."

"Ah, that she did, but she's doin' some better now, all praise to the Lord A'mighty. She's sleepin' now, though, so I'm afraid you won't be able t'visit with 'er."

"That's fine. I mainly wanted to learn her condition. I'm relieved to hear she's some improved."

Solomon nodded. "She had a bad spell with nausea and got real sick. I went for the doc straightaway. He gave her a good lookin' over. Afterward, he seemed mighty puzzled-like, an' said he didn't think her stomach episode correlated with them tumors."

Jess frowned. "What do you mean?"

A sort of mysterious glint lit in the kindly man's eyes. "He suggested might've been somethin' she ate or drank what didn't set right. Thing is, she got sick shortly after drinkin' a bit o' hot tea."

Confused, Jess asked, "Her stomach rebelled at a few sips of tea?"

The large man leaned forward and whispered, "It's plain strange, if y' ask me."

Jess didn't know what to make of his secretive statement. He glanced around and saw no one. "How so?"

Solomon folded his hands in front of him, straightened his somewhat curved spine to the best of his ability, and set his feet close together. "I don't know as I should say, Mistuh Quinn."

Now he had Jess's full attention. "You think there was some sort of foul play?"

The old man's face twisted into a pained frown. "Oh, suh, I ain't sayin' that. No suh, I don't dare say that. But...." He paused, glancing briefly behind him. "See that table there?"

"Yes."

"Well, I see'd Mistuh Hall standin' there, doin' somethin' with Missus Brockwell's teacup."

"Doing something? I don't understand what you mean. He was here when she took ill?"

"Yes, suh. He say he wanted to speak with her 'bout weddin' matters, namely, movin' up the date and gettin' her blessin' on the nuptials. Missus Brockwell ain't in favor o' changin' the date, 'case you didn't know. Anyways, I come round the corner from the kitchen an' sees him doin'somethin' with her tea, but I got no idea what, and I can't even say it was foul play. All I got t' go on is a hunch that he put somethin' in it, but nothin' more. That's why I ain't tellin' nobody but you. I knows I can trust you."

Jess's stomach curdled at the mere thought of Hall doing something malicious to the elderly woman. "But now that you've told me, my hands are just as tied as yours, Solomon. Can you think of anything else that might've been suspicious? Anything at all?"

"No, suh, not a thing. Except...."

"Except what?"

"Well, I asked 'im if he needed anythin', and he looked a little startled at first, then fumbled a bit and said he was jes' comin' to the kitchen fo' some sugar. He tol' me the sugar bowl was empty, but it weren't, Mistuh Quinn, 'cause I done filled it to the brim just before Miz Nellie delivered the tray to the parlor."

"That is odd," Jess admitted, "but it's not proof of anything."

Solomon's suspicions baffled him. He didn't know Conrad Hall well enough to accuse him outright of deliberately causing harm to Mrs. Brockwell, nor could he imagine what he would possibly gain from doing so. After all, the woman was already dying. What purpose could he have in attempting to hasten her demise? None of it made sense—not that he trusted Conrad Hall any more than he trusted a bear roaming around in the same room with him. What he really needed to do was discover more about the attorney—his family background, where he'd grown up, his education, and whether he genuinely loved Grace or was merely after her inheritance. The question remained, where and how to learn these things? It wasn't as if he possessed any investigative skills. He supposed he could start by asking Conrad's colleague Gerald Wadsworth a few innocent questions about his partner. Shoot, he could have done that today when he'd passed him on the sidewalk outside the post office. Instead, he'd merely tipped his hat at the bearded fellow, who didn't know Jess from Adam.

"No, suh, it ain't proof. All I gots to go on is my instinct, and that ain't always accurate." He gave a weak grin.

Jess had tried to come across as nonchalant regarding Grace, but he couldn't resist inquiring as to her whereabouts. "I suppose Grace is with her betrothed right now."

"Actually, she went to the preacher's house fo' supper," Solomon told him. "I dropped her off some time ago. The preacher said he'd bring 'er home later."

A small wave of relief swelled within Jess. "That's interesting. Maybe he and his wife will talk some sense into her."

Solomon chuckled. "I s'pose if anyone can, it'd be them, Miz Joy primarily. She's got a good head on 'er shoulders. Fine woman and talented seamstress, the best around. She sewed Grace's weddin' dress."

Just the mention of the wedding dress soured Jess's belly, and it must have shown, because Solomon grimaced. "Sorry, suh. I shouldn't've mentioned that."

Jess shrugged. "It's all right. I should be used to the whole notion by now."

"That ain't true. If you love Miz Grace, then you gots to fight hard for 'er. You give up, and she just might find herself married to the wrong man. That Mistuh Hall puts on the charm, I tell y', and I'm convinced she done fell for it. Might be you can do some charmin' of your own next time Mistuh Hall sets off fo' Chicago."

His ears perked up. "You wouldn't happen to know when that will be, would you?"

Solomon pulled back his shoulders and presented him with another gold-toothed grin. "Why, yes, suh, I does. He goin' on Monday and comin' home Tuesday. Miz Grace just tol' me that this mornin'."

"No kidding."

"You goin' to put your own charms to good use when that man's out o' town?"

"Might be," Jess said. Then again, he might do something altogether different that didn't involve one ounce of charm. His brain began busily spinning out the possibilities.

⌣

That night, satisfied to see Aunt Iris breathing steadily and sleeping soundly, Grace tiptoed down the hall to her own room and began the business of preparing for bed. She gazed once more at her wedding dress, which she'd brought home that evening, folded loosely and secured with a thin piece of twine. My, but Joy had done a fine job of stitching it. Too bad Grace's thoughts were a cluttered tangle that seemed impossible to unravel. Would she walk down the church aisle or perchance the grand staircase at Brockwell Manor in this gown on October 15 to meet her groom, Conrad Hall? Or would the dress lay wrapped in twine for weeks, months, or possibly even years? Or...dared she think it? Would Jess Quinn be the one to whom she spoke her vows while wearing white satin?

Good gracious, what was she thinking? Idalene Berry had caught his eye, and Grace still couldn't quite shake the vision of them sitting together in church last Sunday. Had he spent the last few days attempting to get to know her better? Pretty girls like her didn't just appear out of nowhere. Surely, Jess would make every effort to see her again.

She'd been surprised to hear that Jess had stopped by the manor that evening, and chagrined to find that he hadn't awaited her return. According to Solomon, he'd come to pay a call on Aunt Iris; the butler had made no mention of his wanting to see Grace.

Oh, phooey, what was wrong with her? She suspected that the origin of her doubts about going through with her marriage to Conrad was the heart-to-heart she'd had with Joy after dinner. Her whirlwind romance with Conrad had been just that—a whirlwind, fast, fervent, and perhaps a trifle foolish. But then, didn't countless couples fall in love with very little forethought and wind up happy as two fish in a pond?

She slipped on her lightweight cotton nightgown, then crossed the room to the window and lifted it open, glad for the screens that kept the mosquitoes out. Screens were somewhat of a luxury, and she didn't for one minute take them for granted. Leaning forward, she sniffed the evening air, listened to a distant owl, picked up the song of a chorus of crickets, and viewed a million stars through the wire mesh. "Lord God," she whispered into the dazzling night, "Your love is all around me, and yet I've failed to wholeheartedly acknowledge it for so long. Oh, I know You're here, I know You've been walking alongside me all this time, and I recognize Your faithfulness, even in spite of my lack

of commitment and dedication to You. It seems as if my main concern
has been finding the right man to marry. While it's true that I'm not
getting any younger, I don't want to settle. Did You truly bring Conrad
into my life because You intended us to marry? Or would I be settling
by agreeing to marry him? O Father, I want to follow Your will, not my
own. I want my life to be about You and Your desires, not about what I
want. Help me, Lord, to live according to the plan You've set out for me,
and not according to some plan I manufacture without Your approval
or leadership. Help me to discern Your desires for me, Lord, and give
me strength to walk away from Conrad if he is not the man You would
have me to marry. As for Jess, my first love, reignite that love relationship if You so desire. Bring us back together in perfect unity of spirit.
In Your name I pray, amen."

She left the window, tears stinging her eyes, and walked to the bureau
to retrieve her Bible from the bottom drawer. Taking it in her hands, she
reveled in the feel of the leather cover, the plumy pages as she flipped
through them, and the sheer weight—it was a Book with authority.
Far too much time had passed since last she'd studied it, and she felt a
sense of urgency to reacquaint herself with its truths and promises. She
settled into the wingback chair next to the fireplace and opened God's
Word. The first passage her eyes alighted on was Hebrews 10:22–23:
*"Let us draw near with a true heart in full assurance of faith, having our
hearts sprinkled from an evil conscience, and our bodies washed with pure
water. Let us hold fast the profession of our faith without wavering; (for he is
faithful that promised)."*

"Please, Lord, speak to me as I read from Your Word," she prayed.
"Guide me and instruct me. Reveal Your divine will and direction for
my life. I want only You, dear Father—nothing more, nothing less."
When she uttered that last statement, she broke into a sob, for she knew
that the words had indicated a full surrender on her part—a yielding of
herself to the plans of the Lord, even if it meant walking away from both
of the men who claimed to love her. It startled her to realize that she was
prepared to do just that, if God should ask it of her.

24

Jess climbed aboard the train several cars behind Conrad Hall, completely undetected. The lawyer wore a business suit and carried a black case under one arm and a folded newspaper in the other hand. Seated now, the guy was so engrossed in reading said paper that it seemed he'd taken this particular journey more times than he could count.

Jess had no idea why he felt compelled to follow him; he didn't even know what it would accomplish, if anything. Good grief, he was missing two days of work for this spying venture, and he couldn't even guarantee he'd have a job waiting for him when he returned to Paris. Suffice it to say, Bill Hansen hadn't been too thrilled about his leaving. He'd made it clear that he would cut his pay or, worse, hire somebody else if the right person came along. "I'll make it up to you, Mr. Hansen," Jess had assured him. "In fact, I'll work free my first two days back." At that offer, the man had given a spiteful nod.

In contrast with Conrad's professional attire, Jess had dressed in shabby, overlarge Levis; a stained, baggy shirt; holey boots; and an old straw hat he'd acquired from a secondhand store. He'd even gone so far as to smear dirt on his face, all in the hopes of achieving a hobo-like appearance. He worried that he'd overdone the charade, but, so far, no one had given him a second glance.

The ride to Chicago was anything but a straight shot. However, compared with the alternative—horseback or stagecoach—the eleven-hour trip went quicker and smoother than expected, his hastily eaten meals and short naps in between making the minutes move right along. He got up a few times to stretch and even walked through a few cars, always keeping a watchful eye out for Conrad Hall, lest the attorney recognize him. At one point, and with utmost caution, he stepped into the back of Conrad's railcar and found him dozing, his briefcase propped upon his lap, his hands clutching it tightly even in sleep, as if he feared someone might snatch it. Not daring to linger, lest his subject awaken, Jess meandered back through the cars till he reached his seat, then plopped back down to await the train's arrival at its final destination—Chicago's Grand Central Station.

They arrived twenty minutes ahead of schedule, whistle blaring and brakes screeching like a howling banshee. When the giant locomotive finally came to a stop, Jess stood, along with several others in his car, and stretched, then crouched to peer out the window at the station platform. Dozens of people milled about, either awaiting incoming travelers or preparing to board an outgoing train. A good five minutes passed before the doors squawked open and began releasing the travel-weary folks. Jess hefted his satchel, which contained a change of clothes and his shaving supplies. He planned to travel home on a different train from Conrad Hall, in order to avoid having to dress like a vagrant again. At his first opportunity, he stepped into the aisle and followed the slow-moving line to the nearest exit door, impatient to escape the confines of the smoke-filled car so he could locate Conrad. He only prayed they wouldn't have a face-to-face encounter. Explaining his presence, not to mention his appearance, would be a difficult thing, indeed.

Dusk had not yet fallen, but the sun had definitely started making its descent, so he had to move swiftly yet discreetly to locate Hall. At first, he panicked that he wouldn't find him amid the crowd of people on the platform, many of them pushing and shoving, shouting greetings and waving, corralling children, or preparing to board but being forced back by the conductor to give incoming passengers a chance to debark. Jess worked his way through the muddle, keeping his head down and his hat low. Finally, he spotted Conrad sitting on a wooden bench outside the station, heedless of passersby, sifting through his briefcase. He pulled out several sheets of paper, then opened a folder and scanned its contents. In time, he returned everything to the briefcase, secured it shut, glanced around the station, and rose from the bench. Jess stood hidden behind a post and observed the attorney's every move, prepared to follow at a distance. He'd come all this way, and he did not intend to lose the guy now.

Conrad looked around, then advanced on a taxi driver standing nearby, his horse's reins in hand. Great! If Hall hired a driver, Jess would be obliged to do the same if he intended to keep up. He watched as the two men exchanged a few words, and then Conrad gestured in the direction of a street marked Harrison. The driver nodded, and the next thing Jess knew, both men were mounting the horse-drawn vehicle.

As soon as they started off, Jess jogged over to the next taxi in line. A short, stubby fellow in a black suit and a top hat stood beside it, hands clasped in front of him.

"Can you follow that taxi that just pulled out?" Jess asked.

The guy turned to Jess and looked him up and down through squinty eyes.

To wipe the dubious expression off his pudgy face, Jess yanked a few paper bills from his pocket and held them out to him.

The driver's eyes widened.

"Well? Can you catch up to him?"

The man gave a hasty nod. "Been doin' this job for nigh onto thirty years, an' I ain't never lost nobody yet."

"Here." Jess handed him an entire dollar. "That's to ensure you keep your word."

"Climb aboard," the driver said.

As Jess hopped into the open carriage, the driver stuffed the money into his jacket pocket, then huffed as he grasped hold of a bar to pull himself up. He situated himself on the seat and picked up the reins in one hand, a whip in the other.

"You want me to foller 'im, I'll foller 'im. You want me to wait for ya, I'll wait. Long as ya keep payin' me, I'll do your biddin'; and furthermore, I won't ask a single question of ya."

"Sounds fair to me."

With a "Yah!" and a crack of the whip from the driver, the horse took off at a fast trot.

They followed at a distance, the driver doing a good job of tracking Conrad's taxi. Jess leaned forward and said, "You act as if you've done this sort of thing before."

"More times than you can count," the fellow chuckled over his shoulder. "I'm hangin' back, assumin' you don't want t' be seen."

"You assume correctly."

"I said I ain't askin' no questions, so don't tell me nothin', hear? If there's trouble, I ain't playin' no part in it."

"Don't worry, there won't be any trouble," Jess assured him. "At least, I pray that's the case."

Conrad's taxi turned at the next intersection, drove three more blocks, turned again, drove several more blocks, and then turned again. Jess would be hard-pressed to find his way back to the station on his own. Good thing he had his driver's promise to do his bidding.

When, at last, the driver of Conrad's taxi moved his vehicle to the side of the road and pulled to a stop, Jess's driver did the same, having lagged behind by the distance of a good block or so. Jess stayed low and watched as Conrad climbed down from the conveyance, briefcase in hand. He looked both ways, then disappeared into what appeared to be an alley.

"Ya wanna get out, or what?"

Jess sent up a silent prayer asking God for wisdom. "Uh, can you approach slowly? I need to see where the guy went."

"Ya got it."

The driver directed the horse back into the flow of traffic, and Jess slid down in the seat to stay out of view. As they approached the alley, the driver pulled back on the reins, giving Jess the opportunity to investigate. Though the sun still shone overhead, its rays did not reach the heavily shaded lane; Jess's view was further blocked by a fog of steam escaping from a vent in the side of one building. He did see the silhouettes of two male figures, though, one of whom he presumed to be Conrad Hall. They stood under a stairway attached to the dingy brick building bearing the name Cotter's Warehouse. Why Hall found it necessary to meet someone in a dark alley, Jess didn't know, but he resolved to find out.

The alley wasn't particularly long, just narrow, and the light peeking through from the other end revealed a stack of crates or waste containers piled high next to the building. "Can you proceed around the block so I can enter the alley from the other side?" he asked the driver.

"Sure thing." The driver clicked at his horse, and they started moving forward once more. As they passed Conrad's taxi, Jess peeked at the driver, who looked to be dozing while he waited, arms crossed over his chest, chin down, the bill of his cap blocking the setting sun. It took a couple of minutes to maneuver the taxi halfway around the city block. Once the vehicle came within yards of the alleyway, the driver drew back on the reins. Jess jumped to the ground, then turned and whispered, "Wait for me."

"I ain't goin' nowhere," the fellow answered in an equally hushed tone. "Long as ya pay me for my time, I'm at yer beck an' call."

Jess nodded, then advanced stealthily, head down, knees bent, body crouched. He rounded the dark alley, thankful for the stacked wooden crates, which served as a barricade. Unfortunately, they also blocked his view of the two men. As he crept along, hugging the building, he picked up the sounds of male voices, their heated conversation bouncing off the brick walls.

"I told you I brought your blasted money. It's right here."

A large rat skittered past Jess's feet, making his heart jump. Any other time, he might have reacted with a small gasp, but he managed to hold it in. He could only assume that an angel had reached down and clamped his mouth shut. He made it to the crates and ever so carefully peeked his head around to get a view of the men. He immediately made out Conrad Hall, a shaft of light capturing his livid expression.

The other fellow stood too deep in the shadows for Jess to discern his facial features. Jess slipped back behind the crates and tuned his senses to their keenest level.

"How much did you bring?" an unfamiliar voice growled.

"I told you when I sent the wire that I intended to pay off the entire loan," Conrad replied, his tone dripping with disdain. "Apparently, you don't trust me."

"And why should I?"

"Well, it's all in here." Jess heard him pat the briefcase. "And I had to do a lot of finagling to get it. Let's just say that a few of my clients' trust funds have dropped considerably—for the time being."

The other fellow chuckled low in his throat. "You swindled your own clients, eh? Well, ain't you clever."

"I didn't swindle them; I merely took out a loan without their knowledge."

"Pfff. I'd like t' know how you plan to put the money back in their accounts."

"I'm about to be married, if you'll recall, and I'll step into a sizable inheritance. As soon as my new wife's great-aunt kicks the proverbial bucket—sooner than later, if I have my way—money will be no issue for me."

Uncomfortable silence prevailed before the other guy cleared his throat. "If you have your way? What does that mean, exactly?"

Having the strongest urge to retch, Jess swallowed a mouthful of bile and prayed for restraint.

Conrad chortled. "Ever hear of arsenic?"

"O' course I heard of it, you idiot. You tried to poison the old biddy?"

"Why not? She's dying, anyway. Put a little in her teacup. Apparently, it wasn't quite enough."

The other fellow spat and swore. "You're a blamed devil, ain't ya, tryin' t' kill somebody who's already dyin'? I been told I'm scum, but I think I met my match."

A spurt of icy laughter erupted between them.

"Hand over my money," the other guy said next. "I'm gettin' impatient."

All talking ceased, and the click of briefcase snaps and the crackle of papers filled up the silence. "Here you go," Conrad said. There was more rustling, clacking, and snapping, as Jess envisioned the men transferring the money from one briefcase to another.

"Wanna go get a drink to seal our bargain?" the other fellow asked Conrad.

"Can't. Got me a hot date at Ruby's Saloon, and the quicker you and I part ways, the quicker she'll be in my arms."

"You dirty dog. Didn't you just say you're engaged to be married?"

"Since when does that mean I still can't have the occasional fling?"

There came a wicked cackle. "You won't hear it from me, that's for sure. I'll see you around, then."

Conrad released another cold chuckle. "Yeah, next time I see you, you'll be asking *me* for a loan."

"Fat chance."

"You keep your mouth shut about what I told you. I have plenty enough on you to put you behind bars for a good long time."

"I ain't sayin' nothin', creep. Have a happy life." He spat again.

Jess inched backward, then crouched behind a tall crate to hide, just in case the other man meant to exit the alley the way Jess had come in. Thankfully, both men went in the direction from which Conrad had entered. Jess found a crack to peer through, and he watched them part ways at the sidewalk. Then Jess raced back to the taxi, where his driver sat at the ready, and jumped aboard.

"You ever heard of Ruby's Saloon?"

"I know right where it is. Why?"

"That's our next destination."

"Ya got enough money? It's a little jaunt."

"Yeah, just get me there."

"Ya sure that's where ya want t' go?"

He paused for only a second. "Yes, I'm sure."

The driver swiveled his body around and set his eyes on Jess. "Y' ain't playin' with fire, are ya?"

"I might be, but God is with me."

The guy lifted both eyebrows. "Hm. Ain't nobody better I can think of t' have on yer side. All right, then." He faced front once more and set his horse in motion, the wagon taking off with such immediacy that Jess lurched backward.

Once he'd regained his balance, Jess sat back, his spine rigid, his stomach churning, and his mind a mess of ugly thoughts about what he'd like to do to Conrad Hall once he got his hands on him. Of course, he knew he had to do the godly thing and leave justice in the hands of those who enforced the law. Still, if it weren't for his strong faith, he'd strangle the last breath of air out of the stinking snake. Before he went to the sheriff, though, he had a few more details to ferret out about the crooked attorney.

25

When the driver parked the taxi across the street from Ruby's Saloon, Jess saw no sign of Conrad's taxi. Either his own driver had left after dropping off his passenger, or he had yet to arrive. Jess wrestled with whether to go inside the establishment. It had been years since he'd set foot inside a saloon, the last time being when he and Josiah had still been busy sowing a few wild oats.

Dusk had begun to settle, making it a bit trickier to see. This was a busy corner, despite its being a Monday night, and people by the dozens were milling around. He figured many a fellow had left work and gone straight to the tavern for some refreshment before heading to his place of residence.

"Ain't that them?" his driver asked.

It humored Jess that the man had involved himself in the caper, despite his having no idea what Jess had up his sleeve or whether he himself might be in danger. At least he'd kept his word about not asking for specifics. Jess would be sure to tip him extra for his time and efforts.

"Where?" Jess scooted forward in his seat and glanced around.

The guy nodded at a taxi pulling directly in front of the establishment on the other side of the road.

Jess squinted to get a better view of the passenger. "It's them," he affirmed, his heart jumping. "You've got keen eyes."

"Have to, in this business."

Jess watched as Conrad exchanged a few words with the driver, handed him his remuneration, and then climbed down. As soon as his feet hit the ground, the driver urged his horse into action, navigating him right past Jess's taxi without so much as a glimpse in their direction.

With another hasty prayer for wisdom, guidance, and courage, Jess climbed down from the conveyance and studied the façade of the tavern, the door swinging continually open and shut as men of all shapes, sizes, and ages came and went. He looked at his driver. "I don't know how long I'll be inside."

"Like I said, ya want me to wait, I'll wait—long as ya got the means t' pay me. I don't mean t' be judgmental, but ya don't 'zactly look as if you're rollin' in the dough."

Jess managed a weak smile. "I'm not as destitute as I look. I'll pay you."

"I'm takin' ya at yer word. Just don't come out drunk as a fish."

"No worries there."

He waited a few moments for the street to clear enough for him to cross. After several horses and a streetcar had passed, he ambled across the road, trying to blend in with the crowd. A barrage of smells—most noticeably manure, smoked fish, and rancid garbage—accosted his senses, bringing back memories of Boston and its pungent miasma. At the saloon entrance, he uttered another prayer for protection, wisdom, and discernment. His aim was to gather as much knowledge as he could in as short a time as possible so he could hurry back to Grand Central Station and board the first train back to Paris.

He lowered the rim of his tattered straw hat, hefted up his sagging pants, and entered the dingy, poorly lit, smoke-filled space, hoping his disguise would be enough to fool Conrad Hall, in the event that he spotted him. He kept to the periphery of the room, thankful in some ways for its crowded state, and yet worried that it might also prevent him from locating Hall. His gaze roved over every patron, some standing or sitting at the long bar, others seated at round tables. There were a few clusters of men playing cards—gambling away their last dollars, no doubt—while others simply shot the breeze with their cronies. Several men sat alone, staring blankly into their glass of brew.

When he finally located Hall, the guy had his back to him, and he was speaking to a buxom older woman with long white braids who stood behind the counter.

"Hey there, handsome. You lookin' for a place to sit?"

Jess jerked to attention and swiveled around. A woman carrying a tray of drinks awaited his answer. "Uh, no. I mean…sure, I guess."

She neither smiled nor frowned. "Stand if you like. Makes no matter to me. There's a table over there if you want to snag it." She nodded behind him. "What d' you want to drink?"

"Water will be fine, thanks."

"Water?" She laughed. "What'd you come in here for, mister?" Then she grinned. "You go sit yerself down over there, and I'll bring you somethin' that'll sweat the hair right off'n yer cute head."

She was right, of course. One didn't walk into a tavern and ask for a drink of water. He'd given up booze some time back, but he'd go along with the charade to keep her happy. It also might work to his advantage if he played the game right. He returned her sly grin. "All right, then. Suit yourself, Miss—"

"Abernathy. And it's *Mrs.*, although it may as well not be, since my husband left me five years ago for another woman. Ruby, the owner, is my mother." She gestured at the very woman standing on the other side of the counter from Conrad.

"Oh? You mean, the woman talking to that gentleman?"

"That's her, yes. And a 'gentleman,' as you refer to him, he sure ain't; but then, when has a gentleman ever walked through Ruby's door— except maybe you?" She fluttered her eyelashes at him, a futile attempt at flirtation.

He forced a smile. "I'm a gentleman through and through. But I'd be interested to know why you think that fellow your mother's conversing with isn't."

"And why's that?"

"Maybe I want to know what it is you find attractive in a man." His only hope seemed to be in keeping up the charade.

She wiggled her eyebrows at him. "You jus' go sit yerself down over there. Let me deliver these drinks, an' I'll be right back to talk to you. Well, I'll mix your drink first."

He snagged her by the arm before she turned, careful not to grab so hard as to make her drop her tray. "Forget about that drink for now, Mrs. Abernathy. Just come and talk to me, why don't you?"

A nervous giggle bounded out of her. "Oh, my living stars! Ain't no man asked fer my attention since…well, I can't rightly remember the last time. Oh, and 'Lila' sounds less formal. That's my given name."

He rubbed her elbow and swallowed a pang of guilt for leading her on. "Hurry back, Lila."

She tittered again before hurrying off.

He checked to see that Conrad hadn't moved, then walked to a small round table in an obscure corner of the establishment.

Lila returned a few minutes later and plunked her plump self in the chair next to him. He'd situated himself so that Conrad remained in his line of vision.

"Where you from, stranger?" Lila asked. "I know I ain't seen you in here before."

"I'm—just passing through," he said, not wanting to give her any specifics. "What about you? You live in Chicago all your life?"

"Sure have. Been helpin' my mama in the business since I was this high." She tapped the edge of the table to indicate a height of about three feet.

Jess raised his eyebrows. "You've been serving booze to men since you were a little girl?"

"Well, I ain't *that* kind, and Mama saw to it when I was little that nobody messed with me. Don't think bad of her. She's a good woman. Yeah, there're the Lorindas and the Mabels and the Irenes, but I ain't interested in doin' what they do. Mama don't manage them, neither. She jus' rents 'em rooms and minds her own business."

"She rents rooms to ladies of the night, eh?" He tried to keep the judgmental tone from his voice.

"Call 'em what y' want. Lorinda's the most popular of 'em all."

A hushed murmur arose from around the room, and both of them followed the others' gazes to the stairway.

"There she is now, in fact. Ain't she pretty?"

The woman coming down the stairs fairly floated in her long, fitted purple satin gown, which hugged her narrow waistline, its hem flowing behind her, its low-cut bodice with the cap sleeves pulled down over her shoulders, revealing smooth, perfect skin—and way too much bosom for Jess's taste. He felt a little grimy just looking at her, but he knew he couldn't leave quite yet—not when he still had so many unanswered questions.

Ignoring the chorus of low whistles from admiring men, she walked with purpose straight to Conrad Hall. Conrad spun around and held out his arms. Rather than go into them, she took one of his hands and pulled him away from the bar, leaning into him and whispering something in his ear. Conrad tossed back his head and laughed as he allowed her to tug him toward the stairs.

The bile in Jess's gut went as sour as bad milk, and he swallowed hard to keep the ensuing nausea in check. What a rotten piece of scum, that Conrad Hall. The sooner he educated Grace on his true character, the better.

"See what I mean regardin' that fellow you asked about?" Lila asked. "He ain't no gentleman. From what my mama tol' me, he's engaged to be married in a few weeks—and not to Lorinda, neither. Don't think for a minute any weddin' vows will keep him away. Lorinda has him under her spell, just like she has dozens of other men. She makes a pretty penny at it, too."

Jess couldn't quite take his eyes off the pair as they ascended the stairs together, Conrad's arm now draped around Lorinda's bare shoulders. The guy made him utterly sick. "Is he from around here?"

"Yeah, but he joined a law firm somewhere down in Tennessee. I grew up with the guy, actually."

Jess tamped down his eagerness to learn more and tried his best
to maintain a casual demeanor. "Is that right? You mean, he lived with
you?"

"Heavens, no. He grew up down the street, Chicago Poorhouse
and Orphanage, a no-good place. Story is, his mama left him wrapped
in rags in a box on the top step of the orphanage right after he was
born. The woman who runs the operation don't have much compassion.
Never did. Don't even know why she does that job, 'ceptin' for the fact
that she gets donations from outsiders and is likely usin' 'em fer her own
pleasure. Don't go quotin' me on that, though. It's pure hearsay.

"I used to feel sorry for Conrad. That's his name, by the way. But I
quit that after he started treatin' me like some kind o' low-class person.
Just because he's got that lawyer degree an' all don't mean he's better
'n me. He likes to throw himself around now, if y' know what I mean.
Comes walkin' in dressed all fancy-like and actin' like he's somebody.
Mama says he prob'ly cheated his way through school. She don't like
him much, but she still caters t' him. Truth is, he's got charm, and he
knows how to use it to his advantage. His wiles don't work on me none,
though. Not that any man ever makes much effort on sech as me. I
know I ain't much to look at. That's why I'm shocked you wanted to
talk, but now, listen to me, goin' on and on. No wonder men don't want
me hangin' around. I always seem to dominate the conversation. Mama
says I oughtta learn to shut up and listen. She always tol' me that. I
s'pose it's true."

"No, no, I like to listen to you talk," Jess assured her, not wanting to hurt her feelings. "You have a lovely speaking voice, and I see no
reason why men would shun you. Maybe if you took yourself away from
this place and started afresh somewhere else…. You seem plenty smart
enough to go out on your own."

She dropped her chin and studied the untouched bowl of peanuts
in the middle of the table. After a few moments, she took a couple and
popped them in her mouth, then raised her head and studied him.
"You're not who you seem to be, are you? I never did get your name, by
the way."

"I guess you didn't."

"Are you gonna give it to me?"

He gave a simple shake of the head.

She pushed her chair back but didn't stand. In her expression, he read a hint of suspicion. "What'd you really come in here for? You the police or somethin'? You ain't gonna shut down my mama's place, are you, just 'cause she lets rooms to them ladies? You should know she don't take no profit from their business."

"No, no, nothing like that, Lila. You can rest assured I'm not a cop. I'm not even an investigator. I just needed to learn a few things about a certain somebody, and you helped me with that."

"What do you want with Conrad? Did I get him in trouble?"

"No, but he got himself in trouble," Jess answered steadily. "You had nothing to do with it. And on that note, I should go."

She gave him a hangdog face as he scooted back in his chair. "So, your wantin' t' talk t' me had nothin' to do with me but everything to do with tryin' to get some information."

"I'm sorry."

She flicked her wrist. "Don't worry. I'm used to it."

"You're a nice person. Thanks for chatting with me."

"But you never told me one thing about you. Where're you from? What's your name? Are you ever comin' back here?"

He prepared to stand so he could exit the smoky room. "To answer your last question, no, I doubt I'll be back. I reside in Boston, but I'm staying in a town in Tennessee for now. My name is Jesse Quinn, but I go by Jess. It was nice meeting you, Lila." He stretched a hand across the table. "Friends?"

She reached out and took his hand, and they shook, just three brief pumps. "Friends," she assured him.

On the way back to Grand Central Station, it dawned on Jess that he'd neglected to impress upon Lila the importance of keeping his identity a secret. Surely, Lila would know not to mention him to her mother—or anyone else, for that matter. He didn't want it getting back to Conrad that his fiancée's former beau had followed him to Chicago.

26

$\mathcal{C}$onrad could not believe he missed the next train to Tennessee. Through a series of questions posed to a young ticket clerk, he discovered that Jess Quinn had obtained passage on the 6:30 a.m. train to Memphis. From Memphis, he would hitch another train to Paris. If Conrad figured right, that put him a good two hours behind Quinn, barring any unforeseen delays on either train.

It was Ruby who'd informed him, when he'd come downstairs for a cup of coffee that morning, that a man named Jess Quinn had been in the saloon last night, asking questions. The rat! What was he doing following him around? And what, exactly, had Lila told him? Had she spewed the details of his entire background? All Ruby knew was that a fellow named Jess Quinn had visited her place last night and, according to Lila, had witnessed Conrad following Lorinda upstairs. Ruby said she'd tried to interrogate her daughter but couldn't get much out of her, other than the guy's name and the fact that he hailed from Boston. If all he'd seen was Conrad walking upstairs with Lorinda, Conrad could come up with an explanation convincing enough to put Grace's mind at ease. He had mastered the talent of turning on the charm and making folks believe pretty much whatever he told them. Given enough time, he could probably convince a university student that two plus two was three.

Something nagged at him, though. How would Quinn know enough to go to the saloon if he hadn't overheard him telling Carl Petrie where he was going? And if he'd heard that exchange, it was quite possible that he'd heard Conrad talking about the money he'd borrowed from Petrie and telling him how he'd siphoned funds from his clients to pay him off.

Assuming that was the case, he had to do something before Quinn told Grace—or the law, for that matter! And he had to act quickly. He began forming an idea in his mind, and because of his superb cleverness, he had no doubt he had come up with something that would shut Jess Quinn's trap for a long time, if not forever.

⁓

The train came chugging into Paris at six thirty that evening. Seldom was Grace within hearing distance of its whistle, but tonight was an exception, as she'd been invited by Joy Jennings to a meeting of the Paris Ladies' Quilting Club, held at the home of Mercy Connors. Solomon had driven her to the Connors residence with a promise to return for her at half past eight. In the meantime, he'd decided to visit one of his friends who lived on the outskirts of town.

Ten ladies had shown up for the club meeting and now sat around the Connorses' large dining room table, upon which lay the beautiful triple sunflower quilt. It looked very near completion, in Grace's estimation, with its bright yellows, greens, browns, and splashes of blue. Grace had never participated in making a quilt, and while she knew how to sew, it wasn't her passion. Still, she happily stitched where Joy instructed her to, and she especially enjoyed the lively conversation around the table.

"How are your wedding plans coming along, Grace?" asked Flora Connors, Mercy's mother-in-law, whom Grace had just met.

Grace nearly cringed at the question. Lately, her head had been spinning almost out of control at the fast-approaching wedding date. Everything was in order, to be quite truthful—with the exception of her heart. She still found herself questioning whether the love she thought she had for Conrad was authentic or manufactured, and even more so as she made it a matter of prayer and as she dug more deeply into God's

Word. She'd been asking herself some tough questions: *Do I know enough about Conrad to marry him? What made me fall in love with him in the first place? Is he strong enough in his faith to be a spiritual leader of our family? And, if not, is he committed to growing more in his faith? How much have we discussed our future together?* And the really tough one: *Does Conrad love me for the person I am or for the money I am sure to inherit?*

At Mrs. Connors' question, all eyes came to rest on Grace, and the ladies' fingers ceased working. She glanced around the table and gave a pathetic smile. "The plans are...materializing quite well. Thank you for asking."

"You must be getting very excited," said Gladys Froeling, Mercy's aunt.

She wouldn't call it "excited"; no, more like petrified of the possibility of making the wrong choice. Still, with the exception of Joy, these ladies knew nothing of her misgivings, and she wasn't about to clue them in at a quilting meeting. What would they all think if they knew the truth—that her former fiancé, whom she'd thought dead for two long years, had really been sitting in a jail cell and, when finally freed, had come all the way from Boston to Paris to tell her that he still loved her? Why, she could just about hear their tongues flapping now as they spouted their various opinions, suggestions, and pieces of advice.

Her thoughts wandered to Jess. She'd noticed him sitting next to Idalene Berry at church for the second Sunday in a row, and it had nettled her plenty. But why should it matter to her with whom Jess chose to associate? She was a betrothed woman, for heaven's sake. And yet, seeing him with Idalene made her seethe inside, and the mere thought of him kissing her rattled her right to the core. She hadn't seen or talked to him in days, which only made matters worse. Did he intend to stay in Paris and pursue Idalene Berry?

"Are you...getting excited?" asked Mrs. Froeling.

"Yes. Er, no. I—I'm not quite sure how I feel right now," came her delayed, feeble reply.

"Of course you're not sure," said Hester Connors, Mercy's aunt by marriage. Seated next to Grace, the woman reached over and patted her hand. "It's called wedding jitters, dear. There's not a woman in this room who didn't experience them before she said her vows. Isn't that right, ladies?"

"Oh, yes," Nora Trumble affirmed. "It's been forty-three years for Doc and me, and I still remember those last days as a single woman wondering what in the world I was getting myself into." Several murmurs of agreement arose. "But don't you worry; once you say those vows, they're forever, and when you realize there's no turning back, why, you just start loving your man like he was the last one on earth."

"That's the truth," said a woman whose name Grace couldn't recall—and no wonder, considering she'd met many of them for the first time tonight. "Why, I don't think I even liked my Edward all that much when we first married." A number of ladies giggled at her admission. "My parents arranged the marriage, don't you know." She cast her eyes upward and curved her mouth into a minute smile. "Neither one of us cared too much for the other, but time took care o' that. For the first few months, we just sort of tiptoed around each other, makin' polite conversation. He'd go out to the fields to work and come in at mealtime. We was just like a couple o' ships goin' past each other in the dark of night, not knowin' enough about the other to even talk much. Then, slowly but surely, we started noticin' little things about each other's personalities, we began laughin' together and enjoyin' life, and before we knew it, why, we was startin' to like each other. I will say it surprised us both. 'Course, I ain't sayin' that's the way of it with everybody. Some folks marry out of obligation or because their parents force 'em into a union, and they never do accustom themselves to the notion. They end up living miserable lives together. That would be about the worst nightmare I can imagine."

At the mention of living a miserable existence with someone she didn't truly love, Grace found herself squirming. What did this mean? Was she about to marry the wrong person?

Everyone nodded or murmured in agreement as they all resumed their needlework.

Just then, Grace made eye contact with Joy, who winked and said, "Well, ladies, how're your gardens doin'?"

Grace let out a deep breath of relief for the change of topic, which quickly put the ladies on another path and took the attention away from her. After discussing the fruits and failures of their flower beds and vegetable plots, they moved on to the topic of families and then of homemaking chores. They exchanged recipe ideas, discussed the latest fashions, and even talked about the horrid forest fire in Hinckley, Minnesota, that had claimed 418 lives.

While stitching and talking, the ladies took turns revisiting the snack table for a refill of their punch glass or another baked goodie. Overall, it turned out to be a most pleasant evening, and Grace even put the matter of her impending marriage on a back burner just so she could engage in conversation and enjoy the ladies' company. The worry didn't go away, however; it kept simmering on that back burner.

Jess rode like the wind to Brockwell Manor, only to learn that neither Grace nor Solomon was about. According to the woman who answered the door, Solomon had taken Grace to somebody's house and then gone visiting himself. She couldn't tell him to whose houses they'd gone or when they planned to return, but she said he was welcome to sit in the parlor and wait, if he felt so inclined.

He declined the offer, saying he would return in the morning. Mr. Hansen would have several deliveries lined up for him, so he would swing by the manor along his route, even if it meant going out of his way.

He considered going straight to the sheriff's office, but after giving it some thought, he decided it only fair that Grace learn first what a scoundrel Conrad Hall was, and how much better off she'd be without him. If this new information didn't convince her, Jess didn't know what would.

That night, he chatted a bit with Miss Phoebe. She inquired about where he'd been the last two days, and so, to keep from lying outright, he told her that he'd gone to Chicago on business. She must have doubted him by the way she squinted at him. A man working for Paris Feed Sale and Livery Stable had business to conduct in Chicago? At least she didn't hound him for further details.

Over the past few weeks, he'd grown to like Miss Phoebe Arbogast. She was charming in her own quiet, somewhat humorous, way. Upon first meeting her, he'd found her harsh and no-nonsense, seeming to lack any sort of sense of humor; but now he knew better. Yes, there was a hardness about her, but he saw now that it came from sheer tenacity, a will to succeed on her own without an ounce of assistance. He didn't know too much about her, but what he did know, he liked, and he'd even gotten her to accept a bit of help from him. He'd repaired the hinges on her front door, replaced some broken boards on her back stoop, fixed a section of kitchen flooring that had started to bubble from excessive heat and humidity, and even mended the crooked door on the old outhouse. She'd tried to pay him for his services, but he wouldn't hear of it, saying he appreciated that he had a place to stay and wanted to do what he could to make it more presentable to potential guests. He'd even offered to repaint her front porch to give it a more welcoming appearance, but she claimed not to have the money for paint. Sadly, he believed her. And he would try to find some way to help her.

While they sipped coffee and munched on cookies, she asked him what had brought him to Paris. It was the first time the subject had arisen between them, and he decided to be completely open about the matter. He started at the beginning, telling her about his former engagement to Grace, his job on the ship, his subsequent kidnapping and wrongful imprisonment, and his eventual release. "When they finally unlocked that cell door, I rejoiced in my freedom because I believed it would mean going back to Grace and starting right where we'd left off. I never foresaw her falling for someone else while I wasted away in a jail cell."

Miss Phoebe chewed and swallowed, then fingered the edge of a crocheted doily in the middle of the big oak table, upon which sat a small pitcher of cream, a sugar bowl, and a small vase of garden flowers. "Two years is a long time for a woman to pine away over someone she believes is dead."

"But I wasn't dead."

"Well, she didn't know that, Mr. Quinn."

He grinned. "Have you been talking to her?"

"I don't even know her, but I know her aunt, Iris Brockwell. She's a fine lady. I can't imagine how much money she's donated to good charitable causes, but it's a great deal, I'm sure, the hospital fund bein' the one that stands out the most to me. What does the inside o' that mansion look like?"

"It's beautiful," Jess conceded, "but it's just a big house, nothing more. I believe Mrs. Brockwell and Grace would like to see it put to use for something very worthwhile, for the benefit of the entire community, after Mrs. Brockwell passes."

"I would expect nothin' less from her."

They talked for a few minutes more, until Miss Phoebe excused herself, saying she had grown weary and could do with some beauty rest. Jess admitted to being exhausted himself, having boarded that train in the wee hours of the morning and barely gotten a minute's rest on his long ride back to Paris, for all the thoughts that had been running through his head. After helping Miss Phoebe turn down the wicks of the kerosene lamps, he gave a great yawn and trudged upstairs to his room, praying that his mind would quiet itself enough to allow him some much-needed slumber.

27

With a lantern in hand and a weighty knapsack slung over his shoulder, Conrad skulked up North Poplar Street at two thirty in the morning, one thing on his mind: ridding the planet of Jess Quinn before he went to the police.

Conrad had no way of knowing whether Jess had reached Grace yet, but he did know he hadn't gone to see Sheriff Marshall; otherwise, the sheriff and his deputies would certainly have met him at the train station upon his arrival in Paris and placed him under arrest. He had to believe Grace knew nothing, either, or she would have been waiting on the platform, ready to give him what for. He'd told her that he would come out to the manor first thing Wednesday morning, which he still intended to do. After all, she would want him there to comfort her when she learned of the fate of her former beau. With Jess Quinn fully out of the picture, Conrad's strengthening presence would help get her through each day. Naturally, their wedding would follow soon after, and once they married, he could easily complete his work of hastening Iris Brockwell's journey to the other side—before anybody started formulating a contract to transform Brockwell Manor into an old folks' home.

With every step he took in the direction of Miss Phoebe's Boardinghouse, his already racing heart sped up by a degree. A raccoon sprinted across his path, giving him quite a start. Sweat drops popped out on his forehead. Good grief, could it get any hotter? He continued advancing stealthily up the road, drawing closer, closer. A dog barked, breaking the silence. The keen-eared creature probably heard his footsteps, even though he was doing all he could to creep along as quietly as possible, keeping his body crouched low.

When he at last arrived at Miss Phoebe's Boardinghouse, his gut wrenched with a bit of guilt about the innocent proprietress, but no way could he alert her, or she'd discover him doing the deed. He grimaced at the condition of the place. Its shabbiness reminded him of the orphanage where he'd grown up—a dump, really. He doubted any of the residents of Paris would miss the ugly eyesore.

He heaved the bag of kindling to the ground—a collection of sticks, papers, and whatever else he'd managed to find prior to leaving his place—and began arranging them under the rickety porch, close to the house's foundation. Working fast, he moved to each corner of the house and did the same, making as little noise as possible. When he'd used up all but one stick, he tossed the sack on the pile of kindling and ignited the stick with the wick of his lantern. When the stick caught fire, he held it to the feed sack, which immediately awakened a good flame. Grinning, he stood back and watched the fire progress, an almost sick excitement rising from his chest at the glorious sight.

Next, he hurried to the other corners of the house and lit a flame at each one, then rushed around to the front porch to repeat the process. Squatting down, he reached the flaming stick beneath the porch to start the blaze. As he did, he accidentally tipped the lantern, spilling a bit of kerosene on his sleeve. Because the flame on the stick had grown dangerously close to the end, the gaseous fluid on the cuff of his sleeve ignited in an instant. On instinct, he dropped the lantern and batted at his blazing sleeve, panicked by the searing pain of burning flesh. He managed to put out the small fire in a matter of seconds, but the damage done to his wrist and arm would take some time to heal. He crawled out from under the porch and set off on a terrified run, having no time to glance back at the burning structure. His only thought was to race the few blocks to his home on Lee Street and douse his arm in a bucket of cold water.

For the life of him, Jess couldn't sleep. He'd dozed off a couple of times but then awakened, his mind crammed with thoughts of the previous two days. He should have gone straight to the sheriff's office, regardless of whether he'd been able to talk to Grace first. Maybe he ought to get dressed and go over there right now to file a report with the deputy on duty. But what would a few hours' difference make? No, he'd stick to his original plan: go to the livery first thing in the morning, find out his delivery schedule for the day, load everything onto the livery wagon, and then head out to Brockwell Manor. If he worked fast, he'd get there by nine o'clock. He just hoped Hall wouldn't beat him to the manor, steal Grace away, and talk her into doing something stupid—like marrying him on the courthouse steps.

The smell of smoke prompted him to toss off his cotton sheet, get out of bed, and amble over to the window. Who would be burning garbage in the middle of the night? When he peered outside, it took a moment for the reality to reach clear to his bones. The boardinghouse was on fire! Coming fully awake, he snatched up his trousers from the bedpost and jumped into them, threw on a shirt, and then, with no seconds to spare, opened his door and raced barefoot to the stairway. The sides of the house were already engulfed in flames. He raced down the stairs, turned the corner at the bottom, and ran through the dining room, the kitchen, and the laundry area straight into Miss Phoebe's bedroom at the back of the house. One wall was ablaze, and her room fairly reeked with smoke. In fact, he could barely see his way to her bed. An instant later, and her mattress would go up in flames. He hefted the unconscious woman into his arms, exited the way he'd come in, and made for the back stoop. He turned the doorknob, threw the door open wide, stumbled down the steps, and raced into the backyard of the house that butted up against Miss Phoebe's property.

"Help!" he screamed at the top of his lungs, breathless from fear and exertion. "Help! Fire! Fire!"

Within seconds, doors began screeching open and thwacking shut, and neighbors from all directions dashed toward the burning structure, only to realize that its dried, aged wood couldn't possibly survive more than a couple of minutes more. Insufferable heat from the flames pushed everyone back again. A neighbor lady who introduced herself as Dee Baynum directed Jess to bring Miss Phoebe to her house, on the other side of the street. Someone else hollered that he'd fetch Doc Trumble, while yet another shouted that he'd go wake the sheriff.

Chaos broke out everywhere as neighbors formed a bucket brigade. They attempted to get close enough to douse the burning boarding-house but quickly gave up and started tossing buckets of water on the surrounding homes in hopes of keeping the fire from spreading. Jess hurried across Church Street after Dee Baynum, then climbed her porch steps and entered through the front door, held open by the kindly woman. "Here, lay Miss Phoebe on this sofa," she instructed him.

He placed the frail woman on the sofa, where she lay unmoving. Her breathing, while somewhat labored, remained steady; and when he felt for her pulse, he found it good and strong. Straightening, he pitched a loud breath, silently giving thanks to God that he'd been awake and had realized what was going on before it was too late.

"Oh, dear," Dee fretted. "I do hope she'll be all right. Do you know how the fire started? I wonder if she left a lamp on or somethin'."

"I have no idea how the fire started, ma'am. I helped Miss Phoebe extinguish the hall lamps last night, so unless she left one on in her room, it couldn't have been those. The exterior walls caught fire first, so I tend to think that the fire started outside…and, as much as I hate to say it, I suspect arson."

The disheveled woman, still wearing her nightclothes, covered a loud gasp with both hands. "Who would do such a thing? Why, Miss Phoebe never hurt a flea."

Jess had an idea, and it made his blood boil. But he would keep it to himself for now. "We'll have to let the sheriff sort that out, ma'am," he simply said.

◡

Several loud thumps just outside her bedroom hauled Grace out of a deep sleep. Groggy, she stared through blurry eyes at the doors leading to the balcony off her bedroom. Crisp shadows danced across the walls, and she imagined that someone was trying to break in through the window.

"Miz Grace, wake up. You gots to come right now."

"W-what?"

The shadows continued dipping and swirling, and she cowered under her blanket until she recognized the shape of the oak tree just outside her window, swaying in the moonlit night.

"Miz Grace, wake up. You gots t' open this door."

It was Solomon. *Solomon!* She threw off her covers. "I'm coming." She donned a summer robe, tying it closed as she scuttled across the wood floor to open the door. "What is it?"

At the look on his face, she sucked in a loud breath. "It's Aunt Iris, isn't it? What's happened, Sol?" She reached out and grabbed his arm. "Is she—"

"No, miz, it ain't yo' aunt. She's sleepin' sound. It be Sheriff Marshall. He come to pay a call on y'. Wants t' know if you can tell 'im Mistuh Hall's whereabouts."

"Mr. Hall's whereabouts? It's the middle of the night, for pity's sake. What time is it, anyway?"

"It's just after four, miz."

Mystified, she gave her head a little shake, wrinkled her brow, and ran her fingers through her wild mop of hair. "Good gracious, I can't imagine what this is all about. I haven't seen Conrad since Sunday night—before he left for Chicago."

Solomon touched her elbow. "I should also tell y', Mistuh Quinn is downstairs, as well."

"Mr. Quinn—Jess is here?" She sucked in another gasp of air as her heart tripped. "What on earth is going on?"

"I s'pose you'll soon find out. Come on."

Sure enough, waiting at the bottom of the staircase were Jess, the sheriff, and one of his deputies. Although she'd seen the sheriff about town, she'd never officially met him. He stood there with a sheepish expression, turning his police cap in his hand. "Evenin', miss. So sorry to bother you at this hour."

Her eyes traveled from the sheriff to his deputy before coming to rest on Jess. He reached out and touched her arm, then dropped his hand back to his side. A curious sense of dread curled around her chest and tugged with fierce tightness as she returned her attention to the sheriff.

"I'm Sheriff Phil Marshall, ma'am, and this here is Deputy Jordan Leffering. We've come to ask you a few questions. Again, I'm sorry to disturb you at such an inconvenient time."

She raised her eyes to Jess for a sign of reassurance. He licked his lips and swallowed, then curved his lips into the tiniest of smiles. "Why don't we all go sit down?" he suggested.

"Yes, please," she said, gesturing toward the living room. They passed the grand piano and headed for the chairs and sofa, and then she turned to Solomon, still dressed in his nightclothes and a belted robe. "Perhaps you could bring us a pitcher of water and some glasses, please."

"Yes'm." He gave a slight bow and quickly exited.

Grace and Jess situated themselves in the two wingback chairs, while the sheriff and Deputy Leffering settled on the sofa.

"What's this about, Sheriff?" Grace asked.

The sheriff kept turning his hat in his hands. "Well, the reason for my visit has to do with Conrad Hall, who, as I understand, is your fiancé."

"That's right."

"Did you see Mr. Hall at any time tonight?"

"No, I didn't expect to see him until tomorrow. He had gone to Chicago on business."

The sheriff cleared his throat and cast Jess a swift glance before returning his gaze to her. "I see. Do you happen t' know what sort of, um, business he had there?"

"He didn't explain it to me, but he does travel back and forth between Paris and Chicago quite frequently. He used to work for a law firm there, and I understand that he still has some clients with whom he works. Can you please tell me what's going on?"

"Well, the short of it is, Miss Phoebe's Boardinghouse burned down tonight, and we believe your fiancé might be able to shed some light on how the fire started."

"What?" She pulled herself straight, her mind spinning wildly, and her lungs ignoring their need to exhale. She slapped a hand over her open mouth. "Miss Phoebe—is she…?"

"Mr. Quinn, here, smelled smoke." The sheriff nodded at Jess. "He looked out his window and discovered the fire, and thankfully he made it down the stairs in time to snatch Miss Arbogast out of her bed and get her to safety before the building burned clear to the ground. She was unconscious from takin' in so much smoke, but the doc said she'll survive."

The talking ceased when Solomon reentered the room carrying a tray containing a pitcher of water and three glasses. He set the tray down and commenced filling the glasses and handing them out.

"Please join us, Solomon," Jess said. "You have a right to hear this conversation."

Grace appreciated his speaking up. Solomon had keen ears, and she suspected he'd heard everything the sheriff had said thus far, anyway. He certainly didn't miss much, and it seemed pointless to try keeping him out of the loop.

"If you say so, suh." He lowered himself into a plush armchair.

"What on earth makes you suspicious of Conrad, Sheriff?" Grace's heart pounded so hard, she could hear it pumping in her head.

"Accordin' to Nora Trumble, a man showed up at Doc's office a little over an hour ago. When Nora answered the door, she recognized him as the attorney engaged to Iris Brockwell's niece. She explained to him that the doctor had left to tend to Miss Arbogast, whose boardinghouse had caught fire, and told him she'd help him in any way she could until her husband got back. She described his demeanor as 'fidgety' and said he made a point to keep one of his arms behind his back. He asked her if anyone else had been in the house, and she told him that Miss Arbogast had only one boarder—the one who'd rescued her from the fire. Accordin' to Nora, the man's face went immediately white, and he turned to go. He sort o' stumbled down the porch steps, and she caught sight of what she described as a severe burn on his wrist and forearm." The sheriff ceased talking and raised his water glass to his lips. He took a long drink, eyeing Grace over the rim. Then he set the tumbler on the table and faced her squarely. "Do you see where I'm goin' with this, ma'am?"

"Perhaps it's coincidental that he—"

"No, ma'am. Nothin' coincidental about it. We went to his house and found his burned shirt and a pair o' soiled trousers that reeked of smoke. He'd stuffed them in a waste container at the back of his property."

"But it makes no sense whatsoever. It just—it's out of character for him."

"It's really not, Grace." Jess spoke for the first time, his voice uncommonly calm, considering he'd just escaped a burning house. "I followed Conrad to Chicago without his knowledge, and I learned some very interesting things on my trip."

Her gut twisted into a sickening knot.

"Your beloved Mr. Hall is not at all the man you thought him to be. For starters, he's a liar, a cheat, and a thief, not to mention he's also attempted murder—on more than one occasion. Last week, he laced your aunt's tea with arsenic, hoping to hasten her home-going."

At his assertion, Grace's brow beaded with so much sweat that she had to wipe at it. Her extremities started tingling, an awful humming filled her head, and black dots flashed before her eyes. When the wooziness set in, she put a hand to her stomach and released a moan.

"Grace?" Jess asked, his voice sounding distant. It was the last thing she heard before her mind went blank and her world went black.

28

Searing pain burned clear to the bone as Conrad sat alongside a remote road next to his horse. After riding him hard, he'd had to give him a few minutes' rest. With great care and apprehension, he unwrapped the makeshift bandage he'd made from an old shirt and looked at his wound. Several layers of skin had peeled back, and the sight of the oozing, blistered, bloodred burn made him queasy and light-headed.

Yes, he'd managed to put out the fire that had engulfed his sleeve, but the skin had continued smoldering till he'd reached home and dunked his arm in cold water. After soaking it, he'd realized it needed serious tending, so he'd mounted his horse and ridden to the doctor's office, all the while concocting a fib in his mind to explain how the injury had occurred. Everything had started to unwind, however, when he'd learned that the doctor had gone to treat Miss Arbogast for smoke inhalation, and that she'd been saved by her sole boarder—none other than Jess Quinn.

Mrs. Trumble probably hadn't recognized him, since he'd never formally met her; but knowing that Quinn had survived the fire was reason enough to flee. He'd be an automatic suspect, given all that Quinn knew. If only he'd perished, according to plan! Conrad easily could have manufactured some story about dropping his lantern on his way to the privy and catching his sleeve on fire when he picked it up. No one would have questioned it.

After racing back home from the doctor's, he'd ripped up a shirt, fashioned it into a bandage, and secured it as best he could with a poorly made knot. He probably needed to put some kind of ointment on the burn, so he'd have to find a druggist, but not in Paris. Next, after snatching up a few essential items from his house to take with him, he'd dashed back outside, adjusted the cinch on his horse's saddle, filled his saddlebags, and raced away from his comfortable two-story house, all the while wondering if or when he'd ever lay eyes on it again. He'd taken one last glance back before making the turn off Lee Street, then whipped his horse into a fast clip. With little time to spare until dawn's first light, he'd known he had to make his way to the next train station, in the town of Camden—a good twenty or so miles south. It would be a long ride, and he wouldn't arrive until late that night or early the next morning—if he could go that long without sleep. Once there, he'd race to the depot and catch the next train out of town. No one would think to look for him in Camden. No, they'd head over to the Paris depot first, thinking he would want to hide out in Chicago, his old stomping ground. When they didn't find him there, they'd start searching deserted houses and barns all across the countryside.

Now, sitting in the grass on this quiet little road, he pulled out his watch for a gander. It was approaching half past five. The first light of morning came later these days, and right now, that pleased him. He needed to put as much distance between him and Paris as he could before the sun exposed him. Who would have guessed he'd turn into a man on the run? He didn't understand how everything had gone so wrong in so brief a time. He gave a fleeting thought to how Grace would react to the news of his disappearance—and to whatever that idiot Jess Quinn would choose to tell her about him. But he had no time for dwelling on such things now. No time for regrets or for thinking about the fortune he'd come so close to claiming.

Concluding that his horse had had enough time to catch his breath, he rewrapped his wound, crying out like a baby as scorching pain raced through his arm. Then he mounted up and kicked the critter into motion. First on the agenda when arriving in Camden: Find the closest drugstore. Once the druggist had fixed him up, he'd make a beeline for the depot and buy a ticket for a seat on the next train leaving town. Right now, the destination made no difference. He just needed to get away.

⌒

Jess remained at Brockwell Manor for the remainder of the night. Solomon got him settled in one of the spare bedrooms, where he caught an hour of sleep, maximum. This marked his second night in a row with very little slumber; but, exhausted or not, he would lose his job at the livery if he took off yet another day, and he couldn't afford to part with a single cent—not if he wanted to find another room to rent in Paris. He'd already promised Mr. Hansen that he'd work the next two days without pay, and, knowing Hansen, he'd hold Jess to the agreement. Where to stay in Paris became a matter of some concern, but he also knew the Lord had it all figured out, so he chose not to let his mind get all wrapped up in worries. He could sleep under the stars, if need be, and he had enough money to purchase food for the next several days, if not weeks. Right now, his priority was the well-being of Grace and her great-aunt.

When the first rays of morning sun burst through the window, Jess dragged himself out of bed, wiped the sleep from his eyes, and donned the same smoke-saturated clothes he'd taken off just a short while ago. He glanced around the opulent room and imagined someone sick or dying living out his final days in such lavish surroundings. More than ever before, he hoped that Grace's dream of converting the majority of the building into a medical facility would come to fruition. With her nursing degree, Grace would be a prime candidate for managing the place, if they could work out the details with Gerald Wadsworth. Jess had no idea whether he'd ever fit into the equation, but he prayed that he might.

Downstairs, he found a disheveled Grace sitting at the dining table, sipping a steaming beverage. Even at this early hour, the kitchen buzzed with activity, and the aroma of bread baking filled the room. In spite of the few residents of Brockwell Manor, the staff surely stayed busy.

Grace looked up at him with red, swollen eyes. "Good morning, Jess."

"Morning. What are you doing up so early? You need more sleep."

"You should talk. Have a seat." Instead of an invitation, it rang more like an order.

For once, she hadn't done up her long, dark locks in the usual perfect knot with a few swirly strands curling at her temples. Instead, the silky strands hung loosely, giving her a vulnerable appearance, almost like that of the young girl he remembered so well. Her chocolate eyes drooped from lack of rest, and her skin still had an ashen shade left over from her fainting spell.

He approached the ornately carved mahogany table with the glossy finish and situated himself in a chair across from her, elbows on the armrests. "Did you sleep at all?" he asked her.

"Not really. You?"

"Same."

The silver coffee carafe in the center of the table called his name. He lifted it and poured the hot brew into the floral china cup in front of him.

"Cream or sugar?" Grace asked. "Oh, never mind. I just remembered you take yours black."

"You remembered." He gave a little grin as he finished pouring, then set the pot down and brought the cup to his lips.

Nellie rounded the corner. "How would you like yo' eggs, Mistuh Quinn?"

"Me? Oh, don't go to any trouble. I have to head for work in a minute."

She scowled. "You can't leave here without eatin'."

He could see she wasn't about to let him win this battle. "I'll take them over hard, then, please."

"Yessir. Be back shortly."

A ten-second block of silence followed Nellie's departure, before Jess broke it. "How are you feeling…about…things? Last night was rough on you, I know."

Grace inhaled a deep breath, then slowly let the air back out. "Sort of numb." She lowered her eyes but not her face. "I really didn't know him, Jess, and I feel like such a fool. To think I intended to marry that—that awful man…. I asked the Lord to open my eyes, that I might see whether marrying Conrad would only bring me grief. I guess you could say He did just that. Mind you, I'd already pretty much decided to call the whole thing off after having a long chat with Joy Jennings the other evening."

Jess's heart took a little leap. "Really? You were going to break off the engagement anyway?"

Grace nodded. "Joy challenged me to set aside more time for prayer and for meditating on God's Word. I guess that was my turning point. I have completely redefined my sense of what God has in store for me, and I know with certainty I don't have a future with Conrad Hall. In fact, I'd like to find him and wring his scrawny neck. It sickens me to think that he was the reason Aunt Iris's health declined so drastically last week. That rat, putting arsenic in her tea! Has he lost his mind?"

"Maybe he has." Jess shrugged. "Some folks will do irrational things if they think they stand to earn a great deal of money."

She pressed her fingers to her temples and winced. "He had me so fooled, convincing me of his strong faith and of his love for me. How could I have allowed myself to fall for his deceptions? Where was my discernment? He lied outright about paying cash for Brooks Hotel and Restaurant, led me to believe his aunt had raised him from boyhood, and stole money from his clients' trust funds to pay off his debt. To make matters even worse, he entertained a lady of the night in Chicago—not just once but many times! Oh, my stars in heaven, what other lies has he told? And how can anyone be sure he's a legitimate lawyer? Maybe he stole his diploma and board certificate, as well."

"I'm sure his partners at the firm checked his credentials carefully before bringing him on board," Jess reasoned. "Still, they'll be in for a great shock when Sheriff Marshall pays them a call this morning. He'll probably pump them with all manner of questions."

With slumped shoulders, Grace buried her head in her hands and started to sob.

Jess resisted the urge to go to her and wrap his arms of loving assurance around her. She had much to process, and his physical closeness would only add to her confusion. No, she had to work out these new revelations in her own way and in her own time. Even last night, after the sheriff and his deputy had left, and Jess had gone on to share with Grace exactly what he'd learned about Conrad, he'd made sure to keep his hands where they belonged—in his lap or at his sides. Oh, he'd wanted to hold her, to tell her everything would be all right; but it wasn't his role to make that kind of promise. That was God's department.

After a minute or two of silence, she lifted her tear-filled gaze to his. "Do you think they'll find him today?"

Before he could respond, Nellie returned with a plate piled high with eggs, fried potatoes, grits, thick bacon, and buttered toast. His mouth watered at the sight. "Trying to fatten me up, are you, Nellie?" he asked with a grin.

"Pshhh." She flicked her hand at him. "You still needs a little fattenin'." Still chortling, she returned to the kitchen.

Jess took a bite of potatoes and chewed a piece of bacon as he pondered how to answer Grace's question. "I don't know when they'll find him, Grace," he finally said. "Sheriff Marshall said he planned to go straight to the train station and inform the employees that no one was to sell a ticket to Conrad Hall. He also said there'd be deputies on duty keeping a lookout for him. Conrad won't go there, though, and the sheriff knows it. It's too logical, too predictable. My bet is, he won't even go to Chicago. He'll want to head for a place no one would think to look, but I'm convinced such a place doesn't exist, as far as Sheriff Marshall is concerned. He strikes me as exceedingly skilled at what he does. How far can one go on horseback? He couldn't cover much more than fifteen miles a day, and with the little sleep he got, he'll need to stop somewhere for a few winks—some cave, a remote barn, or maybe some deserted house. Lawyer or not, I'd bet my last dollar the guy doesn't realize that cops from all over the state will soon learn he's on the run. Nobody wants a would-be murderer invading his property, so the law will inform the public, too. I'd bet that, even now, the authorities from every surrounding county are out there looking for him. He won't last long as a free man."

"And when they find him…?"

He took another bite of food, then chewed and swallowed before replying. "They'll bring him back to Paris to stand trial—unless he makes a statement of confession and waives his right to one. He'll go to prison, though, and for no short length of time, either. Kind of funny—he's a lawyer in need of a lawyer. Might be a trifle hard for him to find someone to represent him. I doubt even his own firm will offer their services."

"They'd be crazy if they did."

They both sipped their coffee, and Jess resumed working away at the mountain of food Nellie had piled on his plate.

"Thank you for coming out here with the sheriff in the middle of the night."

"Of course. I wanted to be here."

"I…haven't…seen you for a while. Well, unless you count the last two Sundays at church. When you were seated with Miss Idalene Berry."

Did he hear a hint of resentment in her tone? Perhaps even jealousy? The notion rather pleased him. "Yes, I guess I was."

"She appears to have eyes for you."

He grinned. He really couldn't deny it, although he'd done nothing to encourage it, and he'd certainly not sought her out during the week. He'd thought that the first Sunday she'd latched onto him would be her last, but as soon as he'd walked through the church doors the following week, there she was, apparently waiting for him. He'd never known a woman to be so forward in her advances toward a man, and, in truth, he didn't quite know how to handle her without crushing her spirit. He hated hurting people's feelings. He'd admit that she was a pretty thing, but not for a second did she hold a candle to the woman sitting across from him now.

"Miss Grace?"

She turned her head. "Yes, Blanche?"

"It's Missus Brockwell. She's callin' yo' name."

"Oh, of course."

She slid back in her chair and rose, and though Jess hadn't come close to finishing his breakfast, he stood along with her. "I have to get to the livery to make sure I don't lose my job. After work, I plan to go check on Miss Phoebe to see how she's doing. She's staying with a neighbor for the next few days. I imagine she's feeling completely out of sorts, never having had to rely on anyone else till now."

Grace folded her napkin into a perfect square and set it on the table. "Yes, I'm sure she is. Please tell her that she is in my thoughts and prayers."

"I certainly will. Thanks, Grace."

She pressed her lips together and stared at him, blinking away more tears. "Are you coming back tonight?"

He couldn't tell if she'd just asked a simple question or issued him an invitation. "I…I have to go out looking for a place to stay."

"Oh, of course. I hope you find something."

Ah. So, it hadn't been an invitation. He laid his napkin down, as well. "I'll need to go to the secondhand store for a few sets of clothes, and to the general store to pick up a few necessities. I lost everything in the fire."

"Oh dear, that's right." Grace frowned. "How awful."

"Well, it certainly wasn't much—not compared to what Miss Phoebe lost."

Blanche cleared her throat.

"Well, I'd better get going, Grace. Give my best to Aunt Iris, will you?"

"Yes. Yes, I will."

She left the room, and he followed behind until she turned to head up the stairs, at which point he made for the front door. Outside, he drew in a whiff of fresh morning air, then caught a glimpse of Solomon standing at the edge of the garden, talking to Horace McMartin, who appeared to be weeding. At least the household could all relax now that the wedding was off. They had to be pleased about that.

Jess's horse stood right where he'd left him at four in the morning— some three hours ago—now with a bucket of water on the ground in front of him, no doubt compliments of Solomon. He untied the reins from the hitching post, mounted the animal, turned him around, and headed up the gravel drive toward Nobles Road, his heart heavy and confused, his mind overwhelmed, and his body spent. The only thing that brought him a measure of comfort and satisfaction was the fact that Grace no longer wore a diamond on her ring finger.

29

*L*ack of adequate sleep was making Grace's mind fuzzy. Upstairs, she paused for a moment outside Aunt Iris's room to collect her bearings. She didn't quite know what to think of her recent interactions with Jess. Last night, while relaying to her all that he'd learned about Conrad, he'd spoken not a word of his feelings for her, nor had he tried to touch her at all. Yes, he'd followed Conrad to Chicago, but for what purpose, other than to prove to her that he'd been right about him? At least he hadn't said, "I told you so." There was no indication that he'd intended to convince her to marry him once Conrad was out of the picture. In fact, he hadn't even denied it when she'd told him she thought Idalene Berry had eyes for him. Instead, he'd just given her a sheepish little grin, as if the mere thought of it pleased him, which made her want to slap him. How dare he toy with her!

But what was she thinking? He'd come all the way to Paris from Boston to let her know he hadn't perished and to proclaim his enduring love for her, and what had she done in response? Told him she loved another and intended to marry him! She supposed she deserved a bit of snubbing for her idiocy.

She turned the doorknob and entered the room. Aunt Iris's giant four-poster bed practically swallowed up the frail woman, who lay quiet and unmoving, a lightweight blanket tucked securely under her chin, eyes closed, lips parted slightly. Grace tiptoed closer and checked the blanket, out of habit, making sure that it rose and fell with her aunt's breaths. When she saw that it did, she exhaled with relief. Lately, her aunt had shown less interest in sitting in her chair by the window, and even less desire to get dressed and descend the stairs to join the rest of the household—very uncharacteristic for a woman who'd never wanted to miss a thing.

Grace's mind swirled with uncertainty as she pondered how much to tell the elderly woman about what had transpired in the middle of the night. Everyone in the household had agreed not to divulge the fact that Conrad had laced her tea with arsenic. There were certain things a dying individual simply did not need to know.

Grace prayed silently for wisdom and discernment, then sighed deeply as she sat down in the chair at the foot of the bed.

"Come closer, dear."

The shaky whisper startled Grace. "I thought you were sleeping." She tugged the heavy wingback nearer to her aunt's bedside and sat down.

"You look tired," Aunt Iris stated. "Didn't you get enough sleep?" She might be dying, but she hadn't lost an ounce of cognizance.

"I'll admit I didn't sleep well." No sense in lying about it.

"I heard a bit of commotion in the house last night."

Grace's spine stiffened. "Did you?"

"What was going on?"

Her heart tripped over itself. There came that question again—how much should she reveal? She proceeded with great care. "Well, around four o'clock in the morning, we had a visit from Jess, as well as Sheriff Marshall and one of his deputies. I was hoping you'd sleep through it."

"You should know I don't sleep much at all anymore, dear. The pain...you know." Iris pressed a hand to her abdomen. "But that's another matter. Tell me what on earth would possess the sheriff to come here in the early-morning hours."

Grace scratched an itchy spot on her chin and then rubbed the side of her nose, shameless stalling tactics. "I...I don't want to upset you further, Auntie."

Iris flicked her hand beneath the blanket. "Good glory, I've heard enough in my lifetime that nothing surprises me anymore. Tell me what's happening."

Grace took a deep breath. "Well, for starters, I'm no longer engaged to Conrad Hall." She held up her left hand within her aunt's line of vision. "See? No more engagement ring."

Slowly yet determinedly, Aunt Iris lifted her own arm heavenward. "Well, praises be for that news! Tell me, though, what does that have to do with Sheriff Marshall's visit?"

Grace swallowed a lump in her throat. "He and Jess had some news to impart, and they also inquired as to whether I knew anything of Conrad's whereabouts."

Her aunt furrowed her brow. "Didn't you tell me he went to Chicago?"

"Yes, and Jess followed him there—unbeknownst to Conrad. In the course of trailing him, Jess discovered that Conrad was involved in a number of criminal activities. We believe that Conrad somehow got wind that Jess was on to him, and, in order to keep Jess from going to the authorities, he started a fire at Miss Phoebe's Boardinghouse last night. They have no solid proof, mind you, but he's their only suspect— especially since he's skipped town."

"Oh, for all the saints. Is Phoebe Arbogast still with us?"

"Yes. Were it not for Jess's quick acting, she surely would have died. When he went to her room, she'd already lost consciousness due to smoke inhalation. Jess whisked her out of bed and got her to safety. She's expected to recover."

Aunt Iris stared off. "That's certainly good to know. Jess is a hero, then."

"Indeed."

There was a brief pause before Aunt Iris said, "Tell me of Mr. Hall's suspected criminal activities."

Grace bit her lower lip as she pondered how much information to disclose.

Aunt Iris reached out and took her hand. "Just tell me, Grace. I'm not so sick that I can't take the truth. I want to know."

"All right, then. He wanted to marry me for my inheritance."

"No surprise there. I told you I had my suspicions."

"He had taken out a huge loan for the purchase of Brooks Hotel and Restaurant, which he couldn't pay off in a timely manner, so he skimmed money off the top of his clients' trust funds. He figured he could put the money back once he got hold of my—well, *your*— money. And something else…he kept a—a lady of the night. Jess followed him to a saloon in Chicago and befriended the owner's daughter, who clued him in on a few things. It seems Conrad lied about his upbringing and his roots. He has no idea who his parents are, only that someone dropped him off on the steps of a Chicago orphanage shortly after his birth. No well-to-do aunt raised him, and he never acquired any inheritance, as he told me he did. He doesn't even have an authentic faith, Auntie. He's lied about everything."

Aunt Iris gave her head a little shake. "It's a shame he felt the need to construct a life of lies. I'm just glad you discovered the truth about him before you said 'I do.'"

"My gullibility troubles me, Auntie. Why ever did I fall for such a schemer? Folks will view me as naive and stupid for failing to see through him, and I won't blame them a bit. Even Jess treats me differently."

"It doesn't matter what people think. You have a very trusting heart, Grace, and that's a gift. You just need to learn to channel that trust in the right direction. The man blinded you to the truth. It happens, so don't waste time berating yourself over it. Simply thank the Lord for His watchful care over you and for stepping in before you married the clod. As for Jess treating you differently, what do you mean?"

"He hasn't professed his love for me lately."

"He went clear to Chicago, didn't he? He wanted you to see the truth about Conrad before you married him. And thank the Lord he did."

"Or he went to prove a point—that I'm gullible and stupid."

"Oh, for glory sakes! Just come out and ask him how he feels, then. If his affections for you have faded, he may as well go back to Boston."

"But now—now there's Idalene Berry, so I doubt he'll leave."

Aunt Iris's expression darkened. "Hmm. I see."

"He didn't deny that she has eyes for him—and he didn't make any attempt to assure me he doesn't find her attractive."

Aunt Iris closed her eyes. "Seems to me it's your move, Grace."

"My move?"

"Yes. As they say, the ball is in your court. If you still love him—and I think you do—you'd better make it clear to him." Her eyes remained closed. "Make it fast, though. I'd like to know what you decide about your future before I go."

"What do you mean, Auntie? You'll be here for a good long while," Grace insisted.

The woman's wrinkled face puckered in an even deeper grimace, and she opened one eye to assess her niece. "Now you *are* being naive, my dear."

⌒

"I think we've caught him, or at least we know his general location."

Having just come from visiting Miss Phoebe at the Baynums', Jess sat across the cluttered desk of Sheriff Marshall in his office, the sheriff's cluttered desk between them. He needed to keep searching for a new place to stay, but first he'd wanted to see if there was any news regarding the fugitive.

"I got a wire from Sheriff Duncan over in Camden not fifteen minutes ago," the sheriff went on. "Camden's about twenty or so miles southeast of Paris, in case you didn't know. A farmer reported a stranger comin' to his door an' askin' for a bandage, or material for makin' one. The man described the wound as a bad burn, and said his wife gave the guy some ointment and a proper dressing. He said the fellow then asked if he could sleep in his barn for a few hours, and he consented. He said his wife gave him a blanket to use and even prepared him a mid-afternoon meal when he woke up.

"A few hours later, a knock came to their door. A couple o' deputies from Benton County said they were payin' routine visits to all the area farms to inquire about a man on the run—a man with a bad burn on his arm. The couple informed them of the man in their barn, but when the deputies went out to check, they saw him ridin' over the crest of a distant hill. He'd stolen one of the farmer's horses and left his lame one. At any rate, last I heard, they weren't far behind him. Shouldn't be long now."

"That's good news," Jess said. "What's next for Conrad Hall?"

"They'll drag him back to Henry County, and my deputies will bring him in. He'll be entitled to a jury trial, unless he waives his right to one by making an outright confession, in which case there'll be a bench trial, and it'll be Judge Corbett who determines his fate. My guess is, he'll take the latter course. He's an attorney, after all, so he knows that's his best option."

Jess said nothing but merely nodded.

"That was a fine thing you did, gettin' Miss Phoebe out o' that burnin' house," Sheriff Marshall added. "You said you just came from the Baynums'. How's she farin'?"

"She's doing surprisingly well, I'd say; certainly thankful to be alive. She's breathing better and even eating and drinking some fluids, all thanks to Mrs. Baynum's watchful care."

"The Baynums are a right delightful couple," the sheriff said. "He's a retired minister from the Wesleyan Methodist denomination, and his wife used to be a nurse. Seems to me Miss Phoebe couldn't have landed in a more perfect place."

"I would agree."

The sheriff tapped the end of a pencil on his desk. "Did you know folks round here are callin' you a hero?"

Jess chuckled. "I'm far from that. I just did the natural thing. God was with me, no question there. I couldn't sleep, and I have no doubt that the Lord Himself kept me awake so I could escape that fire and take Miss Phoebe with me."

"I must say, I like your logic." The sheriff smiled. "I heard just this afternoon that the Reverend Jennings and his wife have set up a bank fund so's folks from the community and surroundin' areas can donate money to help her rebuild. Hear-tell the money's already pourin' in. Wouldn't surprise me none if a team o' volunteers put up a nice new boardinghouse for her. Paris folks band together in the tough and tragic times. They're a generous, friendly lot. I couldn't ask for a better place to hang my hat."

"I've certainly found that to be true in the short time I've spent here," Jess affirmed. "Just today, I stopped in at Juanita's Café for lunch and happened to mention to Sam Connors my need for a place to rent, and he told me his mother has several spare bedrooms and would gladly put me up. Said she lived alone in a big old farmhouse and would welcome the company. I thanked him but told him I wouldn't want to put her out. But then, this afternoon, she paid me a visit at the livery, introduced herself, and insisted I take one of her rooms." Jess chuckled and scratched the back of his neck. "I guess that means I'll be sticking around Paris a while longer."

The sheriff grinned. "Glad to hear it. You seem like a fine young man. What in the world brought you clear to Paris, anyway? You sure don't talk like you're from these parts. Where is it you hail from?"

"Boston's my hometown, and I came here to claim my former fiancée, Grace Fontaine. I won't bore you with the details, but she and I had been apart for some time—two years, actually—due to some extenuating circumstances. I didn't even know she'd moved to Paris until some good friends in Boston informed me. Anyway, I came here, only to discover she'd fallen in love with someone else and was planning to marry him."

The sheriff gave a little chuckle. "Well, now that Conrad Hall's outta the picture, you can pick up where you left off, eh? Go ahead and stake your claim?"

Jess smiled. "I'm afraid it's not quite that simple. She's a little numb right now from all that's transpired. Can't say I blame her for being confused and baffled. Add to that the declining health of her great-aunt, and I'd say she's a bit too overwhelmed to think about jumping back into a relationship. I'll probably stay around here for a few more months, but if it doesn't look like things are going to pan out for us, I'll head back to Boston."

30

Conrad could not believe this rotten turn of events. What he'd initially considered a fine idea, heading south rather than back to Chicago, wound up as a disaster, and now he sat crammed in the back of a police wagon on his way back to Paris, his hands cuffed behind his back, ankles secured with chains, doors locked on either side of him, and deputies on horseback surrounding the wagon—as if he stood a palm tree's chance in the Arctic of ever escaping. It was a hard pill to swallow, considering how close he'd come to escaping. Were it not for his dumb horse's going lame and his own dad-blamed exhaustion, not to mention his hideously painful wound, he might have outwitted the law.

What a fine fix. And his deepest regret wasn't the loss of Grace Fontaine or even her money. No, truth told, he'd miss Lorinda's warm body more than anything—and he'd never even learned her last name.

‿

Over the next few days, Aunt Iris showed a marked decline in health, so much so that it frightened the daylights out of Grace. Solomon went to fetch Doc Trumble, who rode out to the manor immediately to assess her condition. When he examined her, Aunt Iris roused only briefly and gave a weak moan.

Doc bent close. "Are you in pain, Iris?"

"A little," she managed in a hoarse murmur.

"Which means a great deal," Grace whispered to Blanche as they watched from across the room. "Oh, Blanche, I can't bear to lose her yet." Her throat felt raw from the effort of holding back her tears, so she allowed just a couple to slide down her cheeks. Blanche put a strong arm around Grace's shoulder and tugged her against her plump side. Solomon and Nellie, standing nearby, offered murmured sympathies.

"I'm going to increase the dosage of your pain medication, Iris, but it will mean you'll probably want to sleep more," Doc told her.

"No, not...yet," she muttered in a wobbly voice. She reached out and snagged the doctor weakly by the arm. "Grace...where is Grace?"

"I'm right here, Auntie." She crossed the room and went down on her knees at her aunt's bedside, clasping the woman's unbelievably chilly hand in both of hers. "What can I do for you?"

"I want...to talk to you."

"All right, I'm listening."

"Alone."

Grace turned her head and looked helplessly at the others as they scurried out of the room. The door closed with a gentle click. She returned her gaze to her aunt. "It's just you and me now, Auntie."

"I have...something...to tell you."

Her voice quavered so that Grace had to draw closer to hear her words. As she did, a sense of foreboding came over her.

"I should have told you...long ago." Furrows of pain etched her forehead, and she clutched her abdomen with her free hand.

Grace had to fight the tears that seemed determined to flow out of pity for this beloved woman. She focused on breathing through her nostrils, in and out, in and out. "Aunt Iris, whatever it is, I don't want you agonizing over it."

"I've never told this to anyone...well, except for John, bless his heart." With effort, she turned her head to the side to look Grace in the eye. "He was the dearest of all men, don't you know. He loved me the way a man is supposed to love his wife…the same way God loves His church."

Grace nodded. "Everyone adored him. He had such a tender heart. Did you want to talk about him?"

More wincing. "Yes…and no. I never did tell you…or even your mama…why we never had children."

The unexpected topic gave Grace a slight jolt. "Mama told me she didn't know why, and you never talked about it."

"Yes, well, I could not have children, although I desperately wanted them. I did something horrid and shameful, so shameful that I dared not tell a living soul. For years, I felt God's punishment on me for my awful act." She clenched her teeth as a terrible shudder racked her frail body.

A knot formed in the pit of Grace's stomach, and she found herself having to loosen her grip on her aunt's cold hand. "God loves each of us, Auntie, no matter what we've done."

"Oh, child, I know that now, but it took me an entire lifetime to come to truly believe it."

Grace nodded, then waited while Aunt Iris closed her eyes and took a couple of shaky breaths, as if trying to determine where to begin. At last, she lifted her eyelids and stared at the ceiling. "There was another man…a boy, really…before John. I thought I loved him. He was seventeen, and I a mere fourteen." She licked her dry, cracked lips. "Water. Is there some water nearby?"

Grace reached for the glass on the bedside stand and then, putting a hand under her aunt's head to prop her up, carefully brought it to her mouth. She took several small sips, then collapsed, exhausted, on the mattress.

"Auntie, you don't have to keep going."

Iris lifted her hand. "No, I…must. God has surely cleansed me of all my sins, but I feel as though confessing to you will…make my cleansing…all the more…complete." She took several more labored breaths. "This young man and I, we became…too familiar with each other, if you know what I mean. And, well, I became pregnant."

Grace couldn't quite catch the gasp before it escaped her lungs.

Tears filled her aunt's eyes, so Grace quickly dabbed at them with the hem of her bedsheet before drying her own. It was the first time since Uncle John's funeral that she'd seen her aunt cry. "And you lost the baby?" she asked in a trembly whisper.

Iris nodded. "Yes, but not…in the way…you think."

Grace shifted from her knees to her backside and wrapped her arms around her bent knees as a horrid sense of dread encircled her.

"He insisted I…get rid of…the baby. He said we couldn't be together if I didn't. I remember crying for days and days, but I never told a soul about it, not even Mother or Father. I foolishly thought that if I got rid of the baby, he and I could resume our relationship."

Her voice had taken on a croaky quality, so she gave a slight cough, then swallowed.

Grace went back on her knees and rested her hand atop her aunt's clammy wrist.

"I didn't go to a doctor, Grace. I read…in a book…how I could do it on my own. But in doing it, I…well, I wrecked my whole insides. After marrying my beloved John, I went to a doctor in Nashville. He confirmed what I most feared: I would never conceive again."

She made several attempts to swallow, so Grace picked up the glass of water and offered it to her once more. She declined with a feeble shake of her head.

"I recall that after…doing…the dreadful deed, I bled and bled…for days on end. My utter shame and guilt kept me from telling Mother… and, of course, she was so busy, she never…noticed my pain. I continued washing my own clothes, throwing some of them away, and just suffering through the entire ordeal…alone." She sucked in a breath, then took another and another, as if she couldn't get enough air. Her hand trembled, and Grace caressed the top of it. Iris's other arm lay at her side, her fingers fidgeting with the blanket. She continued to stare through wet eyes at the ceiling.

When she had finally caught her breath, she continued. "Of course, the young man left me. He had…no idea…how to process the gravity of what we'd done. Nor did I. Rather than turn to God for forgiveness, I ran away from Him. And I stayed away from Him for a good portion of my life. Oh, I had known the Lord as my Savior since childhood, but I hadn't dedicated...my whole being...to Him. Thank God for John... for his love, patience, and compassionate understanding. Were it not for the way he modeled Christ's unconditional love and forgiveness, I would not know Jesus...in the way I do...today." A loud sigh rolled out of her, and she closed her eyes.

"Oh, Aunt Iris, Aunt Iris." Tears now flowed freely down Grace's face. "I'm so sorry for you, for the baby, for...for everything that happened to you. But I'm thankful you discovered God's amazing, unfailing love. He would never hold a sin against you—or anyone, for that matter. He just asks that we come to Him with repentant hearts and receive His forgiveness." She moved closer so that she could rest her head on her aunt's pillow.

Neither spoke another word for a time; they just held hands and listened to the birds chirping outside. The breeze drifted in through the open window, billowing the curtains and blowing their damp cheeks dry.

"I will meet...my child...soon," Aunt Iris whispered. "And when I do, I'll wrap him in my arms and speak sweet words of love and tenderness to him. I don't know if it was a boy, mind you, but all my life, I've thought so. It won't matter one bit once I get to heaven. I will recognize that child as mine, boy or girl, as soon as we set eyes on each other."

In this moment, Grace loved her aunt more than ever before. "Yes, Auntie. Yes, you will." There was another round of tears and sniffles. "Thank you for sharing this burden with me. It's time now for you to let it go."

They rested in silence for a while, and then Grace thought Aunt Iris might have drifted into a slumbering state. Slowly, Grace lifted her head from the pillow.

"I've been thinking...."

So, she hadn't gone to sleep. Grace brought her head close again. "What is it?"

"I want you to summon Gerald Wadsworth to my bedside so I can talk to him about our wishes for the manor."

Grace's heart leaped, as a sort of joy bubbled up from down deep. "Tomorrow is Sunday, so I'll tell Solomon to bring him here first thing Monday morning."

Her aunt managed a weak nod. "And I want Gerald to find out how much Phoebe Arbogast needs in order to rebuild. He must…use funds from my account…to cover the expenses she incurs."

Grace's heart swelled even more. "Oh, Auntie, that's so generous."

The woman gave a little gasp, then continued through clenched teeth. "I also want you…to beware of…the danger of allowing a seed of bitterness toward Conrad to grow…in your heart. Those roots will entangle you and squeeze the life out of you. I know…about bitterness."

Briefly, Grace pictured Conrad sitting in a cell in the Paris jail. According to Solomon, who'd done a bit of investigating, he'd waived his right to a trial and had confessed his guilt, both of attempted murder by arson and of poisoning Aunt Iris. He could hardly deny the poisoning, seeing as Jess had overheard him telling the Chicago shylock about it, never mind that they'd found a bottle of arsenic still in the pocket of the jacket he'd been wearing the evening he'd visited her aunt.

"I don't harbor any bitterness toward Conrad, Auntie. In fact, I hardly think about him any longer. God has begun a work of restoration in my heart, and I'll be quite content never to lay eyes on him again."

"Good, that's good." Her aunt smiled weakly. "And what of Jess Quinn?"

At the mention of Jess, her heart stumbled over itself. "I haven't seen him since…well, since the morning after he and Sheriff Marshall came to the manor. No doubt he's busy."

"Or waiting for you to take the next step. It's your move, remember?"

"My mind is so muddled, Aunt Iris."

"Well, don't wait too long to unmuddle it, or he might take up with that Idalou woman."

"Idalene."

Aunt Iris lifted a shaky wrist and flicked it. "Whoever."

Later that evening, as Grace prepared for bed, she laid out her Sunday clothes, not knowing whether she'd go to church in the morning. It would depend on how Aunt Iris was doing. Nellie, Blanche, and Ellen were all taking shifts to sit with her. They'd agreed that, from this point forward, someone would be by her side at all times. Doc Trumble had gone ahead and increased the dosage of her pain medicine in order to help her sleep, but she'd made it clear that she wanted to stay alert enough so as not to miss anything. Even on her deathbed, she was a stubborn soul.

After donning her nightgown, Grace took her Bible and curled up in the armchair across the room. She turned on the nearby floor lamp, opened the Book, and resumed reading where she'd left off that morning, her crocheted bookmark holding the spot in 2 Corinthians. As she read, the sweet presence of the Holy Spirit washed over her with a sense of peace and rest, somehow assuring her that as long as she continued to yield to Him her *all*, He would take full control of *all* her circumstances. In that comforting knowledge, she closed her eyes and drifted asleep.

On Sunday morning, Jess searched the congregation for Grace, to no avail. She must have stayed home to be with her aunt. He decided that he'd stayed away long enough; whether Grace liked it or not, he had to stop by to check on Aunt Iris. She'd been on his mind a great deal lately, and he'd been praying that God would provide peace for her soul and relief from bodily pain.

At the close of the service, Idalene Berry, who'd again sat next to him uninvited, looped her hand through his arm and boldly paraded down the center aisle with him in tow. He'd purposely tried to avoid her that morning, even arriving a bit later than usual in hopes that she would have already found a seat. Instead, she'd been waiting for him by the door, a big, bright smile on her pretty face, her hazel eyes beaming at first sight of him. Had she begun to think of them as a couple, despite the fact that he'd done nothing to encourage such a belief?

"Miss Berry, Mr. Quinn, how lovely to see you this morning."

They both turned at the female voice. A woman Jess didn't recognize held out her hand in greeting, and he stopped to shake it. "Good morning," he said.

"I'm Floretta Grassmeyer. I've not met either of you formally, but I'm on the Paris Evangelical Church Welcome Committee, and I learned your names from the reverend. I wanted to invite you both to a picnic luncheon at my house immediately following the service today. We've had several newcomers to our congregation as of late, and we thought it would be lovely to bring everyone together."

"I appreciate the invitation," Jess began, "but—"

"It sounds wonderful," said Idalene in an altogether too enthusiastic manner, her hand gripping his arm the tighter, as if she owned him. He bristled.

"Oh, please say that you will join us, Mr. Quinn." Mrs. Grassmeyer flashed him a shining smile.

He supposed it couldn't hurt. He would keep his stay brief, though, so he could make it out to Brockwell Manor before it got too late.

Once he agreed, the older woman clapped her hands with delight, then gave him hasty directions to her home before hustling over to greet the next set of newcomers.

In the churchyard, Jess freed his arm from Idalene's hand as tactfully as he could.

She didn't let it deter her. "Might I ride with you to the Grassmeyers' home?"

He wished he could tell her that it wouldn't be possible, since he'd ridden a horse to church. But, alas, he'd driven a rig. Working at the livery afforded him the benefit of choosing from any of the available horses and borrowing any one of the many rigs Mr. Hansen kept in his inventory. "Uh, sure, that'd be fine." What else could he say?

She awarded him a cheery smile, and together they walked toward the rows of wagons and rigs, her hand once more taking hold of his arm on their short jaunt. He helped her up to her seat, then walked around to the driver's side. After climbing aboard, he took up the reins and guided the horse down the rutted driveway toward Morton Street.

Idalene made sure to slide over to the middle of the seat, as close to him as possible. He rolled his eyes to the heavens. How had it come to this? Halfway to the road, a carriage passed. How odd that the driver would be entering the churchyard just as everyone else was leaving. As Jess made the right turn onto Morton Street, he decided that today, when the time seemed right, he would make it clear to Idalene Berry that he had no intention of pursuing a relationship with her.

⌒

Grace had sizzled with ire when she'd caught sight of Jess—with Idalene—riding out of the churchyard. She stared out the back window of the carriage driven by Horace McMartin, trying to get another gut-wrenching glimpse. Jess and Idalene—an actual couple? They'd been sitting so close on that wagon seat, she doubted even a single sheet of paper would've fit between them. With a loud huff, she whipped her head around front, folded her arms across her chest, and narrowed her eyes. She nearly gave voice to the growl that threatened to explode out of her when Horace spoke up.

"There's the preacher right there, Miz Fontaine," he called from the front. "Y' want that I should go over an' summon 'im to the buggy?"

Grace cleared her throat and forced a pleasant voice. "Yes, please."

The brougham came to a stop in front of the church, and Horace jumped to the ground. Grace gazed over the heads of the congregants still milling about the yard and looked toward Morton Street, where Jess's rig was fading into the distance. Overhead, several large gray clouds were moving in from the west, and she secretly hoped for a sudden downpour that would douse the two lovebirds.

"Grace!"

Grace swiveled on the seat and saw Joy Jennings approaching the carriage, baby Naomi in her arms, Annie trailing behind. Grace slid across the seat and stuck her head out the window. "Hello, Joy."

"I just overheard your driver talkin' to Lucas. I'm so sorry to hear your aunt is doin' so poorly."

"Yes, Solomon and the other staff are with her. We thought she ought to have a pastoral visit. I wanted to ride along because I thought I might…um, see Jess. I wanted to invite him back to the manor."

Joy's face fell. "I just saw him ridin' out. I think he went to a new-comers' picnic over at the Grassmeyers' place."

"Yes, I saw him…along with Idalene Berry. They were sitting closer than two birds in a nest."

Joy bit her bottom lip and shifted baby Naomi in her arms. Annie bent over to tie her shoe, then got distracted and started writing words in the dirt with a stick. "I'm sorry about everything, Grace," Joy said softly. "About how your fiancé turned out to be a big fat shyster. I can hardly believe all he did. And I can hardly imagine how you must feel."

Grace nodded. "I'm mortified by his actions, and even more mortified that I almost married him. I'm certain folks must view me as a silly, brainless goose."

"What? No, not at all." Joy shook her head emphatically. "If anything, I'm sure they're happy you didn't marry the lout."

She sighed. "I'm sorry you went to all that trouble making my wedding dress, not to mention that you had to rush to finish it."

"Oh, pooh, it wasn't any trouble. Besides, you'll still get to wear it. Someday."

Grace sniffed. "No time soon, I fear."

A good ten seconds of silence followed.

"Are they courting?" she finally blurted out.

Joy shrugged. "All I know is, they've sat together in church for the past three Sundays."

Another low growl threatened to roll out of Grace, but before it did, Horace returned to the carriage and climbed aboard. "The preacher's comin' out this afternoon, miz." He took up the reins.

"Thank you, Horace."

Joy stepped closer to the carriage window. "Would you like both me an' Lucas to come to the manor? I can take the girls to Mercy's house. She'll be happy to watch them for a couple of hours."

Grace smiled gratefully. "That would be lovely."

31

*J*ess had intended for things to run differently today, but he'd been delayed, and he and Idalene didn't leave the picnic until three o'clock. Floretta Grassmeyer and her husband, Clyde, had planned several activities for adults and children alike, including horseshoe tournaments, balloon tosses, and three-legged races. And since his "date" insisted on participating, he'd had little choice but to hang around. He had played a few rounds of horseshoes with the other men but otherwise hung back and merely observed the festivities, all the while anxiously awaiting the conclusion of the gathering.

When the picnic finally ended, Jess drove Idalene back to the church, where she'd left her horse and rig parked in the shade of a tree. She turned to him and, batting her eyelashes feverishly, asked him, "Would you like to take me out sometime this week?"

He couldn't believe her shameless assertion. He decided to reply with equal boldness. It seemed to be the only language she understood. "No, not really."

She put on a pouty face, clearly taken aback. "Oh."

Jess immediately regretted being so blunt. "I'm sorry, Idalene," he hastened to add. "It's been nice sitting with you in church the last few Sundays, but…well, I'm very sorry; I'm just not interested in pursuing a relationship with you."

"I see." She gave a curt nod. "No doubt it's because you still love your former fiancée. Never mind that she's marrying somebody else."

"I guess you haven't heard. They're no longer engaged."

"Oh."

Rather than elaborate, he jumped off the wagon, walked around to her side, and extended a hand to her. She took it and hopped down, her yellow skirts flaring.

"Well, I suppose we can simply be friends, then?"

Her quick recovery, reinforced by a genuine smile, came as a relief to Jess.

"Of course." He grinned. "Though we probably shouldn't sit together in church anymore. Folks might get the wrong idea."

She grimaced. "I see. All right, then. Bye, and thank you for the ride. And thanks for taking me to the picnic. It was fun, wasn't it?" Without awaiting a response, she turned and headed for her wagon, a little bounce in her step.

"Yes." He scratched his temple and gave his head a little shake as he watched her walk away. "It was."

Women were strange creatures, some more so than others.

After leaving the church, he drove out to his new residence to wash up and change out of his church clothes, which had gotten dusty after an afternoon spent outdoors. He found Flora Connors to be quite friendly and talkative, and he figured living alone probably fueled her apparent passion for conversation. In general, he didn't mind it—even welcomed it; but today, he was especially eager to head out to Brockwell Manor. They talked for a bit, he telling her about the picnic at the Grassmeyers', and then he went upstairs to clean up. When he came back downstairs a half hour later, he got caught up in another conversation, this one about whether she ought to sell her farm and move into town to be closer to Sam and Mercy. They discussed the pros and cons of both situations, but he found himself mostly listening, knowing she probably just needed a chance to air her thoughts. After a bit, he finally excused himself and took off for the livery, where he would switch from a rig to a horse and thereby make better time on his five-mile trek to Brockwell Manor.

Although he'd given Mrs. Connors his first month's rent, God alone knew whether he'd stay that long. It all depended on how things panned out with Grace. He decided to look for a time, perhaps even tonight, if possible, to express his feelings for her and to see if he could figure out where she stood. Even the smallest glimmer of hope would convince him to hang around. Anything less, and it seemed pointless for him to prolong his stay in Paris.

It was five thirty by the time Jess reached the livery, and he worried he might be out of line in dropping by, uninvited, at Brockwell Manor during the supper hour. Still, a sense of urgency nagged at him, so he chose to go with his gut.

As he turned up the long drive off Nobles Road, he saw the Reverend Jennings and his wife climbing aboard their rig in front of Brockwell Manor. He proceeded toward them and pulled back on the reins to stop alongside their wagon. "Evening, folks. Are you just leaving?"

The reverend was busy with the reins, so Joy was the first to see Jess. "Why, Mr. Quinn! I'm...surprised to see you. What are you doin'— I mean, it's nice you dropped over to see— How are you?"

Her greeting didn't come off especially polished.

Lucas smiled warmly. "Good to see you, Jess. Are you here to check on Mrs. Brockwell?"

"Yes. How is she doing?"

Joy shook her head.

"Not so well, I'm afraid," Lucas answered. "Doc Trumble left not so long ago and told us she'd taken a drastic turn yesterday. We all stood around her bedside and prayed for her, but, to tell you the truth, I'm not so sure she even knew we were there. Apparently, her attorney came out earlier today, despite its being a Sunday. Mrs. Brockwell insisted she see him immediately. She appears to be in a great deal of pain, so the doctor has sedated her to help ease the spasms."

"Grace is understandably upset," Joy put in.

Jess nodded. "She loves her aunt very much."

"Yes, she does. And she's had many disappointments and setbacks of late," she added, her eyes nearly piercing him. "How was the newcomers' picnic today?"

Ah, so that explained her cool demeanor. She must have seen him leaving the churchyard in his rig with Idalene snuggled against him, too close for comfort.

"Yes, how was it?" Lucas asked, leaning forward.

"It was nice. The Grassmeyers sure are friendly folks."

An awkward gap of silence followed, so he decided to clear the air. "Just so you know, there is nothing between Idalene Berry and me."

"There isn't?" Joy interjected.

"You don't have to explain anything," Lucas told him.

"No, I want to." He grinned at the reverend and his wife. "I made it more than clear to her today that we won't be sharing any church pews going forward—unless there's a body or two between us. That woman is…well, presumptuous, to put it nicely."

Joy laughed outright now, which gave Jess the ability to relax. "Well, good evening to you folks. I'd best go knock on the door and see if Grace will let me in."

"You might have t' be a trifle persistent," Joy told him.

"Joy, mind your business," her husband muttered. "Good evening, Jess. We'll continue our prayers for Mrs. Brockwell." He tugged at the reins, putting his horses into action.

"And for you an' Grace," Joy called over her shoulder.

Jess rode the rest of the way to the hitching post, dismounted, and looped the horse's reins over the post, then approached the stone steps leading to the front terrace. The door opened before he had a chance to use the knocker. There stood Grace, and she wasn't smiling. Her eyes, red and swollen, bored into his chest like steel bullets. "Yes?"

"Grace." Her name came out as a gravelly whisper at the sight of her in her fashionable full skirt of blue and yellow flowers against a beige background and her white shirtwaist with short puff sleeves and a rounded bodice. She had gathered her hair in a loose bun, from which several strands had escaped. Pearl drop earrings framed her perfect, oval face. He cleared his throat. "I came to check on things. Am I allowed?"

Rather than invite him in, she stepped outside and shut the door behind her, hands clasped at her small waist, gaze still lowered. "She's not doing well at all. It's breaking my heart to see her suffer."

"I'm so sorry. How is the staff holding up? How's Solomon doing?"

"Not well."

"May I…come in?"

She bit her lower lip. "I don't know if she'll recognize you."

"Really?"

"Her condition has declined dramatically. You could have come earlier…a few days ago."

"I…I didn't know if you wanted me here."

Her eyes finally met his, and it was all he could do to keep from opening his arms and wrapping her in an embrace. Did she want him to do that? Or would she recoil?

"You could have come at any time. Aunt Iris asked after you."

"I didn't know. Why didn't you send for me?"

"Why didn't you just come?"

"Would you have welcomed me?"

"Would it have mattered? It's my aunt who's sick."

She had him so stumped, he didn't know which end was up. He shifted his weight from one foot to the other and gathered what courage he could. "Grace, let's start over. I came clear to Paris from Boston to reclaim you, but you were engaged to another and didn't want me."

She challenged him with a teary-eyed stare. "I didn't actually say I didn't want you."

"You didn't?"

"Not in so many words."

"I don't even know what you want from me, Grace. Just answer me this: Are you over Conrad Hall?"

Now she gawked at him as if one of his ears had just fallen to the ground. "What?" she squeaked. "How could you ask such a thing? Of course, I'm over him. Long over him. Now it's your turn to answer me this: If you came all the way from Boston to reclaim me, how is it that you got over me so quickly?" Her voice trembled with anger. "Just answer me that." She pointed a finger straight at his face.

"What are you talking about? Who said I was over you?"

"Nobody. I saw it with my own eyes."

"Saw what?" A strange, unexpected amusement at her ire started rising within his chest.

"You've sat with Idalene Berry at church for three weeks now, and although I wasn't at the service today, I also know you took her to the… the newcomers' picnic. I saw you leaving the churchyard together, all snuggled up like two bugs in a rug." Her finger was still pointed at him, dangerously close to his mouth. An inch or two nearer, and he could bite it.

"Are you jealous?"

"Certainly not."

"Then what are you, Grace?"

"I'm…mad. Yes, that's just what I am."

He decided to open his arms to see if she'd step into them. She did not. "What are you doing?" she asked instead.

He kept them spread wide. "Idalene Berry means absolutely nothing to me. I told her so, just today."

"You—"

"I told her I had no interest whatsoever in starting up a relationship with her, not when my heart belonged to another. Well, I didn't use those exact words, but she got the drift."

Her shoulders dropped a smidgeon as a tiny sigh rolled out of her. Yet she still didn't budge.

"I am not over you, Grace Fontaine. Far from it."

She lifted her chin a notch. "Then why were you sitting so close to her in the wagon seat?"

"Um, she's the one who slid close to me. I did not invite her to do so. What were you doing there?"

"We thought Aunt Iris would appreciate a pastoral visit. Reverend Jennings isn't her actual pastor, but he happily came. I rode along with Horace because I wanted to see if I could find you." She looked at his arms, still spread open wide. "I wanted you to come, as well. I needed you to come."

He took a step closer, sudden wetness pooling in his own eyes. "I'm sorry, honey. I'm here now. Does that count?"

She crossed her arms in front of her and shifted her weight to one side, tilting her head and studying him in a most indecisive manner. "It might."

With his arms still outstretched, he said gently, "Come here, would you?"

She unfolded her own arms and moved into his embrace, cutting loose a sob that quieted only when he pulled her even closer and held her tight. With a contented sigh, he rested his cheek on top of her head and closed his damp eyes, reveling in the sweet moment—the feel of her face pressed against his collarbone; the floral scent of her soft, supple hair.

"Oh, Jess, I've been so foolish. I should have left Conrad much sooner. I love you, Jess. I do. I love you." She spewed the words almost frantically, then stepped back and looked up at him. "Will you forgive me?"

He drew her back against him, closed his eyes once more, and breathed deeply to control the whelming tide of emotion generated by her request. "Of course I will, silly. I don't happen to have an engagement ring on me at the moment, but I'll get one very soon if you'll promise to marry me for real this time."

She pushed back again and lifted her chin, tears still dripping down her cheeks. With the pads of his thumbs, he brushed away the wet streams. "I promise. Do not get me some whopping thing, though. I never did like the one Conrad gave me. It was far too lavish for my taste, and that's not me."

"I'll get you whatever your sweet little heart desires. I am not a pauper, Grace."

"Let's not even discuss the ring right now. Let's discuss kissing to seal the deal, shall we?"

He chuckled. "You don't have to ask me twice." He hauled her tight against his chest, and she looped her arms around his neck, going up on tiptoe to meet his lips. The kiss meshed them together in wondrous ways, and it continued for a while, a sort of search for relief from all the waiting and questioning and longing that had separated them for so long. His hand went to her spine and caressed it in tiny circles, while her fingers threaded through his coarse hair. Seconds passed, perhaps even minutes. With her, Jess lost track of time. Breaths came in short supply. He couldn't get enough of her—and yet, she wasn't quite his yet to fully partake of, so he ended the moment by grasping her waist with both hands and stepping away, then bending forward to plant a tiny kiss on the tip of her nose. "I love you back, my dearest Grace. One day—soon, I hope—I'll prove to you just how much."

She gave a slight shiver and smiled, her lips a bit swollen now to match her eyes. "I hope soon, as well, although everything depends on Aunt Iris."

"I understand. Shall we go inside?"

"Yes. I need to check on her."

He filled his lungs with a deep breath of air, then let it slowly escape. "Let's go, then."

She started to push open the big door but stopped and turned to look up at him. "Thank you for loving me, for being here. I feel stronger already."

He gave her arm a gentle squeeze and followed her inside.

32

All of the staff, save for Horace McMartin, who'd gone out to the barn to muck stalls and feed the stock, stood around the dying patient. The room held a somber air, and yet it was simultaneously pervaded by a strange kind of peace. How extraordinary that these two very different passageways into eternal glory could meld together with such ease and sheer beauty. At the sound of Grace and Jess's entrance, all heads turned. The two of them were holding hands, and Grace appreciated the smiles of approval that lit their faces. That meant the world to her.

"How is she?" she whispered.

"She be 'bout the same, Miz Grace," said Solomon. He stepped away from the foot of the bed and extended a hand to Jess. They shook, and their eyes met in a sort of silent understanding. She liked that they'd become friends so quickly.

Nellie and Blanche sat in chairs near the bed, while Ellen stood on one side of Aunt Iris, caressing her arm, and Zelda stood on the other. So much love filled the room that Grace could barely contain her emotions. She could tell by the tear-stained faces that they'd shed a good number of tears, Solomon included.

"We been singin' hymns, and she seems t' like it," said Ellen. "She ready t' meet her Maker, tha's fo' sho'."

Grace had shed a waterfall of tears over the course of the day, but now she found a certain strength she hadn't known before. She credited

311

her increased faith in an unfailing God, as well as her darling Jess, who even now squeezed her hand to reassure her of his love.

"O God, how good You are to have brought all of us together in this place for this particular time," Grace prayed aloud. "Would You kindly grant Your divine peace and all-surpassing love to Aunt Iris in this hour so that she might sense You in her heart and in her spirit? Please remove all fear or anxiety that she may have of the passage from this place to the next. We thank You, dear Father."

"Yes, we does, Lord."

"Amen."

"We all knows we need Thee, Lord."

Several additional murmurs and whispered prayers followed hers.

Then Aunt Iris issued a moaning sound, to everyone's surprise. For hours, she'd lain silent and sleeping; but now her eyelids fluttered in a valiant attempt to open. Blanche and Nellie both stood, as if expecting something wonderful to unfold. Ellen moved aside to make way for Grace, who leaned over her aunt. "Auntie, I'm here. Do you need anything?"

The woman winced slightly, her brow crimping. It must have been the pain that had roused her.

"Oh, Lord…" Grace whispered.

Jess stepped forward and took the woman's hand in his. "Aunt Iris, it's me, Jess."

One of the woman's eyebrows flicked, and both Ellen and Blanche gave quiet gasps.

Crouching so that he came within inches of her face, he continued, "I want you to know something. I am going to marry Grace. She is a precious gift from God, and I love her very much. I proposed a second time, and she said yes. I promise to cherish and take excellent care of her. She'll be fine with me, Aunt Iris, rest assured." He eased away, and they all waited, holding their breath.

The tiniest hint of a smile touched her lips, followed by a clear pronouncement of "Good. Thank You, Jesus."

A moment of awe filled the room.

Grace scooted closer. "I love you, Auntie."

"We all does," said Solomon.

Blanche went to the butler and put an arm around his hunched shoulder. He leaned into her. Ellen started singing "What a Friend We Have in Jesus," and several others joined in. Aunt Iris didn't acknowledge the song, nor did she make any more attempts to lift her eyelids. The singing ended after two verses, and the room fell into a hushed repose, as all eyes came to rest on the blanket covering Aunt Iris's chest, still rising and falling, albeit more slowly than ever. At one point, the movement stopped altogether, and everyone waited, some weeping quietly, Grace most of all. One shallow breath followed another, and then, suddenly—nothing, only silence of the stillest kind. Even the wind that had been blowing outside, creating quite a stir as it caused the curtains to swell and dance about, had ceased, as if in honor of the soul passing by on its way to heaven's gates.

In the days that followed, a continual stream of friends and neighbors stopped by Brockwell Manor, not only to view the body of Iris Brockwell, laid out in the parlor in a coffin of rich, hand-carved wood in the parlor, but also to drop off casseroles, soups, breads, meat dishes, and more cakes and pies than anyone knew what to do with. Clearly, the people meant well, but it was far more food than the household needed, considering Zelda cooked and baked almost round the clock just to stay busy.

As was customary, Blanche and Ellen drew the drapes and closed all the shutters, darkening the house to a drab gray. For three days, folks came and went, paying their respects to the deceased and offering their condolences to Grace and to all the staff. Jess kept up his work schedule at the livery as well as he could, but Grace was his main concern; and if Mr. Hansen didn't like it, he could fire him. Besides, he'd been giving serious thought to bringing his father to Paris so they could open up a cooperage together. So, he spent most of his time at Grace's side, sometimes leaving the manor as late as midnight to make his way back to

Flora Connors' place to catch a few hours of sleep before starting all over again the next day. Grace had suggested he take one of the spare bedrooms at the manor, but he'd said that it wouldn't be proper, despite the number of staff who could readily attest to the couple's upright behavior. He didn't want any tongues wagging before they spoke their vows—vows that he was growing quite impatient to recite.

The funeral service, held at Brockwell Manor, drew a large crowd— no surprise, since the fact of Iris Brockwell's decades of generosity toward the local community was well-known. Her most recent financial gift had been made to Phoebe Arbogast, bringing the sum of the donations to an amount that far exceeded what was necessary for rebuilding the boardinghouse. Miss Phoebe's entire demeanor had changed to one of joy and gratitude, and Jess had no doubt that her misfortune had ended up working for the betterment of the community, drawing folks together and expanding their hearts of compassion as it had.

Several men had volunteered their time and talents to build a number of wooden benches to provide extra seating for the funeral, which was held in the parlor. Even so, dozens of attendees crowded into the living room, the hallway, and the adjoining rooms to either sit or stand. An overflow of guests even stood outside the front door in reverent silence, the relentless sun in the cloudless sky beating down on their shoulders.

Grace held up well throughout the service, and it was Jess's great honor to sit next to her and hold her hand. Her strength and fortitude surprised him, considering how deeply she'd loved her aunt and how dearly he knew she missed her. He appreciated the way Joy Jennings and Mercy Connors arrived early to attend to her, taking her to the living room for a time of conversation and prayer in order to take her mind off things for a bit before the service began. Reverend Jennings and the pastor of the church Iris had long attended conducted the service with utmost compassion and tact, having gathered stories from many community members about Iris Brockwell's generous spirit and feisty temperament. Grace later told Jess that there had been some stories she'd heard for the first time at the service. The preacher had also offered words of encouragement and shared many pertinent Scripture passages to lend comfort to the bereaved.

After the funeral, they laid the body to rest in the cemetery where her husband was buried, behind their longtime church. The reverend offered a few final words and a closing prayer, then invited everyone back to the manor for a mid-afternoon meal, to be served on the well-manicured lawn. Several rustic tables had been arranged in the front yard and covered with colorful tablecloths made by women from the church. The meal itself had been prepared by a host of ladies from area churches, who insisted that the staff of Brockwell Manor stay clear of the kitchen and take a break from work in general. It was a remarkable sight when Sam Connors, Lucas Jennings, and Doc Trumble escorted the staff to one of the tables set up on the lawn and instructed them to sit so that the women of the community could serve them.

It had been a long, tiring day—a taxing week, to be sure—and when the events were over, and the women finished the chore of washing every last dish and setting the kitchen to rights, Grace, Jess, and the rest of the household fairly collapsed in the living room.

"She was a fine woman, a fine friend," Solomon said in a reflective tone.

"Yes, indeed," Blanche affirmed. "She could be a real whippersnapper, though."

"Oh, don't I know it. My, my." Solomon gave his gray head several shakes.

"Soft around the edges, though," Ellen put in.

"Yes'm, she was that." Solomon nodded in his slow, methodical way. "When she wanted somethin', though, you knew you best not get in her way whilst she was goin' fo' it. You might get yo' foot stepped on."

That comment gave rise to an eruption of dog-tired laughter.

"You knowed her best, Sol," said Zelda. "I s'pect it's gonna take y' some time t' recover. We all here for y'."

Jess marveled at the love, the camaraderie, and the familial fellowship shared by the group, even though the McMartins were the only ones truly related.

He sat on the sofa next to Grace, his legs stretched out in front of him, his knee touching hers, his arm draped over the back of the sofa behind her head. He had never loved her more.

"I wonder wha's next for Brockwell Manor," Blanche mused, staring at her clasped hands.

Grace tilted her head up at Jess and smiled. He squeezed her shoulder and gave a reassuring nod, so she looked around the room at each person resting his or her weary body. "It's interesting you should bring that up, Blanche. I would love to talk to all of you about that, and I don't see why we can't do it right now.

"In the weeks before her passing, Aunt Iris and I did some talking. First, I want to make it clear that you will all have a place to stay for the rest of your lives—in your quarters on the third floor. Brockwell Manor is your home as much as it is mine. In fact, it's probably more yours. Gerald Wadsworth informed me that he will be reading the will next week, and he asked me to see to it that each of you is present."

Several of the staff shifted in their chairs, their cocoa-colored eyes wide, the whites surrounding the irises standing out like crescent moons in a dark sky.

Grace went on to tell them about the ladies' picnic she'd attended and the challenge she'd heard concerning the need for a medical facility for the sick and aging. Then she shared her idea about transforming the manor into something that could provide the community, and even all of Henry County, with an interim residence for those in need.

"Nothing will happen immediately. Gerald Wadsworth said there'll be lots to consider and plan for—permits to bring before the city council, contracts to carve out and agree upon, architects to hire, contractors to draw bids from…the list goes on. It sounds like an overwhelming task, and yet my aunt and I were in agreement that we wanted the manor to be put to good use—and we wanted to dedicate this place and its grounds to God."

"Y' might have t' hire some mo' staff," said Ellen, her face pinched with obvious concern. "I don't think we can—"

"Oh my, yes. We'll be hiring medical personnel. They won't live here, mind you; they'll commute to and from work. Of course, we'll have to hire round-the-clock staff. I'm a nurse, as you know, so I'll be diving in to do my part. I don't see myself taking care of the administrative tasks, though, so, again, we'll hire someone." She glanced up at Jess. "Perhaps my husband will assume that responsibility."

His stomach did a complete flip. "I don't know about that." He'd never considered himself a business-minded man. He was more a hands-on sort of guy. Josiah and Ruth Woodbridge came to mind, and his thoughts started running off in all kinds of directions as newfound excitement built in his chest. His beautiful fiancée had him broadening the scope of his imagination regarding the future.

Jess surveyed the room. Everyone was silent, most faces bearing contemplative expressions.

Finally, Solomon broke the quiet. "Well, I think it's good. Sho' are a lot o' folks out there needin' care. We jes' seen our beloved Missus Brockwell give up the ghost, but with a whole slew of us surroundin' her. Don't 'magine that happens with some folk. An' this way, we'll all be here fo' each other when our time comes t' leave this here earth."

Several heads nodded in agreement.

"I was thinking we could name it The Iris Brockwell Facility for the Sick and Aging," Grace mused.

"That's kind o' long," Ellen remarked, her brow crumpled.

Grace laughed, and the sound warmed Jess unlike any blanket. He tugged her closer and murmured, "It is a little cumbersome, honey."

She giggled. "Okay, then what do you suggest?" She threw the question out to everyone.

"Brockwell Manor," at least three said in unison.

"Folks'll know it's changed by word o' mouth alone. Ain't no need to change what's become a well-known landmark t' all o' Henry County," Zelda argued.

"Well, aren't you all the berries?" Grace said, clapping her hands. "Here I am, making it far more complicated than it needs to be. Brockwell Manor it has been; Brockwell Manor it shall always be."

That statement alone seemed to introduce a new sense of calm to the room.

The group talked a while longer about the idea until they'd exhausted their questions, many of which Grace was unable to answer.

"We're in the very early stages of development," Jess interjected, "so there'll be a fair number of questions with no answers until a professional steps in and clears them up. One thing is certain, though: As Grace already stated, none of you is to worry about having a place to stay or a livelihood. Understood?"

Nellie raised her chin and grinned broadly. "I isn't a bit worried. Me, I'm lookin' up the road, an' I's seein' a few twists 'n turns, an' even some bumps; but, y' see, it's God what's buildin' that road, so what's t' worry about?"

"Amen t' that!" Blanche exclaimed.

"Ain't that the God's truth?" Zelda asked.

"Personally, I'm likin' the looks o' that windin' road," Horace chimed in. "God's been mo' 'n faithful. Ain't no reason to think that'll change."

"Well then...." Grace put her hands on her knees as if preparing to stand.

"Wait jes' a minute 'fore we all goes about our business," Solomon said. He'd been quiet for most of the discussion, taking in all the information and giving the occasional nod, and Jess supposed he had another question pertaining to the transition. "I know we ain't even opened them drapes or shutters yet, but when are you two gettin' wed?"

Jess would have to remember to thank the man for broaching the subject. He hadn't wanted to bother Grace with the question just yet. She scooted back on the sofa once more and snuggled against him. He leaned down and planted a kiss on her forehead, then arched an eyebrow at her, waiting for a response.

She gave a lazy smile. Funny how, despite the fact that they'd laid Aunt Iris to rest today, they were already discussing such matters as change and new beginnings. His heart took a leap at the twinkle in Grace's eye.

She cleared her throat. "What if we stuck to the original wedding date—October fifteenth?"

Jess wrapped her in his arms so tightly, he probably came near to squeezing the breath out of her. After a moment, he released her from the embrace and held her at arm's length. "Are you serious?"

"Indeed I am," she said, kissing him square on the lips in front of everyone.

A round of applause broke the kiss.

"Well, I'll be dipped in sauce," said Blanche. "I s'pose that means we gots ourselves a lot o' work to do."

"We'll be fine, jes' fine," Solomon said. "A lot of the work was already done. We'll use them tables where we ate the funeral lunch. They'll work plenty nice with fancy tablecloths an' fresh bouquets o' flowers."

"You leave the fancy stuff up t' Nellie an' me," Zelda told him.

"It won't be nearly as big an affair as today's assembly," Grace said. "For the wedding, I'll want a far more intimate gathering."

"You'll have it exactly as y' want it," Ellen told her.

"I'll have to send my pa a letter and tell him to travel here with Josiah and Ruthie," Jess mused aloud. "I'll wire him some money for the fare. Oh, and I'll ask Josiah to stand as witness. I'm sure someone will be happy to tend to Edith Ann during the ceremony."

As if the sun had just risen after a long winter night, everyone came to life, and Jess figured there hadn't been this much enthusiasm at Brockwell Manor for a long time. From what he'd heard and known of Iris Brockwell, she liked to run a tight ship, and her staff likely wasn't accustomed to much joviality—certainly not in the past few months. He could envision Grace loosening the reins a great deal and allowing freedoms these folks had never experienced. They were her family, after all, and soon to be his, too.

"Oh, my!" Blanche said, silencing the room. "What do y' think Missus Brockwell would say to all this excitement on the same day we done put 'er in the ground?"

Everyone looked to Solomon for the answer.

He grinned, showing that one gold tooth, and cleared his throat. "I say she be real pleased that we is goin' about life as usual, not t' mention we's plannin' Miz Grace's weddin'. Why, she might be lookin' down on us right now and puttin' in her two cents. We bes' keep our ears tuned 'case she decides t' chime in."

Everyone chuckled, and soon the enthusiastic din resumed, with the women discussing the wedding plans and preparations. Jess looked around the room and realized he'd come to love them all.

33

In Grace's mind, the morning of October 15 could not dawn soon enough. In just two days, she would become Mrs. Jess Quinn, and every time she thought about it, her heart reacted with a wild flutter. In the last two weeks, she had gone over and over the details with Blanche and the rest of the staff—the menu, the flowers and other decorations, the table linens and dinnerware, the seating arrangements, and so forth. She was frequently tempted to fret, but Blanche assured her that she had no need to worry—she had everything under control.

How thankful she was to have such capable friends to handle the preparations. Even Mercy and Joy had stopped by a few days ago, insisting that Blanche put them to work. She had tasked them with polishing the silver, and Grace had joined them. The three women had sat at the dining room table and polished for three hours, chatting, laughing, sipping sweet tea, and simply enjoying one another's company. She'd had no idea that so much silver existed in all of Tennessee.

Not a day passed that she didn't grieve the loss of Aunt Iris. While everyone stayed busy around the manor, accomplishing day-to-day tasks on top of preparing to host approximately sixty wedding guests, no one could deny the cloud of grief hovering overhead. But fond memories of the feisty woman kept her alive in their hearts, and Grace enjoyed the reminiscences they shared around the dinner table—at her insistence, the residents and staff had started partaking of every meal together.

Jess's father, Fergus, as well as Josiah and Ruth Woodbridge and three-month-old Edith Ann, arrived by train that afternoon, and they all enjoyed the reunion, even amid the chaos of the wedding preparations. Blanche put the Woodbridges up in one of the seven bedrooms on the second floor, and Jess had arranged with Flora Connors for his father to stay in one of her spare rooms. Ruthie oohed and aahed over the spacious manor and its lovely gardens, while Fergus gawked in disbelief. "This ain't no house—this here's a palace," he said upon first entering through the front door. "Quite a place, I tell ya. Ya two gonna live here after ya wed?" was one of his first questions.

"For the time being, Pa," Jess responded.

Soon he and Grace ushered everyone into the living room, where they situated themselves on their choice of furniture. Solomon announced that he would return presently with cold drinks for everyone. Jess and Grace sat close together on the sofa, knees touching. He took Grace's hand—the one with the shiny new diamond engagement ring, which he'd purchased with money his father had taken out of the bank in Boston before traveling there—and looked at her before addressing the rest of them. "We haven't decided where we'll live down the road—whether in the manor or in a smaller house we'd build on the property. In time, we plan to convert this place into a home for the sick and aging. A great deal has to happen beforehand, so it will take a while, perhaps a year or even longer. We have attorneys working on all the legalities as we speak."

"Hmm," his father muttered. "That's interestin'. Seems like a mighty commendable cause."

Grace noticed a healthier demeanor about Fergus since the last time she'd seen him. His shoulders weren't quite as slumped, his personality was perkier, and his eyes no longer looked droopy and bloodshot. She prayed that he'd given up his habit of heavy drinking.

Josiah and Ruthie wanted to hear more about their plans for the manor, so they shared their vision in greater detail. Josiah, with his business background, had many questions and brought up several interesting points for discussion. Grace could almost envision him and Ruthie fitting in quite well at the manor, and she couldn't help but wonder if they'd ever consider a move to Tennessee in order to work alongside them. She also foresaw Jess talking his father into moving south and didn't think it would take much to convince him. The two men needed to spend time rebuilding their relationship after their long separation from each other. Surely, Horace McMartin could use an assistant grounds-keeper. Then again, Jess had brought up the possibility of opening a cooperage in Paris, and Grace realized that the possibilities for their future were endless. Whatever happened, one thing remained clear: She and Jess, with God's help and divine direction, would build a happy life together.

The day before the wedding, she barely saw Jess at all, since Blanche had assigned him a number of last-minute duties, which he completed with his father and Josiah tagging along. While the men ran errands, Grace and Ruth walked the grounds, checking periodically on Edith Ann, who napped in a makeshift bed Blanche had fashioned for her by lining a bureau drawer with soft blankets. Grace related to Ruthie all that had transpired between Conrad Hall and her, even detailing his poisoning of Aunt Iris in an effort to expedite their wedding date. "His aim all along was this manor and all its wealth. Thank goodness, Jess followed him to Chicago to play detective, or I don't know what would've happened. I do know I'd already decided against marrying him, but what might he have done to me when he learned of my decision? I shudder to think of it now that I know what a brute he truly is. God had His hand upon me, that's for sure."

"And upon Jess and the boardinghouse proprietress," Ruthie put in.

A cool breeze had kicked up, but the sun still shone bright overhead. Both women looked up when a trio of crows flew over, cawing vociferously. "I am blessed, and I'll not deny it," Grace said softly. "God has been faithful to me in so many ways, even when I failed to seek His guidance and went for long periods of time without even opening my Bible."

Ruthie nodded. "He's not only faithful, He's patient."

Across Nobles Road, the maple trees had just started changing into the faintest shades of reds and yellows. "Autumn's in the air," Grace mused.

"Yes, and tomorrow's going to be the loveliest day of the year—I just know it," Ruthie said. "You must be beside yourself with joy and excitement. Think of it—your dream of marrying your childhood sweetheart is finally coming to fruition. And then, to think he's whisking you off to the Atlantic shore for an entire week of honeymooning! My, you're living a dream, my darling friend."

⌒

Every second he wasn't with her, Jess missed Grace more than anything, but spending the day with his father and Josiah proved gratifying. Besides talking about everything from politics to farming to business, his father confessed that he'd been reading the Bible Jess had left for him and, in so doing, had decided—all on his own—to simultaneously surrender his heart to the Lord and give up drinking.

The news made Jess give a little whoop while they drove up East Wood Street on their way to the general store. "I knew something was different!" he exclaimed. "Well, glory hallelujah!" His jubilant shouts drew a few curious stares from pedestrians wending their way up the sidewalk.

His father told him about the church he'd started attending and how the folks there hadn't exactly treated him with utmost kindness. When Jess told him about Paris Evangelical and said that he thought he would fit in well, an attempt to ease him into considering a move to Paris, Josiah glanced at him over his father's head and winked.

During supper that night, Jess and Grace soundlessly exchanged foot caresses under the table. He wanted to make her scorchingly aware that tomorrow night there'd be a whole lot more going on between them than mere brushes of skin on skin. He'd waited a good long time to make her his, and he intended to do a thorough job. The conversation around the table ran on as bright as could be, but Jess heard none of it, and he doubted Grace did, either, for neither of them contributed to the banter.

They had very little time alone after supper, either, as Jess's father started yawning when the evening was still young, compelling Jess to drive him back to Flora Connors' place before it got very dark. Prior to leaving, he took Grace by the hand and hauled her to the back of the house, near the cellar door off the kitchen.

"What are you doing?" she asked as she skittered along behind him.

He pressed her against the wall in a darkened corner and cupped her face gently in his hands. "Did you enjoy our little game beneath the table tonight?" he asked with a conspiratorial smile.

She feigned shyness and gave him a playful slap. "A game—is that what you call it? I couldn't decide what you were doing."

He lowered his face and gave her a fervent kiss that left her gasping after just a few seconds. "Jess Quinn, you—you take my breath away."

He laughed, caressed her cheek with his thumb, and kissed her again, this time with even more passion, until her knees began to buckle under her, so that he had to hold her up. She ended the kiss by planting her hands between them and pushing him away from her. "You'd best get going, Mr. Quinn, before I melt into a puddle of mush. I'll be no good to you at all tomorrow if that happens."

He chortled. "You'll be just fine, my darling." He touched her nose and winked. "Sleep well."

He turned and left her, still leaning, breathless, against the wall.

⌒

On October 15, Blanche gave a light knock at Grace's door at precisely 3:50 in the afternoon, then peeked inside to inform her that most of the guests had found their seats downstairs, and it wouldn't be long now. She added that her groom looked dashing, then asked if either she or Ruth needed anything. Since neither did, she smiled, told Grace how very beautiful she looked, and then left as quickly as she'd come.

Grace felt surprisingly calm, in spite of the fact that she could hardly contain her excitement at the notion of becoming Jess's wife in less than an hour. She and Ruthie stood side by side, holding hands as they studied their reflections in the tall mirror. Joy and Mercy had both come in earlier, Joy to help Grace into the beautiful dress she herself had fashioned, and Mercy to style the hair of both the bride and matron of honor into fancy, fashionable buns, complete with an elegant pearl comb for Ruthie and a lovely headpiece with fresh flowers for Grace that included the long, lacy veil Joy had made. They'd had a relaxing, unhurried time together, and before she and Joy had headed back downstairs, Mercy had offered up a beautiful prayer, asking for God's blessings upon the already sparkling day, that quickly chased away any remaining nervousness Grace had been feeling.

"Are you ready, honey?" Ruthie asked her.

Grace took a deep breath. "More than you know."

Their cue to leave was when Wendy Hodgin started to play "Love's Old Sweet Song" on the parlor piano, an accompaniment to the solo sung by Debbie Stinehart in her lovely voice.

Blanche had been right when she'd told her that her groom looked dashing. Why, when it finally came time for Grace to descend the stairs, Ruthie having already moved into position on the ground floor, and Wendy Hodgin pounding out Mendelssohn's "Wedding March," she caught his green eyes and never allowed her gaze to waver.

The ceremony went off without a single snag, Jess clinging to her hands, squeezing them gently at just the right times. After they spoke their "I dos" at Lucas's prompting, they dutifully recited their vows. Finally came that precious moment when the preacher looked them in the eyes, moving his gaze slowly from one to the other, and said, "I now pronounce you man and wife. You may kiss your bride, Mr. Quinn."

The kiss was nothing like the ones they'd shared last night, but then, they had an audience today. Briefly, Grace recalled his promise that, tonight, he would make her thoroughly his, and a tremor of excitement ran the length of her.

After Lucas spoke a blessing on their marriage and they processed down the aisle, the guests descended on them, shaking Jess's hand and enveloping Grace in warm embraces, some tight and snug, and others gentle. Everyone offered words of congratulations, blessings, and best wishes. Tears filled the corners of her eyes, not only due to the love pouring in from every direction, but also due to the sad fact that Aunt Iris had missed the celebration.

In that very moment, Jess turned to her and leaned down, his lips brushing her ear. "She's well aware, honey. She may be watching, for all we know."

She smiled up at him, the love for him so great, so boundless, that she could hardly contain it. "I hope she is."

The luncheon turned out to be a lovely affair, with delectable dishes arranged attractively on exquisite china plates and served with perfectly polished silverware. However, the menu could have consisted of nuts, berries, and dried leaves, for all Grace cared in her euphoric state.

Cheerful conversation drifted up from every table, but as Grace and Jess arose from their meal to begin mingling, she could think of only one thing—escaping the guests so that she and Jess could be alone. They would spend the night in her room and then, first thing in the morning, board the train as a married couple and head for Savannah, Georgia, where Jess had reserved a seaside cottage for their honeymoon. How he'd arranged it, she did not know, but she had married a well-traveled man, so she figured he had his connections. Whatever the case, she was packed and ready to go. All she knew for now was that she could hardly wait to experience more of his kisses and discover the mystery behind what it meant to be thoroughly his.

The handshakes and good-byes took a monumental amount of time, but finally the last guest departed. There were dishes to wash, vases of flowers to clear away, the tablecloths to fold, and tables and chairs to carry to the barn. Thank goodness for Sam Connors and Lucas Jennings, who helped with the heavy lifting, while Mercy and Joy lent a hand in the kitchen. It must have been well past nine by the time everyone finally cleared out, except for Jess's father, who had given in to Blanche's insistence that he stay in one of the spare guest rooms.

At long last, the latch on the bedroom door clicked, and the bride and groom found themselves facing each other in the shadowy space, lit only by a single low-flaming lamp on a side table.

"Hello, Mrs. Quinn."

Jess stood with his feet planted several inches apart, one hand hanging loosely at his side, the other unfastening the tie at his neck.

"Hello, Mr. Quinn." Her heart took a strange little dive that made her breathless. He seemed to have that effect on her.

He yanked off his tie and tossed it on the floor. Then he glanced around the room, his eyes lingering on the four-poster bed, with its fresh sheets and bedding. Sometime in the hours since the wedding, someone, no doubt Blanche, had slipped in and laid a bouquet of red roses on the coverlet. The intoxicating scent wafted across the room, enhancing the already dreamy moment.

He focused his gaze on Grace once more. "Are you ready for me to make you thoroughly mine?"

She swallowed. "I'm not entirely sure I know what that entails."

"Then let me show you," came his raspy reply.

They moved into each other's arms, first heart to heart, then mouth to mouth, and, finally, man to woman. Pure, unadulterated passion bloomed between them, a culmination of all the months and years of waiting for this one fine, perfect moment—a moment wrapped in love and tied with ribbons of hope.

Questions for Discussion

1. Aunt Iris questions Grace as to whether she truly heard God's still, small voice in regard to her plans to marry Conrad Hall. How would you explain God's still, small voice? Have you ever experienced it yourself?

2. When Grace relays to Aunt Iris that Jess is alive, Aunt Iris responds with an interesting question: "Do you think any of this comes as a surprise to [God]?" Have you ever found yourself in a troubling situation in which you had no idea which way to turn? (Feel free to share.) Is it reassuring to you just to know that God already saw it coming, or do you wish He would have clued you in?

3. When Iris Brockwell manages to make it to church one Sunday morning with an almost divine sort of strength girding her up, Jess reflects that with God, all things are possible, right down to healing the sickest of individuals. Have you ever experienced dramatic healing of a divine nature or known others who have?

4. At the ladies' church picnic, when the speaker presents the town's need for a medical facility for the sick and aging, Grace experiences a divine nudge in her spirit. Yet, she finds herself wondering what she can do to help; after all, she is "just one person." Have you ever wondered how you could possibly make a difference when a need seemed far too great for you to handle alone?

5. As Grace makes a complete surrender to God regarding her choice between Conrad and Jess, she takes Hebrews 10:22–23 to heart—a passage that includes the phrase *"for he is faithful that promised."* Can you give an example of a specific time in your life when God proved Himself faithful to you?

6. Conrad blinds Grace with his charms. How often our enemy, Satan, does the same thing, for he is called the deceiver. What is the best and surest way to avoid allowing him to envelop us in a web of deceit?

7. We learn that immediately after aborting her baby, Aunt Iris turned away from God rather than turning to Him in repentance and receiving forgiveness. How often do you see others growing bitter in their sins, whatever they may entail, and running away from God's forgiveness instead of seeking it? Have you done the same? Share if you feel compelled.

8. Aunt Iris warns Grace not to allow a seed of bitterness over Conrad's acts to grow in her heart, telling her that those roots could entangle her and squeeze the life out of her. How does one escape from the bitterness of unspeakable hurt?

9. Grace shares with Ruth about God's faithfulness, even when she failed to seek His guidance and went for long periods without even opening her Bible. How has God shown you His unflagging patience and faithfulness?

10. Life doesn't always bring happy endings. How do you handle life's struggles when things don't go exactly as you wish? Read Romans 8:28 and reflect on its implications in your life.

About the Author

Born and raised in west Michigan, Sharlene MacLaren attended Spring Arbor University and graduated in 1971 with a degree in elementary education. In 1975, she married her childhood sweetheart, and together they raised two daughters, both of whom are now happily married and enjoying their own families. Over the course of thirty-one years, Shar taught both second and fourth grades before retiring in 2003. Besides writing, Shar loves to read, sing, decorate, travel, and spend time with her family—in particular, her five adorable grandchildren!

Shar has enjoyed dabbling in writing since high school, but it wasn't until more recently that she felt God's call upon her heart to take her writing a step further. In 2006, she signed a contract for her first faith-based novel. With sixteen of her books now gracing store shelves nationwide, she daily gives God all the praise and glory for her accomplishments.

Through Every Storm was Shar's first novel to be published by Whitaker House, and in 2007, the American Christian Fiction Writers (ACFW) named it a finalist for Book of the Year. The acclaimed Little Hickman Creek series consists of *Loving Liza Jane* (Road to Romance Reviewer's Choice Award); *Sarah, My Beloved* (third place, Inspirational Readers' Choice Award 2008); and *Courting Emma* (third place, Inspirational Reader's Choice Award 2009). Shar's popular series The Daughters of Jacob Kane comprises *Hannah Grace* (second place, Inspirational Reader's Choice Award 2010), *Maggie Rose*, and *Abbie Ann* (third place, Inspirational Reader's Choice Award 2011). Her historical series River of Hope includes *Livvie's Song*, *Ellie's Haven*, and *Sofia's Secret*. *Gift of Grace* concludes Shar's latest series, Tennessee Dreams, which also includes *Heart of Mercy* and *Threads of Joy*. And in 2014, Shar published a stand-alone seasonal novella, *Christmas Comes to Little Hickman Creek*.

Shar does numerous countrywide book signings, has made countless television and radio appearances, and thoroughly enjoys speaking for various women's gatherings, retreats, banquets, charitable organizations, libraries, and the like. She has a strong heart for women and is currently involved in a women's mentoring program. She and her husband, Cecil, are active in their church. They live in Spring Lake, Michigan, with their beautiful white collie, Peyton, and their loving Ragdoll cat, Blue.

Welcome to Our House!

We Have a Special Gift for You ...

It is our privilege and pleasure to share in your love of Christian fiction by publishing books that enrich your life and encourage your faith.

To show our appreciation, we invite you to sign up to receive a specially selected **Reader Appreciation Gift**, with our compliments. Just go to the Web address at the bottom of this page.

God bless you as you seek a deeper walk with Him!

WE HAVE A GIFT FOR YOU. VISIT:

whpub.me/fictionthx

WHITAKER
HOUSE